ANSWERING
THE CALL

Praise for Ali Vali

Lammy Finalist *Calling the Dead*

"So many writers set stories in New Orleans, but Ali Vali's mystery novels have the authenticity that only a real Big Easy resident could bring. Set six months after Hurricane Katrina has devastated the city, a lesbian detective is still battling demons when a body turns up behind one of the city's famous eateries. What follows makes for a classic lesbian murder yarn." —*Curve Magazine*

"The plot is engrossing and satisfying. A fun aspect of the book is the images of food it includes. The descriptions of sex are also delicious." —*Seattle Gay News*

"In *Calling the Dead*, Vali has given us characters that are engaging and a story that keeps us turning page after page."—*Just About Write*

Beauty and the Boss

"The story gripped me from the first page, both the relationship between the two main characters, as well as the drama of the issues that threaten to bring down the business...Vali's writing style is lovely—it's clean, sharp, no wasted words, and it flows beautifully as a result. Highly recommended!"—*Rainbow Book Reviews*

"This was a story of love and passion but also of surprises and secrets. I loved it!"—*Kitty Kat's Book Review Blog*

The Romance Vote

"Won by a Landslide!...[A] sweet and mushy romance with some humor and spicy, sexy scenes!"—*Love Bytes*

Balance of Forces: Toujours Ici

"A stunning addition to the vampire legend, *Balance of Forces: Toujour Ici* is one that stands apart from the rest."—*Bibliophilic Book Blog*

Blue Skies

"Vali is skilled at building sexual tension, and the sex in this novel flies as high as Berkley's jets. Look for this fast-paced read."—*Just About Write*

Beneath the Waves

"The premise...was brilliantly constructed...skillfully written and the imagination that went into it was fantastic...The author managed to insert a real fear and menace into the story and had me totally engrossed...A wonderful passionate love story with a great mystery."—*Inked Rainbow Reads*

Second Season

"Whether Ali Vali is writing about crime figures or lawyers, her characters are well drawn and extremely likeable. Indeed, writing so the reader really cares about the main characters is a trademark of a Vali novel. *Second Season* is no exception to the rule...This is a rich, enjoyable read that's not to be missed."—*Just About Write*

"The issues are realistic and center around the universal factors of love, jealousy, betrayal, and doing the right thing and are constantly woven into the fabric of the story. We rated this well written social commentary through the use of fiction our max five hearts."—*Heartland Reviews*

Carly's Sound

"Vali paints vivid pictures with her words...*Carly's Sound* is a great romance, with some wonderfully hot sex."—Midwest Book Review

"It's no surprise that passion is indeed possible a second time around."—*Q Syndicate*

"*Carly's Sound* is a great romance, with some wonderfully hot sex, but it is more than that. It is also the tale of a woman rising from the ashes of grief and finding new love and a new life. Vali has surrounded Julia and Poppy with a cast of great supporting characters, making this an extremely satisfying read."—*Just About Write*

Praise for the Casey Cain Saga

The Devil's Due

"This is an enthralling, nail biting and ultra fast moving addition to the Devil series…once again Ali Vali has produced a brilliant story arc, solid character development, incomparable bad-ass women in traditionally male roles, leading both the goodies, baddies and cross-breeds."—*Lesbian Reading Room*

"A Night Owl Reviews Top Pick: Cain Casey is the kind of person you aspire to be even though some consider her a criminal. She's loyal, very protective of those she loves, honorable, big on preserving her family legacy and loves her family greatly. *The Devil's Due* is a book I highly recommend and well worth the wait we all suffered through. I cannot wait for the next book in the series to come out." —*Night Owl Reviews*

The Devil Be Damned

"Ali Vali excels at creating strong, romantic characters along with her fast-paced, sophisticated plots. Her setting, New Orleans, provides just the right blend of immigrants from Mexico, South America, and Cuba, along with a city steeped in traditions."—*Just About Write*

Deal with the Devil

"Ali Vali has given her fans another thick, rich thriller…*Deal With the Devil* has wonderful love stories, great sex, and an ample supply of humor. It is an exciting, page-turning read that leaves her readers eagerly awaiting the next book in the series."—*Just About Write*

The Devil Unleashed

"Fast-paced action scenes, intriguing character revelations, and a refreshing approach to the romance thriller genre all make for an enjoyable reading experience in the Big Easy…*The Devil Unleashed* is an engrossing reading experience."—*Midwest Book Review*

The Devil Inside

"Not only is *The Devil Inside* a ripping mystery, it's also an intimate character study."—*L-Word Literature*

"*The Devil Inside* is the first of what promises to be a very exciting series…While telling an exciting story that grips the reader, Vali has also fully fleshed out her heroes and villains. *The Devil Inside* is that rarity: a fascinating crime novel which includes a tender love story and leaves the reader with a cliffhanger ending."—*MegaScene*

"*The Devil Inside* by Ali Vali is an unusual, unpredictable, and thought-provoking love story that will have the reader questioning the definition of right and wrong long after she finishes the book… first time novelist Vali does not leave the reader hanging for too long, but spins a complex plot of love, conspiracy, and loss."—*Just About Write*

"[T]his isn't your typical 'Godfather-esque' novel, oh no. The head of this crime family is not only a lesbian, but a mother to boot. Vali's fluid writing style quickly puts the reader at ease, which makes the story and its characters equally easy to get to know and care about. When you find yourself talking out loud to the characters in a book, you know the work is polished and professional, as well as entertaining. Ever just wanted to grab a crime boss by the lapels, get in their face, and tell them to open their eyes and see what's right in front of their eyes? If not, you will once you start turning the pages of *The Devil Inside*." —*Family and Friends Magazine*

By the Author

Carly's Sound

Second Season

Blue Skies

Love Match

The Dragon Tree Legacy

The Romance Vote

Girls with Guns

Beneath the Waves

Beauty and the Boss

Call Series

Calling the Dead

Answering the Call

Forces Series

Balance of Forces: Toujours Ici

Battle of Forces: Sera Toujours

Force of Fire: Toujours a Vous

The Cain Casey Saga

The Devil Inside

The Devil Unleashed

Deal with the Devil

The Devil Be Damned

The Devil's Orchard

The Devil's Due

Heart of the Devil

Visit us at www.boldstrokesbooks.com

ANSWERING THE CALL

by
Ali Vali

2018

ANSWERING THE CALL

ISBN 13: 978-1-63555-050-4

This Trade Paperback Original Is Published By
Bold Strokes Books, Inc.
P.O. Box 249
Valley Falls, NY 12185

First Edition: December 2018

CREDITS
Editor: Shelley Thrasher
Production Design: Stacia Seaman
Cover Design by Sheri (hindsightgraphics@gmail.com)

Acknowledgments

Thank you to Radclyffe for your overall awesomeness and for giving me the continued opportunity to be a part of such a great organization and family. Thank you to Sandy Lowe for all you do for us and for being awesome as well.

Thanks to my editor, Shelley Thrasher—I think we're getting the hang of this writing business. You always teach me something each go-round, and for that I'm grateful. A big thank you to my beta readers Cris Perez-Soria, Kim Rieff, VK "Super Cop" Powell, and Carsen "Law Woman" Taite. You guys were great, and I thank you for all that expertise along the way. Thank you Sheri Halal for another great cover. It's like you can read my mind every time.

Thank you to all the readers, especially the ones who kept writing and asking for a sequel to *Calling the Dead*. It took a few years for the right story to come to me, but your encouragement helped the writing process. Every word is written with you in mind.

Thank you to C for all the fun times, and for all the ones yet to come. *Verdad!*

For C

For my parents

CHAPTER ONE

Please," New Jersey Detective Thomas Branson said as he tried his restraints again. He struggled to lift his head an inch—the only freedom he had.

After a night of fun with his buddies to celebrate another successful arrest, he'd woken up to this nightmare. Even scarier, he recognized the walls of his bedroom. This fucker was going to kill him a foot from his own bed, and he was glad to die alone. The family his mother, Myrna, had bugged him about, but he'd never gotten around to acquiring, would've only complicated this scenario.

"Please what?" The person on the bed spoke, their voice muffled by a leather mask.

Tommy couldn't even tell if it was a man or a woman from the way they were dressed. Except for the short questions, the only sound was the scraping of a knife against the sharpening stone. He'd screamed at first, but the slice into his chest warned him not to repeat that mistake. The deep cut stung, and trickles of blood ran down his sides. The scraping stopped, and he took a deep breath in preparation.

"I asked you a question. Please what?"

"Let me go." That wasn't going to happen. From the moment he'd opened his eyes, the situation was ominous, and he knew exactly what came next. He'd testified in court step by step how this would go and what the police would find.

"That's exactly what I plan to do," the person said, still out of his sight. "This should be a lesson to you."

"A lesson in what?"

"Hubris, Detective Thomas Neely Branson, hubris." The large, shiny knife slapped down on his wound, and Tommy screamed, opening his mouth wide enough for the gag to go in. Once he was silenced, his executioner strapped his head down. Now he was no better than a bug pinned to a board.

He would be the next victim of the butterfly killer. The large owl butterfly tacked to the ceiling above his head was the killer's only calling card and the only clue. The big butterfly had been left at the twelve murder scenes they'd investigated, along with the FBI, until Eugene Paul Masters had been apprehended on a fluke. And it had been a fluke, since Eugene hadn't left one bit of evidence at any of those crime scenes that could in any way be traced back to him.

The arrest had come from luck, but he and his team had been thorough and made it stick. Eugene was now waiting his turn on the table where his life would end for the atrocities he'd committed. With all the evidence against him, it'd taken the jury only two hours to come back, and an hour of that time had been their dinner break. Eugene was the guy, but who the hell was this fucker?

"Your ego was hard to swallow after you captured Mr. Masters," the person said, stripping away the rest of Tommy's clothes with the sharp blade. He knew they'd be neatly folded, even though they were ripped, and stacked in a very precise way. His shoes would top the stack, and his eyes would be found inside. Eugene never gave up why he put them in the shoes, no matter how hard the headshrinkers had pushed him on that little tidbit.

"You could've said you were doing your job, but even then Eugene dropped in your lap. That's the truth, because it certainly wasn't your stellar detective skills." Tommy saw a gloved hand point to the butterfly on the ceiling. "Did you notice the edge of the wings? The butterfly uses it to scare off predators because it looks like a snake's head. That, along with the owl eyes, makes this species almost untouchable in the wild. Its greatest enemy is man. Eugene wanted you to understand that freedom shouldn't be taken away from something so beautiful only to beat your chest at the capture. Winning the game by chance shouldn't go without punishment."

The knife came into view next, so Tommy sent a silent message to his mother. It wasn't his job to die before her, she'd said over and over after he'd gotten his shield. I'm sorry, Ma, he thought as the carving began. I failed you, but don't give up on life. I love you.

"But even in nature some mindless animal gets lucky and kills something that seems so deadly it should be by all accounts untouchable." The killer hesitated a moment before going back to work. "Luck ran out today, so look at the butterfly, Detective, and know you should've left well enough alone."

He bit down on the gag and bowed his body as much as he could when the knife plunged deeper and started the filleting process. It was the only way he'd been able to describe it. The sadistic bastard followed the same shape as the bug on his ceiling. The skin flap shaped like the butterfly would be his death shroud when it covered his face, his empty eye sockets matching the owl spots on the insect's wings.

"This should make Eugene's fate interesting, but don't worry. He's not going anywhere."

Tommy moaned when the blade rested under his balls.

"Your shoes need something to show what a bad boy you've been. This little trick should guarantee this as a copycat crime, but your buddies will be busy trying to figure out what it means to find you like this."

The cut was clean, and his scream was swallowed by the rubber ball in his mouth, but the killer only chuckled. "Come on. It's not like you were using them for anything useful. Mama wanted grandkids to spoil, but you could only get it up for those cheap whores who charge twenty for a blow job. Myrna's little boy was a figment of her imagination, so she'll cherish the memories, but you'll be forgotten in no time. No more twenties to buy some friends in your future."

Tommy struggled in one last attempt to free himself, but feeling the skin on his chest come off made him lose consciousness. The sweet relief of blackness saved him from knowing when the blade went through his heart. Tommy Branson was just a statistic now.

The hunter finished the staging necessary from the notes committed to memory. Only Tommy's testicles in his shoes would differ in this crime scene his fellow detectives would comb over. Eugene's trophies weren't their style, but the snips removed Tommy's small toe, which appeared ghoulish when dropped in a small bottle of alcohol. It went into a small bag on the bed, since it was a calling card for the next place. New Orleans was going to be fun.

"Time to move on and make Father proud."

❖

The small boat rocked on the smooth lake surface, but Keegan Blanchard could give a damn as her lover Sept Savoie slammed her fingers in, bringing her closer to orgasm. Six months together hadn't blunted the ferocious need to have Sept touch her and love her.

"Don't stop, baby," she said, digging her own fingers into Sept's shoulders to keep her in place on top of her. "So good…don't stop."

Sept pumped her hips into her as if to make her thrust upward more powerful, and Keegan wanted to cry now that Sept was completely healed from the gunshots that could've taken her away from her. The remaining souvenirs of Sept's last case had left scars on her left forearm and leg, but she was alive and in love with her. Keegan felt that emotion in every touch and every time she made her completely insane like now.

The end came quickly, and she fell into Sept, content to float and listen to the birds around them. "I can't believe I've never liked fishing before now," she said, and Sept laughed.

"Good." Sept pulled her hand free and held her. "If you'd learned this technique from someone else, I might've gotten jealous."

"Your jealous days are over, Seven," she said, using her favorite nickname for Sept since her name was actually the French word for the number seven. "Your only job now is to get Della to love you." Della Blanchard was the current head of the Blanchard restaurant empire and Keegan's grandmother, and she lived to tease Sept until she cried for mercy.

"Your grandmother can pretend all she wants, but I know she loves me," Sept said and laughed. "Want to head in and take a shower?"

"Don't tell me you're tired."

"Nothing's biting but you, so I want to get more comfortable before we continue our afternoon. Tired has nothing to do with it." Sept wiggled her eyebrows as she pulled her shorts on, and Keegan laughed along with her. "We've got four more days of vacation left, and I'm not interested in catching another fish."

"What can I interest you in then?" She straddled Sept's legs when she sat up. It had taken Sept three months to be cleared from desk duty, and Keegan had enjoyed every single day of it. Sept had closed one of the worst cases in New Orleans history, but not without penalty. The serial killer she, along with the rest of the department, had hunted for weeks had shot her twice before he was taken into custody. The normality of the hours and having Sept next to her every morning had spoiled her. "You want lunch?"

"Yes, I do, but I'd like an appetizer first," Sept said and kissed her.

"Della was nice enough to rent us that cabin, so let's go practice some of that happily-ever-after."

She nodded and leaned forward to press against Sept. Her grandmother had arranged their getaway with the hint of them starting the family Della wanted. "I love you," she said, and Sept kissed her.

How they'd made it to this place from such a gruesome beginning she didn't know, but the death of the Blanchard pastry chef had brought Sept into her life. All the deaths that followed hadn't blunted what was happening between them, and their relationship had only deepened. Sept Savoie was everything Keegan wanted in a partner, and she was looking forward to the rest of her life because she'd spend it with Sept.

"What are you thinking so hard about?" Sept asked, cupping her butt and tugging her closer.

"I'm thinking about you, and it's all good." She lost her smile when Sept's phone rang and understood why Della always looked like she was sucking a lemon when she heard the damn thing go off at their Sunday brunches. "Tell them you're off until Monday."

"Hey, Dad," Sept said, nodding and listening for a few minutes. "We won't be back in time for that, but if it's important I'll swing by your office Monday morning before I go in. I'll do that, but are you sure you don't want to tell me now?" she asked as Keegan rested her head on her shoulder and sighed. "Love you too," Sept said and hung up.

"Something wrong?" Keegan asked, not moving.

"He wanted to talk to me about something that's not work, but he can wait until Monday, so it can't be that important." She kissed Keegan's temple and rubbed her back. "Let's go in and talk about china patterns."

She lifted her head and stared at Sept, trying to figure out what she meant. "China patterns?"

Sept slid the tackle box closer and opened it. The velvet box was in the corner compartment, and the sight made Keegan press her hands to her mouth. "Last week I had lunch with the three most important people in your life, and I'm going to tell you what I told them."

"What?"

"The best day of my life was the day you basically told me off, which guaranteed I'd be back for more because you're damn beautiful when you're angry." She smiled at the memory of Sept accusing her of murder. "The *more* has been the best days of my life, but I'm greedy. I want all your days, and I'll spend them making you happy. I love you,

Keegan Blanchard, and I promise to love you for the rest of my life. Will you marry me?"

"Yes," she said, kissing Sept through her tears. "I love you so much."

"Before I open this, you need to know I love you too, and Della loves you as well," Sept said and smiled. "After she asked for my fingerprints, a DNA sample, a physical evaluation, and following a thorough interrogation under a naked lightbulb, she asked a favor of me."

"Considering what a hard time she gives you, I'm shocked you haven't cuffed her yet. Your patience with her does prove how much you love me." She combed Sept's hair back, kissing her again. "What was the favor?"

"To consider this ring instead of the one I'd gotten." Sept opened the box, and Della's ring fell into Sept's palm. Della had inherited it from her own grandmother, and Keegan had loved it from the first time she saw it. The large diamond flanked by two sapphires was simple but beautiful. "She told me how much you loved this ring and that she'd promised it to you."

"You bought me a ring?" She loved Della's ring but didn't want to insult Sept.

"I did, but the most important part of this was the girl saying yes, at least to me it is. Della also told me how much happiness her own marriage had brought her, and she wanted the same for us. I love you, and you love this ring, so," Sept took the ring and held it close to her finger, "marry me."

"I love you, and my answer will always be yes."

Sept slipped the ring on her finger and kissed her.

"The setting could've been more romantic, but I couldn't wait any longer," Sept said as she held her hand. "I'm looking forward to spending my life with you."

"You could've proposed at the landfill, and I would've loved it, and my answer would've been yes. I can't believe you actually had lunch with my family and I didn't figure it out." Sept was such a no-nonsense person, and that wasn't her family at all. They loved her, but they were hard to take all at once if you weren't used to them.

"When I said the three most important people, I didn't mean at the same time. Even I'm not that brave." Sept came closer and kissed the side of her neck. "So you better be nice to me."

"You *are* too good to be true," she whispered in Sept's ear before sucking on her earlobe.

"And you're a lucky woman." The way Sept hugged her warmed her body. "I already knew this before talking to them, but your mom, sister, and grandmother love you very much."

"Thank you for doing that. I'm sure it made points with all three of them."

"If that's your fishing technique for more information, it needs work," Sept said and laughed. "Come on. Jacqueline gave me some champagne that she promised would knock your pants right off."

She sat next to Sept and pinched her side as she lifted anchor. "She didn't say that."

"I'm sorry, but have you met Jacqueline?"

Sept guided them back in and carried their gear to the large wrap-around porch overlooking the lake. The hanging bed at one end had a bouquet of yellow roses next to it, and a bottle of champagne waited in an ice bucket. Keegan couldn't believe how much trouble Sept had gone to. Then again, Sept knew instinctively what made her happy, so it wasn't such a shock.

"To the years to come," Sept said, handing her a glass. "And the joy we'll experience."

"Definitely."

CHAPTER TWO

"The meeting is set up for Monday, but Sebastian Savoie seems to be on board," Gwen Berger said in her very succinct manner, wanting to get off the phone as soon as she could.

Gwen had been Nicole Voles's secretary for the last five years and three best sellers, and Nicole appreciated how the young woman could almost think for her. The flight to New Orleans wouldn't leave for another hour, so Nicole had used the time in the United concierge lounge to look over the file her mole in the NOPD was able to get a copy of.

There was still plenty to see, but the district attorney's office would have the complete file, as well as a record of Detective Sept Savoie's cooperation in putting the serial killer, Alex Perlis, away. The legal system was only a few months from the trial they hoped would land Perlis on death row. That Savoie had apprehended a crime-scene technician working his own crimes after going on a killing spree was impressive, but she was more interested in Alex Perlis.

"Sept Savoie agreed?" Nicole asked as she stared at Tameka Bishop's crime-scene photos. The call girl had met a horrific end, but Alex Perlis hadn't stopped there. He'd killed again and again, twisting the Santeria religion to meet his needs. She planned to use the story of why Alex had turned to murder and how Sept Savoie had captured him as the subject of her next book.

"Not yet, but Detective Savoie promised she'd be at the meeting Monday. I'm sure you can use your charm to persuade her to agree to whatever you want." She could hear Gwen typing as they spoke, but that was her norm. Her assistant prided herself in her ability to multitask.

"Oh, believe me, she'll agree." She pulled out a newspaper article written after the case had concluded. It was fairly standard but did include a large picture of Sept Savoie.

Sept wasn't, in appearance, what she was expecting. The detective was young, but the full head of white hair made her memorable, as well as incredibly attractive. Maybe this assignment wouldn't be as boring as usual, and maybe the detective would be interested in a little fun along with telling her story. After the phone call with Jacqueline Blanchard, she doubted it, but she loved a challenge. And sometimes after the reality of a monogamous relationship set in, the challenge was as trying as stepping over an ant hill.

Nicole studied the picture a minute longer, then skimmed the article. The subject of her book, at least one of them, wasn't real talkative when it came to giving anything up to the media, but that was good. Sept was a mine she was getting ready to strip of information. The detective simply didn't realize it yet.

"Keep after our contact," she said, starting to pack. She still had time to get a drink before her flight. "I want the whole case file along with Savoie's notes, if we can get them."

"I'll try, but don't count on it."

"Try some of that charm you used on me when you convinced me to give you this job."

Nicole ordered a drink, rested her head on the back of her chair, and closed her eyes. Of all the stories she could've tackled next, Alex Perlis had been at the top of her list because he'd come up with an almost ingenious way to kill people. As a crime-scene technician working his own crimes as a way to control evidence collection, that made him almost perfect. If it hadn't been for Sept Savoie, Alex would still be killing and trying to get his gods to resurrect his wife and son.

Luck had led Sept to Perlis, according to her father, after Nicole had shared the file with him. Nicole had read six months earlier that her dad, Brian Voles, was coming to the end of a distinguished career with the FBI, but his contributions would be remembered long after. He was the division head of counterfeiting operations in Los Angeles but could've done anything within the bureau because of his brilliant mind. Telling the stories she did, in her opinion, paid tribute to her father and his work, and she wanted the world to know how special he was.

"Ms. Voles?" A woman stood close to her chair with a hopeful expression. "I hate to bother you, but could you sign this for me?"

Nicole accepted a copy of her latest best seller and smiled. Having your eyes closed should be the universal hint for leave me alone, but unautographed books seemed to trump every rule of common courtesy. "Sure. I'd love to."

"I really should stop reading your stuff at night since you scare the hell out of me, but I can't help myself. I'm addicted to you."

She smiled as she flipped to the title page. "So should I make this out to 'addict,' or would you prefer your name?"

"Kelly...can you sign it to Kelly?"

"Sure," she said as she wrote her usual phrase but added "sweet dreams" before she finished with her signature. "I hope you're enjoying it."

"This is my second reading so I can say I totally loved it. You're one of the only authors I read more than once."

"Thank you. That's kind of you to say." She handed the book back and wanted to laugh when the woman made a move to touch her hand. "Where are you headed today?"

"Going home to New Orleans," Kelly said, and seemed to lose her shyness as she sat on the arm of her chair. "Are you on my flight?"

"Looks like it." She didn't move when Kelly put her arm around her shoulders and leaned closer. "Maybe we can find something to make the trip more interesting."

"My thoughts exactly," Kelly whispered in her ear, then stood. "The restroom is right over there." She pointed to the right and smiled, her book pressed against her chest.

"The nap I thought wasn't going to happen might be possible, depending on how talented Ms. Kelly is," Nicole said softly, hoping a bit of fun would relax her enough to sleep. This was her last frivolous dalliance before she concentrated on bending Sept Savoie to her will.

"Tell me what you want," Kelly said after Nicole entered and locked the door.

"Everything, so get on your knees."

❖

"I still can't believe it," Keegan said as she sat between Sept's legs in front of the roaring fireplace Sept had lit after cranking up the air conditioner.

"You shouldn't be too surprised." Sept kissed the side of her neck before pouring her more wine. "I had to ask before someone else came along and tried to steal you away from me."

"You're good at flattery, baby."

"Not really." She scratched Keegan's abdomen, making her laugh. "You're a beautiful, sexy woman. I can flatter all I want. It's in the contract, especially since you're mine."

"That last part is right. I am yours, and I'm incredibly happy about that." The sun had set, and she wanted to enjoy every bit of their alone time, so she ran her hands down Sept's thighs. "And in case you didn't realize how much I loved this trip—I do."

"I've got one more thing to give you."

She turned and knelt between Sept's legs. "You're sure about this, right? If you think I'm rushing—" She stopped when Sept pressed her fingers to her lips.

"I waited on the proposal this long so you wouldn't think I'm some kind of stalker, so stop talking. I'm where I most want to be." Sept kissed her and smiled. "Before we left I asked my father for a job downtown."

"Downtown?" She put her hands on Sept's shoulders and squeezed. "What does that mean?"

"It means a desk job and regular hours. I don't think it'll be hard to get because of the last case I cleared."

Keegan had waited to hear these words since the first time Sept kissed her. She closed her eyes and pressed her forehead to Sept's. She'd wanted the safety and comfort of the words, but not at the price it would cost her lover. Detective Sept Savoie was a cop who came from a long line of cops, and it's who she was. Taking her position away from Sept was like asking Keegan to leave the kitchen of Blanchard's and run her family's corporate finances. She could manage it, but she'd be miserable anywhere except as head chef at their flagship restaurant.

She couldn't help the tears that started to fall because of Sept's giving nature. No matter what they'd been through, she'd found someone who not only loved her, but understood her. That was rare.

"Hey. Why are you crying? Trust me, the only danger I'll be in now is from a paper cut."

"Thank you," she said, swiping at her cheeks impatiently. "The way you love me is beyond perfect." Sept held her gently as she kissed her and waited her out when she leaned back so Sept could see her face. "That you would do that makes me very happy, but you're really good at your job, so I don't want you to quit. I also don't want Nathan to hate me forever if he's stuck behind a desk alongside you," she said of Sept's partner, Nathan Blackman.

"I told Dad to reassign him," Sept said, sounding like she wasn't ready to let the idea go.

"Do you honestly think he'd do that? Believe me, Batman, your Robin isn't going anywhere." The muscles in Sept's neck were tense, but she tried to smile. "Believe me, honey. I may not always love what you do, but I do understand why you have to do it. More important, I don't want you to stop."

"This is about both of us," Sept said, placing her hands on Keegan's hips. "If it makes you nuts every time I go to work, I'm afraid you'll get tired of it and leave."

"You asked me to marry you and gave me a ring, so you're crazy if you think I'm going anywhere. I love you and I'm stubborn like Della, which means you're stuck with me." She put her hands over Sept's and kissed the tip of her nose. "But you do have to promise me something besides picking out china with me."

"Name it."

"Swear you'll do your best not to get shot again."

Sept laughed and nodded. "That's an easy one, and if you were wondering, the way you love me is perfect too. All I want is a long happy life with you."

"We'll have that, since the Alex Perlis case has to be a once-in-a-career one, right?" In her heart she truly believed that. Perlis had to be an anomaly that would probably define Sept's career, but surely she'd be involved in only run-of-the-mill murder cases from now on. "Tell me crazy serial killers aren't the norm."

"They aren't, and I pray to God no one like Perlis ever enters our lives again. Crime is down right now, but it's only a matter of time before that trend's over. As people start to come home after Hurricane Katrina, they'll start killing each other, but one at a time."

Keegan jumped when someone pounded on the door. "Were you expecting anyone?"

Sept shook her head. "It's probably Della making sure I didn't screw up the proposal, and if I didn't, she's had the prenup drawn up."

She laughed as she got off Sept to answer the door, since whoever it was didn't seem to want to stop knocking. "I'm coming," she said, with Sept right behind her. "Or I could be if someone wasn't at the door," she said softer to Sept.

The UPS delivery guy had his fist up to knock again when she opened the door, almost falling forward into her, but she stopped his momentum. "Sorry to bother you, but I have a delivery for Detective Sept Savoie. Is she here? She has to sign for it."

"From who?" Sept asked. The box in the guy's other hand was small and nondescript.

"I don't have any information on that." He held up his electronic clipboard. "You her? If so, please sign right here."

Sept did as he requested and asked the guy for his name as she directed him to place the box on the kitchen counter.

"What's wrong?" Keegan asked as Sept told the guy to hold on after he followed her directions. On a blank sheet of paper, she had him press his fingers down to get a good set of prints. "Seven, you're freaking me out. What's the matter?"

"Do you think Della or anyone in our families sent us something through a carrier service? When we open it, I want to know everyone who touched it."

The delivery guy didn't seem to want to leave after Sept said that.

"If Della did send us something, I doubt it could kill you." She tried to joke, but Sept's grim expression didn't change. "What is it?"

Sept shook her head and, with as little contact as possible, opened the package. She sat down with a thud when the small jar rolled out.

"Is that a human toe?" Keegan took a few deep breaths, but they weren't helping much with her nausea. "It is, isn't it?"

"I'm going to need all the information your company can send me on this delivery," Sept said to the driver. "Let's start with where it originated." She put her arms around Keegan. "You okay?"

"What's happening?" Sept's last case had been so bizarre that it had shook her, and she didn't want to repeat the experience.

"I wish I knew, baby, but it's not good." Sept stepped in front of the counter, blocking the disgusting gift from her view. "If I had to guess, it's like an invitation."

"To what? That's fucked up...sorry," the delivery guy said.

"He's right about that," Keegan said, nodding and shivering at the same time. "Everything we'll get invited to from my end will only involve hors d'oeuvres and drinks. Nothing like that will ever be given as a party favor." Sept finally laughed as she held her tighter. "What now?"

"We call the local police and hope they're willing to punt to the NOPD."

The delivery guy snorted, then stopped when Sept glared at him.

"You're not from around here, are you?" She and Sept shook their heads. "The local sheriff, Earl Boonebury, has waited his whole life for something like this. Do you get me?"

"Totally," Sept said.

"So, no punting?" Keegan asked.

"More like trying to block a brick wall wearing mirrored sunglasses, once he gets one look at this," Sept said, turning her head a little to glance at the counter again.

"Ah," the guy said. "You really do understand."

CHAPTER THREE

The NOPD headquarters appeared to still be in hurricane-recovery mode like much of the city, as a cleaning crew moved around the main entrance with lethargic movements that nonetheless stripped grime off the floor. A few others were wiping the walls with a strong-smelling cleaner, but they too were moving in slow motion.

It was Monday morning so they couldn't blame a hard, long workweek for their utter laziness. Seven months had passed since Katrina, but still most of the city was uninhabited and slow to rebuild, so it was easy to understand why the cleaning crew was so low-energy. Nicole studied them for a moment and thought of a few lines for her book.

"Can I help you?" one of the officers manning the desk asked.

"Hello, I'm Nicole Voles, and I have an appointment with Captain Savoie. Could you let him know I'm here?"

She moved to the spot the guy pointed out and tried to imagine the desperation of this city in the hours and days after the storm. Nothing she'd read or seen in the news had captured the darkness of those moments, followed by the fear that began when Perlis started killing. That was the angle she was trying to aim for in her book.

"Ms. Voles," a tall, handsome man said, and he seemed to instantly size her up.

"Captain Savoie?"

"No, ma'am." He pointed to her seat and took the one across from her. "Captain Savoie was called away on business and apologizes for not being here."

"Nothing bad, I hope," she said, trying not to show annoyance at the wasted morning. She'd been sitting around since she'd arrived on Friday and was ready to get started.

"It's not anything I can discuss at this time, and he really does send his regrets for not calling you sooner to save you the trip. I'd reschedule, but there's no way to know how involved he'll be for the foreseeable future."

"I'll give you a few days and call back." She stood and plastered on a smile.

"I have your number, so I'll call you. Are you staying in town?"

"This project will keep me busy for at least three months, maybe more, so I rented a place in the warehouse district." She took a card from her purse and handed it over. "There's my contact information, so please call me. The books are always better with local cooperation, but I can proceed without you. Only then, don't complain about any misunderstandings that are open to interpretation."

"Captain Savoie has been my boss for five years, ma'am, so trust me, he doesn't respond well to threats. The facts of this case, like any other we bring to the district attorney's office for prosecution, are black-and-white. They're not open to any interpretation, so if I were you, I'd stick to the facts." He placed her card in his jacket pocket and stood. "I'll call you when the captain wants to reschedule."

"Shit," she said under her breath, realizing she hadn't played that one smart at all. Local cops were either eager to spill everything about themselves, or they wanted to keep quiet as a way of hiding any mistakes. The quiet ones were the kind that loved to sue if you exposed them to the world for their incompetence.

"You're done already?" Gwen asked once the call connected, and Nicole could sense the smile on her assistant's face. "Was it a meeting to simply schedule interviews?"

"Savoie wasn't there, and his gatekeeper wouldn't tell me where he was. Today was a total waste of time." She crossed the street and stared at the building where Sebastian and his like ran the city. Everything her father had said about local law enforcement made sense. "Have you talked to our friend in the department?"

"I did, and I need more time. The files we got are all we're getting. I've put everything together in a report." Gwen typed something, which added to Nicole's aggravation. "It's in your email."

"Text me the contact information. I want all the case files, and I'm going to get them."

"Be careful. I'm sure you've done this before, but heavy-handedness could derail any cooperation we might get."

"Thanks, but I know what I'm doing. Just send me what I asked for." She hung up and flagged a cab. The only thing she could do while in limbo was read all the facts again. "Let's see what makes you tick, Sept Savoie."

❖

"Are we really going to court over this?" Sebastian said, sounding like he'd lost every ounce of patience he possessed. "It shouldn't matter where the jar was sent—"

"It matters who it was sent to," Sheriff Earl Boonebury said, leaning back in the office chair that appeared to be original to the hundred-and-forty-eight-year-old courthouse and police station. "The problem is," Earl said, seemingly enjoying his captive audience, "the jar arrived here. And because it did, it's my case."

"Court it is, then," Sebastian said, throwing up his hands.

"Dad," Sept said, patting him on the back. "Sheriff, how about a compromise, since it is your case."

"What you thinking, little lady?" Earl said, and her father snorted.

"You keep the jar and investigate from here, but you let us bring our forensics team in to take a look. Once they're done, we share whatever we find to help your guys crack the case." Sept winked at Sebastian, deciding to let the little-lady condescension go for now.

"And if I say no?" The sheriff really was a brick wall and appeared to be digging his heels in.

"Then we go to court and drag it out as long as it'll take to suck up the rest of your department's budget for the rest of this year and maybe cut into next year's coffers. I don't want to sound threatening—" Sept explained, smiling the whole time.

"Ha." Earl slammed his fist on his desk. "It sure as shit sounds like it."

"Believe me, I'd love nothing more than to drive back home and forget this and let you handle it. My last case gave me enough excitement for a lifetime, so why not compromise and everyone goes away happy?" Sept asked.

"They'd do the tests here?"

"Yes," Sebastian said. "They're right outside, so all they need is a place to work." Earl grunted, which they all assumed meant yes, so they left before he changed his mind.

Sept's uncle, George Falgout, was standing out in the hall with a young woman who Sept assumed was Alex Perlis's replacement on the crime-scene unit. "Hey, Uncle George. You're set to go?"

"Let me introduce you to Jennifer Shultz," George said, making the young woman put down the cases she was carrying. "She just started on my team."

Sept wondered why Jennifer had joined his team but would never bring it up. Her uncle was in a way the most haunted by their last case, having worked with and mentored one of the worst killers in the city's history. Her father had told her George had wished she or her partner Nathan had pulled the trigger. In his opinion, Perlis didn't deserve to live, and given the chance, George would've ended his life.

"Welcome aboard, Jennifer," Sept said, shaking her hand. "You two have the go-ahead, so take all the time you need. Dad will go with you to keep George from strangling Sheriff Earl."

"Where are you going?" George asked.

"To pick up Keegan and relieve the deputies the sheriff assigned to her."

"Tell her congratulations from me and your Aunt Mary. You finally wised up and snagged the best girl in town," George said and hugged her. "Having Keegan keeping you in line will give your poor mama a rest."

"Don't tell people I'm already whipped, Uncle George. I'll lose all my street creds."

Sept drove back to the cabin, glancing in her rearview mirror occasionally to make sure no one was following her. The chance was nil, and her gift in the mail probably wouldn't amount to much, but she wasn't taking any chances. She had so much more to worry about now that she was with Keegan, and she didn't want some sicko touching anything in Keegan's world.

"Learn anything?" Keegan asked when she got out of the car.

"The mailing information was a dead end, and Uncle George and his new assistant are working on the mystery toe." She waved to the deputies, who didn't seem inclined to leave but were staring at them like they expected *her* to commit a crime. "We can stop at the courthouse and check on their progress, but if they don't need us for anything, we can go home."

"George's new assistant doesn't have any marital problems, right?"

She laughed at Keegan's ability to stay upbeat even when she was afraid. Even before Alex Perlis had started his killing spree, he'd been a serial abuser, his wife and young son his first victims. "She came across okay, but I'll check her personal life later. You ready to go?"

"We're all packed, but will you promise me something before we head out?" Keegan pressed against her, and the deputies leaned forward and removed their sunglasses as if shocked and wanting to get a better look.

"Name it."

"When we go on our honeymoon, can we skip stuff like this? Not that I don't love your family, but I prefer the non-work-related stuff instead."

She laughed, since her father had spent the last two nights with them, mostly using his time to fight with the sheriff from hell. "You got it, baby, and I promise to open the door only to room service."

They packed the car and got the okay to leave, so she started the five-hour trip back, which would give her time to think about what this was all about and how best to tackle it. Usually when someone wanted to send a message or make a point, there *was* actually a message. Body parts were good for shock value, but nothing beat a handwritten note.

"What are you brooding about?" Keegan asked.

"The delivery, considering where we were, is strange," she said hesitantly, not having her thoughts in order. "Like I said, it's almost an invitation to something, but I'm not interested. Don't you think it's someone else's turn to hog the headlines?"

"Maybe it's an invitation to play with the cop who captured Perlis."

"I doubt they're interested in playing with our dog, babe," she said, and Keegan elbowed her.

"Mike is brilliant, but he can't take credit for all your hard work. And I almost forgot. What did your dad call you about a few days ago? It slipped my mind to ask when he arrived."

"Some woman called him and Chief Jernigan about writing a book on the Perlis case. She wants to interview me and everyone who worked the case, but she's concentrating on me."

"That's wonderful," Keegan said, squeezing her hand. "Isn't it?"

"You know how much I love media and being the center of attention." She laughed along with Keegan, but what she'd said was true. "The job and doing my best is enough for me, and it's not me against the world. I have a good team and plenty of support."

"I know that, love, but if Fritz Jernigan okayed this, you know how he is, so I doubt he'll let it go if it's something he wants you to do. After some of the stuff about the department that made national headlines during the storm, he's going to want all the good press he can get." Keegan rested her head back and ran her hand up and down Sept's arm. "And I know how you are. If you're forced to do this, you won't make it about you."

"I'm ready to get back to work, but I'm nervous about it too. Perlis took a little of what I most believe in and count on, and I'm trying to convince myself it was a one-time thing." It had been a long time since she'd taken time off simply to have a good time, and she couldn't wait to do it again with Keegan. "You're the one thing I can count on, and I'm happy about it. It's good to have you all to myself."

"That's always going to be true, but tell me what you think he took from you."

"Trust, and I mean absolute trust in my team. I've never worried about the people who are supposed to have my back. Getting shot by one of my own isn't the way it should go."

"Alex Perlis is a crazy bastard who fell through the cracks, so don't lump everyone else you work with in with him. You're a good cop, and I'm going to be blissfully happy sharing my life with you since, aside from being the noblest person I've ever met, you're sexy as hell. You just have to promise me that you'll talk to me no matter what." Keegan moved and kissed her cheek, then her neck. "You promise?"

"I promise, and the same goes for you. If anything's worrying you, don't clam up on me."

"I'm not the tough, stoic one in this relationship, baby, so that's a given." Keegan's phone rang, and she put it on speaker after her tease. "You didn't burn the restaurant down, did you?" she asked her sister Jacqueline.

"Be nice to me. I'm calling to congratulate you and stud muffin, and to check on you guys. Gran said Sept's dad had to go up there and meet you two for something. Are y'all okay?"

"How in the hell does Della know everything that's happening in the city?" Sept asked, and she and Jacqueline laughed. "Someone sent us a toe as an engagement present, so Dad came up and tried to take charge of the investigation."

"A human toe?" Jacqueline paused as if not knowing how to respond. "Never mind. I don't want to know right this minute, since I'd rather hear about the happy, hot time you two had."

Keegan rolled her eyes and laughed. "We're not talking about our sex lives no matter how often you ask, so drop it already."

"It's spectacular. That's the only thing you need to know on the subject," Sept said.

"Thank God one of you is sensible. When are you getting home?"

"By six, if the traffic's decent," Keegan said, and she nodded.

"Good. Meet me at Blanchard's at eight, and do not put on the muumuu outfit. We're celebrating your engagement, so you can start cooking tomorrow."

"We'll be there, and thank you for the champagne," Sept said.

"In case you haven't figured it out, we're glad you're going to be a part of our family."

"Thank you," she said as Keegan said her good-byes. "Let's hope your family always feels that way."

"You're stuck with us now, Seven, no matter what happens."

CHAPTER FOUR

The rules are clear, so if this is some weird shit, I'm out of here." Bonnie Matherne was easy to find, and even easier to entice once lured off Airline Drive right on the edge of the city limits.

The area was a string of fast-food joints, cheap hotels, and the kind of prostitutes glad to spend the night with you for a hundred bucks. Bonnie, though, had laid down the law once she entered the room that smelled of mold and age, and she didn't appear to want to back off her demands.

"How much for the night?" the hunter asked, knowing the mask was putting Bonnie on edge, but the roll of money on the dresser was enough to keep her feet planted. Bonnie had been an obvious victim of a harsh life, but the hunter didn't feel any sympathy or remorse for what had to happen. "The whole night and a little bondage?" The odor of the place was nauseating, but it was important to keep the outer façade in place.

"What exactly do you mean by light bondage?" Bonnie asked, swaying from foot to foot like she was restless for something that most probably wasn't sex, and she appeared high on something that wasn't alcohol. "And what's with the mask?"

"I need to know you won't touch me during our session. I don't feel comfortable being touched in any way that I don't initiate, but I'm willing to pay extra for your discomfort. My face isn't what people expect, so this is better."

Bonnie glanced at the money again, and it was easy to read what was most probably going through her drug-addled brain. That roll would keep Bonnie high for weeks, if the idiot didn't overdose before the cash ran out and she was actually lucky enough to make it out the door. "Do we have a deal?"

"You want something more than straight sex? I'll suck your dick, but no back-door stuff." Bonnie came a step closer, which was a good sign. Why did stupid people never have an ounce of instinct, that little voice in the pit of your stomach that told you to run in situations like this, the hunter thought as Bonnie inched even closer.

"Trust me, nothing like that. So how much?"

"Five hundred," Bonnie said, almost like a question, since the hunter knew she'd never made that much off a john in her pathetic life.

"Five hundred it is." Even Bonnie, with her cheap spandex dress and bad teeth, was worth more than five hundred dollars, but bad things happened to you when you thought so little of yourself.

"What's your name, honey?"

"Hunter." The name seemed appropriate and would make the night easier. "Come here." It was an order, but Bonnie's mind was obviously on spending the cash, so she complied without another complaint.

"No kissing either," Bonnie said, leaning away. "That's extra, if you want to take that mask off and do it."

"Kissing isn't required," Hunter said and leaned toward Bonnie. The needle caused only a moment of discomfort, but Bonnie was out a moment later, landing at an odd angle on the bed. "You'll thank me later when I release you from this hellish existence."

It was easy to load Bonnie into the old Ford sedan, since the last room was the only one occupied on this side of the hotel. What came next would take some time, so privacy was necessary. The city had made tremendous strides in their cleanup effort, but New Orleans East was still a flood-ravaged, mold-riddled ghost town. It was as perfect now for Hunter's plans as it'd been months before, when Alex had picked it as the place to start his fun.

The way Bonnie's eyes widened when she came to was almost comical, but they were one of the only parts of her body she could still move. Her screaming stopped when Hunter's knife pressed under her right eye and a gloved finger came up to the mouth of the mask as a cue for silence. Her gaudy dress and shoes were folded and stacked next to her, making her look pale and sick on the patch of cleared floor.

"Do you feel special, Bonnie?" The furniture in the place had rotted from the flood and neglect, so Hunter crouched next to her, surprised the wood floor was still relatively flat. At least flat enough for the stage it would become.

"What the fuck is this, you sick fuck?" Bonnie screamed, pulling the ropes taut. The nails Hunter had driven held fast.

"It's time to start my game, and you get to go first, which makes you special." The supply bag was next to Hunter, and everything in it was arranged in the order it'd be needed. The research phase of this process had been new and completely foreign from the early exploits Hunter had accomplished. It wasn't often Hunter was this excited to start a new game. "Do you read the papers, Bonnie?"

"No." She sounded strained as she fought her bindings again.

"Shame." The red candle that came from the religious store seemed garish, but this ritual required certain steps. The flame flickered very little in the stale air as the smell of sulfur from the match lingered for a few seconds. "If you'd read the papers, you'd appreciate what's going to happen more."

"Fuck," Bonnie screamed again when the sharp knife that gleamed in the candlelight cut into her left wrist. "What the shit is this?"

The blood that streaked from Bonnie's wrist didn't seem as dark as with previous victims, but that didn't matter. Hunter used it to draw the number three on Bonnie's forehead and then the number two on the top of one foot and a one on the other. "All this nonsense doesn't mean anything to me, so don't fault me for it." Bonnie was shaking her head, making the number three streaky, so Hunter retraced it. "It's weird, isn't it, what some people will do for religion's sake? I've always been of the mind that you make your own path, your own luck, and most important, your own fate."

A potato-sized rock came out next, painted half black and half red. "This goes here." The rock rested perfectly against Bonnie's sex, and she didn't move when the knife pressed against her abdomen. "These gods are so particular when it comes to color and numbers, but that's like everyone, I guess. We all have our little quirks." The crime-scene photo and the actual scene were very alike so far, but Hunter checked once more to make sure.

"Look, do whatever you want, but leave me the fuck alone. Keep your fucking money," Bonnie said, crying now.

"Everyone likes and dislikes things," Hunter said, not paying attention to her plea, "so gods shouldn't be any different. We all want what we want." The knife went into the left side of Bonnie's abdomen, and her scream was rather satisfying and not something that could be indulged in very often. It stopped when Hunter sliced to the right, effectively gutting Bonnie like a deer that had to be field dressed. Her guts spilled, but not as much as Hunter would've thought.

Bonnie's heart was still warm when Hunter reached in and ripped it out, a feat not as easy as it had sounded when it'd been mentioned in the police report. Hunter held it close to the light of the candle and squeezed, surprised at how much blood squished out. "This is for Elegua, the god of beginnings and roads. Open the path for me along with Eshu Afrá, your companion, who gathers the bodies of the dead. This road will be long and unending between us."

Hunter held the heart up as the prayer was offered to the god being called, almost sad the ceremony was almost over. "Thanks for the great night, Bonnie," Hunter said and chuckled. The heart went next to the candle in the circle of salt the ceremony called for, followed by the bath of water and rum.

"Mr. Perlis, you're a truly sick fuck, as Bonnie so eloquently said, but I have to admit this was rather fun." Everything so far was textbook from the case, so it was time to either stick with the plan or improvise. "A number seven on each breast seems so amateurish." The bag held one more thing, and it seemed a better fit.

"Let the games begin."

❖

"Just remember one thing, Sept," Della Blanchard said as the waiters at Blanchard's served drinks. "You hurt my beloved granddaughter, and I know people."

"I know you do, and I live in fear of you, so don't worry. I'll cherish Keegan forever because I love her, not because you threaten me," she said, causing Keegan to squeeze her thigh. "And if you don't behave, we're not naming any of our kids after you."

"I want plenty of great-grandchildren, so don't skimp on the number," Della teased back, and the rest of the family laughed. "You've certainly brought excitement into our lives, Sept, and I feel blessed you're now part of our family."

"Hopefully our excitement days will stay at a minimum, Gran," Keegan said, waving off the menus. "Tell the kitchen to feed us," she said to the waiter. "It's good to be surprised every so often."

"Your vacation certainly sounded like a surprise," Melinda, Keegan's mother said, and Jacqueline groaned.

"Please, Mom, don't ruin my appetite," Jacqueline said. "There's plenty of time for Sept to fill us in, just not right before dinner."

"It was a surprise, ma'am, but good people are working the case, so I'm hoping whoever did this will be in custody soon," Sept said, realizing it would take time for the Blanchards to get used to the ugly side of life they were seldom exposed to. "Starting tomorrow I'll be back on active duty, so I'll keep you all updated."

"Tomorrow?" Della asked. "Are you sure you're fully recovered? I don't need to make any calls downtown, do I?"

"You don't need to call anyone, but I appreciate it. I'm back in top form, ma'am. If not, Keegan would have locked me in the house."

Della nodded and smiled at Keegan. "Don't let anything happen to you if you're going back out on the streets, Sept. Think of how long it'll take you to get back in my good graces if you defy that order."

"You all keep this up, and I'll need to hog-tie her to get her to an altar," Keegan said, pointing at each person in her family. "And the vacation included more than our gruesome delivery, Mom." Keegan held up her hand. "She asked and I said yes. Thanks for this, Gran."

"Accepting the gift of my ring proved to me that you're the right person for Keegan," Della said to Sept. "My grandmother wore it, and like her grandmother did for her, she left it to me before she passed. That ring represents so much more than a family heirloom. It holds within that stone a lot of happy memories and happy years to the women who've worn it." Della took her hand and smiled at her. "That you understood what this ring means to our family history makes me think you'll put Keegan's happiness first throughout your lives together. Anyone else's ego might've gotten in the way."

"I have ego for a lot of things, but when it comes to the things that are important to Keegan, that won't ever be the case," she said as the appetizers came out.

"So when are we having a ceremony?" Melinda asked.

"I'll leave that up to Keegan and you. You tell me when and where, and I'll be there in a nice suit." Keegan pinched the top of her hand hard, and Jacqueline repeated the move on the other hand, meaning her answer had been dead wrong. "Or you let me know when you want me to start making plans, and I'll be there to help out."

Jacqueline kissed her on the cheek. "Why the hell can't I find one this trainable?"

"Don't say stuff like that out loud, Jacqueline," Keegan said, and Della winked at her. "There's no need reminding her she's still in the learning phase."

The waiters surrounded the table and placed all the appetizers at once with their usual flair, making all the Blanchards quieten as they tried the first course. They all appeared to be judging a cooking competition, but Sept had long since gotten used to the food peculiarities of this family. The Blanchards really were restaurant royalty and took every aspect of their business very seriously.

"Thank you, and let Louis know this is delicious," Keegan told the head waiter.

"It is good, but I'm not forgetting that you think me and Mike are in the same boat," Sept said about their dog. Mike had actually been a guide dog to Perlis's second victim and had been adopted by her and Keegan when he'd had to be retired. "But on a different topic, my mother invited everyone over for Sunday lunch, so would y'all mind missing our usual brunch date for once?"

"Camille's already called us, and I talked her into coming to the house," Jacqueline said. "It's been too long since our kitchen's been used the way Great-granddad intended. She and your sisters-in-law will be there early to help with the cooking."

"Well, I guess I'll just have to worry about my job from now on." She was joking but was happy their two families were getting along so well.

"True, and I'll be taking plenty of notes from Camille on how to make you behave, so consider yourself warned," Keegan said, and Sept couldn't help but kiss her. "And I'll let you off the hook for our first couple of meetings for our ceremony, if you'll tell me what you want."

"I want you standing next to me saying I do," she said, and Jacqueline gagged, along with Della.

"You two are sickening," Jacqueline said, "but put me down for the planning parts of the happy occasion. And I didn't mention this before, but some woman called and wanted to talk to me about some book she's writing."

"Did she say why?" Sept asked, thanking the waiter for bringing her another plate of the garlic toast the restaurant made.

"Somehow she knew you live with me and Keegan, and she said she wanted a full picture of what it was like when you were trying to solve this case. I'm not sure what I can add aside from you're quiet except when—" Jacqueline stopped but laughed when Keegan kicked her under the table. "You're watching football on television," she said, sticking her tongue out at Keegan. "You're dedicated to your job but don't talk about ongoing investigations no matter how much we beg you to."

"That's not remotely true. I give you plenty of inside scoop, but I appreciate you not passing that along to someone I've never met."

"Who is this person?" Della asked.

"Crime writer Nicole Voles. She's after the story of Alex Perlis and the detective that caught him," Keegan said as one of the hosts came up and whispered in her ear. "Excuse me for a second. I'll be right back."

"Problem?" Della asked.

"A little snafu in the kitchen," Keegan said, waving her hand toward the host. "It shouldn't take long."

"I've heard of this woman," Della said. "But why would she want to talk to any of us at all when you should be the center of this story?"

"Probably because I'm not interested in being the center of her book. I'm sure Perlis's crimes fascinate some people, but I had to live the situation, and I'm not too hyped to go back there. I don't believe that sick bastard's atrocities should be celebrated or sensationalized."

"You won't have any problems from us, babe," Jacqueline said. "I love you for you, and for what you do."

"It's not that I'm shy," Sept said, and Melinda laughed.

"That's true. You've given Mama an earful since you met her," Melinda said and glanced at Della. "And I happen to think she secretly loves it."

"I know she does, but being the center of attention also makes Keegan and you all the center of attention too, from people I don't want anywhere near you."

Della put her hand up as if to ask for Sept's attention. "What does that mean?"

"It means the world is full of crazy, evil people. My world is more than my job, so I don't want those kinds of idiots reading about what's most important in my life. If all I do is my job and move on from case to case, then I'll be satisfied." She placed her hand over Della's and kissed her cheek. "I'm not ashamed of my love for you and your family, but I don't want to advertise it to anyone who might want to get back at me simply because they don't like what I do."

"You're going to make it impossible not to mention you in my will," Della said and laughed.

She smiled and stood when she saw Keegan coming back with Melinda's new girlfriend, Dr. Carla St. John. "I'm so sorry I'm late, but I got stuck in surgery," Carla said as she shook Sept's hand. "Congratulations on the engagement. We're lucky to have found such beautiful women, huh?"

Keegan rolled her eyes where only she and Jacqueline could see her, and Sept felt for them both, since they were still in the process of accepting Carla into Melinda's life. Melinda's longtime partner, who'd raised the girls with Melinda, had died a few years prior, and their mother had only recently started dating.

"Thanks, but they're much more than that, so we are lucky," she said, and Keegan kissed her for that remark as well. "I'm glad you could make it."

"Mrs. Blanchard, how are you?" Carla asked. She hadn't made a very good impression on Della, and the ice wasn't melting on that relationship any time soon.

"I'm well, thank you. Shall we begin?" Della said, cutting off any other small talk.

The meal was delicious as they worked through a few small plates so the kitchen could bring out a variety, and they ended up with a mini wedding-style cake as a surprise. Sept put her arm around Keegan when the waiter placed it in front of them and suddenly couldn't wait to start planning a day where she could tell the world how she felt about this woman.

She raised her glass, and the others followed suit. "To Chef Donovan," she said, remembering the pastry chef who'd been killed right outside the back door of the restaurant, bringing her into Keegan's life. Donovan had been one of Keegan's good friends, and Sept knew how much she missed him. "He died too young, for no good reason, but his parting gift was special. I wish I'd met him, but I'll be forever grateful for his sacrifice."

"Well said, sweetheart," Della said. "And to Keegan and Sept, may your days be filled with happiness, love, and good fortune. And, most important, children for me to spoil."

They finished dinner, and Sept walked Della down the stairs, enjoying her quick wit. "Thanks for everything and for agreeing to change your Sunday routine."

"That I don't mind, but you need to do me a favor."

"Name it, aside from jailing your enemies in the food industry," she joked, and Della shook her head.

"I've got other people for that, so concentrate on what and who you love. Tomorrow you're going back to something you enjoy doing, but don't ever stop talking to Keegan about everything. That's the secret to making something last."

"And don't forget to take care of yourself," Melinda added. "Don't worry about Mike until you get off work. I've enjoyed having him around."

"Thanks, Mom, from both of us, but we'll pick him up tonight before we head home," Keegan said. "Come by tomorrow and have lunch with me, and we'll get started on our rough draft." She went willingly into her mother's arms. "I love you."

"I love all three of you," Melinda said as she hugged Sept, then Jacqueline. "And this was a nice night to celebrate and give Sept a good send-off to start work again. I know you've missed it."

"I have a little, and I'm sure it'll be boring for a while, but I won't complain." She crossed her fingers and smiled, but figured she'd just jinxed herself simply by mentioning the word "boring."

❖

"What was that like?" Terri Schultz asked her daughter Jennifer as she finished preparing dinner. "You've wanted this job for so long, and now you're mixed up right in the middle of it. I don't like it."

"Ma, calm down. It was simply a quick trip out of town to test some evidence." Jennifer picked a cucumber out of the salad and sat on a stool at the kitchen island. "It's not a trip to the gallows."

She'd grown up in a family of lawyers, but no matter how much her parents had pushed, she wasn't interested in the firm her great-grandfather had established. She didn't want to walk a beat either, so she'd picked forensics, applied to work with George Falgout, and persisted until he said yes.

"The drive up there was good, since I got to pick George's brain and get to know him better. You don't often see something like the Perlis case, and that bastard was working the scenes. He cleaned up any mistakes he'd made while the city was paying him to do it." The realization still made her angry because people would point to Perlis when they wanted to blame the police for something.

"Sweetie, you're going to have to let that one go and concentrate on doing a good job," Chloe Johnson, Jennifer's partner, said as she put her arms around Jennifer and kissed her. "I'm glad you're home. How'd it go?"

Chloe had gone to work for Jennifer's father and quickly become one of the firm's frontrunners to make partner, even without the added bonus of dating David Schultz's daughter. They'd actually met in the courtroom when Jennifer had been the officer who'd explained the evidence against Chloe's client to the jury. No matter how hard Chloe had tried, she hadn't been able to rattle her. That had come much later, after their fourth date. Now Chloe could rattle her plenty, but the tone of the questions was very different and very personal.

"It was okay," she said, resting her head on Chloe's chest. "I missed you."

"I missed you too, but I caught up on my caseload so I can spend the entire dinner with the family. No cutting out early, but I can't say the same for Dad." Chloe scratched her back and kissed her forehead before hugging Terri. "Thanks for cooking, Mom."

"Can't you use some of your womanly wiles to convince this one to go back to law school? She's been assigned to her new team for a whole whopping three days, and something strange has already happened," Terri said, kissing Chloe's cheek.

Chloe stared at her with wide eyes, as if Jennifer had lost her mind. "I use those to get her to take out the trash and cut the grass, but I guess I can refocus," Chloe said, holding her hand out to her. "Come on. Let's go sit outside so I can seduce you to the dark side."

She and her mother laughed, but she wasn't foolish enough to turn Chloe down. "I know what you're thinking," she said when they shared a chaise lounge by the pool.

"If it's that I'm shocked you're sharing war stories with the most overprotective, paranoid mother in the world, then yes, that's what I'm thinking." Chloe undid a few of Jennifer's shirt buttons and slipped her hand inside to scratch her abdomen. "Am I right?"

"You usually are," she said, closing her eyes and enjoying the attention. "But you know better."

"So what happened? Think carefully before you give me the company line," Chloe said, pinching the skin by her navel.

"We made a deal, sunshine, so try again." She grabbed Chloe's hand before she pinched harder. "We never know when our jobs will overlap, so I'll tell you the same thing I told Mom. I went with George to test some evidence—end of story."

"More like incomplete story, hardhead. Any particular reason you and George are going that far to test anything?" Chloe moved up a bit so she could whisper in her ear. "You know you're dying to tell me."

"Actually, I'm dying to make out with you, but Mom is probably glued to the window spying on us. So we'll save that for later, and you'll be too engaged to ask any more questions."

"Are you usually this delusional?" Chloe asked, turning her head and kissing her passionately. "And maybe Mom is trying to learn something from you aside from what you were doing in North Louisiana."

"Nice try, but not going to work."

"You're no fun, Schultz. Let's go eat so we can get naked."

She laughed, standing so she could help Chloe up. "You're definitely the idea person in this relationship."

"I'm also the ovulating person in this relationship, so you've got some work to do when we get home. With any luck this will be the surprise everyone will be excited about for the holidays." Chloe held her in place by the belt and lifted her face to request a kiss. "I love you, Officer, so make sure you've got your cuffs later."

"You live to make me blush in front of my mother, don't you?" she said but slid her hands down to cup Chloe's ass.

"It is one of the things I live for, since your mother gets such a kick out of it." Chloe wrapped her arms around her waist and pressed the side of her face against her chest. "Thank you for choosing me and introducing me to your family. They and you have been the greatest gifts I've ever gotten."

"You're easy to love, baby, and my mother and father love you more than me and Davie. As a matter of fact, I think you're their favorite." And that wasn't far from the truth. Chloe had been in the child-welfare system from age six, so how she'd come through so whole and happy was something Jennifer gave thanks for.

"That simply means Mom and Dad are very intelligent people." Chloe kissed her on the chin and gazed into her eyes. "Promise me you'll be careful."

"I'm always careful, so that's not going to change."

"The scope of what you'll be doing will change, though, and it makes me a little nuts. We both know George and the people who work for him are the leads for major crimes, which will put you in the thick of it." Chloe cupped her cheek with a very serious expression. "If you get hurt, I don't know if I can handle it."

"Would it help if we talk about some new terms to our deal?"

"Like what?" Chloe sounded suspicious.

"You or the firm can't be in any way involved with the case."

Chloe shook her head, hugging her again. "I want you to talk to me only if something's bothering you. That's the deal."

"You got it, and the same goes for you."

"I will, but tonight I'm only interested in using your mouth for purely pleasurable pursuits."

CHAPTER FIVE

Sept finished getting ready by clipping her holster to her belt and her badge on the front. The sigh Keegan let out behind her as she sat on the bed made her turn around and smile. She knelt between Keegan's legs and kissed her for a long moment, wanting to put her at ease.

"I doubt we'll be doing anything that'll keep us late, so I'll pick you up tonight."

"I'll get Jacqueline to give me a ride then, so we don't have two cars tonight," Keegan said, pressing their foreheads together. "Now start channeling that badass cop I met months ago." Keegan waved her to her feet and held her hand as they walked down the stairs. Their dog Mike was already in the kitchen since Jacqueline took him on her morning runs.

Sept was surprised to find her partner Nathan in there as well. "Did you get lost?" she asked, heading for the coffee pot.

"If Keegan invites me over for a meal, I'm coming. I'm not an idiot, and partnering up with you has been the smartest move of my career so far," Nathan said, and the sisters laughed.

"Leave him alone, honey," Keegan said, pointing to the table so they'd sit. "I need Nathan at full strength to keep an eye on you. You know how you get into trouble if left to your own devices."

"What are you two up to now that you're back to wearing the capes?" Jacqueline asked, pouring everyone orange juice.

"We'll be back in rotation, so we'll work cases as they come in," she said, her stomach growling when Keegan took a breakfast casserole out of the oven. "Hopefully, I don't have to chase anyone after I eat my weight in that."

Nathan's phone rang, and she laughed, thinking of how obnoxious

Della considered being interrupted during any family dinner. "Sorry, it's Royce," he said, mentioning their supervisor. "Yes, sir."

He stayed on the phone for five minutes and pinched the bridge of his nose when he wasn't writing anything down. "What?" she mouthed, and he put his finger up. "We'll be there in twenty."

"What?" she asked again, reaching for her jacket.

"I don't want to tell you," he said, glancing at Keegan's breakfast. "But we have to go."

"Nathan," Keegan said, filling two paper plates and handing him one. "Take care of her, or I'll sic my grandmother on you."

"Yes, ma'am. I promise not to take my eyes off her."

"Be careful, and call if you get a chance," Keegan said, kissing her again. "If you're not too late, we can have the big talk with Jacqueline."

"You got it. Have fun at work today," she said, kissing Jacqueline's cheek since she'd wandered over at hearing her name. "No hints until I get back, so cut Keegan some slack."

Nathan was in the car shoving casserole into his mouth when she joined him and waited for him to swallow before asking questions. "I'm not going to like this, am I?" she asked, and he shook his head.

He slapped the blue light on the roof and took off down St. Charles Avenue, headed for the interstate. "Royce said some fucker called in asking for you and got bitchy when you didn't come to the phone. After Royce talked to them, he or she gave up an address."

"He or she?" She took a bite of breakfast, thinking this would be her last meal for some time.

"Royce couldn't tell since they used one of those voice manipulators. He said it could've been his mother and he wouldn't have recognized her."

"Did our mystery person give a hint as to what this was about?"

"No, but the address is in New Orleans East, a block from where we found Tameka Bishop."

"Fuck," she said, and Nathan nodded. This nightmare couldn't be starting over already. "Royce," she said, calling him and hearing a lot of talking in the background. "Shut that scene down if you haven't, and call George, but tell him to wait until I get there."

"Already done, and I've got plenty of uniforms out here locking down a block perimeter. The news folks are already here, kid, and they're asking some pretty informed questions."

"Your tipster most probably made more than one call then, and if they did, it's only going to make this harder." Nathan reached the on-ramp and gunned it.

Alex Perlis had chosen New Orleans East because it'd been pretty much deserted after Katrina, and now months later it wasn't much better. The water had stagnated here longer than anywhere else, so the area still had that gray, desolate feel about it. Some people had come back, but not enough to put anyone remotely close to where Tameka had been killed.

"Just get here, and I'll call Sebastian," Royce said and hung up.

"This is too close to Perlis, and there's no way we got the wrong guy," Nathan said.

"I won't argue that point, but this sounds like Perlis minus the phone call. He called but not until he'd killed numerous times." She ate the rest of what Keegan had given her before calling her. "Hey, have Jacqueline drop you off at work and take you home. We might be late, but I'll call you if I'm going to be real late."

"You've been back like thirty seconds, so what can keep you out late already?"

"I'll tell you later, but I'm headed to a crime scene in New Orleans East. Don't put a lot into that statement, but this could be more involved than I was expecting on my first day."

"I love you, so please be careful."

"I love you more, so keep those pretty eyes open."

It took them another fifteen minutes to reach the first blockade Royce had set up, and the uniform made them walk in. She would've complained, but Royce had given explicit instructions to keep the crime scene as uncontaminated as possible.

The houses lining both sides of the street were all still abandoned, and some appeared vandalized, which was ridiculous. These people had lost everything, and now that the water had receded, addicts had flooded their homes, looking for a place to shoot up. The police were having to canvass this area again, but instead of drowning victims, they were searching for dead junkies.

"This place is creepy during the day, so can you imagine at night?" Nathan said as he flipped his pad to a new page.

"Let's have patrols beefed up and round up some of the crank heads around here. It's iffy, but one of them might've seen something," she said and stopped to stare at the next block down. The house where Tameka had died would definitely be her next stop. "Hey, John," she said to the sergeant at the end of the cracked driveway. "Send a couple of guys to that house and lock it down too." She pointed to the place, and he nodded. "Tell them not to go in, and we'll be over when we're done."

She entered the house before Nathan and walked to the center of the first room. The scene was like stepping back into Perlis's nightmare. "Should we get in touch with Dr. Munez?" Nathan asked.

Dr. Julio Munez was a professor of sociology that centered on religious studies, but he was a devout believer in Santeria. It was the religion Perlis had twisted to get what his sick mind wanted, helped by the voice in his head he called Teacher. Perlis had killed his wife and son, then had killed numerous times in the name of what Sept and Nathan had learned were the Santeria orishas, or gods. The altars Perlis had constructed were his way of getting his family back, each one dedicated to an orisha that would bring him closer to that goal.

Julio had helped them navigate the scenes they'd come across when Perlis was on his killing spree, and he'd also helped introduce them to the leaders of his faith within New Orleans.

"Can't hurt, so hopefully he's not in class." She put on some booties and stepped close enough to see the victim's face. The beam of her flashlight highlighted the dust particles floating in the air, but Sept didn't recognize the dead woman. The scene, though, was more than familiar, down to the red candle and the numbers drawn on the woman's head and feet. It would've never occurred to her that Perlis had a partner, but perhaps Teacher wasn't in his head and was someone real who wasn't with Perlis when they caught him.

"It's the same but different," she said as she stood next to the body studying the room.

"What's different?" Nathan asked, standing across from her.

"Perlis did what he did to open some door between our world and the world of the dead to talk to the wife and child he sent there. Every crime, with the exception of the first two, were these altars he erected for these gods. He was methodical, but he evolved as he went, adding the messages we found." She pointed to the candle, stone, and folded clothes. "All that matches, but this scene seems more organized somehow. And they added the statue of St. Anthony. If Julio's willing, we need to get him out here."

"I called him, and a unit's on the way to pick him up," Nathan said as he wrote something down. "Do you think Perlis's lawyer is going to use this to try to get him out?"

"No way in hell that works, but if he had an accomplice he's going to be keeping that sick bastard company on death row if he misses him that much." She wanted to start picking stuff up, but she had to wait for George and his crew. "I'd rather set my feet on fire, but we're going to have to pay Perlis a visit."

Perlis's mental stability had only deteriorated during the months he'd been in lockup, and she'd heard the medical staff had no choice but to start medicating him, if only to keep him from beating his head against the walls of his cell. He'd been trying to quiet the voice in his head he kept accusing of making him mad. Sept had thought it was all horseshit, but maybe Perlis's playmate was sending a message of how much Perlis was missed.

"Sept." She recognized her father's voice outside.

"Put some booties on and come in, and if Uncle George is with you, have him join you." She took one more glance around the room to see if anything else was out of place in a space where everything was out of place. The dead woman with the religious stuff around her was the only neat spot here. "Look familiar?"

"Holy shit," Sebastian said, combing his hair back in apparent frustration. "We just got the media to not lead with all this crap, and we get a copycat?"

"Let's not jump to conclusions," she said, waving to George and Jennifer. "I doubt you'll find any, but go ahead and dust for prints."

"There's no way someone got it this right," George said as they prepared to start.

"Not unless they had intimate knowledge of the case or Perlis was their best friend," she said. Sebastian whipped his head around to stare at her. "That doesn't leave this room, but it's a possibility, Dad."

"Believe me, Sept, we don't know each other well yet, but I'm going to work hard with George to get you what you need," Jennifer said.

"I know, and I know your dad, so you're good people," Sept said with a smile. "Now if my dog's got a problem with you, I'm taking you down." She laughed, since it was Mike that had first reacted when he'd caught Perlis's scent. Since Mike had belonged to her second victim, he'd been there when Perlis killed Robin Burns. The growling and aggressive barking Mike had directed at Perlis's office chair had prompted Sept to go to his house.

"I'm more of a cat person, but you still don't have a problem."

Sept watched them set up away from the body and start dusting for prints. "Step out for a minute," Sebastian said, and Nathan followed her out. "What do you think?"

"It's too early to make any conclusive statements, but if it's a copycat, it's a damn good job."

Her father sighed, and she almost repeated the action when Chief of Police Fritz Jernigan sprang out of his car, and the media came to life. "When is he going to learn to not feed the animals," Sebastian said, shaking his head. "And no comment from either of you about that."

"No problem, sir," Nathan said. "I'll go wait and escort Julio in when he gets here."

"Have the line moved back even more after Chief Jernigan is done, and do your best to keep Julio under wraps. These guys don't need any further encouragement to sensationalize this," she said, and Nathan saluted her.

"What are you really thinking, so I can try to steer Fritz the showboat in the right direction?"

"I need to finish here, and then I'm going to have to sit with that son of a bitch Perlis again. This scene is too perfect not to be somehow related to what he did." She scrubbed her hands over her face and took a deep breath. "Maybe, and I really mean maybe, Perlis's imaginary friend Teacher isn't so imaginary."

"Why now though?"

"I don't know, but there might've been a breach in security, and he might've finally either gotten a message or been able to get one out. In his sick mind, he didn't finish what he set out to do, and this is the only way to complete his fucked-up mission."

"Great, just great," Sebastian said, elbowing her when Fritz headed their way. "Hello, sir."

"Hey, you two," Fritz said, shaking hands with both of them. "Let's go right inside since my only reason for being here is to welcome Sept back to active duty. At least that's my excuse as far as the media is concerned. From what Sebastian said, though, we might have another clusterfuck on our hands."

"Take a quick look, sir, but it's not good." She could hear him cursing under his breath when he saw the body. "I'm sure the media out there will give you crap about Alex Perlis if they find out about this, but there's no way this will spring him." She saw Nathan lead Julio through the back of the house and joined them a few minutes later.

"I know what happened last time, Sept, and everything you and

Nathan gave to this case," Fritz placed his hand on her shoulder. "I want you on this, but if you'd rather have someone else to handle it, I'll reassign you."

"Thank you, sir, but Nathan and I have a good team in place. If this is a copycat looking for fame, it's the first of many murder scenes we'll be facing. We're the best bet you have of catching this asshole," she said, and Nathan nodded.

"Good. I'll trust you to handle it."

"About this writer you want us to meet with," she said, now not feeling obligated to go forward with that. "This case will take up most of my time."

"I gave her my word, but one meeting should do it," Fritz said and shook hands again. "Keep me updated, and let me know if I need to give you more people."

"You heard the man, Nathan." She slapped Nathan on the back after her father followed Fritz out. "Let's get to work."

❖

The two uniform officers were pissed to be pulled away from an active crime scene to watch some dump, but complaining in front of Fritz wasn't a good career move. They walked, since their supervisor said not to attract any attention.

"I don't know why the fuck we're here, but go check out the back," Bob Vito said to his partner. They were part of the first class that had graduated from the academy after the storm, and the timeline to get them on the street had been somewhat shortened since the city needed patrol officers to fill in the gaps.

"Will do," Erik Rawling said as he picked the side with the clearest path to the backyard. "Hey, sorry." Erik stopped when he turned the corner and spotted someone facing away from him. "Is this your house?" He walked closer, trying to figure out what the person was doing there. "I asked if this is your house."

Hunter waited until the snap of the strap holding his gun in place came undone. The cop had good instincts, but it was already too late. "Not my house, but I've been waiting for you." The silencer was in place, and the cop died with a shocked expression frozen on his face.

"Yo, Erik, you find anything?" the other cop yelled. "Come on, man. Stop fucking around."

It took five more minutes, but both of them were dead in the one spot that would teach the best lesson. If Teacher was what Alex had wanted, Hunter would give it to him, if only to show him how to do it without getting caught.

"Nothing against either of you, but Sept Savoie needs to get the message that her participation isn't voluntary," Hunter said, dragging them both inside.

The spot where Tameka had died still showed some signs of fingerprint dust, but it didn't stop Hunter from setting the stage for Sept. "You can think about how close I was to you and that you couldn't stop me from killing your own."

The space Perlis had cleared had been cleaned of all the blood he'd spilled, which was strange considering the shape of the house. The blood was gone, but some of the litter in the room showed the spot had been visited plenty of times since it'd happened. The crack pipes and other drug paraphernalia meant it was a popular place to get high, so Hunter was glad to add to the allure of Perlis's first altar.

"Do you know what's coming, Sept?" The blood oozing from the two wounds was still warm, and since the guys were dead they wouldn't mess up the seven on their foreheads. "I hope you enjoy my gift."

CHAPTER SIX

Nicole stared out the window at the small glimpse of the river her studio loft afforded her and followed the string of barges being led by a tugboat that seemed to be struggling in the current. She'd fleshed out the first chapter, but she needed the interviews with Sept Savoie to progress.

"Though…" She stood and stretched, making her panties ride down a bit. It was the only thing she'd bothered to put on, and she didn't care if anyone saw her through the large windows. "Maybe I should start where this story did."

She took a shower, put on a business suit, and took only a small field notebook. The place she'd leased was five blocks from the streetcar line, but she decided to walk to catch a streetcar. The exercise would help her decide if she needed to rent a car for her stay in the city.

This area of town was really beautiful, with the grand homes and moss-draped oaks, and set New Orleans apart from anywhere else in the States. Some of the trees appeared damaged from the storm, but in a few years they'd sprout new limbs like they had for the hundred or so years they'd grown here. She had to take a cab from where the streetcar stopped because of damaged lines and tracks, so Blanchard's was open when she arrived.

"Welcome to Blanchard's," the beautiful hostess said as a team of wait staff stood ready to escort her to her table. "Do you have a reservation?"

"I'm sorry. Did I need one?"

"Yes, ma'am. We're completely booked for our first seating."

"And if I decide to wait?" she asked, not planning to go anywhere.

"It'll be at least a couple of hours, so if you're not interested in sitting around that long, we'll be glad to make a reservation for later this afternoon," the other beautiful hostess said.

"Do you have a bar where I can entertain myself until then? I'd love to speak to Chef Blanchard if she's in."

"Is she expecting you?" The women both lost their smiles, as if overprotecting their boss.

"No, but a girl can hope for a few minutes of her time," she said as sweetly as she could manage.

"Charles will show you to the bar, and I'll check for you. Lunch is steadily hectic so I can't promise you anything," the older of the two said. "May I have your name?"

"Nicole Voles, and all I need is an introduction. Once that's done I can make an appointment for a longer visit." She followed the guy through the first-floor dining room to the small oak-lined bar that didn't seem to get a lot of traffic. No, Blanchard's was a world-renowned dining establishment, and they concentrated on eating. The Blanchards obviously wanted guests to drink at a table accompanied by dishes of good food.

"Could I interest you in a twenty-five-cent martini?" The bartender smiled as he placed a cocktail napkin on the bar in front of her.

"Twenty-five cents? That sounds too good to be true."

"It was the owners' twist on marketing to drum up business after the storm, and it stuck. There's no going back now."

"I'll take a dirty one with two olives." She crossed her legs and watched the guy work. The dining room was starting to fill and get noisier, so maybe she would make a reservation to dine here if the place was this popular. "Is it always like this?"

"The crowd?" He poured her drink and slid it closer to her hand. "Yes, it is. Blanchard's has produced some famous chefs, but Keegan surpasses them all. And she's not going anywhere."

"Not ambitious?" she asked, humming when she tasted the excellent drink.

"Her last name is Blanchard. She belongs here, and she's responsible for the crowds in there."

"Don't let her hear you say all that, or it'll swell her head even more than that *Bon Appétit* article last month," a tall, gorgeous woman in an equally gorgeous suit said, and the bartender laughed. "Ms. Voles, it's a pleasure to meet you. I'm Jacqueline Blanchard, Keegan's sister."

"You're not dressed to cook?" she asked, holding Jacqueline's hand longer than she should.

"If I were, there'd be a mad rush to the door. Keegan is the family rock star in the kitchen, and she's got only a few minutes before the team kicks into high gear, so please follow me."

The kitchen staff was a lot bigger than she would've imagined, and at the center stood one of the most beautiful women she'd ever seen. Jacqueline was a classic beauty, but Keegan captured your imagination for reasons that were not readily obvious but still undeniable.

"Ms. Blanchard." She held out her hand and smiled when Keegan took it. "Thank you for seeing me."

"I'm guessing you're the author Voles?" Keegan took her hand back and pointed to a table on the opposite wall from the cooktops.

"Guilty as charged." She sat and crossed her legs again, hoping Keegan would join her since she'd offered her a seat.

"What can I do for you?" Keegan remained standing shoulder to shoulder with her sister.

"I'm sure Jacqueline told you my assistant called about an interview. I'm in town working on a book about the murders Alex Perlis committed, and I'd like to talk with you. Though, I have to say, you'd be a fascinating subject to write about. Maybe we can discuss that possibility." She cocked her head to the side and smiled. This might be a great way to kill time while she waited for her main target, because she'd grown bored with Kelly, who she'd seen a few times after their flight. She broke eye contact with Keegan when Jacqueline laughed for some reason.

"What would I have to do with your book, Ms. Voles?" Keegan said, glancing at Jacqueline with the same obvious confusion she was feeling. "And I very much doubt anyone would want to read a book about me."

"Don't sell yourself short, Ms. Blanchard," she said and winked as she folded her hands on her knee. "As for the book I'm working on now, you're a very important part of the Perlis story. Wasn't your employee one of Perlis's first victims? I'm sure you'd have plenty to say about that," she said, trying her best to sound sympathetic.

"Donovan wasn't just my employee, Ms. Voles—"

"Please, call me Nicole."

"Donovan was also my friend, so I'm not going to turn his loss into something sensational to sell books," Keegan said, sounding as if all her emotional walls were shooting up. "So, if that's all, Ms. Voles, this isn't the best time."

"Why don't we try to find a table so you can at least enjoy lunch for today," Jacqueline said as Keegan turned her back on them. "Ms. Voles, if you would." Jacqueline pointed to the swinging doors.

"Can I at least talk to you about Sept Savoie?" she asked a little louder, and Keegan whipped around with anger very clearly marring her expression. "She is your partner, isn't she?"

"That and everything about my life is none of your business," Keegan said.

"I'm not your enemy, Ms. Blanchard." She smiled again as she slowly uncrossed her legs and stood. "If anything, I think we can be good friends." She winked again to soften Keegan up, but the ploy backfired when it appeared Keegan might hurl a pot at her head.

"Ms. Voles," Jacqueline said, snapping her fingers as if trying to get her attention. "It really is time to go."

"Could you put in a good word for me?" she asked Jacqueline as she chose leaving over lunch. "I really would like to know Donovan, as well as Detective Savoie, from Keegan's point of view as well as yours."

"I have a feeling that's not all you're interested in, Nicole." Jacqueline lengthened her name. "If that's true, forget it, and I'll ask, but don't wait up for her call. Donovan was a close friend, and his loss, the way he was killed, has been hard on her. And neither of us will ever discuss Sept outside our family."

"I'm not sure what you mean." She didn't enjoy reprimands no matter where they came from. "Here's my contact information, so please let your sister know I'll respect Donovan's memory as well as whatever relationship she has with Savoie."

"That'll be up to her, so please respect her privacy and wishes."

"Does she really need this much interference run on her behalf?" Jacqueline followed her outside, and in any other scenario Nicole would've made a play for her, guessing Jacqueline was the easier of the two sisters to bed.

"Believe me, running interference isn't my job, but that position *is* filled, and her pit bull takes that job very seriously." Jacqueline waggled her fingers at her and started back inside. "Thanks for dropping by, but in the future, it might be a good idea to call ahead. That's especially true if you're here to enjoy the cuisine."

"Interesting, but I don't quit that easily."

❖

"Well?" Sept said as Julio Munez stood close to the dead woman, not saying anything. His eyes, though, were a different story. His gaze flitted around the room, not staying on any one thing too long. "Is this another altar to," she referred to her notes, "Elegua?"

"I almost don't want to call it that because it's another abomination to something I love." He was quiet, as if he didn't want to disturb the dead woman. "How is this even possible?"

"It's not Perlis, but whoever it is seems infatuated with his work," she said, standing next to him. "It's an obvious copycat because of the subtle changes. Can you shed any light on that scenario?"

"The statue of St. Anthony is the saint associated with Elegua, only this one is much bigger than those you found in the throat of the first murdered people." He bent his head in the direction of the statue. "Did it have a message in it?"

"It has to go back to the lab before we open it, but I did see something folded up in there." George and Jennifer were working their way around the room while the rest of the team worked outside. So far though, no one had found anything. It was like a ghost had brought this woman here and slaughtered her, but her father had always preached there was no such thing as ghosts. "What about the salt?"

"Whoever this was, he knew a lot about the orishas." Julio stopped for a moment and glanced around again. "Did you find any candy or other food item?"

"Over here," Jennifer said, pointing to a pile of hard, multicolored candies.

"Perlis picked Elegua first because he's the key to reaching all the other gods, but Perlis didn't mention any of his pathways or roads."

"Roads?" Nathan asked.

"Elegua is known for having a hundred or so roads, but they're named." Julio sighed and closed his eyes momentarily. "Hopefully the note, if that's what it is, has a hint as to what road he's interested in opening. If it does, we might be able to understand why this happened."

"A hundred roads?" she asked, and Julio nodded. "And I thought the Catholic Church had a lot of saints to keep track of." Nathan and Julio laughed, and she led them outside. "Thank you for doing this again."

"I've only recently been able to sleep without the nightmares the last time left me with, but I'm available whenever you need."

"Let me know if it's too much for you," she said, and she shook his hand.

"You know how I feel about my religion. I'll do whatever I can so someone doesn't twist it for their own sick reasons."

"Thank you, and hopefully this is finally the last of this crap."

"Sept." One of the uniform officers came running up out of breath. "You need to come with me."

"What now?" She followed, ignoring the media that had decided to stick around. Julio and Nathan kept up. Her skin grew clammy when they stopped at the house where Tameka had been killed.

The place was surrounded by a number of cops who'd gone looking for the rookies they'd originally sent. What their superior had thought would be an ass-kicking for deserting their post had escalated into something quite different. The only people inside were their direct superior, John Loveless, and two of his more experienced guys.

"What the fuck?" John said angrily when Sept's group made it into the house. "Why didn't you tell me you thought this would be dangerous? I would've never sent rookies."

"John, it could've been you or me, and the same damn thing would've happened." She saw the drag marks from the back of the house and the seven drawn in blood on their foreheads.

"What's that supposed to mean?" John combed back his thinning hair with both hands.

"They were ambushed." She pointed to the closest guy's gun. The strap was undone, but the gun had never been drawn. "He reached for it but didn't get a chance to shoot back. We need some guys canvassing the backyard."

She followed the blood-streaked drag marks to the door leading to the backyard. The dead grass wasn't much help, but one of the guys had dropped his hat at the corner of the house. "That's one spot," Nathan said. "Where's the other one?"

"It had to be more this way," she said, pointing to the center of the yard.

"Yeah. That makes sense," John said. "Even a rookie would've backed a brother up if he'd seen the guy get shot."

"I wanted the house shut down because our victim was killed so close to another crime scene," Sept said, slowly making her way back to the bodies. "There's a chance the killer would've been here. A connection to this scene is probably the only reason for the killing a block away. It's definitely a copycat, and whoever it is wanted to show Perlis how much he thinks of his work."

"So why murder these guys?" Nathan asked, and John and Nathan stared at her as if her answer would be the key to solving all this.

"Maybe they saw whoever was watching from here, partner." She studied the numbers on their foreheads, and the style of writing was different from Perlis's. Whoever did it had drawn a small line through the stem of the number seven.

"That's different than when Perlis did it," Nathan said.

"It's used to distinguish a seven from a one," she said, taking a deep breath. These officers looked so young. Did they have someone waiting at home, or maybe kids?

"There's also no slash through it, like in a no-smoking sign," Nathan said, comparing it to the victim they'd found by the river where she'd sat with Keegan when they'd first gotten together. That guy had served as much as a message as the two dead cops she was staring at. The small pain behind her left eye was starting to grow.

"That slash from our first case means something different than this. Perlis wanted me gone right away, but I don't get that sense here." She glanced at the officers' bodies to make sure nothing was out of place. "Have the coroner go over every inch before releasing them to their families."

"What's different about the messages?" John asked as more of George's crime-scene guys came in. "I didn't work the first cases, but you won't be able to keep me out this time. These were my guys, and I'm going to help you catch this fucker and take him down."

"No one's keeping you from anything, John. Perlis put the line through the number on that guy as a warning to me to get off the case, since my name means seven, but this strikes me more as an invitation. It's the second one I've gotten this week." A button at the top of the shirt on the victim farthest away from her was slightly out of the hole. "I need some gloves," she said, and one of the techs handed them over. She unbuttoned only three before she saw the rest of the message.

"What does it say?" John asked, leaning over her.

"Afrá." She spelled it out. "Julio?"

"It's the road the killer's taking," Julio said, blowing out a long breath. "It's the road who gathers the bodies of the dead."

"*Who?*" she asked. "Is it a road or a person?"

"Yes to both. It's a living entity," Julio said as he fingered the beads around his neck.

"So, the message says it'll be our job to clean up after this guy, since he'll keep killing until he tires of it?" she asked, buttoning the officer's shirt back up.

"That's just fucking great," John said.

"Exactly." She resigned herself to the weeks ahead. "Exactly."

CHAPTER SEVEN

H as Sept called?" Jacqueline asked as the lunch crowd started to thin and they sat to eat in Keegan's office.

"Not yet, and I heard from some of the servers that something big's going on. The diners were getting updates on their phones, which is so rude when you're at the table with someone."

"Let's focus, Miss Manners," Jacqueline said as the waiter put their food down. "What are you going to tell her about Nicole Voles?"

"That I don't want to dish about my murdered friend," she said, looking at Jacqueline and not understanding what she was talking about.

"So, you're not going to tell her about ole Nicole hitting on you?"

"She wasn't hitting on me. That's more something that happens to you." She laughed at the absurdity of what Jacqueline was implying.

"Trust me, she was, and as usual, you missed it."

Keegan's phone rang, and she pointed at Jacqueline to shut her up. "Hey, honey, what's going on?"

"Our first case out of the blocks is a doozy, so I might be running late," Sept said, and Keegan heard people talking in the background. "I just wanted to call and tell you to be careful. Please go straight home after work, and that goes for Jacqueline too. To be extra careful, call Melinda and Della and tell them the same thing."

"Hon, you just started working cases again today, and you're already scaring the hell out of me." Jacqueline stood and moved closer to her.

"Sorry." Sept seemed to move since it grew quieter on her end. "Is the troublemaker with you?"

"If you're talking about Jacqueline, then yes."

"Stay put, and I'll stop by before we have to check out some stuff."

"We'll wait for you." She hung up and put her hand over Jacqueline's when she placed it on her shoulder. "That doesn't sound good, and please don't mention Nicole when she gets here."

"Sure, but why?" Jacqueline sat back down and unfurled her napkin. "I totally understand you missed the vibes she was sending out, but why keep her visit from Sept?"

"We talked about this book Nicole is writing on our trip, and Sept wants to be the subject of it as much as she wants to shoot herself in the head. If she's working on something bad right off, I don't want to stress her out or distract her."

They ate, and Sept walked in with Nathan as they finished, but Sept asked him to wait in the kitchen. Sept hugged Keegan and held a hand out to Jacqueline. "You both know how much I love talking about an open case, but the scene we showed up at today was like starting Perlis's case all over again."

"What?" Keegan asked.

"I'm still in shock a little, and I don't have any idea what this is about, but I need you both to watch yourselves." Sept kissed her forehead and sat at the small table. "From the first crime scene, we got another call to the house where Tameka was killed. The killer was watching, I guess, and left two more bodies for us. This time it was two cops with sevens on their foreheads."

"Jesus," Keegan said, remembering the body they'd found by the river. "The killer knows about you?"

"I think so, which is making me crazy, but not because of that. I'm worried that if he knows me, you and the family might be in his sights as well. That's why you need to promise me you'll all be careful." Sept extended a hand to them. "I love you, and it'll kill me if anything happens to either of you."

"Don't worry about us. We'll be careful. But I do want to know one thing. What did you two want to talk to me about earlier?" Jacqueline asked, as if trying to change the subject.

"The house Della grew up in is your home," Sept said.

"You want me to move out?" Jacqueline asked, seemingly genuinely hurt.

"Such a pessimist," Keegan said, leaning over and kissing Jacqueline's cheek.

"The first rule of police work is don't jump to conclusions," Sept said, kissing her other cheek.

"If it's not too weird, we'd like for you to stay. I want you to, but if you feel crowded, we'll move out. It's only fair." Sept nodded at what Keegan had said and wasn't surprised when her sister's eyes grew glassy with tears. "I hope we all stay put, but I'll understand if you need your own space."

"I won't understand, but Keegan thought we should ask," Sept said and wiped at her own tears. "I've missed having a sister."

"Thanks for asking, and I guess I was a little terrified that things would change if you guys made this more permanent," Jacqueline said, sounding a bit embarrassed. "My sister's lucky to have found someone who understands both of us so well."

"I love you, and cooking-lesson night is my favorite of the week. If you weren't there it wouldn't be the same." Sept stood to hug them both. "And because I love you, I need you all to be hypervigilant of your surroundings. We'll talk more about it later, but I'm afraid this is the beginning of another hard case."

"That goes for you too, Seven," Keegan said, pressing up against Sept. "If it's a copycat, then it sounds like they want you involved."

"I think that's part of it, so call me if you see anything out of the ordinary."

Jacqueline stared at Keegan, but she stayed quiet. "Do you and Nathan have time to eat?"

"If it's fast. We need to get started on some follow-up," Sept said, thankfully missing Jacqueline's silent cues.

Sept and Nathan left thirty minutes later with a promise that they'd try to be done early enough to give Keegan a ride home. She stared at the door after they left and said a silent prayer to keep Sept safe.

"Do you have time to go over the books before you head home for a few hours?" Jacqueline asked.

"Can we do it at home? I'm shorthanded tonight, so I'll have to come in earlier."

Jacqueline nodded and sighed. "I don't mean to harp on this, considering there's a slight chance I'm wrong, but don't start a life with Sept by omitting things you think might upset her."

"Come on, Jacqueline," she said, frustrated. "Voles is a non-issue, and you heard Sept. This is going to be hard on her. I don't want her worrying about unimportant things."

"I'm on your side, but think about what I said. I really love Sept, so I don't want her upset either," Jacqueline said softly, taking her hand. "I just don't want anything to get in the way of your happiness."

"Nothing will." And she'd do whatever she needed to make sure.

❖

"Where to first?" Nathan asked when he started the car. Sept stared into the side-view mirror. This wasn't what she was expecting so soon after returning to work, but she needed to get her head back in the game.

"Jennifer texted and said she and George are in the lab now, so let's stop there," she said, turning her attention to the area around them. If this guy was really watching them and came anywhere near Keegan or her family, this time she'd pull the trigger if she had the chance. "I want to see the note."

"I guess they didn't find anything else, huh?"

"That's something else this killer has in common with Perlis. No fingerprints, no clues, and no mistakes. With the first scene that makes sense, because he took his time, but it was the same thing with the second place. This fucker killed two cops right under our noses and didn't flinch or leave a clue." She flipped through her notebook, trying to prioritize her steps.

"You're right, but why now?" The area was almost back to normal, but construction was still going on, with plenty of out-of-town contractors. It made their suspect pool that much harder to nail down. "If this really is Teacher, he's had months to begin. Why now?"

"You should know the answer. If your name had a number in it, it'd be on those bodies next to the seven." Her phone rang, and she groaned when she recognized the number from police headquarters. "Savoie," she said as Nathan turned, heading away from downtown.

"Hold for Chief Jernigan," a woman said.

"Sept," Fritz said, barking her name as if she had a hearing problem. "I'm not sure how in the hell this happened again, but I'm putting you in charge of the new task force I'm forming. I'm not willing to put up with two dead cops."

"Yes, sir," she said, thinking this had gone from bad to clusterfuck at lightning speed. "As long as we can stay in the field investigating, Nathan and I'll do whatever you want."

"Don't agree just to get me off your ass, Savoie. Two rookies were killed today, which doesn't exactly scream that the city is safe and open for business. The mayor and city council have taken a chunk out of my ass since this broke, so this won't go away by telling me what I want to hear."

"Sir, I'm just saying that whoever this was has only begun. He's going to keep killing until we find a clue to who he is and drop him into a deep, black hole." Nathan swerved through traffic and laughed quietly at what she was saying. "We can't do that if we're stuck at the precinct managing the troops."

"Do it however you like. Just get fucking results," Fritz screamed, obviously taking a cue from the mayor and passing along his frustration. "One more thing."

"Yes, sir." Whatever came next wasn't going to be good.

"Call this Voles woman so she doesn't think we're afraid to talk to her. We may not like it, but she's popular, so I'd like us to have some input about what goes in this book."

"I'll take care of it, but if the cases are related, I'll be limited on what I can share."

"Call and get it over with." Fritz's voice started to rise again, but he hung up before she had to pull the phone away from her ear.

"Problems, Boss?" Nathan asked as he took the exit leading to the lakefront where George's lab was located.

"Christmas came early this year, and Fritz gave us a task force. And as a bonus, we have to talk to the author for our fifteen minutes of fame."

"Until the papers get ahold of you again," he said, and punched her arm.

"I'm a giver, so I intend to make sure your name is in every article. If the *Picayune* and the *Advocate* want to portray me as incompetent, I'm not going to be alone."

"You're a riot." He parked by the door and left the blue light on the roof blinking so the crews making repairs wouldn't block them in.

"I'm hilarious, so don't forget it." They took the stairs to where George had set up until the flood damage of the lake's storm surge had been cleared away. "What's my love letter say, Uncle George?"

"We got problems, kid," George said, and Jennifer nodded.

"What? The paper was a grocery list instead of the nicely typed confession with directions of where to find this guy?" George and Nathan both snorted as if they couldn't help themselves, but Jennifer stared at her as if she didn't understand her humor. "You need to loosen your wind a bit if you're going to survive what's coming, Schultz."

"Stop terrorizing my people and get over here," George said, walking to a work station with bright lights over it. "There's a definite difference between this one and Perlis's notes. This one is handwritten, but like his, it gets to no point at all. Cryptic is like a hobby for these sickos."

It was short and might as well have been typed, considering the block, very uniform letters. "It's different, but this guy has insight to every part of Perlis's playbook," she said.

Second chances will show you the error of the gods.
I want back the victory promised by the gods,
and I want to strip you of the title of warrior.
You are no child of Chango.

"What do you think?" Jennifer asked.

"The condensed version is, we caught Perlis, but that's not how it was supposed to go down. The gods he believes in were supposed to favor him, not me," she said, and Nathan took a picture of the note. "Thanks, Uncle George, and let me know if you find anything else."

"Where to next?" Nathan asked when they got outside.

"I want to walk the first scene again before we head to the morgue."

They went back out to the east side of the city, and she walked the outside of the house as well as the couple next to it on both sides. "Are you looking for anything in particular?" Nathan asked. He walked beside her but put a few feet between them.

"See if we can find a hint as to who the victim is. From the clothes, I'd guess prostitute, but knowing exactly who she is might give us a clue about the part of town she worked."

The area was scattered with weeds and debris that had washed out of the houses around them. All the litter was a grim reminder of the lives that were only a memory now that the houses were completely uninhabitable.

"I'd think the killer would've taken the information," Nathan said but didn't give up the search. "You know, like a trophy."

"If he's following Perlis's playbook, the only trophy he's collecting is the kill."

She followed the path to the second crime scene of the day and noticed a denim purse floating in the cracked and faded kiddie pool with enough putrid water to make it seem like the purse had been there for months. The water smelled horrible, but she stuck her pen in and pulled the purse out.

"Shit," Nathan said, following her to the sidewalk out front. "How'd they miss that?"

"Happens," she said, texting George. "That's why I like to come back when the circus folds up and rolls out." She put the purse down and watched the water ooze out of it. "Everyone concentrates on finding something small, and stuff like this blends in."

Fifteen minutes later, Jennifer showed up and, at Sept's request, spread out a plastic sheet. They opened the purse and removed the five items in it. A pack of cigarettes, American-flag lighter, a box of condoms, bottle of Scope, and a small coin purse with thirty dollars in it. Nothing gave a clue to the woman's name or address.

"Well, it could be hers since the cigarettes aren't a complete mush, but why wouldn't she have any ID on her?" Jennifer said, bagging each item separately.

"If she gets popped for prostitution, she can give another name, and people like her think there's no way to verify it," Nathan said. "See if you can lift any prints from it, and we'll know for sure."

"True, so let's go by Gavin's office and run her prints and see how many names our working girl gave," Sept said of Gavin Domangue, the coroner.

The sun was starting to set, but Sept headed to the morgue to check the prints and anything else Gavin had found. Despite the late hour, the place was full of police personnel, and Gavin was wearing bloody scrubs, meaning he'd actually been performing the autopsies. Gavin usually came down for the major crimes, but his talented staff handled the day-to-day stuff.

"Where have you been?" Gavin asked as he signed the files his assistant handed over. "It's been a shit show in here today."

"We've been at the same show, so I'm late, but you know I can't stay away from you, sexy man," she said, making Gavin suck in his large gut and pose with his fists on his hips. "Let's go, handsome. Tell me a story."

"You're here about the girl, I'd think," Gavin said, pointing to the room to his left.

"Actually, I want to know about all three bodies, since I think the same perp did them all, and I have a feeling you're about to get as busy as when Perlis was working, but let's take them in order. Did you run the prints on our Jane Doe?"

After being photographed, the woman on the table had been cleaned up more in the last hours than in her entire life, Sept guessed. She appeared middle-aged, but street life had a way of piling on the years. From what she could see, the victim didn't have any tattoos or marks on her chest, and the large wound had been closed.

"If she had any prints I would've done that," Gavin said, standing at the gurney's side. "Someone shaved off the tips of her fingers. You probably wouldn't notice at the scene without a close inspection."

"I think I would've noticed if her fingers were bleeding," Sept said, bending down to stare at the woman's left hand.

"You would've in most cases, but the animal who killed her applied some kind of adhesive to prevent bleeding. It was a good move to throw you off finding out who she is, but she doesn't seem to be the lynchpin to figuring out who the killer is," Gavin said, placing his hands on the table. "I've seen so many like her in my career, but they usually come here because of an overdose or a bad turn with a john."

"We're going to work for all the answers we get this time. That's what all this is about," she said, shaking her head as an idea came to her and she exposed the woman's feet.

"I checked that first after conferring with George. All her toes are there, so your gift might not have anything to do with this."

"My gut tells me it does, but have you found anything on that yet?"

"Patience, Grasshopper. We sent the sample in for DNA testing so it's a waiting game now," Gavin said. "Now get out of here so I can work on our two fallen brothers. I want to finish tonight so I can turn them over to their families. They deserve that kind of respect."

"They do. Call me if you have anything."

"I will as long as I get an invitation to your wedding," he said and winked. "Congratulations, kiddo. I'm happy for you."

It was dark by the time Sept and Nathan got outside, so she called Royce, their supervisor. "Have the troops started arriving?" she asked, knowing Fritz had formed a task force.

"Fritz called, and tomorrow morning should start with a crowd. Where are you?"

"We're leaving the morgue, so we'll see you then. I want to check one more thing before we call it for today." She asked Nathan for the keys and drove slowly to where Tulane Avenue turned into Airline Drive, not wanting to miss her quarry.

"Who are you looking for?" Nathan asked as she covered another two miles.

"You remember Brandi Parrish?" She pulled into a small gas station and convenience store.

"Yeah. Do we need to stop by the Red Door?" he asked, sounding excited about visiting the infamous brothel in the French Quarter.

"We need to find you a girlfriend, buddy, or I'll have to see if Brandi has any gift certificates available for your birthday. And no, we're not going to see Brandi, but that's Tiny Mongo Williams." She pointed to a guy who was anything but tiny.

"Is that a joke?"

"No. Tiny is a pimp, but none of his girls have ever turned on him, so he's still in business." She got out and walked to the four-hundred-pound, older white guy with a ponytail and a T-shirt with the Saints logo on it.

"Detective Savoie," Tiny said with a high-pitched voice that didn't fit his size. "Long time, but you're famous now. No time for slumming, I guess."

"Tiny, don't make me embarrass you in front of all these potential customers," she said, bending over his chair to get in his face. "Especially since I'm here offering a get-out-of-jail-free card."

"Sept...baby, you know I always get out of jail free," he said, and laughed until she flicked him on the forehead.

"I'm talking about not having to wait in that lockup for a month while they continually lose your paperwork." She flicked him again. "You know I'd do it."

"What do you want?"

"Tell me who this is." She showed him a picture of her victim that Gavin had taken. "If you don't know, I'm giving you until tomorrow to find out."

"Let me see," a young woman said when Tiny reached down for his glasses. "What's wrong with her?"

"She was murdered today and had no identification on her," Nathan said.

"I think that's Bonnie, but she don't work with us. Her boyfriend watches out for her."

"You don't know her last name?" Sept asked.

"No, but she works close to that place with the palm trees on the sign," the girl said as Tiny snatched the picture out of her hand.

"Thanks, and, Tiny, I'm coming back soon and often to check on my friend here. If she's got one little bruise on her, it won't make me happy. Pray she doesn't trip before then." She patted Tiny on the head and laughed when he jerked away. "What's your name?"

"Misty, and that's fucked up that Bonnie got killed. She was nice."

"Thanks for your help. I won't forget it."

She drove to the Palm Court Motor Lodge but didn't recognize the young guy in the office. "How long do you need the room? And towels are extra," he said, sounding bored out of his head.

"Let's start over before you piss me off," Nathan said, putting his badge in the guy's face. "What room did this woman rent yesterday?" He slammed the picture down and jabbed it with his finger. "Think carefully before you say you don't know, because two dead cops are involved."

"Bonnie killed two cops?" the guy said, seeming truly shocked. "Man, I didn't see that coming."

"Bonnie's dead, followed by two cops, so give us a last name," Sept said, taking out her phone.

"I'm pretty sure it's Matherne, but don't quote me on that. We aren't exactly friends, but she hung out here when the weather was bad." He picked up the photo and stared at it. "She never got the rooms, though. That was up to the guy, but if they wanted to screw in the car, they couldn't do it here."

"So yesterday, did you have any really generous customers who paid extra in cash so they wouldn't have to sign the register?" She knocked on the dingy vinyl counter and smiled. "Think about what my partner said and what'll happen if you say you don't know."

"One of our regulars came in and paid a hundred," he said, and she tapped the counter again. "Okay, two bills for the room on the end. I don't know who he took in there."

"Son, do we need to keep pulling teeth here?" Nathan said.

"It was Crazy Nick, but I haven't seen him since," the guy said, putting his hands up. "That's the truth."

"We'll get to that, but for now have you rented the room again?" she asked.

"No. The maid said it was like he never used it, so it's available."

Sept pulled out her cell. "Royce, I need a warrant for room…" he looked at the clerk, who mouthed the number, "thirty-nine at the Palm Court on Airline. Then run someone named Crazy Nick and see what you find. Get George and the forensics team down here as well."

"I thought you were calling it a night?"

"Something came up, so get me that warrant," she said and stared at the clerk. "I'm sure our friend over here would let me in without one, but we're doing this by the book. I don't want any questions when we wrap this investigation."

"And we need this warrant because?"

"Our Jane Doe got snatched here. At least I'm fairly certain that's true. We'll wait here, but call me if you get a hit on this Crazy Nick character."

"You got it."

"When the cavalry gets here, send them down to the room. We're going to make sure no one gets in there before we do." The guy nodded, and she glanced in the direction he pointed.

"This could be good since he went to such trouble to hide Bonnie's identity," Nathan said as he drove them to the end. "If we weren't supposed to find this, maybe something's in there."

"Maybe," she said and got out close to the room, intending to examine how the killer could've gotten Bonnie out or if she left voluntarily. If she was lucky, some camera would be pointed in this direction that recorded what happened. "If the guy pulled his car up here, he could've gotten in and out without being seen unless someone was in that room." She pointed across the parking lot as Nathan followed her around.

"I'll go check with Mr. Answers in the office," Nathan said as he started walking to the office.

He was twenty feet away when an explosion leveled the room they were waiting to enter. Nathan started running, dodging all the burning debris strewn along his path. "Sept," he screamed.

"Sept," he yelled again, already hearing the sirens in the background. "Fuck, fuck, fuck."

CHAPTER EIGHT

Hello, Daddy," Nicole said, smiling into her laptop camera. "I've missed you."

"My darling girl," Special Agent Brian Voles said, the bookcases in his office the background for his head. He liked having these conversations at the office so her mother Gail wouldn't interrupt. "Are you set in your new place?"

"It's small, but functional." She took a sip of her neat scotch. It wasn't her favorite, but he loved the amber liquor, so she didn't mind sharing a drink with him when they were miles apart. "I got here just as something was going on, so I haven't gotten very far."

"I read what you sent me about Sept Savoie." The knot of his tie and his hair were still perfect, even though it was after nine in the evening in California. Brian had always taken pride in his appearance and had insisted on the same from her.

"I'm trying to find ways in, so I'm not worried about it."

"This might not be the kind of cop you're used to, baby. She's ambitious, but not in the pursuit of power. The job and the reputation of her family name seem to be the only things that drive her." He lifted his glass and took a healthy sip. "Law enforcement is her family business, and they're all good at it."

"I'm interested in her, but the real focus is Alex Perlis. This guy picked a unique path and would continue killing if they let him out tomorrow."

"The file on him has some holes, but I don't think he's crazy. He knew what he was doing when he killed his family. And after he armed himself with this Teacher person, he found the rest of his victims." He drained his glass and chuckled. "He was planning ahead on the chance he got caught, which proves to me he was definitely not mentally deranged."

"The jail hasn't gotten back to me, but his attorney approved an interview. She wants the world to see Alex for what he is."

"That he's crazy, you mean?" Brian shook his head, and from the set of his mouth she could tell he was getting angry. "You know my take on that. Everyone always has an excuse for their behavior, and that excuse is their reason for why they shouldn't be punished for their actions." He balled up his fists. "Give credit where it's due, baby. Your Detective Savoie did a good job. This guy needed to be taken off the streets, and she did that."

"The first book I write from the police perspective will be about you, Daddy. You're the only one in the profession I respect enough to spend the time researching." She leaned back and winked at him. "For now, gore and blood sell, so I'm not messing with a winning combination."

"They're forcing me to take some time off, so I'm thinking of going away with your mother for a week or so," Brian poured himself another drink and sat back down. "That wasn't in my plans, but the clueless people in Washington want to see how the twelve-year-old they sent to eventually replace me works under pressure."

"You could come here," she said, trying to sound nonchalant.

"You're working, so I don't want to intrude."

"Until I figure out how to really start this book, I've got time. I could also use your input. I'd actually appreciate it if you came."

"I'd enjoy that, but you know how your mother is."

"I'm sure between the two of us we can figure out something for her to do." She held her glass up and winked. "Please, Daddy. It's been way too long."

"You're sure that's a good idea?" he asked, and she nodded. "I'll make arrangements and let you know. Think about what I said, and shift your attention to Savoie."

"We'll talk about it when you get here." This was the first time he'd ever tried to convince her to change anything she was working on, so the detective must have impressed him.

"We'll do that, but you know I'm right." He finished his second drink and loosened his tie. "Have you connected with anyone socially?"

"Just a quick thing on the way here, but I've found someone new and interesting here in town." She smiled, thinking of Keegan Blanchard and her curves. "She put me off, but I don't quit that easily."

"I can't wait to hear all the details, and if you're good, there will be details."

She'd worried about coming out to her father, but he seemed to enjoy hearing about all her conquests, something she'd never share with her mother. The relationship she had with each parent was as different as she could manage, and if she had to sacrifice one, her mother would always win that contest. Her father was not only her mentor, but the kind of partner she knew she'd never find, so she'd continue to have her fun and entertain him with each woman she bedded.

"Trust me. I'll have plenty to share before you arrive."

The screen went blank, and a rush of energy running through her made her antsy. She needed to work, but that could wait.

"If I can't tell him about Keegan, then there has to be something else." She had to search extensively but eventually found what she needed and made a quick call to set up an appointment. "Thanks for the idea, Daddy."

❖

Nathan stood as close as he could to the hot fire that was quickly spreading, but he still couldn't see any sign of Sept. Doors to the other rooms were opening as guys ran to their cars, probably wanting to leave before an official inquiry made their names public.

"Sept," he yelled again but got no response. If she was standing in front of the door when the explosion happened, he didn't want to be the one to find her, since she probably hadn't survived.

He was sweating and couldn't move. The ringing cell phone in his pocket finally made him focus. "Why the hell isn't Sept answering?" Royce asked.

He didn't have time to sugarcoat it, so he told Royce what had happened and that he was still looking for her. "Forget the warrant, and get some guys over here to help me search." He started to walk to the side of the building where part of the brick outer wall had collapsed and the roof was on fire. "This can't be happening," he said, forgetting he was still holding the phone.

"Be careful and hang on. I'm on my way." That was all Royce said. Their boss wasn't a soft guy, but he cared about Sept and her entire family.

Nathan kept moving to the side of the building to get closer and almost started crying when he saw the arm sticking out of the pile of splintered wood and brick. "Sept," he yelled, not caring about anything but getting her out of there.

Some of the wood was smoldering, so he wrapped his jacket around his hands and started throwing the lumber off Sept. Her eyes were closed, and her face was covered in blood, but she was still breathing. It probably wasn't a good idea to move her, but he didn't trust that the rest of the wall wouldn't give way under the intense heat.

"I need an ambulance, officer down," he yelled into the radio as soon as Sept was clear of any danger.

"We've got a few on the way," the dispatcher told him, so he went back to Sept. The last thing he wanted to do was call Keegan, but she'd never forgive him if too much time passed and something else happened. He dialed the restaurant and asked for her.

"I'll connect you to the office. Hold, please."

A woman he knew wasn't Keegan answered. "Blanchard's. Can I help you?"

"This is Sept's partner, Nathan. It's important I talk with Keegan," he said as he flagged the ambulance in their direction.

"Nathan, this is Jacqueline. Tell me what's wrong." She said "okay" a few times during his short explanation, then asked him to hold.

"Nathan, where are you?" Keegan asked, clearly upset. "Is she okay?"

"She's alive, and we're on our way to the hospital. Hold on," he said, putting his hand over the phone. "Where are we going?" he asked the EMT.

"Tulane downtown. You can ride with us if you want," the woman said as they carefully lifted Sept onto the gurney.

"They're loading her up, so meet us at Tulane," Nathan told Keegan. "Call when you get there, and I'll come get you. She's going to be fine, so don't worry," he said, hoping to hell Sept wouldn't make a liar out of him.

❖

"I've got to go," Keegan said, grabbing her bag and heading to the door. This couldn't be happening again so soon after Sept had recovered from her injuries.

"Not without me," Jacqueline said, shouldering her purse, keys in hand. "Let's go, and I'll call Mom and Gran on the way. Where are they taking her?"

"Tulane," Keegan said, her stomach hurting so much she was nauseous.

"Carla's got privileges there so she might actually be useful to us for once," Jacqueline said, giving the kitchen a brief explanation before leading Keegan to the car. "Gran, we're on our way to Tulane Hospital. Sept's been in an accident."

"I'm watching it on television, so keep your sister away from the news. Melinda's here and is calling Carla. We'll meet you there once I'm dressed." For once, Della sounded subdued.

"Thanks. Call me, and I'll tell you where we are."

"Why does this keep happening?" Keegan asked, staring out at the neighborhood as Jacqueline sped downtown. She thought about their conversation after Sept had proposed. "She offered to get a desk job to make me stop worrying so much, and I talked her out of it."

"Don't, sweetheart," Jacqueline said, grasping her hand. "This isn't your fault, and you were right to do that. You knew going in who Sept was and what came along with that. If you love her, and I know you do, you have to let her be who she is."

"Lately, she seems to be a target for crazed killers. I can't lose her, and I'd never ask her to quit, but this is making me nuts."

"It was an explosion, so it could just be a freak accident." Jacqueline turned in the direction of the emergency room and sighed when she saw the number of police crowding the area. She was going to have to park five miles away but stopped when an officer stepped in the middle of the street and flagged her down.

An older policeman tapped on her window and asked, "Are you Keegan Blanchard?" when she lowered it.

"Yes, sir."

"Pull up right here, and we'll watch your car for you. They're waiting for you inside."

Jacqueline held her hand, and she didn't start crying until she saw Nathan talking to Sebastian and Sept's older brother, Gustave. "Am I too late?" she asked in barely a whisper.

"No. The doctor's in there now, so Nathan was filling us in," Sebastian said as he and Gustave put an arm around her. "We're waiting for the boys to pick up Camille, so I'll let Nathan take you in until she gets here."

Nathan and Gustave walked her and Jacqueline into a room, and she was relieved to find Carla in there with the ER doctor. "Hey," Carla said, smiling. "Her vitals are good, and she's coming around from what seems like a hard blow to the head from some flying debris. We'll know more once we run some tests, but let me squeeze you in before it gets any crazier in here."

"Thank you," she said, taking Carla's hand but not letting Jacqueline's go. Sept's face still had traces of blood and soot on it, but her eyes were open to slits, as if the bright lights were bothering her. "I can't let you out of my sight," she said, and Sept's lips twitched in a smile. "Are you okay?"

"Perfect now," Sept said softly. "Sorry about this."

"Don't be sorry. Just be okay."

"Let's let these guys finish, and then you can fuss at her for not ducking," Carla said, placing her hands on Keegan's shoulders. "I just wanted you to see her before she went."

"I love you, and I'll be right here when you get back," she told Sept as Carla moved to allow the medical transporter to take Sept. "Will she be okay?"

"She's talking and is aware of her surroundings, so I'm optimistic everything will be fine." Carla walked them back out, where a lot of the NOPD was waiting and giving Nathan support.

Keegan saw Sept's mom and immediately hugged her.

"I'll walk Sept through her tests and come get you when she's done," Carla said before she headed back in.

"Did you see her?" Camille asked when Keegan relaxed her embrace a little.

"She's awake and talked to me, and Carla thinks she'll be fine. They're just being cautious."

"I swear one or all of these kids are going to drive me into an early grave," Camille said, taking Keegan and Jacqueline's hands. "Let's go sit and wait."

"Nathan," Keegan said when she saw the guys he'd been talking to walk off. He hugged her and then Jacqueline. "What the hell happened?"

"We followed a lead to the Palm Court, where we think our victim was taken, and wanted to check it out. While we were waiting for a warrant she ordered, the damn place blew up." He scrubbed his thighs with his hands and shook his head. "Either this was a big coincidence, or the bastard booby-trapped it."

"Man, that's messed up," Jacqueline said.

"Why would it have blown up right when you and Sept were there?" Gustave asked when he joined their group with one of Sept's other brothers, Francois. "If that was the first stop in your investigation, and the perp didn't have time to clean the room, it could explain what happened."

"We never got close enough to the door to trip any trap, and the clerk said the maid had checked the room and nothing happened." Nathan and Keegan watched him visibly pale. "Do you think this guy followed us?"

"I've got Alain and Joel over there with the bomb squad to make sure nothing is missed," Francois said about their other two brothers. "If you were followed it won't happen again."

"No, it won't," Della said as she entered with Fritz. "How are you?" she asked Keegan. "And how's Sept?"

"She'll be okay, and I'm starting to calm down a bit. This job of hers takes some getting used to."

"It's hard to believe this rarely happens, but our kid sister is an overachiever," Gustave said, finally making her laugh.

"The full force of the police department is on this, Ms. Blanchard," Fritz said, sitting next to her when Jacqueline moved. "We've already lost too much today, so this is our top priority. You have my word."

"Thank you, and knowing Sept, she'll be back at work as soon as they discharge her," she said, and they all nodded. "If she's ready, then let her do just that."

"She's going to appreciate that," Fritz said. "This job is hard enough without the support of our families and those we love."

"Just take care of her," Della said. "She put a ring on my granddaughter's finger, so we're having a wedding no matter what's going on."

"Gran, I'm sure the chief has things to do," Jacqueline said, as if trying to reel Della back in.

"And one of those things is not getting banned from any Blanchard establishment, so I'll do anything to keep Della happy." Fritz took her hand again and kissed her cheek. "I'm a call away if you need anything, so stay in touch. It's good to see you again, Camille."

"Thanks, Fritz," Camille said as he went to talk to some of the others standing around. "Don't worry. He means well," she told Keegan.

"Keegan," Carla said, coming in and smiling at Melinda. "We put her back in the same exam room. The results shouldn't take too long, so if you want to go in two at a time, I'll come back with the attending to give you the rundown."

"Thanks so much," she said as she gripped Camille's hand so

she'd come with her. "Hey, baby," she said, glad they'd dimmed the lights. Sept seemed more comfortable now.

"Hey. I see you picked up some company," Sept said as Keegan leaned over and kissed her. "Sorry to get you out so late, Mama."

"Are you kidding? The coffee here is worth the trip," Camille said, kissing her hand. "Now don't lie to your mother. Tell us how you really feel."

"My head hurts, but I'm okay. I was on the side of the building, so a bit of the collapsing wall hit me, but I was lucky. If it'd gone off while I was in front, I wouldn't have been so fortunate." Sept seemed more alert than before, which helped Keegan stop thinking of the worst. "Is Nathan okay? No one told me."

"He's a little unhinged from thinking he'd lost his partner, but he'll be okay if you don't shoot him on sight," Keegan said and kissed her again. "Let's wait for Carla and the other doctor, and then I'll go get him."

"I don't think we need to wait that long," Camille said. "I'll get him, but it might take a minute, so behave until I get back."

"I really love your mom," she said when Camille closed the door. "And she had a good point. You really feel okay? If you don't, you can tell me."

"Just a headache. I got a couple of stitches that might mess up my good looks, but I'm fine. The blast itself knocked me for a loop, but it wasn't serious." Sept raised her hand and cupped Keegan's cheek. "Nothing's going to stop me from meeting you at the altar, my love."

"You make me crazy, but only because I don't want to lose you. Thank God you're okay. I don't know what I'd do without you."

"I feel the same way, so you really have to be careful. Losing you or you getting hurt would kill me."

"No one's dying for a very long time, Seven. I want...no, I demand a long and happy life with you. That includes plenty of good days, good memories, and a gaggle of grandchildren who'll either cook or fight crime."

"That sounds good, and I really am sorry for worrying you," Sept said, stroking the slope of her neck. "You didn't burn anything to get here, did you?"

"There isn't anything I'm not willing to do for you, stud, but I draw the line at burning something." She smiled and kissed the tip of Sept's nose. "I'm worried, though, that whoever this is might be watching and following you. If that's true, then they're really determined to hurt you."

"Someone's going to a lot of trouble to get my attention and to copy what Perlis did," Sept said as Keegan enjoyed their closeness. It was helping fight back the terror of that initial phone call. "But now they have my undivided attention."

"I hope that's not completely true," she said, rubbing Sept's abdomen. "I'm not going to enjoy being left alone too often."

"That'll never happen. Even when I'm in the middle of everything at work, at the center of me, you're always there."

"God, the things you say to me."

"Detective." The ER doctor interrupted at the worst time when he entered with Carla.

"Hey. I'm ready to go whenever you get the paperwork done," Sept said, and Keegan pinched her side.

"Della wanted me to remind you she's right outside with a rolled-up newspaper if you get out of hand," Carla said, pointing over her shoulder. "I'd take her at her word, since she scares the hell out of me."

"Uh-huh," Sept grunted.

"Our life together will never be boring, baby. You have to admit that." She kissed Sept's temple, ready to head home herself.

CHAPTER NINE

Keegan was surprised the next morning when she came down and found Jacqueline and their dog Mike entertaining a bunch of cops in their kitchen. They'd all left the hospital together the night before, after Carla promised to make a house call to check on Sept. They'd gone to bed, and Sept had thankfully gone to sleep right after she was under the covers. She was a little bruised, but fine in the light of day, so she was planning to do her best to take care of her while Sept was still in the house.

"Cousin Mackey's delivering breakfast, so don't cook anything," Jacqueline said when she spotted her. "Gran called him last night after asking plenty of questions while you were with Sept."

"What kind of questions?"

"The police-procedure learning curve we have no clue about. If the lead investigator can't work because some nut tried to hurt her, the investigation comes to her." Jacqueline spoke softly as Joel Savoie, the only remaining single brother Sept had, stood next to her sister with his arm around her, nodding at everything she said. "I came back from my run with a police escort."

"Well, the investigator is finishing up so she shouldn't be too long," Keegan said, headed for the coffee.

"You might want to wait for Mackey, since whoever made that knows nothing about coffee or how it's supposed to taste," Jacqueline warned her.

"Is he bringing everything?" she asked, noticing more people arriving.

"He said not to sweat anything. It's handled. All you need to do is relax and eat."

She nodded and opened her arms when Joel seemed to reluctantly release Jacqueline to give her a proper hello. "Did you have to stay out late last night?"

"The bomb guys got a hand from the feds, so it wasn't too bad. Once Smokey gets down here, we'll give y'all a rundown," Joel said, and Keegan appreciated his humor. Joel wasn't much older than Sept and was the only Savoie still in uniform every day. It was something he loved, so it had no bearing on his ambition. "She did okay last night? I'm sorry I didn't finish in time to see you guys."

"She slept fine and is ready to go, so I should be grateful for that hard Savoie head," she said, and he laughed as he knocked the side of his own head.

"Thanks for making things easier on her," he said and hugged her. "She's really lucky for a lot of reasons, but the main one is finding you. She loves you, and it would really bother her if you didn't understand what we do."

"I'm going to worry no matter what, but I'm trying my best not to add to her slate."

"These guys would line up to have Sept's back, so you don't have any concerns there. She's earned their loyalty and respect by always doing the same for them." He hugged her again and kissed the top of her head. "And there's going to be food and way better coffee than the department buys."

"You're hilarious," she said and noticed Mackey's guys setting up in the yard. When he said everything was covered, he meant all the way down to tables and chairs. "Let me go see if they need anything."

"I'll do it," Jacqueline said as Joel moved back to her side. "These guys are here to see you, not me."

"I think they're here to see Sept," she said, folding her arms over her chest.

"You're with Sept, so you're part of not just our family, Keegan, but part of the NOPD family, so get used to it. They're here for you too. We all are," Joel said.

The rest of the Savoies came in as Joel was finishing his pep talk, so she accepted hugs from the Savoie brothers, ending with Sebastian. "Thanks for coming, and if you give Mackey a minute, he'll feed you," she said as she turned to watch Sept come down the stairs.

"Hey, guys," Mackey said, starting another round of hugs. "I've got everything set up outside, but how about I put the family and Nathan in here? Gustave told me you all have some stuff to go over, so I figured that would be good."

"Thanks, man," Sept said, embracing Mackey and kissing him on the cheek. Ever since they'd met, Sept had really come to enjoy their cousin's company since they'd bonded over steaks and bourbon when Sept had been recuperating.

"Shit. You're the one with the hard job. Eggs are easy. Go sit, and I'll get you guys fed." Mackey patted Sept on the back before going outside.

"You want us to go eat with the masses while you talk to your family?" Keegan asked, taking her hand but not getting too close so Sept wasn't uncomfortable about showing too much affection. Sept seemed to notice and tugged her closer. "I'm sure we can find a seat out there."

"Are you going to run to the papers?" Sept asked, clearly joking. "If you think you can handle it, I'd like you to stay. I think you'll feel better if you're aware of what's going on."

"That *would* make me feel better." She kissed Sept's chin and led her to the head of the table.

Once everyone had a plate, Sebastian pointed to Joel to start. "From what we found last night, we can definitely say the explosion was the result of a device and not a gas leak, but they're still gathering information about how it was put together and detonated." Joel read from his notes and passed Sept a file with pictures of what they'd found.

"That was a quick, hot fire," Sept said, flipping through each picture. "Do they at least know what kind of accelerant was used?"

"You know those bomb guys, and then mix in the feds, so until they've tested every inch, they're not going to give us anything," Joel said.

"The device had to be activated remotely. If not, the maid would be dead." Sebastian covered Keegan's hand as if to comfort her from the words. "This person definitely has eyes on Sept."

"If that's true, though, he had every opportunity to kill me when I was closer. If he was watching, he waited until I understood he could've killed me but then spared me," Sept said.

"What the hell then?" Nathan asked.

Sept smiled as she looked at Keegan, who nodded as if understanding this wouldn't be a cinch. "We have to guess this is our killer and he's showing me how smart he is. It's a taunt that we caught

Perlis, but this time won't be so easy." The headache was mostly gone, but the frustration of being in the dark was starting to drive the pain in the base of her skull up to the middle of her head. "Who'd Fritz put on this task force?"

"Me, for one, so tell me who you want," Sebastian said. "You get your pick as long as most of the people around this table are on your list. This is your investigation, but you're my kid, so I want family looking out for you."

"Thanks, Dad, and I think we'll start with the folks we had last time and add to that. These crimes have a twisted meaning of the Santeria religion, so we need to pull Lourdes Garcia from whatever patrol she's on."

"Are you okay to work today?" Gustave asked.

"I am, but one low-pressure day won't set us back too much," she said, and Keegan squeezed her fingers. "In my gut these killings aren't related to Perlis, but it's time to move forward, so I think the best thing to do is go back."

"What are you talking about?" Francois asked.

"Nathan and I need to go down to central lockup and visit Perlis. He's not going to give up if Teacher's real, but we need to push him to start talking."

"Make sure you go through his attorneys. His trial's not for another few months, but you don't want to throw anything into that path to slow it down," Gustave said.

"I'll make the call," Nathan said and headed for the front of the house.

"If we can get in to talk to that bastard Perlis," Sept said, smiling when Keegan pushed her plate closer and pointed to it, "then let's meet this afternoon and go over what they're able to pull out of that motel room."

"How about the crowd in the yard?" Jacqueline asked.

"They just want to make sure I'm still breathing," Sept said and laughed. "The fact there was food was an added bonus, so they'll leave once all those chafing dishes are empty."

Sept took some time outside chatting with the folks who'd stopped by before she went in search of Keegan, who was changing for work. The staff at Blanchard's had taken care of the lunch prep, but Keegan wanted to be there for the lunch rush, since she'd left the night before.

"Changed your mind about saying yes?" she asked when she

walked up and put her arms around Keegan from behind. The chef pants were on, but Keegan hadn't reached for the pristinely white top with the restaurant's logo over the right breast pocket.

"You're not getting off that easy." Keegan fell back against her, wearing only her bra. "I remember the first time we made love and what you told me."

"Consistency," she said and kissed the side of Keegan's neck. "I'll leave every day and I'll come back. If I ever break that promise, it's not because I want to. I love you too much to leave you."

"You waited until I fell madly in love with you before you added that last part," Keegan said, and Sept could tell she was crying. "I was so scared."

"I'm so sorry." It was all she could think to say.

"You don't have to be sorry, baby," Keegan turned in her arms and pressed her face into her chest. "This isn't your fault or something you need to apologize for, but it terrifies me that someone's out to kill you."

"I'm always careful, and I know you don't want to hear this, but I can't quit now." Keegan nodded against her chest. "I'll never show you the crime-scene photos, not because I don't trust you, but because they're horrible. Nobody deserves to die the way that woman did, no matter what they do for a living."

"I know that, but I'm selfish." Keegan leaned back a little and gazed up at her. "I want a long life with you, and I don't want to be robbed of one second of it."

"And you won't." She kissed Keegan and slid her hands to her ass. "It's going to take all those years for me to express how much I love you."

"Go to work, then, before I strip you naked and handcuff you to the bed," Keegan said, hissing when Sept pinched one of her nipples. "Not nice, Seven."

"You'd better get dressed before I have to toss the dog off the bed and strip *you* naked." Mike was lying on his back with all four paws in the air, gently snoring. "And he'd probably bite my ass if I tried."

"Call me later so I won't be completely insane all day."

"I promise, and if I'm done early enough, I'll come by and have dinner. Only I promise to ditch the crowd before then."

"I have a veal chop with your name on it," Keegan said as her head cleared her T-shirt that she wore under the chef's coat. "And we both know what you'll do for one of those."

"True, so I can't wait."

❖

"Ms. Harrison." Nicole took the tall, blond woman's hand and shook it briefly. "Thank you for agreeing to this."

"Please call me Gretchen." Gretchen waved her to a seat at the small conference table in her office. "And I think this might be good. I did a little research, and you're not opposed to interviews before your books are published."

"That's true," Nicole said as Gretchen's assistant placed cups of coffee in front of them.

"It wouldn't hurt for the world to see that my client has come untethered from reality," Gretchen said, raising her hand. "That's the best way I can describe it."

"How did you come to represent Mr. Perlis?" The firm, the partnership, the corner office—all the wins in Gretchen's career added up to her being way out above Alex's pay grade.

"His parents and mine are lifelong friends, and they insisted on paying for his defense," Gretchen said, shrugging slightly. "I'd rather our association not go too far in your book. That's not the most pertinent thing in his case, and his family's been put through enough."

"Not a problem. I've focused all my time on Mr. Perlis, so I don't know anything about his family. Is that something we can talk about?"

"Alex's father is a part owner in a very successful oil-field supply company, his mom is a professor here at the UNO campus, and his two younger brothers work for their father." Gretchen seemed somewhat hesitant, but obviously the Perlis family had agreed to this part of the conversation. "They're all horrified that Alex was capable of this, but his past mental issues have made it clear to all of us that he deserves to be hospitalized, not put on death row."

"Understandable, but I don't believe diminished-mental-capacity cases do well in Louisiana, so that might be a stretch," she said, letting some of her father's argument out to play. "Your jury pool is full of black-and-white thinkers."

"Once you talk with Alex, we'll meet again and see if your opinions stay the same," Gretchen said, shrugging again. "The family and I agree to give you full access but do reserve the right to have final say in what you print. Alex isn't always talkative, but I can't allow anything he might volunteer to torpedo his defense. That would be negligent on my part."

"Yet you agreed to this?" she asked, briefly touching Gretchen's hand. "That doesn't fit with the type of woman who was given such a prestigious office."

"I earned this office one successful case at a time, but Mr. and Mrs. Perlis are determined to show the world how sick their son is, Ms. Voles. All I can do is follow their wishes while still doing the best job I can to protect my client."

"Ah, I see," she said, picking up on Gretchen's reluctance. "If he's nuts, the blame doesn't taint the old family name."

Gretchen smiled but shook her head. "Your words, not mine, so let me know when you'd like to go visit him, and I'll arrange it."

"Ms. Harrison," a woman said over the intercom. "I hate to bother you."

"Excuse me a moment," Gretchen said, lifting the receiver and not saying anything for a long moment. "Not without me there," she said eventually, not sounding pleased. "He has legal counsel, so that's out of the question. Did she leave her number?"

"Problem?" Nicole asked.

"The police want to question my client again." Gretchen folded the page she'd written on and stood. "I apologize, but if you have anything else, we'll have to reschedule."

"Do you mind if I come with you?" She tucked her notebook back into her bag and placed it in her lap as a signal she was ready to go. "I can observe how Alex interacts with the police and might gain some insight into how to get him to open up to me."

"As long as you stay quiet, I don't see a problem."

❖

The jail had a peculiar odor Nicole couldn't quite place, but it reminded her of some kind of cold cut. There were more people than chairs in the waiting area, but that was fine since she didn't really want to touch anything in the room. The place defined physical misery.

"There she is," Gretchen said, cocking her head toward the door marked Official Business Only.

Nicole recognized Sept Savoie and her white hair from the numerous pictures of her but wasn't prepared for the woman's presence. Sept's face was bruised over her left eyebrow, but she seemed to exude confidence with a healthy dose of cocky. It made her even more attractive, since Nicole figured she wasn't a pushover no matter the circumstances.

"Gretchen," Sept said, offering the lawyer her hand.

"Sept." Gretchen answered in the same tone. "What's this about?"

"Not out here, okay," Sept said, leading them into an interrogation room complete with a two-way mirror. "I need to talk to him even though he probably won't say anything real."

"Give me a good reason." Gretchen spoke, but Sept's focus wasn't on her.

"Who's your friend?" Sept asked, and Nicole smiled at the question. She was used to both women and men looking at her with the same curious and wanting expression.

"She's with me, so forget that and answer my question," Gretchen said.

"I'm not going to discuss this situation in front of someone I don't know, so who's your friend?"

"Detective Savoie," she said and held her hand out. "I'm Nicole Voles. I've called you numerous times, but we haven't connected yet."

"Nice to meet you, and if you don't mind waiting outside, I need to speak to Ms. Harrison about her client," Sept said, her face losing all expression.

"Ms. Voles isn't just writing a book. She's helping me, Roger, and Fred with this case," Gretchen said, picking her briefcase off the table. "If you can't handle that, then my client's off-limits for any conversation."

"I really need to talk to him, preferably without the circus."

"Nicole, excuse us a moment, won't you?" Gretchen said as she left with Sept, whose partner stayed behind.

"Busy day?" she asked the man.

"Not yet, but it's still early," he said as he sat and concentrated on the glass wall.

"With any luck, it'll pick up for you." She crossed her legs and waited. She didn't see any reason to waste breath on someone who couldn't give her what she wanted. "It'll give me something to write about eventually."

"Maybe," he said, not looking at her.

"Maybe indeed."

CHAPTER TEN

W hat are you saying?" Gretchen asked, slumping into a chair.
"There was another ritualistic murder last night," Sept said,
holding her hand up when Gretchen opened her mouth. "I know what
you're going to say, but it won't exonerate Perlis. I can't get into it, but
there were plenty of differences."

"Then why talk to Alex?"

"I don't have the authority to deal the needle out of his arm, but if
Perlis had an accomplice he hasn't given up, we might be able to save
his life." Sept raised her hand higher. "We can do that if he's ready to
answer questions."

"Let me talk to him," Gretchen said, taking a thick file from her
bag. "I'm not promising anything, but I'll see what I can do."

"We have to leave Nicole Voles out of this for now. She might be
helping you, but I'm not going to lose control of my investigation to
some sideshow when she starts talking to the media to hype her next
book."

"Have Nathan walk her out, and give me the room to talk to him."

Nicole didn't appear amused as Nathan escorted her back out to
the waiting room. How Nicole Voles thought she could help the defense
made Sept curious, but she didn't have time to think about that now.
Every one of her conversations with Perlis took concentration, because
he usually divulged something, and all of it amazingly played into his
defense of not being responsible because he was nuts.

"And I'm about to give him his strongest argument yet," she
muttered as she drummed her thumbs on the table.

"Are you talking to yourself?" Nathan asked, reaching up to feel
her forehead, but she slapped his hand away. "So, what do you think
about the writer? She's hot, huh?"

"She's also here for a story that'll make you and me look like idiots." She put her hands in her pockets. "Remember that before you decide to do something cute."

"Don't worry. No meetings or conversations without you," Nathan said, then shut up when Gretchen came back in.

"Let's lay some ground rules," Gretchen said.

"It's not warfare, just a conversation," Sept said but sat down.

"I'm taping this, and nothing he says can be used against him or to strengthen his case."

She laughed, but Gretchen didn't join her. "That's a redundant statement."

"I get paid by the word," Gretchen deadpanned. "I'm just being careful, so if you can live with that, we can talk."

"Off the record then," she said, and Gretchen nodded. "You want me to get an ADA in here before we start? I know you, so I'm thinking this isn't your favorite case, so don't do anything that'll come back to bite you."

"Thanks, Sept, and maybe that'll be the best course of action."

It took twenty minutes for the district attorney's office to send the prosecutor's second chair. Allison Chase agreed to Gretchen's demands, and only then did Gretchen divulge that Alex had been medicated by necessity to keep from hurting himself. Sept remembered the first time she'd seen him after his arrest, and he was bloody from beating his head on the wall, supposedly to quiet Teacher's voice in his head.

The doctors had started calming him pharmaceutically, but Sept had no idea just how many drugs they were giving him. When Gretchen shared the list with her, she figured this would be a waste of time as Perlis was led into the room. With this cocktail, Perlis was probably close to comatose.

"Alex," Sept said, surprised how quickly he went from a doped catatonia to being alert and aggressive. The cuffs the deputy had locked to the table were the only things that had kept him in his seat. "Take a breath."

"What the fuck do you want?" Alex asked, barely opening his mouth.

"There are ladies in the room, so calm down. I want to talk to you." How was he fighting the effects of the sedative so well?

"You should be dead," Alex said, the spunk in him suddenly gone. "I should've killed you."

"Alex, when you talked about Teacher, you always said he spoke to you in your head, but it's time to tell me who he really is." She rapped her knuckles on the table, trying to get him to stop his chant about killing her.

"Who he really is? What do you mean by that?" Gretchen asked, putting her hand up to keep Alex quiet. "What's going on, Sept?" Gretchen asked as if they hadn't had a conversation a few minutes earlier. "You think Teacher's real?"

"I need him to tell me that." She pointed to Perlis. "Now's the time to save yourself, so you need to talk to me."

"Teacher's mine. He wouldn't dirty himself by talking to you. He'd never allow it." Alex yanked hard to try to free his hands.

"A repeat of the crime isn't going to open the door to this place for you. So, who is he?" Sept said, raising her voice. "If you don't tell me, I promise I'll put the needle in your arm myself."

"The sacrifice was the same?" Alex stopped moving and stared at her. "That can't be right. He wouldn't do that."

"Alex, if you know something, it's okay to tell us. It'll take the death penalty off the table," Gretchen said, sounding like a soothing kindergarten teacher trying to calm a small, unruly child.

"Teacher wouldn't do that," Alex screamed. "He's mine. He's here with me, and you're trying to steal him for yourself." The tears and anguish in Alex's tone seemed real, but Sept wasn't ready to completely believe him.

"He said he could do it better, so he doesn't need you anymore. You screwed up, so he's doing it on his own." She spoke softly, which quieted him enough for him to hear her. "He betrayed you, but you can punish him by answering my questions. Who is he?"

"He's mine," Alex mumbled. He suddenly pitched himself to the left, fell over, and hung by his hands, beating his head on the side of the table. "He promised," he yelled as Nathan and the deputy tried to get him up. "You promised not to leave me. Talk to me. You promised."

"I don't think we're going to get anywhere, Sept," Gretchen said and nodded when the deputies came back to remove Alex. "Let me talk to him when he's more receptive and see if I can make progress. If I can find any answers I'll let you know."

"This is important, Gretchen, especially if whoever this is decides to repeat all the crimes. You don't want that on your head."

"I give you my word I'll talk to him as well as his parents. Maybe they can get through to him, especially if Allison is serious about dropping the death penalty. I know the DA really wants to bury Alex."

"Thanks, and if he gives up the Teacher, I'll do whatever's necessary to at least save his life. This is about saving more lives and nothing to do with politics." Sept watched Gretchen leave, taking Allison with her. It was time to go back and take another look at where Bonnie had died, but she had time to see Keegan before they did. "Hey," she said to Nathan after he got off the phone. "You want to meet me at the precinct in an hour?"

"That was Gavin's office," Nathan said, holding up his cell. "From the mug-shot photos, they've identified Bonnie Matherne as our victim. Royce is sending someone to pick up the boyfriend."

"Good. Maybe he has some clue about what happened last night."

"You need a ride somewhere?" Nathan asked, and she shook her head. "Give Keegan a friendly kiss for me then, and I'll see you later. She still looked freaked this morning, so it's good you're stopping by."

"Thanks, man, and keep your eyes open."

She waited for Nathan to go out the back of the building, where they'd parked before she went out the front. She had a hunch. Nicole Voles sat in the waiting area, appearing as out of place as a porn star in a convent, but Sept knew she'd still be there. If the surroundings bothered her, Sept couldn't tell as Nicole uncrossed her legs and stood.

"Detective." Nicole held her hand out again. "I hope you have a few minutes to spare."

"My apologies for not calling you back before," she said, wrenching her hand from Nicole when it didn't seem she was ready to let go. "It's been a hectic few days."

"Sounds like it from the news." Nicole reached to touch the bandage on her forehead, but Sept cocked her head away. "Sorry. It looks painful with the big bruise."

"I've got to be tougher than that to get my job done. What can I do for you?"

Nicole glanced at the door and smiled. "How about I make all my demands over a cup of coffee? I noticed a place next door."

Sept hadn't planned this, but maybe it was the best way to get rid of Nicole and the project she wanted nothing to do with. Sept followed her, not saying a word until they both ordered coffee and sat. "It's your two bucks," she said when the waitress brought their cups.

"I'm sure the chief has explained the book I'm working on, so I'd like to interview you about the Perlis case. I understand the trial is pending, but you can still brag about how you caught someone who could've been at this for years."

Nicole was a beautiful woman who spoke in a way that sounded like you were the center of her world and she was sharing a deep, fascinating secret with you. She was apparently used to getting her way because she knew how to flatter. If you were in the market to spend time with a beautiful woman, she would be hard to turn down.

"We don't know each other at all, and I'm not familiar with your previous experiences, but I'm not the bragging kind." Sept smiled as Nicole's flirty façade slipped just enough for her to notice. "I also just left a meeting where the defense attorney said you were helping them, so I don't see us talking too much, even if I wanted to beat my chest."

"I think Gretchen exaggerated my involvement," Nicole said slowly, as if trying to recover.

"I've known Gretchen since college. The only things she exaggerates are her golf scores, so I wish you luck with the book."

"Without any input from you, don't be upset when I'm done."

"Crime novels aren't my thing," she said, being totally honest. "I don't want to relax by reading something that centers on what I do all day. And I can't stop you from writing your opinions. I seldom give interviews, but I won't mind a few to set the record straight if you wander off the path paved with facts."

"What do you enjoy reading?" Nicole asked.

"A good historical novel is more than just an escape. I like learning new things about interesting people." She glanced down at her watch. "If I can do anything else for you, please don't hesitate to call."

"I realize you don't want to do an interview, but could I ask a favor that might help us both?"

"I'll try. What is it?"

"My father is coming to town in a few days and would like to see the first crime scene," Nicole said, tapping her nails against the white ceramic cup. The noise was irritating, but Sept didn't plan to stay much longer. "Would you walk us through it?"

"Wouldn't he rather go on a riverboat dinner cruise?"

"He's an FBI agent, not a tourist. I'm sure Chief Jernigan can accommodate me, if you're not available."

"Are you interested in the first scene or in the first ritual scene?" Maybe if she did this, Nicole would forget about the rest.

"The first two are more like practice runs, in my opinion, so the one in New Orleans East. That's what he's interested in."

"It's an active scene now, but I'll see what I can do." She removed a ten from her wallet even though Nicole protested. "I'll call you once I arrange it."

"Thank you. You might find we can help, if you're not so rigid about the rules."

She laughed. "It's the rules that keep us from chaos, Ms. Voles."

"Or they bind us from achieving true greatness."

"In writing or in life?" Sept asked, uncharacteristically disliking the woman.

"In all things, Detective. I'll wait for your call."

"The sooner you're in my rearview mirror, the better," she said once Nicole had slithered away in what she assumed was supposed to be a sexy gait. "The sooner the better."

CHAPTER ELEVEN

Did you enjoy yourself?" Brandi Parrish asked Erica Median as Erica unpacked her bag. After Sept had taken Erica to the Red Door months before, Brandi had noticed how Erica had blossomed in a safe environment. Granted, Erica was still working as a prostitute, but under Brandi's watchful eye, eventually she'd have a new life away from this. "Looks like you got some sun."

"I had a blast, even if it was a working vacation. Lauren was really sweet, and all she wanted was not to show up at her class reunion alone. It's the first time I ever had to talk someone into having sex with me, considering that's what she was paying for."

"Then you did a good thing, and you're a miracle worker." Brandi laughed and lay back in Erica's bed. "Lauren Goldberg makes a date every couple of months, and no one's been able to get her pants off. She books dinner and conversation, but nothing else. She must've really liked you."

"I was with my asshole boyfriend for about a year, and he was never as nice to me in all that time as she was in the last week." Erica opened her makeup bag and took out a necklace beaded with pearls and other stones. "She got me this because I told her I liked it."

"Did you not like it?" she asked, hearing what sounded like sadness in Erica's voice. "That was sweet."

"I love it, actually, but I felt funny taking her money. That's never happened to me before."

"She didn't mind handing the money over, but it might be more than that, so don't worry that it was wrong." Brandi patted the spot next to her and put her arm around Erica when she joined her.

"What's that supposed to mean?"

"It means she's already called for another date and asked if she could phone you directly." That was the first step in losing Erica, but the kid deserved some happiness. "I told her it was up to you to make whatever arrangements with her you want."

"Really? You don't mind?" Erica asked, squeezing her middle.

"You have a home with me for as long as you need one, and no matter what, you can always come back if whatever you find out there doesn't work out."

"You don't think this is a lot crazy?" Erica asked and laughed.

"Crazy is not taking the chance to be happy, so call her and set up your own damn dates," she said, pinching Erica's cheek. "And I'll be happy for you no matter what."

"Thanks." Erica finished unpacking and catching up on the latest gossip. "So, what happened while I was gone?"

"Do you have time to show someone the ropes?" Brandi followed Erica out and smiled when she headed to the kitchen. Her young friend made a lot of money as an escort, but she never lost that innocent air that made her so popular. "She reminds me a lot of you."

"What, a loser who a cop took pity on?" The pile Erica had taken out of the refrigerator was the ingredients for her favorite sandwich, and something she made Brandi often.

"Cut the bullshit," she said as she took the twisty tie off a loaf of bread. "You simply didn't know all your options back then, and you should thank God Sept isn't some opinionated asshole. So now it's time to pay that back."

"What's the new girl's name?"

"Lee Cenac, and she's related to me. At least that's what her mother claims. If she's telling the truth, Lee and I are third cousins. Supposedly she has experience, but so far she reminds me of a nervous little Chihuahua."

"Man, she and her mother must have a very understanding relationship. Mine's a piece of shit, and I'm still not telling her what I do."

"Her mom's also in the business and probably figured if her kid is going to make money at this, she might as well shoot high. After I left southern Mississippi a million years ago, I never looked back. She could be my cousin or she could be lying, but she's a sweet kid." She took a sip of the beer Erica handed her and laughed. "Now if only we can get her over that shivering, nervous thing she's got going."

"I'm sure she's not that bad," Erica said, laughing. She threw a piece of pickle at Brandi and stuck her tongue out at her. "Did you send her on any dates yet?"

"A couple, and she did okay, but she still seems hesitant. I thought if you talked to her she might have a better time of it. Kind of what Tameka did for you," she said, and Erica shivered, not really having gotten over her friend's death.

"I'll talk to her, no problem." Erica slid a plate toward her and sat. "You need anything else?"

"Not a thing except this," she said and took a bite of her sandwich. "Have you heard from Sept? I read the news online. She's got her hands full."

"I think you're right, so be careful. For some reason these assholes always go for what they think is the easiest target."

"You taught me well, so don't worry so much." Erica wiped her mouth and reached into her pocket. "And before I forget, I got you something." She took a freshwater pearl bracelet out of the silk bag and swallowed around the lump in her throat. "I saw it on one of our stops and thought you'd like it."

"Thank you," she said and had to take a deep breath to bury her emotions. It had been so long since she'd allowed anyone so close to her. "I'm going to really miss you."

"I'm not going anywhere, no matter what. I love you, and you're going to have to accept that."

"I love you too," she said and noticed Lee Cenac hovering outside the door. "Come here and meet Erica."

Erica started on another sandwich, and Lee sat next to her. "Let me feed you. Then we'll go up and talk."

"Brandi told me about you."

"Hopefully not everything." Erica winked, and Lee laughed. "We're neighbors, so it'll be good to get to know each other."

"I have a date later," Lee said.

"No problem. I'll help you get ready." Erica moved closer, put her arm around Lee's shoulder, and kissed her cheek. "It's easier when you have a friend."

❖

"We've got nothing from Perlis or from either scene," Nathan said three days later as they met with the task force. "We didn't find any useable prints or Nicholas Newton, aka Crazy Nick."

"If it's the Crazy Nick I'm thinking about, let's pray he's not so high he doesn't know who he is, much less who hired him to pick Bonnie up," Joel said. "The guy we busted a few years ago was a major tweaker."

"Hopefully he has some clue about who hired him, because I doubt he could've pulled off that murder if he was high as hell," Sept said, studying the pictures on the board. "These are a lot of steps to follow and get right even if you're sober."

"See something?" Alain asked.

"Not yet, but something's off." Sept kept staring, moving slowly but not stopping at any one thing.

"Something's off?" Ronnie Bachlet, Alain's partner asked and laughed briefly. "You mean aside from the dead woman with her heart ripped out?"

"You know what I mean." She smiled and slapped him on the back. "It's not Perlis, but in a way it is."

"Heads up, everyone," Lourdes Garcia said, coming in out of breath. "We got another call." She placed a phone in the center of the table and pressed the intercom button. "Go ahead and cue it up."

"Nine-one-one, what's your emergency?"

"You need to go to the Governor Nichols Wharf," a mechanical voice said before they stopped to hum, or that's what Sept guessed they were doing. *"The work, it's not done."*

"I'm sorry. What work?" the EMS operator asked, suddenly sounding interested. *"Is someone in danger?"*

"Someone has been set free. Tell the warrior I'm waiting."

"That's it?" Sept asked, and Lourdes nodded.

"The chief sent the info over and ordered us not to broadcast it. That should keep everyone out until we get there," Lourdes said, handing over a transcript of the call. "You want to head out?"

"Yes, but let's start with a small group. Okay, everyone. We're going in, but Nathan and I'll clear the scene." Nathan got up, but the others didn't appear to be behind that course of action.

"You, Nathan, and I will clear the scene, so forget about bitching. That's the way it's going to be," Gustave said.

"I don't have time to argue with you. Call George and have him meet us there. It'll be nice to get in before a hundred people walk through my scene."

They all left together, and her team set up along the wharf, but they had no way of knowing exactly where the caller was talking about.

The Port of New Orleans was a major operation, and the Governor Nichols Wharf was one of the largest on the Mississippi River. Gustave got the operations manager to let them in to walk around with someone familiar with the layout.

"I'm not sure what your caller's talking about, but if we got a dead body somewhere, someone would've noticed by now," the older man wearing an orange hard hat with flames on it said. "I think they were fucking with you."

"Are there any empty areas right now?" Gustave asked.

They were walking together about ten feet apart to make sure they didn't miss anything. "And what's the most secluded spot in here?" Sept asked. If there was a dark place anywhere, no telling what was waiting for them.

"Not really," the guy said, rubbing his jaw. "With all the rebuilding and stuff, we've been going hard."

"How about shifts? You guys go twenty-four-seven?" she asked.

"Pretty much, so I doubt anyone would have time to do anything and not be seen." He lifted the hard hat and scratched the top of his head. "Not to mention, security is a real bear to get through."

"Are you sure there isn't one spot that's not real busy? Even if you're working around the clock, you can't be all over this place every single day. Has any cargo been sitting for a couple of days waiting to go out?" she asked, stopping at the office to check the main manifest.

"We've got about five shipments that fit that description." He didn't seem to mind when they followed him up the stairs to the elevated offices.

The view of the cavernous space was pretty good, but unless it was right below them, she doubted anyone would see anything happening behind the stacks of cargo filling the space. An army of forklifts in constant motion moved around stacking and removing other pallets of cargo.

"At night, do you have this level of activity?" she asked as she tried to study every inch she could see from here.

"The night crew is half this, so no. We run at night, though, since the river never closes, and we have to be here to unload." He pointed to a board with ships they were waiting on.

Sept's phone rang, and she slid it from her pocket. "Sept," Royce said. "George is here."

She hung up and dialed her uncle. "George, don't make a big deal of it, but start taking pictures of anyone standing around watching, and don't forget the rocks along the levee. We haven't found anything yet, so hang tight."

That's where Perlis had hidden on the night she'd taken Keegan to the river to talk. Later that night, he'd killed a jogger and left him on the bench she'd shared with Keegan to show her how close he could get without her catching him.

"You got it," George said.

"Here you go," the manager said, handing over the list she'd asked for.

"Can you show us where these are?" Gustave asked, and the man nodded. "And can someone have something shipped and picked up here?"

"Like I said, security is a bitch about stuff like that. It doesn't happen often, but it's possible. It has to be something really big, though, since we mostly deal with shipments that will be going out to distribution centers across the country."

"Where's this one?" she asked, pointing to the one at the bottom of the page.

"What is it?" Gustave was peering over her shoulder.

"A shipment for Immaculate Conception Jesuit Church on Baronne. They were vandalized during the storm," she said.

The manager nodded and punched the order into his computer. "They were doing some repairs as well, so we kept the statues they were gifted from Rome until they're ready for them. They're in the back in the next section of the building. My boss told them we'd hold them as long as they need."

Nathan called outside and reported where they were going. The building was separated by only a ceiling-to-floor, twenty-foot divider, and two of the five shipments that had sat for a while were off to the left. There wasn't as much activity here, but still some, so she figured at night with a smaller crew, this section would be dead.

"Hold up." She stopped the manager from getting any closer. "This fucker's going down for this."

CHAPTER TWELVE

Hunter stood naked, looking out the large window at the river traffic. All the lights were off, and the only sound breaking the silence was the classical music on the stereo. The bomb had come close to ending the game before it got interesting, but Sept Savoie was proving to be a worthy adversary. Savoie had gone back to work the next morning, so she'd earned Hunter's respect.

It was time to move on and erect the next altar, because Sept had probably found the gift at the wharf by now. It was the best that could be done to replicate what had happened to Sept's dog, so that didn't take a lot of effort.

"FIOG Enterprises. How can I help you?" A woman had answered the call, tearing Hunter's eyes away from the water.

"I'd like a date for tonight," Hunter said softly.

"Any special requests?"

"Someone fresh. I'm not a big fan of domineering women, so I want someone who can follow implicit instructions. Can you accommodate me?"

"Certainly," the woman said and paused to type something. "All I need is a credit card and the hotel where you'd like to meet."

"Anything else?" Hunter started packing the kill bag, smiling from anticipation. "And I'd prefer to pay in cash. It won't be acceptable to have this transaction appear on my statement."

"The fee is twenty-four hundred, but it's an additional five hundred if you insist on cash, and it's due four hours before your date."

"That's not a problem."

"Leave it in an envelope with our company's name on it with the front desk, and we'll call with the escort's contact information."

"Thank you." Hunter disconnected and made one more call before getting ready. "I need you to drop off something and pick up some room keys for me."

"Where do you want me to drop them?"

"Meet me in the same spot, and I'll have everything you need."

Crazy Nick was an idiot, but an idiot who followed directions. This would be his last job, but it was best for him to pick up the keys to the room at the JW Marriott on Canal Street. Hopefully, whoever the escort service sent was really good at following orders, because that would be the easiest way to walk out of the hotel without making anyone suspicious.

The parking garage at the Hilton Riverside had cameras that covered all but a few spots on each floor, and Hunter had doubled the dark spots by short-circuiting the camera on the fifth floor closest to the stairwell no one seemed to use. Crazy Nick was waiting and said he understood what Hunter wanted.

He returned shortly and handed over the keys. "Here you go, and what are you going to do about the cops? They've been asking about me. They think I had something to do with Bonnie. Fuck that. I ain't going down for that."

Why the hell did people complain so much when most of what happened to them was a direct outcome of their own bad decisions? "All you did was rent a room. That's all they have, so don't get stupid. Keep your mouth shut and stick to the plan."

"Look, Bonnie's dead, and I don't know if you're deaf or slow, but I ain't going to take the rap for that."

"And you won't, if you listen to me," Hunter said. It was becoming obvious why this guy was called Crazy Nick. He was sweating and didn't seem to have the ability to keep his hands still. "Are you going to listen to me?"

"Yeah," he said, but his leg was bouncing up and down at a rapid-fire rate. "Fuck. What choice do I have?"

"You have plenty, believe me. You need to tell me now if you want out," Hunter said, and Nick looked away as if he couldn't face admitting just that. "Here's what I owe you." Nick turned to accept the offer, and as he glanced down for his money, Hunter buried the small filet knife in his neck.

Nick immediately brought his hands up, but it was too late. The amount of blood running through his fingers meant his time and usefulness were done. Now to find Bonnie's boyfriend and tie up that loose end before the date who'd be waiting at eight got antsy.

Hunter pocketed the money and took the extra jacket out of the trunk. The real loss here was the old sedan Nick had stolen the week before, along with new plates. Next time that had to be accounted for before any blood was spilled, rendering the vehicle useless.

"Three minutes should do it," Hunter said, handling the pipe bomb that would more than get rid of any evidence, along with the few cars around it. "Deviations from the plan are never good, but nothing's going to slow me down."

The stairwell was thankfully empty again, so getting to the street and away before the fireworks went off wasn't a problem. A bonus here was the large parking lot next door and the endless number of cars available. This time Hunter chose a newer model so as not to set off any alarms later on. Anyone who could afford to pay twenty-four hundred for sex needed to portray a certain image.

Everyone on the street stopped when the fireball shot from the side of the parking structure, the explosion loud enough to shatter windows in a one-block radius. More than one car alarm was going off, so it didn't draw any attention when the Lexus sedan's alarm started blaring after Hunter got the door open.

"I hope you're well rested and recovered, Sept, because tonight will be fun."

❖

"This sucks," Nathan said as he and Sept waited for Nicole Voles and her father. They'd decided to meet in front of their precinct and allow the Voles family to follow them to Tameka's murder scene. Sept hadn't figured out yet why an FBI agent whose area was counterfeiting was interested in this case. It seemed too simple to think it was all just about helping Nicole with her book.

She'd stared at the file they had so far, including the body this asshole had left them at the wharf for two days, and she still had no idea where to head next. At least the poor street mutt that had been stabbed twice, though still in critical condition, was improving. Unlike Mike, this dog had been lying with an altar around it.

Mike had been a random victim because he'd tried to protect Perlis's true target, visually impaired Robin Burns. Mike had been a service dog that almost sacrificed himself to save his owner, but the dog they'd found barely alive at the wharf wasn't at all random. The killer had chosen him because he resembled Mike, which chilled her.

"What sucks? You said Voles was hot." She leaned against the car, smoothing down the new sweater Keegan had bought her. The weather had turned cool, though it would most likely warm up until at least December.

"I read her last book about the killer in Los Angeles. This animal killed thirteen people, and that bitch Voles almost glamorized him and shredded the cops. That's probably what she wants to do to us."

"Probably, but we can't think about that now." She noticed a car approaching slowly, so she nudged Nathan. "Let's get rid of these guys and then get back to our new case."

"Detective," Nicole said, emerging from the passenger side and waiting for the handsome, neatly dressed older man to exit the driver's seat. "This is my father, Special Agent Brian Voles."

"Please, Detective." Brian shook hands with her, then Nathan. "Call me Brian."

"Thanks for giving us the tour today," Nicole said.

"No problem, so please follow us." The traffic was heavier than normal because of an accident, but Brian Voles had no problem keeping up. "This guy looks uptight."

"The feds are a different breed, but I agree. Mr. Voles has a longer than usual stick up his ass," Nathan said, driving as if he didn't care if Brian got lost.

She laughed and glanced at her phone. "Hello, beautiful."

"Do you have a minute?" Keegan asked.

"I'm playing tour guide to Nicole Voles and her father today, so I've got until we reach the house Tameka and the two officers died in." She pressed her fingers against the dash when Nathan had to slam on the brakes. "When I called earlier, I forgot to tell you I'd met her. I didn't have a good enough excuse to ditch her, so Fritz stuck us with this assignment."

"Sounds fun," Keegan said, and Sept heard Mike barking close by. "Do you think you can make dinner at Gran's tonight?"

"I love spending time with Della and the hard time she gives me."

Keegan hummed a second and clucked her tongue at her. "She loves you, and I have that on good authority, so no complaining. Tonight, though, Mom and Gran are cooking to start the planning process."

"I'll be there, or God knows what Della has in mind for me."

"Be careful and I'll see you later tonight," Keegan said, whistling for Mike. "I love you."

"Love you too."

Nathan took the exit that led to the neighborhood where the house was, and Sept started scanning the area for anyone who stood out or was studying them in turn. If the killer had already come back twice, he could do it again.

"Are you ready to be taken back to school?" Nathan asked, and she laughed.

"He does resemble my disapproving gym teacher," she said as Brian got out with an expression of superiority. Sept was used to the feds treating them like the Keystone Cops, considering the hard time they gave her over her friendship with the alleged crime boss Cain Casey. Cain consistently made the feds look like idiots, so the local agents sometimes took it out on the local police because they didn't treat Cain like Satan on steroids.

"How did you originally find Tameka Bishop?" Brian asked, reading from a file he didn't seem to want to share with them.

"The crews were still working after the storm, searching for bodies and marking the places as they went. When they arrived here, they saw the candle burning through the window. We connected it to the second murder because of the strange designs on that victim's chest." She walked to where Tameka had been found and pointed to the holes in the floor. "This was the first official altar Perlis made to his gods."

"Makes sense," Brian said, walking around the four holes, his attention on the empty space. "The silence out here even now would make it ideal for what he had in mind."

"What he had in mind was to torture and kill a young woman who had nothing to do with him, so try to remember the real victims, Ms. Voles, when you start your book. The very vivid details of this crime won't be made public until the trial, but believe me, what he did was animalistic." She glanced around, trying to see if anything was different. If the killer had come back, something might be out of place.

"She wasn't exactly innocent," Nicole said, her eyes on her father. "And please, I asked you to call me Nicole."

"So, we should feel only for the morally pure?" Nathan asked, sounding rather shocked at Nicole's attitude. "If that's the case, no victim should be mourned. No one deserves what happened to Ms. Bishop and the others, no matter their station in life."

"It's rare to find a cop not jaded by his job," Nicole said, and Brian cleared his throat.

"So this Julio Munez came and explained the significance of what you found?" Brian asked.

"The murder isn't part of any ritual of his religion, but the things left at the scene were specific to these gods. Every scene focused on a new god with a different message." She stopped him from stepping into the cleared spot. "I don't want to compromise the scene any more than I have to, just in case we need to come back for something."

"I understand." Brian moved to her side and tucked his file under his arm. "And the reason for all this was?"

"He was calling the dead. He messed up with the murders of his wife and son, and it was his way to get them back," she said, and Brian snorted. "Something funny?"

"You testify like that, and you'll guarantee his attorney will get him into some cushy hospital where he'll get out in no time. It's time to stop coddling these bastards and hold them responsible for what they did."

"No one's coddling Alex Perlis, sir. If you're afraid of that, then perhaps you should talk to Ms. Voles, since Alex's attorney seems to think she's going to help the defense. Part of our job was to catch him, and we'll finish it in the coming months by making sure he stays locked up awaiting execution."

"Are you sure you'll have the time?" Nicole asked, and Sept turned and glanced at her briefly.

"Am I supposed to know what you're talking about?"

"You caught Perlis, but what happened today?" Nicole peered at her like she'd sliced through her with her verbal assault.

"Be careful, Ms. Voles. Nothing's more sensitive to the public than a young officer killed in the line of duty, and we've had two of those. Our department is working hard to solve those murders, and if you do anything to stand in the way of that, you risk turning the mob against you. As a popular writer, you can't imagine that's a good idea."

"So, someone killed two officers here as well?" Brian asked.

"Sir, I appreciate your input, but I'm not going to discuss this subject with you. Especially since your daughter is profiting from the Perlis murders."

"This would matter only if the cases are related," Brian said.

"You can speculate all you want, but if you're done, we have to close up. Nathan and I need to get going. We have work to do." The way Brian faced off against her was a clue that he wasn't at all in a mood to be defied. "Would you like to see anything else?"

"We're done for now, but please don't let your ego get in the way of finding the truth in your open case," Brian said, and Nicole smiled.

"If you're in town long enough, you'll see that Nathan and I are the least egotistical people you'll meet." She lifted her arm and pointed to the door. "Are we ready?"

"Yes, Detective, but this isn't the end of this."

"I'm not sure what you mean, but rage all you want downtown. I'm sure the chief will listen, but the mayor wants answers. We aren't opposed to assistance, but Anabel Hicks, the local FBI bureau chief, has more than capable people."

"I'm sure Anabel does have good folks, but I have time to help."

"I'll give you a call if I need anything at all."

"That's quite the brush-off, Detective."

"I play in the sandbox just fine, so it's more of a promise," she said, sighing when he and Nicole dragged their feet. "Can you find your way back?" she asked as she padlocked the door shut.

"It's amazing what I can find when I'm motivated," Brian said.

"I'll keep that in mind as well, and your number on our list," she said and walked to the car, letting Nathan drive. "Let's stop downtown so I can give my father a heads-up, and then we'll call it a night."

"What an asshole," Nathan said.

"Your investigative skills are improving, partner."

❖

"Do you think she's holding something back?" Nicole asked Brian as she watched Sept standing next to their car with her fists on her hips. She was incredibly sexy in a butch sort of way, and the kind of woman Nicole liked to break to her will.

"The two crimes are related, but there's something else," he said as he sped up, obviously wanting to be on the interstate as fast as he could manage it. "She obviously takes me for an idiot who didn't notice all the crime tape a block down. It hasn't hit the news yet, but something happened close by on top of the two dead cops."

"I've got a contact at NOPD. By the way, Sept told Alex's attorney, Gretchen, something, but she talked her into keeping the conversation private."

"There are ways around that, sweetheart, so let's start with a visit to the FBI offices here. I'm going to offer my services, so Sept Savoie can take her objections and cram them. Only piss-poor cops don't accept help, especially when it's superior to what she's got on hand."

He drove as if they were in a car chase through the thankfully light traffic.

"It'll be nice having you around, so if Mother wants to go home, you can stay with me." She couldn't think of a better scenario than collaborating with her father on her book.

"I'm sure once I explain it to her, she'll gladly go back," he said and briefly glanced at her as he placed his hand on her knee.

"Thank you," she said, covering his hand with hers.

"It'll be fun—I'll make sure of it."

CHAPTER THIRTEEN

I stocked your favorite, so hopefully you're off duty," Della said as she held up a bottle of Grey Goose vodka.

"Just one, so Keegan won't fuss," Sept said, getting a swat from Keegan.

"We're in the coupe, Gran, so she can have two."

"Are you okay?" Melinda asked as she stopped stirring to hug Sept, then Keegan. "Carla told me she's been checking on you, and you're recovering well."

"Once the headache was gone I didn't have any problems. Your daughter's been taking very good care of me, and it doesn't hurt to know a doctor who makes house calls." Keegan kissed her for that as she sat at Della's kitchen table. It was the largest room in the house, even though she'd downsized when she'd given the girls the family home.

"Jacqueline called, and her flight's delayed, so let's go sit outside," Della said.

"How's the new place coming in Houston?" She picked a rocker so Keegan could sit in her lap. "We've been missing each other at home lately, so I never get to ask Jacqueline."

"Once we approve the chef, Blanchard's will open our first franchise location, but between Melinda and Keegan that could be a long process," Della said, rubbing Keegan's shoulders as she moved to sit next to them. "My loves expect perfection, and speaking of that, Jacqueline did tell us you talked about her staying. It almost makes me feel bad that I've given you so much shit."

She and Keegan laughed as Melinda shook her head. "That remark translates to, thank you for understanding my children and what makes them happy. Growing up as an only child, I loved the attention but wanted to give my girls someone they could always count on," Melinda said, smiling.

"If I get my way, we'll all grow old together, if only to have a built-in babysitter," Sept said, and Keegan squeezed her shoulder.

"You'll work on that right off, right?" Della asked with her hands pressed together. "I want to enjoy babies before I can't remember my name or how I'm related to all of you."

"We'll do our best, Gran, but I want to be an official Savoie before this one gets me pregnant." Keegan's comment kind of surprised Sept. They'd never really talked about that subject, even after she'd proposed.

"Are you sure you don't want them to be Blanchards, in case they're born with a spoon in their hands?" she asked, not knowing if this was the best time to ask.

"Everyone in our family is going to have the same name, baby, so Keegan Savoie has a nice ring to it."

"How about Blanchard-Savoie? If we sign like that, I get free dessert for life."

"Don't do anything to get rid of this one, baby," Melinda said as she and Della stood. "Let's finish so we can eat and plan when Jacqueline gets here."

"It shouldn't take too long." Sept put her empty glass down. "Joel's getting off in fifteen, and he promised to stop by and pick her up. I wanted to make sure she was okay."

"You're not playing matchmaker, are you?" Keegan asked but kissed her anyway.

"I might've mentioned that Joel likes girly girls," she said, repeating a line Jacqueline had told her at the first Sunday brunch Keegan had brought her to. It had been the encouragement she'd needed to kiss Keegan for the first time. "I wasn't kidding about how much I love Jacqueline, and it's time she was cherished instead of being treated so disrespectfully."

"My mom's right." Keegan pressed her lips to hers and passionately expressed how she felt. "You're a keeper."

"The only thing I am is lucky, and if you kiss me like that again, you're going to be in big trouble," she said and moaned when Keegan took her up on her challenge. "So before we start all this, what do you want out of a wedding?"

"I'll give you my honest answer if you tell me what you want," Keegan said, and Sept shook her head.

"Nope. I asked you first, but if you need a hint as to what's in my head, I'd never really thought about any kind of wedding." She ran her hand up Keegan's leg, enjoying the feel of her skin. The weather was still cool, but Keegan had chosen a long skirt with a slit on the side that gave her plenty of access. "I've really sucked at relationships, so I doubted anyone would put up with me for long. That's why weddings weren't ever on my radar."

"Baby." Keegan framed her face with her palms and smiled. Sept smiled as well, knowing she'd never get tired of looking at Keegan because she was incredibly beautiful on the outside, and loving her because she was just as beautiful on the inside. "Are you really sure about this? I'm not exactly unhappy with the way things are."

"You should've let me finish. My mother always told me it'd only take the right woman to change my mind, and my sister told me it would only take a blink of an eye to fall in love."

Keegan nodded and kissed her forehead. "So did it change your mind about a wedding as well?"

"It did, so hopefully you don't mind me standing in front of a really big crowd so I can tell the world how I feel about you." She moved Keegan closer and bit her gently on the side of her neck. "I also want them to know you're mine."

"That's a given, honey, plus I get to put a ring on your finger, which beats a tattoo on your forehead that reads Property of Keegan," Keegan said, and she laughed. "And I'm glad you said 'crowd.' It might be a lot of people we may not know well, but Mom and Gran would be crushed if we say 'intimate affair.'"

"I promise to do my share, but the hospitality-talented people are on your side of the family."

"You got that right, babe, and whoever's not on the invitation list for this thing will be pissed," Jacqueline said, sticking her head between theirs. "I started thinking about it on the way home and started a list on the plane. I also got Joel to promise to shoot you if you complain about any of it."

"Hey, guys," Joel said, coming out and handing Jacqueline a glass. Sept's brother, like every one of her siblings, had taken after Sebastian's side in height and hair color, though his still held a good bit of the dark color Sept had started with. "I'll go if I'm in the way of all this frou-frou."

"Stay and commiserate with this one once we get going, but don't say the word 'frou-frou' in front of Della, or she'll stab you with a paring knife."

"Are you sure? I wasn't invited."

"Gran and Mom always cook like the entire city's coming over, babe, so take a seat," Jacqueline said as Keegan touched the chair next to them with her foot.

"It'll be good to have a normal night," Joel said, and Sept groaned. "What? It's been crazy lately."

"You just had to say it, didn't you?" Sept asked, and Keegan pulled her hair.

"Believe me, I checked before we got here, and it's a quiet night. Nothing but the normal stuff that neither of us has to deal with." Joel opened his hand, and when Jacqueline took it, stuck his tongue out at her. "And if y'all are planning the wedding, can Nathan and I plan your bachelor party?"

"If I hear the words 'strippers' or 'red door,' you'll both be bruised in the wedding photos," Keegan said.

"You're no fun," Joel said, and Jacqueline laughed.

"She's plenty fun," Sept said, and Keegan kissed her cheek. "So we'll have to stick to drinking and steaks at Mackey's place."

"Of course our cousin is known for his love of strippers, so that's not making me feel better," Keegan said.

"Turn your phones off and come eat," Della said, prompting her to stand, still holding Keegan.

Carla was helping put things on the table when they went inside and Keegan walked up and hugged her. The move seemed to make Melinda happy. "Thanks for all your help with Sept," Keegan said to Carla as Jacqueline hugged her as well.

"I was glad to do it," Carla said as everyone sat down.

"To family and the people we love." Della raised her glass.

"Very true." She tapped her glass to Della's. "And you didn't have to open the good stuff. I agreed to the big shindig."

"You're a smart woman, so be glad you went so willingly and I didn't have to rough you up." Della pinched her cheek and took her plate. "Now wrap up all this stuff at work so we can do this right."

"Yes, ma'am. I'm working on it, and thanks for doing this. My brother's right that it's nice to forget everything over good food and wine with people you love."

"You're a good egg, Detective, and you're always welcome at my table."

"Thanks, Della."

"How about you call me Gran and get it over with."

"Gran, let's eat before my phone rings and I'm back in the doghouse calling you Mrs. Blanchard."

❖

"You look great," Erica said to Lee as she finished applying her mascara. "Who do you have on tap tonight?"

"Someone at the JW," Lee said, making one more swipe before capping the tube. "They had some crazy explosion at the Hilton, so I'm glad I'm not headed there with the million cops probably walking around. I don't have a name, but it's probably some convention-goer looking for someone new that ain't his wife."

"True, but never use the word 'ain't' with a date."

"Brandi already told me, and I'm trying to get better." Lee stood and put on the silver cocktail dress Erica had lent her. "Fits okay?" She studied herself in the mirror.

"Like it was made for you. Go have fun, and if we finish at the same time, let's meet down in the bar for a drink and ride back together."

"Now that's a date I'd love to keep. I should be done by midnight, so I'll meet you there."

"See you then, and be careful."

Lee took the car service Brandi had arranged and checked her face one more time before going inside. "I have an envelope waiting for me from Mr. Smith," she told the guy behind the front desk. He handed it over as if expecting her and smiled.

"This just came down. There's been a change in plans. Mr. Smith's running late and is interested in dinner as well. The car's waiting outside to take you to the restaurant."

She held the envelope that didn't feel as if it had a key in it and hesitated. Brandi had lectured her enough about doing anything that wasn't in the plan and questioning it, but dinner would cut down on spending time trying not to gag while some fat guy who didn't know anything about fucking touched her until he got off.

"Thanks," she said, and stepped away to open it. It just said where to meet the car, so she headed out past the valet station to the street. The Lexus was where the note said it would be, and she headed to the passenger side. "Hey," she said, turning her head to close the door and jerking at the stinging sensation in her shoulder.

It was the last thing she remembered as her vision dimmed, then went black.

Hunter reached over and buckled Lee in, not wanting to be pulled over for anything. "Hey, yourself," but Lee was out with her head against the window. "Let's hope you're worth the money."

The date had been expensive, but it was in honor of Tameka Bishop, even though the order of the killings was off. "But if Savoie's the best, then she deserves someone like you."

The drive didn't take long, and Hunter put on the hood and mask before getting out. After a few nights of surveillance, Hunter saw that the neighborhood was still fairly empty, most of the rebuilding happening a mile away.

This was where Alex had gone wrong and had never recovered. But that mistake wouldn't be repeated tonight. Hunter dragged Lee to the yard and placed her where the stakes were already driven in. The drug that had knocked Lee out wouldn't last until the end, so the ball gag was necessary.

Hunter returned with the supply bag and the leather gloves that lessened the chances any cuts would leave DNA behind. "I might have to go back to New Orleans East to hear your fear." Hunter brought Lee around with smelling salts and smiled at the wide-eyed, horrified expression. "The first time was rather intoxicating."

Lee's movements were so similar to Bonnie's that Hunter stopped and watched. "I know you don't see this as an honor, but you're an important part of my game, and you're one more pawn I plan to use to win."

The blue and amber candles came out, and the light they provided with the faint streetlight gave the area an almost romantic feel. This time the circle of salt was larger to fit the pears, grapes, and three pigeons from the city-park traps that Hunter had set in a secluded spot.

Lee moved her head from side to side as the knife sliced into her wrist. "This time I can leave the number that should make the most impact." Hunter put a three on Lee's right foot and a seven on her left, followed by the shepherd's crook on the bottom of them. "Tonight it's time to leave Perlis's playbook for something more interesting."

The bottle of anisette replaced the rum Perlis had used, but that would have to wait. The statue of St. Norbert went to the right of Lee's head, and the prayers to the orisha Ochosi were complete. "Are you ready?" Hunter asked, and Lee shook her head again, the pitiful moaning stymied by the gag growing louder. "Eventually I'll meet you in hell, but not tonight."

That was all that was left to be said as the knife went into the lower side of Lee's abdomen, and Hunter cut toward the right. It was amazing to see the tears running down Lee's cheeks and hear her heavy breathing. The disembowelment hadn't killed her or knocked her out like with Bonnie, and she stared up at Hunter as if not believing what had happened.

"Let go." Hunter reversed the direction of the knife and sliced up until it hit the ribs. Lee's eyes finally closed when Hunter reached up and ripped her heart out and added it to the circle of salt. Once the bottle was empty after pouring it on all the sacrifices, Hunter took a moment to enjoy the kill dedicated to the one god that would not only understand but appreciate what had happened. Hunter also thought the god would appreciate the work it had taken to make it possible.

"I'll keep going if only to show you how poor an opponent you are," Hunter said, thinking of Sept.

A sound from the street stopped any other insightful words, and in the silence, the conversation carried easily to the back.

"This is a fucking nice car, bro." Whoever had said it sounded young. "And the fucking keys are in it."

"Chill, man," another young man said. "Who the fuck left it here?"

"What the fuck do I care. We can cruise for the night. This fucker was stupid enough to leave the keys, so they deserve it."

Hunter moved to the side of the yard and walked to the front to see the driveway. The two Hispanic-appearing teenagers already had the door open, seeming to have made up their minds. It would help with the disposal of the car but wasn't exactly part of the plan. Whatever happened next had to be a snap decision.

"What would be found first?" Hunter whispered, deciding to return to the supply bag. Now it depended on how fast the potential car thieves were. They were still talking it over, so Hunter opened fire, walking toward the car and killing the closest guy, then wounding the other one by the driver's side. How long he lived depended on how fast the cops got there.

"Take deep breaths, and pray to the gods they hear your pleas to live."

The young man looked up and held up one hand, the other pressed to the wound in his chest. "Please don't kill me." The words came out in a harsh whisper.

"The only way you die is if help doesn't respond fast enough. Remember to pray, and let's see what this adds to the game."

Hunter put the gun back in the bag and walked the three blocks up to retrieve the other crappy car Nick had found. That one obviously wasn't an enticing target, as it sat in a driveway Nick said would be safe, the keys under the front mat.

"Nine-one-one, what's your emergency?" the operator asked after about twenty rings.

"Two bodies." Hunter gave the address, having memorized it. "One's still alive, but you have to hurry."

"Do you know who's responsible?"

"It was me, and I left you a short window to talk to the one alive. Sept Savoie will want to know, so call her."

Hunter hung up and headed back downtown. "Let's see where you get with a witness."

CHAPTER FOURTEEN

The dinner had gone well, and Della was entertaining Sept and Joel with funny stories of Keegan and Jacqueline when they were young. It was the type of night Sept had been craving, if only to forget about her case for a little while and remember what was most important in her life now, aside from her family. Keegan was her life, but her family was becoming as important to her as her own.

"Gran." Keegan and Jacqueline both lengthened the name, as if outraged with Della's selection.

"Sleep with one eye open, lady," Sept said but kissed Della's cheek. Della lost her smile when Sept's phone rang. "Sorry, but it's my boss, so I can't not answer it."

"You drive me totally insane with that thing," Della said, but Sept smiled and moved away a bit.

"Sept, we got another one, but this one might get us somewhere," Royce said and explained the circumstances. "Get there, and I'll have John's guys lock down the scene. Since the caller mentioned your name, the emergency operator knew not to broadcast it, so it should stay fairly quiet there for a little while anyway."

"You got it," Sept said, writing the address down and cursing when she recognized it. "That's where Perlis took Erica."

"Are you sure?" Royce asked, releasing a long breath.

"I know this case like it's my religion. I'm sure. I'll call Nathan and let you know what I find." She phoned Nathan, waking him up, but he promised to stop by for Julio and meet her at the scene. A call to the 9-1-1 operator came next, but another mechanical voice with no discernable background noise didn't help her at all. "I'm sorry, everyone, but I've got to go."

"Take my car, and I'll go home with Jacqueline," Keegan said, putting her arms around her waist. "Call me if you're going to be real late."

"Go to bed, sweetheart." She kissed Keegan's forehead and held her tighter. "I'll be a while, believe me. Thanks for a wonderful evening, Gran," she said to Della, and the new name earned her a smile and maybe a little forgiveness. "You too, Melinda, and you both have to believe that I'd much rather stay, but if you'll excuse me, I have to go to work."

She pushed the seat back as far as it would go and thought about the different ways to reach the neighborhood Erica had escaped from that wouldn't take out Keegan's suspension. The killer wouldn't leave by a main thoroughfare, and if they liked the danger of taunting the police and her, maybe they were still around. The back of the area had a park piled higher with debris and other trash than the surviving trees, but that wasn't unusual. Any open area not well patrolled had become a dumping ground for anyone busy gutting their house and not wanting to wait for the trash collectors.

After they finished with the scene, she'd send some people to walk the grounds to see if anything relating to this incident had been dumped along with the ton of Sheetrock and warped doors. Some of the places she drove by showed signs of repair, but she didn't see any FEMA trailers or signs of life, so witnesses wouldn't be possible here either.

The crime-scene house was lit up with blue flashing lights when she stopped and heard one of the uniforms whistle at the car. At least for his sake, the wolf whistle had better have been for the car. "Nice ride, Sept. You're moving up in the world."

"It's a loaner, so don't get used to seeing it. Where's the fun?"

"Out back, but John said he'd rip our balls off if we leave our post."

"That would suck, so stay put, but I might have something for you to do later." She accepted booties and gloves from one of George's guys and followed them to the back of the yard. "Son of a bitch," she said softly when she saw the body. This time the victim had been left tied and displayed like some nightmare from a horror movie.

"We've got another one by the fancy car out front, but I peg it for a kid being at the wrong place at the wrong time," George said as the floodlights came on, accompanied by the whirl of the generator needed to run them.

This one was vastly different from the first copycat murder, at least as far as the victim and what was left behind. Whoever had done this had gone off script because she didn't recognize the saint left behind, and the sacrifice seemed more complete with the other items in the salt circle. The circle was starting to melt into the ground as the late-night dew arrived, and she hoped the rest of their clues wouldn't go with it.

"My Catholic chops aren't the greatest," she said as she finally looked up at the altar and away from the body, and George laughed. "Just don't tell my mother that." He nodded and aimed his penlight at the base. "Who is that?"

"St. Norbert, and I had to get down there and look, which basically means I'm going to hell with you. Another note's rolled up in there, so if you want to see it, I'll send Jennifer back to the office to open it." George pointed to the pile of ripped but folded clothes and the small purse sitting on top. "This is a different caliber than Bonnie Matherne."

"What are you talking about?" she asked, trying to take everything in.

"I'm no fashionista, but the dress is expensive, and the purse is Kate Spade. I'm not sure who Ms. Spade is, but Jennifer said nothing out here is a knockoff."

"What about the kid in the front?" She nodded to Lourdes Garcia and her partner Bruce Payton as they stood close by, taking notes for George. "You guys keep it locked down, and I'll be right back."

"You got it, Boss," Bruce said.

She and George walked slowly as she illuminated the path to the front. "Why does this shit always happen at night?"

"To keep evil hidden. That's what my father and brother always said." George spoke softly of his family, who'd also given plenty of years to police service. "If we're dedicated enough we'll flip the lights on, and the cockroaches can't hide. And since this is your case, your dedication isn't a question to me."

"Thanks, Uncle George." She looked at the scene in front of her.

A body sprawled by the passenger side of the dark sedan, the head held up at an odd angle against the bottom of the door. The way the young man was so haphazardly splayed out meant he was caught by surprise and fell where he was shot. She walked a large circle around the car to the driver's side, where the door was open, and heard the dinging that meant the keys were still in the ignition.

"The other kid fell right over here," George said, pointing to the cones someone had laid out. "From what the EMS guys told me, he'll be lucky to last a few hours, if that."

"Hey," Nathan said, walking up with Julio. "What do we have?"

"Female at the back, that kid, and one on the way to the hospital."

"One survived?" Nathan asked, moving closer to keep their conversation private.

"We need to finish here, so how about we send Gustave to the hospital? It sounds like the kid might not make it, and I don't want to sit around waiting for what might not happen." She squinted when she saw the discarded but new-looking bicycle. "I don't mean to sound like a bitch, but we have plenty to get through here, and I want to do it while it's still fresh. This one didn't go quite as planned, and these two guys might've seen whoever did that in the yard."

"That sounds good. We need someone we can trust, and Gustave and his partner are a good choice."

She took her phone out and dialed her brother as she kept walking the area. Jennifer glanced up from dusting for prints, and she raised a finger to give Gustave all her attention. "Hey, I need you to go down to Tulane Medical and interview a witness from our homicide. From what they told me, this guy's critical, so you better hustle."

"I'm on it," Gustave said, sounding like he was already moving. "I'll get my partner to meet me there."

"Call me when you're done."

"Are you at the new scene yet?"

She stopped in the center of the sidewalk at the front of the house and looked for anything that popped out at her. "It's another fucking nightmare, so try to get to this guy before we run into more bad luck and dead ends."

"Hey, Sept," Jennifer said. "We found an ID on our victim up here. You aren't going to like it."

"Who is he?" A closer look showed the face of a very young man who should've been at home studying and not dead in the middle of this mess. "Jesus, he's only sixteen."

"His name is Miguel Navarro, and he's a junior at McDonogh 35."

"Shit," Nathan said, crouching down to take a look at the guy's face. "What was he doing here?"

"First, let's take things in order." She walked to Julio and shook his hand. "I appreciate you coming out with so little notice."

"No problem, but this looks like a drive-by," Julio said, pointing toward Miguel.

"Like I said, we need to take things in order." She directed him to the back along the fence, since it didn't appear to be disturbed, and Julio gasped at the sight under the bright lights.

"*Dios mío*," Julio said.

"Someone called 9-1-1 and reported the two bodies out front, and when you see this you'll rule out drive-by. I'm convinced they were shot after this," she said, but Julio and Nathan simply stared. "Tell me about St. Norbert."

"He's not one of the better-known orishas, just like St. Norbert isn't well known in the church." Julio stepped closer to see what the woman had around her. "It's an altar to Ochosi, and not something we've seen before with Perlis. Ochosi is a skilled and stealthy hunter. He's known in Santeria as an ethical god who always hits what he's hunting for, using an arrow. That's the only thing I don't see here."

"So the fruit and birds are part of the sacrifice?" Nathan asked.

"Yes, and," he put his face close to the ground, "not rum this time."

Sept joined him and sniffed. "It smells like licorice."

"It's anisette," Julio said. "This orisha prefers it. If you take all this," Julio circled his finger around all the offerings including the woman's heart by the candles, "minus the human sacrifice, he's paying homage to the hunter."

"You're right. This is new, so our guy's going off script," Sept said. "And all this is the planned part." The yard scene was the altar and why the killer had come, so the front was the unplanned part.

"I didn't come to this scene, and the girl getting away didn't allow Perlis to finish his altar," Julio said, not appearing able to turn away from the carnage. "Thankfully it was the end of his killing spree, so I don't know who he'd planned this altar for."

"It wasn't a question of trust, Julio," she said, placing her hand on his shoulder and wanting to break the spell he seemed to be under. "We found part of an altar, but we had a live witness, which took precedence over everything else going on."

"What did he leave with that one?" Julio asked, and Nathan referred to his notes.

"He put down one green and one black candle, and Erica had the remnants of a three and seven on the tops of her feet. The trauma of what happened made her forget what he'd said, but it started with an 'O.'"

"Interesting," Julio said, closing his eyes and shivering. "The orisha's different, but the numbers are the same. Ogun had to be Perlis's altar, and he's known as a powerful warrior who fights for injustice but is also a protective father."

"That's a joke, since Perlis killed his own kid," Nathan said disgustedly.

"The rest of this fits with what you found here at the Perlis scene," Julio said, finally seeming to have hit his limit when he turned his back on the dead woman. "Whoever this is picked something important to them while keeping some of Perlis's choices with the numbers."

"I guess that's true, and thankfully Erica was smart. She used herself to get out of this situation, but this guy seems more focused on the task of killing. Either that or this poor girl froze and didn't have the state of mind to do the same thing."

"I didn't think there could be another cruel animal that could do this again," Julio said, taking a deep breath.

"The world isn't always fair, and it doesn't always make sense, but I appreciate your input. Hopefully we won't have to meet like this again. I'd rather have a drink with you instead of this crap," she said, shaking his hand.

"Do you still have Matilda's gift?" he asked, bringing his hands to his throat where he wore a few strands of colorful beads. He'd introduced them to the city's high priestess, Matilda Rodriguez, during their initial investigation, and she'd given Sept a similar strand of red and white beads. It supposedly provided protection to the children of Chango, the king of all the orishas.

She opened her collar and nodded. "Keegan hasn't let me take it off since the night Perlis shot me and came close to killing Nathan and my brother-in-law. I might not have your deep-set beliefs, but I agree with her. It can't hurt."

"A sacrifice to the hunter probably means your killer is looking forward to battling the warrior and hitting their mark with lethal consequences. That's part of what they want, but I don't know what else they're asking for with all this." Julio waved his hand, still appearing mortified. "Don't take it off, and do accept the protection in which Matilda strung it for you."

"I'll have an officer take you back, and I promise it won't leave my neck. Thanks for your help, Julio, and call me if you think of anything else."

"Now what?" Nathan asked as they stood off to the side while George kept working.

"Now we figure out the rest of what happened here and find the mistakes the two kids out front caused this asshole to make. No matter how much you plan and then work it, variations are going to create cracks that we need to find."

❖

"He's in surgery, Detective, so you're going to have to wait," the emergency-room head nurse said, holding her hands up to keep Gustave back.

"Where can we wait? We really need to talk to him the second he comes to." Gustave waved when he saw his partner Sharon Colbert walk in.

"I'll set you up in our lounge and keep you posted," the woman said and took them behind the desk to a room with snacks, coffee, and comfortable chairs. "Hang on, and I'll get the nurses who worked on him when he came in. I'm not positive, but I think he said something."

"Was he carrying ID?" Sharon asked.

"Wait here, and I'll get what you need."

Two young but tired-appearing nurses came in and handed over a hazmat bag with a cell phone, keys, and a wallet. "It's not dangerous. It was just the only bag handy at the time. His name is Mateo Moreno, and he's a high school senior," the redhead said, sighing loudly. "This job sucks sometimes."

"Did Mateo say anything at all while you were trying to stabilize him for surgery?" Gustave asked, placing the bag next to him. "Even if he was delirious, it might help."

The two glanced at each other and nodded. "I speak a little Spanish," the brunette said, "but I'm not fluent. He repeated *la diabla* a few times and asked forgiveness of someone named Miguel."

"La diabla," Sharon said, writing it down. "She devil?"

"That's the literal translation," the brunette said. "I even looked it up to make sure, but I don't know what he meant. And we don't know who Miguel is either."

"He's the other kid at the scene, but he was killed instantly," Gustave said.

"To tell you the truth, and I hope to hell I'm wrong, but it'll be a miracle if this kid survives," the redhead said. "Hopefully he's a fighter, but that bullet did a lot of damage."

"Thank you, and here's our card if you think of anything else." He handed them over and went in search of gloves to handle Mateo's personal effects. His driver's license showed an address that was a few miles from where he'd been shot. "Francois," he said when his brother answered. "I need you to go by this address and pick up the family. Their son's in surgery, and they need to get here as quickly as they can."

"Detective." The head nurse came in, and he lowered the phone. "Mr. Moreno crashed on the operating table, and they couldn't revive him. He's gone."

"Thank you," he said to the nurse. "Never mind. Meet me at the morgue," he told Francois. "I'll see that his family gets this," he said, and the nurse nodded.

"The surgeon bagged the bullet as well, so if you sit tight, I'll get it for you."

"Murder is never pretty, but it's a fucking shame when the victim is seventeen," Sharon said.

"I'll never understand something like this no matter the age," he said and started mentally preparing to tell the parents their child was dead. The horrific task made him say a prayer for his two boys to always be safe. "We just have to do our best to make sure someone pays."

❖

"This was planned," Sept said softly, walking around the dead woman and keeping her eyes on her face and not her eviscerated middle.

"Do you see something?" Nathan asked.

"This one is different because of that dead kid and the one at the hospital. Those two kids weren't planned, so how do they fit in?" She walked back to the front the way the pretty girl had gotten to the backyard. The drag marks had flattened the grass. "So the killer does that," she pointed to the yard, "and they hear these two out front. The guy comes out and gets rid of any potential witnesses."

"That sounds right, but this doesn't look right," Nathan said, pointing to the dead kid. "The bullet had to have killed him instantly. If that's true, the shooter didn't come from here."

She nodded and slapped his shoulder. "Good," she said, glancing at the other side of the house. "The bullet came from over there, so let's go take a look."

They walked to the other side of the house and found nothing on their first pass, but when she turned around, a small scrap of paper caught the edge of the beam of her flashlight. It had to have blown against the fence, but it didn't show any sign of water or other damage, so it had to have been dropped recently.

"Do you have an evidence bag?" she asked Nathan. He put it in a clear bag and held it up so they could study it. "FI," she said, knowing there was more once, but the scrap had been torn from the main page.

"Any idea what FI is?" Nathan asked.

"Maybe," she said, going back to the yard. "Do you have a name for her?" she asked George.

"The card in her purse had only the name Lee and a phone number." George held up another evidence bag. "That's all that was in her purse aside from some mints and a few condoms. She might've been a working girl."

"Probably, but the clothes and the accessories put her in the escort category. We know only one woman who could tell us more," she said, and Nathan nodded.

"Brandi Parrish." Nathan wrote down the name and number on the card George displayed.

"I'm hoping it's not one of her girls, since she's already had too much pain and loss," she said and glanced over her shoulder when she heard her name called. "Back here," she said, recognizing Gustave's voice.

"Hey. We just finished at the hospital. Our witness didn't make it, but he did say something before he died," he said as they moved to the property line at the back. "Not that it'll do us any good, but he told the nurse it was *la diabla*."

"She devil," she said. It didn't make any sense. "That's it?"

"He asked Miguel to forgive him," Sharon said.

"She devil." She repeated the words to see if anything came to her. "Not that this scene isn't important, but we need to see if those two boys lead us to something. Nathan and Sharon, could you run down the plate on the car in the driveway?"

"I'll do it," Sharon said.

"The killer wasn't stupid enough to leave their car, so who does it belong to?" she asked as Jennifer headed toward George. "And I need to hear the 9-1-1 call. Maybe in the heat of the moment, this bastard made a mistake."

"Hey, Sept, we're ready to move the body, if that's okay," the man from Gavin's office said, and she nodded.

"Did you send someone to notify this kid's family?" she asked.

"I sent Francois to get them after I found out who he was," Gustave said of their other brother. "He's been working the explosion at the Hilton with Jacques but was wrapping up. I talked to the Moreno family, and they said their son and Miguel had been friends since the first grade and loved getting into trouble together. Nothing bad enough to get killed over, so they're in shock."

"What happened at the Hilton?" Nathan said.

"A car bomb that took out five cars and a wall of the parking garage," Sharon said, stopping to talk to someone on the phone. "A Lazlo Watts reported the car stolen this afternoon."

"Where was it when it was stolen?" Sept asked.

"The parking lot between the Hilton and the convention center," Sharon said.

"Shit," she said, calling her father. "We need all the video from the Hilton parking lot and anything that leads to the lot next door."

"We're already working on that because of this damn explosion that thankfully didn't kill anyone on the ground when the damn wall fell. What do you need with it?"

The group around her looked on as she talked and tried to put her thoughts in order. "We've got a stolen car at our scene that came from the lot next to your scene. This guy's smart, but there's no way he was able to disable every lens aimed at the path he had to take from one lot to the other."

"I'll get it done, but we've found a body in the rubble, so give me a few hours."

"Do you mind if Gustave and Sharon go over there and wait? I want to make sure the footage doesn't get erased." Gustave lifted his thumb and seemed anxious to get going. "I bet these two events are related."

"Call me if he has a problem."

"I texted Jacques to see what they have," Gustave said, holding up his phone. "They found a body in the car the bomb was set in, but it's going to be a while before we have an ID, since the fire and explosion did their job."

"We need to wrap up here and have a meeting first thing in the morning. From what happened and when, we can put together a good timeline of what went on yesterday," she said, seeing that George and Jennifer's team was ready to start loading up. "It's as good a thing for us that can happen, since there are too many scenes for something not to have gone wrong for this perp, but a bad thing it had to come at the expense of the people who got killed today."

"We'll get what we need," Sharon said.

"Where are you headed?" Gustave asked.

"Uncle George said there's another love letter in that St. Norbert statue, so we're going to the lab to read it. Unless something else comes up, I'll see you guys at nine. I'm going to find out if Gavin has any luck with Jacques's body."

"Sept, they cued up the call you wanted to listen to," an officer said. It was another dead end. Even though the voice wasn't covered by any type of manipulation, it still could have been anyone, given the harsh whisper and the quiet behind them.

"Have a copy of this sent over to the lab and see if they can filter something out," she said to Jennifer.

"Both of you keep your eyes open. The addition of explosives makes Perlis look like an amateur," Gustave said.

"You too." She put her arms around Gustave when he hugged her and kissed his cheek. "If something happens to any of us, Mama will kick our asses, and then our beautiful women will do the same thing."

"Marjorie's used to me, but Keegan's still feisty, so keep her on your good side."

"I do that like it's my job."

CHAPTER FIFTEEN

Anabel Hicks excused herself from the conference room next to her office, tired of listening to Brian Voles go on about all the things he could do to lend his big brain to her city. The fact that he'd brought his daughter with him had kept her side of the conversation to a minimum and seemed fishy, but he wasn't biting on her subtle hints to end the meeting.

She faced bizarre situations all the time, but Brian Voles was a different breed of animal altogether because of his bragging that seemed only for the benefit of impressing his daughter, so she couldn't figure out his end game.

"Ma'am." Agent Catalina Silva was waiting in the hall for her, holding a sheet of paper.

"In my office," she said to Catalina and her partner Ivan Mora. "What did you find before I ask you to shoot me to put me out of my misery?"

"He's slated for retirement, not his idea," Catalina said, making Anabel chuckle. "He's the head of the fraud division, but it sounds like seniority had more to do with the promotion than merit. DC sent down some wunderkind, and they're grooming him to take over."

"I talked to a friend in LA, ma'am," Ivan said, "and it sounds like they're leaning hard on Voles to retire. They don't know what he's doing here asking to butt in on the NOPD's case."

"It's called going out in a blaze of glory, and it happens to the best of us. Hell. Cain Casey might drive me to do something this obnoxious eventually, but God save me from that," she said, and her new agents laughed. "What's NOPD got that this guy wants in on so bad?"

"Voles's daughter is Nicole Voles, the crime writer, and she's working on a book about Alex Perlis," Catalina said, and Anabel closed her eyes, imagining how cooperative Sept Savoie was being. That case had sent a cold stab of memory through the middle of her skull, since she knew full well the ramifications of having someone dirty in your department. "From what little Fritz is saying, they might be working a copycat scenario, but Detective Savoie and the department have done a good job of plugging any leaks on this one."

"Let me get rid of this guy once and for all so we can take a ride to see Fritz and Sebastian." She stood and waved them back to their seats. "Call and see where they are. Now that I know the score, this won't take long."

She shook her head as she headed next door and took a breath to release her impatience before she entered. "Sorry to keep you waiting, Agent Voles."

"I realize you've got things to do, considering what you're facing here, but all I need is for you to talk to Fritz Jernigan and get me access. If the FBI needs to be brought in, I'll call you."

"I'm planning to talk with Fritz, but I'm not going to force the issue. We've got a good working relationship with the locals, and I don't want to jeopardize that." She didn't sit and left the door open, all hospitality gone. "I'll call you with Fritz's answer, but if you'll excuse me, I'll have someone escort you out."

She turned and left as Brian opened his mouth, but he'd have to tackle her to get her to stay and listen to anything else he had to say. An entire career of putting up with overbearing and condescending men telling her how to do her job was enough.

"Well?" she asked her agents when they entered the elevator that descended below street level to the parking garage. "Where is he?"

"Sebastian Savoie is actually with Chief Jernigan at the Hilton scene, ma'am. They said they'd wait for you since some of our guys are over there as part of the investigation," Ivan said as Catalina unlocked the black sedan.

"Good." She sat in the back, knowing it wasn't far to where they were headed. "Check in with our team, and I'll join you when I'm done with the NOPD brass."

They made their way through the media line and the people who appeared to be waiting to start the cleanup. "The animals are rattling the cage bars over this," Catalina said as she blew the horn to get a news van to move.

"This is a little out of the ordinary, even for New Orleans, and two bombs in such a short time seems suspicious," she said, waving to one of the detectives she'd met before and following him into the parking structure. "Fritz…Sebastian," she said, joining them at the table that had been set up. "What do we have?"

"We must rate if we got you to leave the building, Special Agent Hicks," Sebastian said, smiling at her. She'd met the chief of detectives the first week she'd arrived in New Orleans, and he'd proved himself a good friend from that first day.

"Maybe I missed you, so tell me what happened before I change my mind about that."

"The older model there," Sebastian said, pointing to the car second from the wall, "is where the blast originated. It damaged everything around it, but your people and ours both agree it was planted in that car."

"It's the only one with a body in it as well, so this was a hell of a way to cover up a murder," Fritz said, straightening his tie. "I hate to ask, but can you rush the tests? We need to know if this is the same kind of device that almost killed one of our people."

"I heard about Sept. Is she okay?" she asked, placing her hand on Sebastian's forearm.

"She's back at work, so she's fine, and I just got off the phone with her. She might've found something."

"What?" Fritz asked, his voice rising at the end of the word.

"We need to collect the video feeds from every camera in this place all the way next door and beyond," Sebastian said and explained why. "It is too much of a coincidence not to check out."

"We've already requested the ones from the hotel," Fritz said.

"We can help you with the rest, and you have my word this is your investigation. That's a given, but that's not why I'm here."

"Have we missed something?" Fritz asked.

"Agent Brian Voles and his daughter Nicole came to see me about twisting your arm to allow him access to your investigation into the recent murders. They obviously met with Sept and her partner, and she cooled his jets on any illusions he had." Both men seemed to puff up with anger.

"Are you asking us for that?" Sebastian asked, sounding cautious.

"Not in this lifetime, but this guy isn't the type of person to simply let go."

"I'll talk to him and tell him to go fuck himself, nicely, of course," Fritz said. "I, or anyone else on the force, don't have time for this."

"Let me know if you need any help burning the tick off," she said, and shook Fritz's hand when he had to leave to give a statement.

"Let's go get those videos," she said to Sebastian. Her bomb experts were still working, so they headed to the security office. "Is Sept really okay?"

"She and her partner Nathan caught Perlis, but we have a copycat on our hands, and she's running that investigation as well. So far we have two of these ritual killings and two dead cops." Sebastian stopped, not wanting to share their conversation with anyone else. "She thinks today and what we have here are connected to the scene she's working now."

"I know your kid, and she's not an embellisher. If she thinks that, it's probably right. Let's get what she needs to prove her theory."

It took an hour, but they had copies of all the footage from a three-block radius that could've caught something on their security cameras. The casino was their best bet, so she hoped it wasn't too far away to make out anything.

"Thanks, Anabel," Sebastian said, holding the CDs.

"Our enhancement capabilities are pretty good, so let me know if you need our resources," she said, now curious about the case herself. But she wouldn't worm her way into the middle of it to take the credit at the conclusion.

"You'll be my first call, and if this Voles character contacts me, I'll send him back to you."

"I thought we were friends," she said and winked. "Thanks for trusting me, Sebastian, and I meant what I said. I'm a call away, and that goes for Sept or anyone else in the department. We can't afford any more of the bad press that comes with this kind of murder spree, so our agencies need to work together."

"Thanks, and I'm sure Sept will be in touch if there's a chance our perp's on video."

"With the bomb angle, if it's someone we're looking for on a federal level, it's a win-win."

"No one's that lucky," Sebastian said and walked her back outside. "Take care, and try not to feed the animals on the way out."

The reporters shouted questions, but she got into the vehicle again, ready to go. "I want a report on what they find up there," she said to Ivan. "Sept Savoie is a good friend to us, so I don't want to miss anything."

"If anyone can find the answers, ma'am, it's Sept," Catalina said.

"Let's hope so, and before this nutcase burns down the whole city."

❖

"Hey, honey," Keegan said, and her voice made Sept close her eyes and smile when she answered on the third ring. "Are you okay?"

"You're supposed to be sleeping," she said, opening her eyes when she heard some noise and saw the coroner loading up the body in the backyard.

"The bed isn't the same without you, and my bedmate at the moment has horrible kibble breath. I couldn't sleep, so stop trying to change the subject and answer my question."

"It's not good, but I'll tell you about it later. I'd rather be sitting with Della giving me a hard time instead of here."

They'd spent two hours checking the trajectories of where the shots had been taken and established that the killer had stood on the opposite side of the house to kill the two teenagers. The young woman had, from the drag marks, been taken from the car to the spot in the yard that was a good twenty feet from the place Perlis had used when he'd brought Erica out here. "This guy is using the same concept, but he's off."

"I'm sorry this is happening to you again, baby." Keegan's voice sounded like honey and silk, and it beat back the horrors of her night. "Are you mad at me for talking you out of the desk job?"

"Right this second, I'm sick that someone is capable of this, but I'm where I'm supposed to be," she said softly, wanting to put Keegan at ease. "At least Nathan's getting better than me, so my chances of getting hit by friendly fire are decreasing dramatically."

Keegan laughed and groaned at the same time. "Don't even joke about that, and I'm sure he's got a way to go before he catches up to you, Batman."

"Go to sleep, baby. I'm fine, but I probably won't see you until late. We've got to do a lot of follow-up." Nathan nodded, and she held her hand up to put him off for a moment longer. "I'll call you if it's sooner than that so I don't scare you coming in."

"I love you, so be careful and take care of Nathan. Know you're missed. Even Mike looks mopey without you here."

"I love you too, and make sure the dog knows I'm coming back eventually so he won't get too comfortable in my spot." She disconnected the call and took one more glance around the yard. They did have plenty of follow-up, but she needed to find out exactly who Lee was and if she was, like she suspected, one of Brandi's girls.

"Did you get a chance to call the number?" she asked Nathan about the card in Lee's purse.

"It connected me to FIOG Enterprises," he said and smiled. "When I identified myself, the receptionist asked if I was interested in vinyl siding for my house. If the salespeople all look like Lee, I might consider it."

"It's Brandi's idea of a twisted joke. FIOG Enterprises stands for fucking is our game, and all the saleswomen do look like that. You might want to put it in your contacts for when you save enough of your lunch money, Skippy."

"I might have enough in my savings already."

"Don't make it a habit, then. The price tag on Brandi's kind of fun can get overwhelmingly expensive and quick."

"I'll keep that in mind. Captain Savoie has the video from the Hilton and is on his way back to the precinct. You want to go there first?" he asked, holding up his middle finger.

"He'll wait for us, so let's go by Brandi's before we head back and see if Lee's one of hers, and who her date was. If this is like Tameka, it happened after her official date, but we need to know where she started. We know where she ended up, so it'll be easier to fill in the middle."

"George said he'd call when he was ready for us."

"Let's go. Follow me, because I'm not leaving Keegan's car out here." She walked to the front as Gavin's crew did their best to place Lee in a body bag without doing any more damage. John was directing his guys to keep the small number of news crews that had arrived back from the house. "John," she called out, getting the reporters to come to life and start shouting questions. She ignored them all and waited for him to reach them to ask for a reassignment for some of his men.

"You guys done?" John asked, taking his cap off and stuffing it under his arm.

"Gavin's guys are almost done, so leave enough of a presence out here to keep the curious folks over there out of the yard. I want our team to check out the perimeter in daylight and before it's on the morning news."

"You got it. Don't worry. Anything else?"

"Think you can get the cadaver dogs out in that trash pile in the park?" She had a hunch that the perpetrator had chosen this spot for more than an homage to Perlis's crimes.

"You think this son of a bitch did two in one night like this?" John appeared shocked.

"I don't know if it was two in one night, but not like this for sure. If you find anything in there, it's going to be a dump job."

"This is fucking crazy," John said, and she nodded. "Okay. I'll call you."

"Who do you think is in there?" Nathan asked as Gustave and Sharon joined them after delivering the warrant to Sebastian and making it back.

"I've got two candidates, since our guy has two loose ends. Bonnie's boyfriend and Crazy Nick are still at large, and our killer doesn't seem like the type to let two idiots trip him up."

"You going back to the precinct?" Gustave asked.

"We're stopping at Brandi's first, but we still have plenty to do, so see if we can get everyone together. We can check out all this stuff while it might lead us somewhere."

"You got it, and don't let Nathan linger," Sharon said, teasing Nathan.

"If any of you need any ideas for his birthday, he wouldn't turn down a gift certificate."

"Fuck all of you," Nathan said.

"Not on your life, but I'm sure Brandi's got someone who'll be happy to do that," she said and rubbed her knuckles along the top of Nathan's head. "Come on, and I'll drive slow so your blush will calm down before we have to face your crush."

She drove the coupe and glanced back a few times, and Nathan was right behind her. The sense of déjà vu hit her, as she'd come to Brandi's door before to tell her one of her girls had been brutally murdered, and Keegan had called her right after that. That call and that she'd gone to Keegan after leaving Brandi had been a turning point in her life, and she'd stopped running. Now she'd instead rush toward the life she wanted with Keegan.

"Hey, Sept," Wilson Delacour said after he opened the door and waved them in. "Been a while since you've come by for a visit."

"Sorry, Wilson. I don't have an excuse for my bad manners." She followed him to Brandi's office as he walked to a chair and put his hands on the back to encourage her to sit.

"You want a drink? You look like you could use one." Wilson moved toward the phone. "Bad news?" he asked before picking it up.

"We're still on duty, so no to the drink, and a maybe yes on the news. Let me ask you first so you can help me with Brandi if I'm right." Wilson nodded and sighed. "Life is making me older than I have to be, I swear. What's wrong?"

"We caught a case tonight, and the only thing in her purse was a card with a name and the number to FIOG," she said, and the news made Wilson fall into Brandi's office chair.

"Can't be Erica, since you know her, so who was it?" He tensed as if preparing for a blow.

"Lee," she said, and Wilson closed his eyes and lowered his head. "Pretty blonde who appeared to be in her early twenties."

"Lee Cenac, and she's related to Brandi. Supposedly she was Brandi's third cousin, but you know her history with her family. I don't think I'm talking behind her back, since Brandi loves you," he said, and she nodded. "She didn't want the kid to be in this life, but her mama got her in it first, and you can't force anyone into choosing a path they don't want."

"I'm sorry, Wilson, but I have to tell her."

"Yeah. Let me go get her." He stood and smoothed his vest. "She's out back."

"We'll go if you want," she said.

"No. Sit and relax. We'll be right back."

"Man, this is going to be rough, especially if Lee was related to her," Nathan said, and she cocked her head back and blew out the deep breath she'd taken.

She'd recognized the scrap of paper and the partial initials on it, but she still hoped she'd been wrong, since lately she only showed up on Brandi's door with bad news. Her friend was going to eventually stop letting her in. "It's not her fault, since no one is here out of obligation. If this is the life you choose, Brandi gives you a safe place to work from."

"It can't be that safe, sugar, if you're here at this hour," Brandi said, and her voice brought both her and Nathan to their feet.

"Did Wilson tell you?" she asked as Brandi took a step toward her.

"One of you just spit it out." Brandi reached for her hand, so she raised it palm up.

"We found Lee Cenac tonight," she said, and Brandi's eyes instantly filled with tears. "I'm so sorry." She put her arms around Brandi when she fell against her.

"What the hell happened?" Wilson asked, placing his hand on Brandi's back.

"She was killed in the same place Erica was attacked last year. That's all I can really tell you right now, so let's sit down." She walked Brandi to the sofa against the wall. "Who was her date tonight?"

"She and Erica were both meeting their dates at the JW on Canal. Oh, God." Brandi sat up, appearing panicked. "Sept, we need to find Erica. She mentioned she and Lee were having drinks together after they were done. If she's there all alone, she could be in danger."

"I'll go," Nathan said.

"Stay put, and get all the information of how Lee started her evening." Sept cared deeply for Brandi, but Erica had been a lost soul who'd been turned out by an abusive boyfriend when they'd met. Sept had taken her off the streets and brought her to Brandi, knowing her old friend would eventually make it possible for her to leave the business if that was what Erica really wanted. From the day they'd met until now, Sept had felt somewhat responsible for Erica and what happened to her.

Nathan looked nervous as she stood to go. "Are you sure?"

She took him into the hall and knocked her knuckles against his forehead. "Right now, Brandi is a woman in pain, so be gentle with the questions, and be a good friend."

"Okay," he said, glancing back at the office.

Sept took off and sped to the downtown hotel, flashing her badge at the valet to keep Keegan's car close. Erica was sitting in the bar peering at her watch as some older guy tried to talk to her. She seemed too polite to tell him he had no chance, probably even with the large fee tucked between his teeth.

"Hey, beautiful," she said from a few feet away, and Erica's head whipped up, an expression of relief on her face.

"Hey." Erica hopped down from the barstool and hugged her. "I'm so glad to see you."

"Excuse me," the wannabe Romeo said. "The lady and I were talking, so get lost."

"Let me see some ID." Sept held her badge a few inches from his face and snapped her fingers. "I said, let's see some ID."

The guy fumbled for his wallet, and his apparent nervousness made Erica smile. "Here," he said practically throwing his license at Sept.

"Nebraska, huh," she said, holding it next to his face and taking out her phone. "This is what your options are here, Mr. Archer. You can either go up to your room and stop bothering the ladies, or I'm going to call Mrs. Archer and have a frank conversation about your habits when you're out of town. What's it going to be?" She held the license up and wasn't surprised when he snatched it back and ran out.

"That was mean but entertaining as shit," Erica said. "I'm so glad to see you. Do you have time to wait with me? I'm meeting someone for a drink."

"I'm so sorry, honey, but Lee's not going to make it." The explanation made Erica hysterical, so Sept ordered a shot of whiskey, and the bartender waved off her money. "Let me take you home."

"How did she die?" Erica asked, never moving away from her as they made their way to the car.

Sept told her as much as she could on the way back and, when they walked in, found Nathan holding Brandi. The crying started again when Brandi and Erica saw each other. Erica hadn't been with Brandi that long, but they'd built a solid friendship that both really cherished.

"I've got everything we need for our end," Nathan said. "The fucker paid in cash."

"She was dropped off at the JW?" she asked, and both Brandi and Nathan nodded. "Okay. We need to head back over there and see what we find."

"Do you think this bastard forced her to leave?" Brandi asked, now holding Erica.

"That's what I need to find out but, Erica," she said, kneeling between Brandi and Erica, "remember what I said. I think this is more about the location than the girl, but I want you to be extra careful. If something happens to you, I'm going to be pissed if it's because you're taking unnecessary chances."

"I won't, I promise." Erica wiped her face and smeared her makeup even more than it already was.

"Brandi, call me no matter what."

"I will. Thank you."

"I'll come by again, and we'll talk about precautions you can take so I don't have to show up on your door for something like this again."

Brandi squeezed her hand and leaned forward to kiss her cheek. "You're a good friend, but don't get into trouble over us."

"I'll quit this job the day that giving someone comfort is rated as bad as murder. I'll be back."

CHAPTER SIXTEEN

I'm exhausted," Nathan said as he and Sept left the hotel.

"If I drink any more coffee I'm going to have a permanent twitch," Sept said, stopping around the corner from the main car entrance, which was actually a block back from Canal. It was the door Lee had walked out of to meet her date. "The front-desk guy said someone called in with the message, and Lee didn't question the directions. The video shows her coming this way."

"Trying to avoid being seen, I guess," Nathan said.

"True, and it's going to be our job to prove him wrong. There's got to be a camera around here somewhere, especially with all these banks and office buildings. We just have to find the one with the best angle."

"You want the uniforms to canvas to see if we get lucky?" Nathan asked as he yawned. She couldn't blame him, since they were about thirty minutes from sunrise. It had been a long night.

"Good idea," she said, getting back into the car. "Follow me home so I can leave Keegan's car."

"No chance she'll be cooking breakfast by now, huh?"

"At four forty-five in the morning? No chance, buddy," she said, laughing.

She actually wished Keegan was up, but she wasn't going to be an asshole and wake her. Her phone rang, and almost as if she'd conjured her up, it was Keegan. "Where are you, Seven?"

"I'm on my way home actually, but only to leave your car. Why aren't you asleep?" She sped up, needing to see Keegan before she had to keep working.

"I missed you, and I was worried about you. Was your entire night horrible?"

"It was bad, but we might get somewhere after this. And if you were wondering, I missed you too. All this crap I see needs to be balanced by something, and I'm glad that's you, baby. Don't get scared, but I'm here, and I'll bring your keys in."

"Don't you dare run off before I get downstairs."

"I'm not alone, sweet pea." She unlocked the door and heard Keegan and Mike coming down the stairs.

"Is it going to embarrass you if Nathan sees me kissing you?" Keegan asked as she put her arms around her. "Do you have time for me to feed you?"

"Yes. We'll make time," Nathan said, coming in and kissing Keegan's cheek. "See," he told Sept. "You just have to throw your wishes out into the universe, partner."

She put her hand on the center of his face, pushed him away, and asked Keegan, "Are you sure you're not too tired?"

"Babe, I wasn't the one running around all night." Keegan pulled her head down and kissed her. "Go start the coffee like I taught you." Keegan moved her hands and slapped her on the ass.

Keegan made omelets and talked to them while they ate. The food was good, but Sept knew it would make her tired, so she had another cup of coffee. "The girl tonight was one of Brandi's girls," she said, and Keegan reached for her hand.

"Do you think that was on purpose?" Keegan asked.

"I do, and he took her to where Erica escaped from. This girl was new to town and wasn't so lucky. To compound our bad night, two teenagers got killed in the front yard of the same house." The thing the kid said before he died popped into her head. Why say "she devil"?

"Was Brandi okay?" Keegan asked.

"She and Erica were pretty shaken up. We might have seen all this before, but the scenes are different."

"The other crime will be hard to duplicate since it was in a place of business, if I remember that right. Maybe this is the end of it." Keegan held up her fork to feed her a piece of omelet. "What happened to the kids?"

"I think they were there to boost the car, and the killer didn't want witnesses. The car was stolen, and the guy was most probably going to abandon it anyway, so I'm not sure why they had to die."

"That's so sad," Keegan said.

"Why do you think the guy was going to leave the car?" Nathan asked, grabbing another piece of toast.

"Patrol didn't find anyone on foot, and the car was already stolen.

Why take any more chances to get caught in a car that had Lee Cenac's DNA in it?" She ate another bite that Keegan fed her. "There had to be another car. And if you think about it, he parked it in a neighborhood where there aren't any witnesses or video cameras for blocks. Those two kids were looking for trouble, but grand theft auto isn't punishable by death."

Her cell phone rang, and she thought about not answering it, but now wasn't the time to start rebelling. "Savoie."

"Sept, it's John. The dogs found something. How in the hell did you know?"

"Lucky guess. I've got two missing guys I want to talk to, and that dump spot is on the way to our crime scene." She took another sip of coffee. "We'll be there in thirty minutes."

"What now?" Keegan asked.

"They found something else. Sorry, sweetheart. I'll call you later, and I should be home tonight."

"Are you sure you can go that long without sleeping?" Keegan rubbed the side of her neck, and Nathan took his plate to the sink.

"I need to see what this is, get the team going, and try to take off early." She cocked her head toward the stairs. "Nathan, give me a minute."

"Thanks, Keegan, and I'll see you later," he said.

"You'll be okay, really?" Keegan asked as she went up a step to even out their heights somewhat.

"I'll be fine, and I need you to make sure of your surroundings. The number-one thing I worry about is how much this guy knows. It's like he's got Perlis's playbook and is using it for his own game. If he knows exactly where Erica escaped from, he knows about us, and if something happened to you, I'd be lost."

Keegan combed her hair back gently with her fingers and kissed her. "Just find your way home, and I'll be here waiting for you. Like you told me about consistency, you need to believe in me. I'm not going anywhere, baby, and you need to start trusting that fact."

"I love you so much," she said, and Keegan kissed her eyelids before she moved down to her lips. "Thank you for the pep talk."

It was tough to let Keegan go, but they had to leave. Her hunch had been right, and the dogs had found a body in that dump. Her killer was an efficient worker who seemed to like to take chances since he'd driven around town with a body in the trunk of a stolen car. Hell, if he thrived on danger, the body could've been in the back seat.

"Who do you think it is?" Nathan asked as he drove faster than normal through the quiet streets.

"It's got to be either Bonnie's boyfriend or Crazy Nick. They don't strike me as master criminals who can elude police this long, and this would explain their absence."

The patrol officers guided them to the entrance to the park they needed to use, and Sept was thankful the sky was lighting up. Her shoes would probably be toast after this, but she wanted to avoid jamming something sharp into her feet so she walked carefully through the piles of debris. The cluster of police stood behind the perimeter the forensic guys had set up, but she didn't find an altar this time. This was your basic dump-and-run.

"Do you know who it is?" she asked Jennifer, since George wasn't in sight.

"Roger Breaux." Jennifer handed over his wallet. "He's got the same address as Bonnie Matherne and a picture of them together."

"Anything out of the ordinary?" The wallet had a hundred in small bills and a picture of a little girl.

"I'm not an investigator, but it seems like someone drove in here because they could turn around and just dump him and not be seen over these piles." Jennifer moved as the guy with her took a series of pictures. "We're almost done, but I'll stick around just in case the dogs find anything else."

"Thanks, and put our numbers in your phone. Text me your contact information," she said, handing over her and Nathan's cards. "Be careful out here. God knows what's mixed in all this shit, and you don't want some raging infection."

"Will do. Thanks. Maybe I'll see you at the lab later."

"Yeah. After we head to the precinct and regroup. If you find anything else, make me your first call." Jennifer nodded, and Sept hesitated when she saw the coroner. "How did he die? Can you tell?"

"Shot in the back of the head. At least I think it's a bullet wound. That's the only injury I see." Jennifer walked her around the body to point to the blood-soaked collar. "I didn't want to move him until we collected everything, so he might have some more of those."

"This bastard is trying to bury us in work, but too much of a vice always brings you down. That holds true in everything in life except when it comes to our SOs."

"What's your philosophy there?" Jennifer asked, smiling.

"Too much of Keegan Blanchard is never going to be a bad thing, but if you don't believe that about Chloe, I'll make sure to mention it to her," she said and winked.

"Please don't since she'll give me shit for weeks. How'd you know about me and Chloe?"

"She's an old friend, but I haven't seen her in a few years. Behave, since she's one of the good ones." Sept pocketed her notebook and waved to Nathan. "Let's see if I can do something about the rotten ones messing up our nights, and we can get back to our better halves."

"Amen to that, sister."

❖

Hunter parked four blocks from the condo and walked leisurely back. The night had been long but not hard. Both Roger and Nick weren't a problem any longer, and the altar in the park had turned out beautifully.

"The only thing to worry about is the kid who lived." The day was cold and clammy, but the frosty temperature was good and helped Hunter keep a cool head. "Maybe that was a mistake," Hunter said but shook off the nagging worry as the silence of the lobby meant no more talking out loud.

The place was dark and even quieter, so the first order of business was to tidy up the kill bag and see what had to be replaced. This task was important and needed total concentration, so adding weak emotions here would lead to mistakes later. Hunter was methodical in taking everything out and placing it on the table in order. When the gun came out, it caught on the paper with Lee's contact information.

"Fuck," Hunter whispered as the torn corner came into view. It had to have come out and dropped when the two car thieves had to be dealt with. "Did I touch it?"

All that planning had been for nothing, which meant no more deviations from the plan. "Think." Hunter stripped and headed for the shower. For now the cleanup was the thing to concentrate on, so the clothes went onto the plastic sheet already on the bathroom floor. Nothing had ever been left to chance because the plan was sacrosanct. No deviations at any time had been the motto to freedom, and it all came down to that—freedom.

The killing was the ultimate high, and the process of carrying it out, knowing it was something that could be done over and over again, was intoxicating. It had been six years, and the body count including last night stood at 114. The thrill was better than sex or anything else the average person thought mind-blowing, and the only way to keep achieving the rush was to be smart. Mistakes like the two boys couldn't be repeated or the game was up.

Even with the errors, the day had been exhilarating. Five kills in one day wasn't an opportunity that came very often, so it'd been fun. The memories would have to last for the next week as normality returned, and Hunter's persona would be put away. The hot shower was steamy enough to wash away the night's activities, but Hunter lingered afterward, enjoying the slightly uncomfortable temperature.

"I'm alive," Hunter said loudly, "and there can be only one warrior."

Alex Perlis had been inventive in his technique—that was true—but he'd erred by not killing Sept Savoie through any means possible. The chance of repeating that enormous mistake was nil, but there was still time for indulgence.

"The game continues."

Chapter Seventeen

"Yesterday and last night left us with plenty to follow up on," Sept said as everyone crammed into the conference room at their precinct. The whiteboard was covered with a timeline of events that Nathan had written out for her, but the most important was the videos they needed to study. "John, we need some guys on St. Charles stopping at every business to see who has cameras pointed at the street from Canal down to Poydras."

"What time span?" John asked.

"Start at noon and go until eight last night. We're looking for any glimpse of that pretty black sedan from our scene." Sept checked off the top item. "The rest of you head back to the house where Lee Cenac was killed and the park dump site in the light of day and see if we missed anything. After last night, we got a late start today, but you still have time." The follow-up everyone had done had pushed their meeting back to late afternoon.

"The canine unit is still out there, so we'll let them finish and concentrate on the house," Gustave said.

"Good plan." Sebastian stepped next to her. "It was a long day, so let's try to wrap everything up and report back here in the morning. I don't want anyone making any mistakes and overlooking anything because of exhaustion."

"Yes, sir, and Royce has a dedicated line if anyone needs to call anything in. Use it, and update everyone," she said as Nathan wrote that as well. "Stay safe, everyone. What happened at the Hilton yesterday proves how dangerous this guy is."

Gustave, Alain, and their partners stuck around after everyone dispersed, wanting to see the video. "Which one do you want to start with?" Lourdes asked as her partner Bruce rolled out the biggest television they owned.

"Let's start from the moment the bomb went off until you pass the car leaving the lot," she said, trying to narrow their scope. "If we see who comes out, walks next door, and steals the car, we'll know who we're looking for going back from there."

The average day on the screen ended at two fifteen in the afternoon, and the camera caught a partial shot of the wall coming down and the panic it set off in the people entering the building from that angle. Most of them turned and ran toward Poydras Street, but five minutes in, a calm-appearing person exited from the garage stairwell.

"Right there," Sept said. This had to be someone to watch.

The person stopped and adjusted the hood of the sweatshirt and never lifted their head. If the garage camera had been tampered with, the rest seemed to be common knowledge to whoever this was, who did their best to obscure their face. The only thing they did show was an eerie calm as they walked from the door to the lot next door. The actual car theft wasn't caught on camera, and the car's heavily tinted windows blocked an image from the side. They'd have to find a straight-on picture to have any luck seeing actual facial features.

"Great. It's the Unabomber," Nathan said because of the hoodie and large sunglasses.

"Let's watch the walk again," she said, and Lourdes cued the disk.

"I know what you're thinking," Lourdes said.

"What?" Sebastian and Gustave asked almost together.

The suspect stopped as if assessing their surroundings and started toward the other lot. "You can hide plenty with clothes and aviators, but your walk is hard to change," she said. "Especially if you're nervous despite the calm because you've just blown a hole in a public building and killed a guy."

"What does that mean?" Alain said.

"Not many men have that much sway in their hips. Well, not many women either, but *that*," Lourdes said, pointing at the screen, "is not a man."

"Back it up again," Gustave said.

Sept watched but reached for her phone when it rang.

"Sept?"

"Yes," she said, glancing at the screen but seeing only a number she didn't recognize right off.

"This is Sergeant Nobles. I'm at the park with the canine unit. Dispatch gave me your number," the man said. "Took us most of the day to cover the whole thing, but we're almost done. While we didn't find more bodies, we did find something you might want to see."

"Make sure you leave someone behind when you're done."

"I'm not about to get on the wrong side of John."

Sept watched the screen, and the only person who acted out of character in the chaos happening around them was the hooded person who never lifted their head. "La diabla," she said softly, and the words sparked an understanding of why the kid had said it.

"I'm sorry?" Nobles said.

"Nothing, and we'll be there in a few." The group ran the loop again, and she was more convinced than before that it was a woman. "They found something at the park, so we're going to check it out."

"You guys concentrate on finding more CCT footage, and give Brandi a call and ask if you can talk to the operator who set Lee up with her date."

"You really think this is a woman?" Alain's partner Ronnie asked. "These crimes are fucked up enough without thinking a woman could do it."

"You don't think women can be as evil and fucked up as men?" she asked, and Ronnie seemed close to squirming in his chair because of her tone. "Believe me, some women can be much more imaginative in thinking of ways to hurt you than a hundred men put together."

"I'll keep that in mind," Ronnie said.

"This could also be another disciple of Teacher," Gustave said.

"True, so I'll meet you guys back here later on. We're going to stop by the lab to see what they've got from last night."

"See you later, then," Gustave said. "We'll take Brandi and the other side of the street from the lot where the car was stolen."

Nathan gladly drove, and halfway to the park, George called her. "Hey, kiddo. You want to stop by? We've got everything set up for you, and the note is as useful as the first one."

"No statement or confession complete with selfies and where to find this guy?" She laughed and rubbed her eyes. The fatigue was starting to really take its toll. "Is an hour okay?"

"I'm due downtown for a review for the chief, so can you come now? I'll be brief. Jernigan wants an update before the six o'clock news. That doesn't give me much time."

"Okay," she said and mouthed the word "lab" to Nathan. "See you in a few." If George was in a rush, they'd still have time to make it to the park.

They were in the elevator at the lab with their eyes closed, leaning against the back of the car, when she sighed. "Damn, I'm tired."

"Me too, so hopefully the rest of this won't keep us out all night again," Nathan said as the doors opened.

"Yeah, the last couple of months didn't exactly prepare us for this." Jennifer was waiting for them, and she actually appeared happy. "Did you win the lottery?"

"Better. We got two prints off your scrap of paper."

George was sitting at his desk staring at his computer monitor. It appeared like he was running the prints as plenty of samples flashed by. "Anything yet?" she asked him.

"Give it another hour or so, and we'll see," George said, standing and moving to the table the note was laid out on. "Here's what was in the St. Norbert statue."

The emergency call went out before they reached the table, and Sept along with everyone with her cursed. Solving these crimes was going to be hard enough without this asshole piling on. Whatever it was, the call included EMS for officers down.

"Where is this?" she asked the dispatcher, following Nathan to the stairwell, both of them forgetting their tiredness. George and his people were already gearing up to do their part after the scene was clear.

"The park where the dogs are working," the woman said.

"Fuck," Nathan said, and she totally agreed.

"Our timing is good, but this asshole has a death wish going after cops like this. Once we figure out who it is, they won't make it to a trial."

"Shit. I'll pull the trigger myself," Nathan said as he sped to the park.

The news had to be crawling all over this, so she got her phone to call Keegan. The last call to the dispatcher had sucked up the rest of her battery, which meant she would have to wait. They weren't that far from the park, and she was right as they passed the two news vans heading in the same direction.

"Let's see what this is," she said as she looped her badge around her neck.

Her father waved them closer, and she saw FBI mixed in with their personnel. "We got another bomb—maybe more than one," Sebastian said. "The group we left behind is buried in there." He pointed to the spot about five hundred yards from where the body had been found. "They started at the street and worked their way in."

One of the uniformed officers was sitting in the back of an ambulance with an oxygen mask on, a large gauze bandage wrapped around his forehead, and from a glance at his name tag it was the guy she'd talked to, Nobles. Sept sat next to him and placed her hand on his back. "What happened?"

"I came out to call you and grab our camera," he said, taking the mask away. "The canine unit was just leaving, and we found this weird altar kind of thing in what was like a horseshoe area."

"Horseshoe?" she asked.

"It was like people backed up there to dump stuff and left only one way in. That's all we'd found and thought you'd want to see it."

The altar was the bait, and bringing down the piles had to have taken more than one device. "Did you hear more than one explosion? And how many guys are we looking for?"

"My partner and two others got trapped. My ears are still ringing, and I was close enough to get hit by some of this stuff, but it sounded like more than one."

The EMT came around and placed the mask back on his face.

"Thanks. We'll talk again," she said. She followed her father to the spot and saw the heavy equipment they'd brought in. "We were here this morning, so why not blow it then? They had plenty more targets."

"Maybe this time you weren't the target," Sebastian said as one of the officers handed him a bullhorn. She knew he had to check before sending in equipment that could potentially finish the job the bomber had started.

"Our guy seems to be targeting cops, then. If not, why put the bombs here at all?"

"That could be, but the garage had nothing to do with police personnel. Let's get through this first, and we'll speculate later."

"Are the dogs still in there with them?" she asked, knowing how much these guys loved the animals they worked with.

"They'd just unleashed them to get them back in the car, so they were ahead of the officers and got clear," Sebastian said, holding up the device in his hand. "Quiet," he yelled, the bullhorn making his command heard over the din. "Listen."

She walked closer to the large pile. The area was quiet, and John called the names of the guys who were missing. Every cop available was there, along with numerous volunteers, and they all seemed to be straining to hear any sound to prove the officers were alive. John called out again, and Sept heard a faint sound that could've come from anywhere in the area.

"Send the dogs back in, but protect their feet," Sebastian said, and the entire canine unit went to work. "If they were at the bottom, we would've never heard them."

"Nathan, give me your phone, please," Sept said half an hour later. The dogs had found one guy and were still working to find the other two. She tried Keegan, knowing she was at work now.

Keegan's phone rang but went to voice mail. "Call me so you won't worry. I'm okay, so don't listen to the news until you talk to me." She handed it back to Nathan as she walked back to the front line. "Let me know if she calls back."

"Found one," someone yelled, and two guys started digging. It took close to twenty minutes, but they pulled the officer out alive and bruised but breathing and talking. Two hours later the two others had come out as well, but in worse condition. All four of them were taken to the hospital.

"Give them some time before you start questioning them," Sebastian said as he left for the hospital as well. "Take some time yourself, and we'll talk before you head to any more crime scenes. Today we were lucky, but I'm not going to take the chance with anyone else by sending you in blind."

"Thanks, Dad, but we'll stick around."

"Go home for the night. That's an order. Get some sleep, and then get back to work. Whoever this is will keep doing it until we catch them, and you aren't going to do that running on fumes."

"Okay, but have one of the boys talk to these guys when they can. I want to see what they found in there and if their story matches the story of the survivor."

Sebastian simply stared at her, but she didn't look away. "You think Nobles has something to do with this?"

"Not necessarily, but I'm not going to skip asking questions because he's one of us. Think about what happened before. Never again." Right as she finished, another bomb went off.

❖

Keegan walked out of her office to get the staff ready for the dinner rush. It had been hours since she'd heard from Sept, but she was trying her best not to worry a lot. From the constant news coverage about what had happened the night before and the body count that had come of it, keeping happy thoughts had been a chore.

"Ms. Blanchard," she heard as the kitchen staff started cleaning their stations before their last few quiet moments abruptly ended and the orders poured in. When she turned to the swinging doors that led to the main dining room, she found Nicole Voles. "Do you have a few minutes?"

"Very few, Ms. Voles," she said, trying not to bleed too much sarcasm into her voice. "I'm not going to talk to you about Sept or the case that started with Donovan."

"Actually, I'm more interested in what's happening now. Some exciting things are unfolding in the city, and the news hasn't been close to accurate in their coverage."

"And you want me to fill in the blanks? You did look around out there," she said, pointing to her kitchen. "I'm a chef. Police work and how the news covers it isn't in my purview."

"No, but you and Sept Savoie are close, aren't you?" Nicole's question sounded teasing, and Keegan thought it was meant to lower her defenses.

"Even if that's true, whatever Sept says to me is none of your business, Ms. Voles."

"So you haven't heard?" Nicole's demeanor changed, and she seemed genuine in her concern, but Keegan wasn't falling for that.

"Heard what?" The back of her neck and head grew eerily cold, as if someone had aimed a freezing vent at her.

"There was another set of explosions, and some police officers were caught in the blast. It was just on the news." Nicole came closer, and her hand on Keegan's shoulder broke her out of the stillness the fear had trapped her in. "Have you heard from Sept?"

She pushed by Nicole and grabbed her phone. Her call went immediately to voice mail, and the pain in her chest was real and acute. She then listened to Sept's message not to worry coming from Nathan's phone, and she called again but got the same result. "No, no, no," she said, not knowing what to do.

"Hey," Nicole said, putting her arms around her and gently holding her. "I'm sure she's fine."

Keegan glanced up and desperately wanted to believe that, even though Nicole was saying the words. It was a bad dream, and then Nicole lowered her head and kissed her. The move paralyzed her, but she finally put her hands on Nicole's chest and pushed her away but didn't break their embrace. That's when she heard the sharp intake of breath and turned to see Sept standing in the door with a totally shocked expression. Then she was gone.

"Wait," she yelled and had to force Nicole to release her by prying her arms off so she could go after Sept. When she made it out the door, all she found was Mike in the fenced yard, which meant Sept had walked over with him. She ran to the street and didn't see any sign of her, but the abrupt departure made her angry and concerned about what Sept thought she'd walked in on.

"When I find you, I'm going to give you a memorable lecture before I show you how happy I am you're okay." In reality, if one of them was the target for women to pursue, it wasn't her. Sept was the whole sexy package, but her reaction showed she might be a little scared that Keegan wouldn't be happy with just her.

"Keegan, everything okay?" Nicole asked.

"Ms. Voles, I'm sure you're really good at your job, but that was inappropriate. I want you to leave with the understanding you're no longer welcome here," she said, putting her hand up to keep Nicole from coming closer.

"You're seriously banning me?" Nicole sounded like she was talking to a small child.

"You crossed a line, so yes. Don't make me get Sept involved in a more official capacity."

"The way she ran out of here leads me to believe you're not as close as you seem to think." Nicole ignored her warning and came closer.

"That's usually her reaction so she doesn't bash someone's face in," she said, crossing her arms over her chest. "Don't mistake it for noninterest."

"Whatever you say. I'll be in touch."

"Communicating or touching is the last thing we'll be doing, Ms. Voles. I meant what I said about you not being welcome here." She grabbed Mike's collar and led him back to the yard. "Don't come near me again."

She closed and locked the gate, trying to decide who she wanted to strangle more, Nicole Voles or Sept. "I can't believe you left," she said softly as she sat and petted Mike. "And where the hell did you go?"

CHAPTER EIGHTEEN

T ell me what's wrong?" Della said as she drove back home with a very pissed Sept next to her. It'd taken threatening her with a drive-by to get Sept in the car, and something was clearly not right. Considering she'd walked out of the restaurant, Della couldn't believe Keegan had done anything to provoke this reaction. "I'm going to bug you until you tell me, so you might as well save yourself the nagging."

"Della, I love you, but I'm tired, and I'm not in a talkative mood."

"It's Gran, remember," she said and rubbed Sept's shoulder. "And tired is something I can help you with."

It wasn't too far to her house, and she was glad Sept followed her in willingly, then into her guest room. She took out fresh towels and pointed to the shower. "Go ahead, since being clean will help you feel better. Once you take a nap, you'll see that whatever's bothering you won't be so horrible."

"Thanks," Sept said and kissed her cheek. "A nap sounds great."

"I'll make you a sandwich, so don't fall asleep until I get back."

It was nice to have someone to fuss over again as she set things out to make Sept a pressed panini. Sept came out before she was done and sat at the counter, appearing as if she'd been awake for days. Fatigue like this had a way of inflating inconsequential things.

"Eat it all, and if you want you can tell me what happened," she said, pouring a craft beer Sept liked, which she now kept in her refrigerator for whenever she and Keegan came over for dinner. "Or you can tell me to buzz off."

"My phone died today, so I went by the restaurant to talk to Keegan and show her I was okay after the hellish day I endured," Sept said, then took a huge bite of the sandwich.

"That was thoughtful, sweetheart. My granddaughter doesn't try to show it, but she worries about you every time you walk out the door."

"I know, and that's why I went. But I didn't expect she'd be kissing Nicole Voles when I got there," Sept said, pushing the plate away and seeming disgusted. "Maybe I should go."

"Eat that," she said, pushing the meal back, "and then you're going to bed." Sept didn't seem to have any fight left in her after that, so she went willingly when she guided her back to the bedroom. "I'll give you ten minutes to strip and get in there, or else I'll see for myself what my granddaughter finds so irresistible about you."

Sept laughed finally, so Della stepped out to clean her kitchen before coming back and finding Sept asleep. The pile of clothes that smelled faintly of smoke was left on the floor, so she kissed Sept's forehead before gathering everything for the wash. "If her clothes are wet, she's stuck here," she whispered as she glanced at Sept one last time before shutting the door.

"Hello," Keegan said, and the roughness in her voice meant she was upset.

"Hello, my darling," Della said, plucking Sept's tight boxers up by the waistband and dropping them into her washer. "First off, Sept's fine, and she's at my house. And secondly, her phone's dead, so she's not totally ignoring you."

"Is she mad?"

"She's not thrilled, but at the moment she's out like I hit her with a cast-iron skillet, which gives you time to explain what happened." The shoes she'd put on to attend their weekly dinner in Keegan's kitchen felt good off her feet as she retreated back to the kitchen, and she smiled at Keegan's snort.

"That bitch kissed me at the worst possible time, not that there'll ever be a good time, and my clueless fiancée ran out of here before I could explain. If she were here, I don't know if I'd kiss her or hit her with a raw fish for thinking I'd do that to her." Keegan's tone had gone from upset to sounding like she was speaking through gritted teeth.

"Sweetheart, in her defense, she's exhausted, and she was worried about you. Cut her some slack and get over here."

"I'm double booked tonight, Gran."

"That was the wrong answer, so try again," she said. Keegan and Sept could have a competition as to who was more stubborn. "I've already called your mother, and I'm changing now. Between the two of us, I think we can run any kitchen," she said, getting up and heading to her closet. Get your ass over here. I've got a naked cop in my guest room who needs a hug."

"Are you sure?"

"About the naked part, the hug, or the kitchen duty?" she asked, finding comfortable shoes and a more casual outfit.

"All of it, I guess."

"I'll never lecture you about marriage, but I'll tell you what I told Melinda. Never get out of bed angry, and don't completely lose yourself to make someone else happy. Someone either loves you for who you are or they don't. You have until she wakes up for that first one. Don't squander the chance. Sept loves you, and more important, she always will."

"Thanks, Gran," Keegan said, sighing. "But this doesn't mean I won't bring a fish with me."

Keegan left, trying to calm down on the ride over, and finally sensing a calm in her soul when she saw Sept asleep. She got undressed and slowly eased in next to her, smiling when Sept immediately rolled over and put her arm around her middle. Most mornings she woke up to Sept behind her holding her. It was good to know they probably spent most of their night in the same position.

She kissed Sept's palm before placing her hand back on her abdomen and closed her eyes. When she opened them again, it felt early, but it was light outside. Thankfully Sept was still behind her, but she didn't feel completely relaxed, which meant she was probably awake. She moved to face her, but Sept held her in place.

"I'm sorry I left last night," Sept said, flattening her hand over her stomach. "I should've known better than to think you'd invited that, and I should've stayed and explained a few things to that aggressive asshole. If you did invite that, it's perfectly acceptable to lie to me."

"I told Gran last night that I was either going to kiss you or smack you with a fish. That comment makes me lean toward dead-fish smacking," she said, turning around. The way Sept smiled at her made her forget any anger she felt. "Nicole told me about the explosions, and you didn't answer your phone." She clung to Sept, remembering that helplessness. "I was upset, and she ambushed me by pretending to be comforting."

"She was facing the door," Sept said, kissing her forehead. "Seeing me might've prompted the ambush, so comforting had nothing to do with it."

"That bitch," Keegan said with heat. "Jacqueline said she'd been flirting with me the first time she came in, but I thought my sister was full of shit. She sees flirting in every situation."

"I'm sorry. The first time she was flirting with you?" Sept moved her hands down and stopped at her ass. "I don't remember hearing about that."

"You were in the middle of that first murder case, and I didn't want to burden you. I'm also rapidly losing interest in this conversation." She threw her leg over Sept and sat up to straddle her.

"I don't want to be possessive, but you're mine, and I don't ever want to share." Sept placed her hand on her hips and sat up as well so she could kiss her. "You're mine," she said, rolling them over and hovering over Keegan.

"All yours, baby, you know that."

"I'm so in love with you," Sept said, tracing her cheek with her fingertips. "It makes me nuts to think I'd lose you, and I've never felt that way about anyone."

"You're never going to have to worry about that, baby." She placed her hands on Sept's face and arched up to kiss her. "I need you." She bucked her hips, a hint for Sept to roll over, and she did just that. "I need you inside me."

"God," Sept said as Keegan maneuvered her onto her back.

Keegan didn't need a lot of foreplay, so she threaded her fingers with Sept's and pressed her sex down on Sept's abdomen. "Do you feel that?" she asked as she rocked her hips. "That's how much I want you."

Sept let her hands go and reached between her legs, seeming to need to see how wet she was. The feel of Sept's fingers stroking over her clit made her tilt her hips forward, chasing more pressure. "Don't tease, baby," she said, reaching down and gripping Sept's wrist. "Go inside."

The way Sept touched her was maddening at times, since she slowed when Keegan wanted fast and softened when she needed firmer. "Don't be in a hurry," Sept said, and she groaned. "I want to enjoy this."

"But I'm so ready." She leaned down and kissed Sept, smiling when she kept her hand between her legs. "Come on. You know you want to," she said and moaned again when Sept's now-wet fingers stroked her hard and fast but only for a moment.

Sept moved the angle of her hand, and when Keegan lowered herself, she didn't move and locked eyes with Sept. "I'm so sorry, honey," Sept said with a slight smile. "I'll never walk away again."

"I only need you to believe there'll never be anyone else. I'd never do that to you."

"I believe you, and I love you," Sept said, lifting her hips slightly off the bed and driving her fingers deeper. "Now let me love you."

It reminded Keegan of their first time in the morning light, only this time she knew exactly how Sept felt about her and what she thought of her body. There was no more hiding what she thought were her imperfections. Sept made her feel sexy and wanted because she was right in that you couldn't hide that. Before Sept, she'd dated more than one person who'd wanted skinny since it was their idea of perfection, but now she knew how much Sept loved her curves.

She rocked her hips and held her breasts so Sept could see how hard her nipples were. That seemed to prompt Sept into action, and she sat up without moving her hand and kissed her. "You are so beautiful," Sept said, placing her other hand on Keegan's ass and tugging her closer. "You feel so good like this."

She held on as Sept kissed her neck and pumped her hand as much as she could. She was disappointed she wouldn't last very long, but she couldn't hold back. She also couldn't hold in the groan that came out as the orgasm hit her full force. "Baby…baby, uh, just like that. Please don't stop."

"Never." Sept leaned back slightly to be able to move her hand better. Keegan knew from experience that Sept was strong enough and had enough stamina to go all day, but this was it.

"Yes—yes—yes." She pumped her hips forward into Sept's body and stopped moving. The orgasm was so good she slumped against Sept and wished they had time for a nap. "You're so good to me, babe."

"The way I look at it," Sept said, lying back and holding her in place, "I have to keep you happy and marry you before the rest of the world figures out how great you are."

"Yes, the world is trying to beat down my door to get at me." She snorted at the joke.

"Should I remind you, Sparky, that a woman I'd love to pistol-whip kissed you last night?" She smiled as Sept massaged down her back to her butt and stayed there.

"That doesn't count since I'm not remotely interested." The smile she was used to seeing on Sept's face was there when she rose a little, and she traced the still-dark eyebrows. "And I made an observation this morning."

"Besides your revisionist explanation, you mean? I didn't say anything about your interest, but the interest of others."

"I don't want to talk about that bitch right now, so pay attention." She pulled the hair at the sides of Sept's head and laughed. "You, Detective Savoie, have an infatuation with my ass."

"You're only now figuring this out?" Sept knocked her off and pounced on her so she lay on her stomach. She shrieked when Sept reached down and bit her butt cheek before kissing the spot. "If you think telling me to kiss your ass is a punishment, think again. Your ass is a masterpiece." Sept took another bite, and this time when she laughed loudly the door opened.

In all the months she'd known Sept, she'd never seen her move that fast as she dove for the sheet to cover them both. Thankfully Jacqueline stood in the doorway with a smug expression and her arms crossed. "Gran sent me up to see what all the screaming was about and to let you know breakfast is ready."

"And knocking was a problem?" Sept asked, standing up and dropping the sheet, giving Jacqueline a peek at her perfect body. "Meet you in the shower," she said before walking away.

"I brought you and the amazon goddess a change of clothes." Jacqueline plunked the garment bag onto the bed and scratched the side of her mouth. "And if I've never mentioned this before, fuck me, she's gorgeous."

"That she is, so commit this morning to memory. No more free shows for you or anyone."

❖

"Thank you, Gran," Nathan said as he finished his third serving of grits and shrimp.

Della stared at him for a minute before smiling and nodding. "You're welcome anytime."

"Don't tell him that. You'll never get rid of him," Sept said, and Keegan kicked her under the table. "Did you check on the guys from last night?" she asked Nathan, knowing her fun was at an end.

"They were all moved to regular rooms early this morning, and the chief assigned an officer at each one's door. There's plenty of stitches and a few broken ribs, but overall, the doctors say they were all lucky."

"Yeah. Those piles were so full of construction debris they could've easily been skewered more than once," she said, and Keegan stood and put her arms around her from behind. "Let's start at the lab today. Then we'll meet with the team again."

"Your dad called and said the chief wanted a quick meeting to review what we have so far. He's got everyone and their brother working on the two fallen officers' case, but he knows they're related to our murders." Nathan smiled at Jacqueline as she cleared the table.

"That only helps us if they find something. We need a break, and I don't care where it comes from," she said, and Keegan held her closer. "Their deaths were so unnecessary, and they both left young families behind. More than one little kid won't know their father."

"The whole force is pissed about this, and if this guy knows what's good for him, they'll turn themselves in. They're chancing getting shot on sight if we can prove anything."

"We're dealing with a psychopath, so turning themselves in isn't in their makeup. Let's go see what we can do about dropping them in a black hole." Sept reached up and put her hand over Keegan's. "Sorry to eat and run, but we need to get going. Gran, thanks for everything, including last night."

"Anytime, even though I might have to burn those sheets," Della said, and Sept shook her head. "Be careful, and don't forget to ask questions, especially if they concern your personal life."

"I won't forget, and I love you for reminding me." Sept kissed Della's check, and Keegan tugged her into the sunroom.

"Did you get enough sleep?" Keegan pushed her into a chair and sat on her lap.

"I did, and I'll be home early so you can fuss if I look tired," Sept said as she combed Keegan's hair back. The thick blond strands always smelled like lemons and flowers. "Will you call me if Nicole Voles comes back?"

"I told her she wasn't welcome, but if she thinks I'm kidding, I'll call you." Keegan kissed her softly, and she wished for another long weekend where she could take the time to build the passion between them. "I love you, so come back to me in one piece, okay?"

"And you keep your lips to yourself, baby. I'm the jealous type, but only because I love you so much."

"My lips and my ass are all yours, Detective."

"You're a great motivator, my love."

CHAPTER NINETEEN

There was another explosion last night, and I need to know what the fallout was," Nicole said icily into the phone. Her contact in the NOPD didn't want to cooperate any longer, and none of her threats were working.

"Look. Do whatever you have to, but I'm not telling you shit. If you decide to turn me in, all they can do is fire me for giving you the information I've already turned over. Fritz Jernigan ordered a complete information blackout unless it comes from his office. That means everything, so if I talk to you again, they'll find me." The guy sounded desperate, but Nicole didn't care. "Considering what happened, he's liable to prosecute me."

"Believe me, if I talk to him, his prosecution will be successful. I want those notes, and you're going to get them for me."

"Hold your breath, lady. It ain't happening."

She gripped the phone when he hung up, but it wasn't the time to give in. She just had to throw more money at him, and things would be fine. It was hard to stay angry while listening to her father cook breakfast. Her mother had finally decided to go home and allow them their fun.

"Are you sure?" her mother Gail had asked, reaching for her hand and trying to sound as if she cared anything about her life and what she did. Her fake sympathy was insulting. Gail's concern should've come years earlier, but she'd been too busy with the martinis at the club and her wardrobe.

She stood in the doorway of her small galley kitchen and smiled at her father concentrating over the omelet he was making. This was as undone as anyone got to see him, with his hair mussed and wearing nothing but his boxers. Brian was the man she'd been trying to find all her life, and until she did, she'd stick to women. Her life was less complicated that way.

"Did you get them?" Brian asked without looking at her.

"What happened last night put Jernigan in a lockdown mood, so no. The officers have some bumps and scrapes, but nothing else is coming," she said, moving close and hugging him from behind. "At least not yet. I'm going to give my guy a few days and then really lean into him for the rest of what we need."

"Jernigan's also got two fallen officers, so it's understandable that he doesn't want anything getting out that would compromise his investigation. You'll have to work around it because things won't change until they have someone in cuffs." Brian grabbed two plates and placed a half in each. "There's always a way around everything, so don't worry too much."

"You always taught us that, so I'm more annoyed than upset. Let's eat and get to work."

"Are you sure you're up to it? It's been a whirlwind week, and it's easy to lose focus."

"Excitement is the main ingredient of any good book. These new developments will only enhance the story." She stood on her toes and kissed his cheek, leaning back to look him in the eye and loving the way he gazed at her. "I know your feelings about the good guys versus the bad guys, but in this case you have to heap the imagination and praise on Alex Perlis." She kissed him again when he took a deep breath to protest. "Savoie solving the case was admirable, but you have to give it to Perlis for not making it easy, not to mention interesting."

"So did Charles Manson, but he doesn't deserve any more praise than this asshole. He was caught, and that's all you need to know."

"If the killer stays free, then you'd change your mind?"

He finally raised his head and studied her, not seeming to completely understand her attitude. "Maybe, but the crime would have to be something worthy of admiration."

"Then this might be the one to do just that."

❖

"Yes, sir. Last night didn't end well, but before that, we might've made some progress," Sept said as she, Nathan, and her father sat in Jernigan's office.

Fritz sat behind the biggest desk in the department and steepled his fingers under his chin. "Tell me this will lead somewhere."

"One thing these crimes all have in common, even when Perlis was committing them, is the order and obvious planning," she said, knowing she had his full attention. "The victims at times might have been opportunistic, but how they were killed and why were never random."

"He's never talked to us, but we have got the transcript of your conversation with him the night you brought him in, backed up by your partner as to its accuracy," Sebastian said.

"And from that talk you got the sense he was a planner?" Fritz asked, spreading his hands out. "Perlis, I mean. He's fucking crazy, but I don't know about a master planner."

"Yes, sir. You have to take it all into consideration. Perlis killed not for the pleasure, but to offer sacrifices. Now we know from the evidence we've collected, he was trying in some bizarre way to get his wife and son back. That does make him crazy, but the way he carried out each murder was not."

The sigh Fritz let out meant he was getting frustrated, she guessed. "What's all this got to do with someone we're getting ready to fry in court?"

"The crimes have the same planning and order in common, but I seriously doubt our killer has the same motives as Perlis. It's in a way a copycat scenario, but that's where the similarity ends." It helped to lay it all out, even if Fritz seemed to be getting agitated. "So last night becomes important when you take it in context."

"I'm sure eventually you'll tell me why you think so," Fritz said but smiled as if to blunt his push.

"The perpetrator first killed Crazy Nick, who we were looking for, and obviously he knew the killer's identity. To cover his tracks, he blew the car with Nick inside. Sometime during the same day, Roger Breaux, our first victim's boyfriend, was killed and dumped in the park. Later that night we know he drove Lee Cenac to the house where Perlis brought Erica. The murder included a Santeria altar, and the items left were all planned," she said, glancing at Nathan. It was time for him to learn to speak up.

"But then he abandoned the plan and all the order," Nathan said. "Two teenagers came up to what they thought was a great opportunity. They found a car with the keys in it and were about to go for a joy ride."

"That's what you think happened to them?" Fritz said.

"Both of them were by the car, and if the killer had stayed in the yard, the only thing lost was a ride out of there," she said, and Fritz leaned in.

"So he went looking for trouble after killing Cenac?" Fritz asked, rubbing his chin.

"I didn't say it's a he," she said, and he placed his hands flat on the table.

"No way this is a woman," Fritz said, and sounded adamant.

"Nathan, show him the video," she said, and walked him through it. Lourdes had reviewed the rest of the video feed for the entire day of the bombing, and whoever had walked to the other lot to steal the car had also driven the old car found where the bomb had gone off. "Crazy Nick drove in the other old sedan parked in the area where the bomb did the most damage."

"You sure this is a woman?" Fritz said, pulling the laptop closer.

"It would explain the drag marks at each scene. We need to talk to Gavin again, and if my hunch is right, it'll explain how the victims are led to the altars. Perlis carried the women to his altars, but this guy doesn't have enough brute strength." That theory had been on her mind since seeing the flattened grass at Lee's scene and with the two police officers after Bonnie Matherne's scene.

"If you're right about what?" Sebastian asked.

"The victim has to be unconscious for the perpetrator to torture and kill her in that way. If we can find out what this woman is using and it's not something anyone can buy on the street, then we can narrow down where and who she got it from." If it was some kind of controlled pharmaceutical, a hoodie and sunglasses would never be acceptable at point of purchase. She would have had to show her face.

"How did this guy know all the particulars of these crimes?" Sebastian asked, and she didn't know.

"I need more time to answer that question, sir. That's one thing I can't guess about," she said. Suspicion usually got you somewhere, but speculation without proof wasn't a smart move in front of her bosses.

"Sept, I've got two dead cops. You remember that, don't you?" Fritz asked the question like she'd just come out of a coma and didn't know what was going on around her.

"Yes, sir. That has been on my mind since it happened, and I realize the need to solve those cases is paramount," she said, meaning that with her entire being. She wanted to avenge whoever had killed the new father. Both men had children, but one had a six-week-old daughter when he'd been murdered.

"I've got to stand in front of the cameras and have whoever's listening believe this city is safe," Fritz said, and she and Nathan nodded. "Get back out there and find this bitch, if it is a woman. At this point I don't care if it's a talented monkey—I want them in cuffs or in a body bag. We understand each other?"

"Yes, sir, perfectly," she said as she stood and shook his hand. Nathan did the same, and she smiled at her father on the way out.

"Where to, partner?" Nathan asked.

"Let's go see George, and then we'll go to the coroner's office. We've got too many hunches and not enough evidence." She slowed before they walked out of the building and grabbed Nathan by the arm and pulled him to a stop.

Nicole and Brian Voles were on their way in, and he had what appeared to be the same file under his arm as when they took him to the first murder scene. It was obvious Nicole had done research for her book, but she was curious if Brian's file contained Nicole's outline of the crimes, or her and Nathan's notes, which were not public. If it was a copy of the official case file, she was going to burn Nicole and whoever had shared it with her.

"Think they're back to give us more shit?" Nathan asked as they stayed out of sight.

"I think they're here to fish and to gloat. At least that's going to be Nicole's job."

Nathan turned his head and stared at her. "What's that supposed to mean?"

"That bitch kissed Keegan last night, so your job until she leaves town is to keep me from causing her any physical harm. If I get suspended, then I do, but if the opportunity presents itself, I'd appreciate it if you lost your eyesight for a few minutes," she said as Nicole and Brian sat down.

"If you get suspended, I'm going to be off with you," he said, bumping shoulders with her. "I'm planning to get a few shots in myself."

"Thanks, partner."

"You're my family, Sept, which means Keegan's my family too. No one messes with that while I sit back and let it happen."

"Keegan was right. You're a keeper, Nathan," she said as she texted her father and warned him what was waiting for him and Fritz in the lobby. "Come on. Let's go out the side. I don't have my temper under control just yet, and this place is crawling with witnesses if I go postal on that bitch."

They ran into a few people they knew before they got outside, but mostly it was the folks Fritz had working on the fallen officers' case. The ride to George's was quick, but the parking lot was full when they arrived, so Nathan parked on the street a block away. It was too beautiful a day to be thinking of all the gruesome shit they were about to see, but that was their fate for the foreseeable future.

"Who you dating these days?" she asked, realizing she very seldom if ever asked Nathan anything personal. While they were on desk duty, she'd found out he was an only child to parents who really wanted him to become a doctor, but Nathan had never outgrown his cops-and-robbers phase.

"Judy Rollings," he said, smiling. "She's a beat cop in the Bywater. While we were on desk duty she came in a few times, and I worked up the courage to finally ask her out."

"Why don't you invite her to dinner one night at Blanchard's? I'll check with Keegan on a good time, but if we can swing it tonight, let's do that."

"Really? Judy would love that, and it'll score me some points," he said, punching her arm.

"You know my girl loves to cook, and the chef's table in the kitchen is a treat. That's especially true if someone sends their food back a bunch of times." She laughed at those memories. It was the only time Keegan had proved how well she cursed.

"Let me know and we'll be there."

George was still running prints when they got upstairs, and Jennifer stood next to him taking notes on some stuff he had on the other screen. "Hey, do y'all have time for a run-through of what you have?"

"We've been waiting for you," Jennifer said as George got up.

"Once you get your briefing, we'll head downtown to bring Jernigan up to speed," George said. "First, the prints we found on the scrap of paper were from two different people. One's in the system and the other one is unknown."

"You're starting with bad news? You're killing me, Uncle George," she said, and George smiled.

"One print belongs to Nicholas Newton," George said.

"AKA Crazy Nick." Jennifer frowned. "We don't have a hit on the other one yet, but we're still trying."

"Bad news bit number one," she said, and Nathan shook his head. "What else do you have that'll totally ruin my day?"

"The note was clean, as usual, but like the first one, it was handwritten. Not that this helps us in any way, but maybe once we have someone in custody, we can compare handwriting." George handed them a copy but left the original on the table.

We offer up a prayer to Ochosi,
The great god who has mastered the art of tracking and
*   killing its prey.*
Stop fighting and searching for what you'll never find.
Surrender and I'll gift you with a quick death.
It's your only way out.
You can't protect your own, and I will take them one by one.
There can only be one warrior.

"That's quite the option." Sept reread it for the fifth time. "But I'm not much on surrender," she said, and George put his hand on her shoulder.

"The car was the same dead end," Jennifer said. "We checked like you wanted, and Lee Cenac was in the front passenger side. Nothing from the interior indicates a struggle of any kind."

"I hate to ask you to go over it again, but check the car one more time for any sign of a narcotic or other medicine that would knock someone out." She placed a copy of the scrap of paper they'd recovered and the note side by side, but it was clearly not the same handwriting. "Was Roger Breaux, Bonnie's boyfriend, in the trunk or in the back seat?"

"Back seat," George said. "We lifted prints from the back and found your missing witness. You might've needed to talk to Breaux, but the cops got plenty of chances before that."

"Rap sheet?" Nathan asked.

"As long as your arm," George said. "And that's all we have. We'll have more once I hear from the bomb squad and the feds' bomb guys. It's weird that someone would mix so many crimes together."

"What was he picked up for?" Nathan asked.

"Mostly petty stuff like shoplifting and minor drug offenses," Jennifer said.

"How did he get involved with someone who's killed eight people in a considerably short period of time?" she asked. "He probably got more money than normal for Bonnie, but once she was murdered, he should've hit the road."

"Unless the killer convinced him he was an accessory," Nathan said.

She nodded. "Or the money was too good to pass up, and after all, Bonnie was already dead."

"Chloe is always saying that money or sex makes people lose their minds," Jennifer commented, and Sept nodded again.

"See if there's anything else in the car. Tear it apart if you have to." She reread the note. "We'll meet you at the impound warehouse, but I need to talk to Gavin first."

"It's on Broad, along with the cars involved in the bombing at the Hilton," George said, and she and Nathan stared at each other. "Call the bomb squad and make sure you include the feds. Do it now," she shouted. George got on the phone and started making calls, so she called her father and asked who was closest to the warehouse. "Make sure all they do is clear the scene, and don't go near the car. I was wrong about the two kids and why they were killed."

"What are you talking about?" Sebastian said.

"Not now, Dad. Make the calls, and I'll meet you there. Get everyone out of the building, and I'm serious about doing it now."

George shouldered a bag as he barked into the phone. The entire lab staff seemed to be on alert, and they were all going to the same spot. "Everyone who knows anything about bombs is on their way over there, so tell me what you're thinking."

"Let's get over there, and I'll give you my theory. If I'm right, we don't have much time."

Nathan concentrated on the drive and made it across town in less than twenty minutes. The alphabet of agencies was present as they pulled up, and she was surprised to see Anabel Hicks at the front of the perimeter they'd set up. At least the building was still in one piece, and every person who was stationed there was safely on the street.

"Hey, Sept," Anabel said. "They're ready to go in, so you want to give us a rundown on what you're thinking."

Sebastian and Fritz joined them and pointed to the tent that had been set up. "Let's move in there, so no one from the media takes off with this more than they will already," Fritz said.

"What's going on?" Anabel asked once they were all inside.

"There's a bomb attached to the car we towed from the scene last night. I just don't know where," she said, and they all stared at her like they wanted more.

"Is this another attempt to kill more cops?" Fritz asked.

"No, sir," she said and stopped when the combined bomb specialists entered the building.

It took over fifteen minutes before one guy came out and reported they'd found a device close to a full gas tank. "We set up electronic blockers to keep whoever set it from detonating it," the FBI agent said. "Good call, Detective."

"How'd you know?" Anabel asked.

"I didn't until George mentioned what other cars were housed here, and then it hit me. Perlis was able to keep killing because he and George, along with their team, worked the scenes. He could clean up and collect any mistakes or missed evidence he left behind before it made it back to the lab. We have no evidence he ever did that because he was talented at leaving a clean scene."

"At least he was good at something, the bastard," George said.

"True," she said, giving George a sympathetic smile. "Whoever has taken up where Perlis left off found a way to do the same thing, even though they're not part of the department. Think about it."

"You're right," Nathan said. "The room where you got hurt was to cover up Bonnie's kidnapping, the Hilton was to cover up Crazy Nick's murder, but the ones from last night don't make sense."

"Cover up isn't quite right," she said, holding up her finger. "The perpetrator wants us to find the murders. Any evidence they might've inadvertently left behind on the murders that have nothing to do with the sacrifices need the extra step. The bombs are their security blanket to avoid any possible mistake."

"By finding one, we can see where the components come from, and that should lead us to who," the bomb guy said.

"Good work, Sept," Fritz said.

"Thanks, sir, but I want to get one step closer to bringing whoever this is down for what they did to our guys and all the other victims."

"You know my feelings about that," Fritz said. "This asshole killed our people, and I want whoever it is brought in. Keep at it until you get something."

"Yes, sir, I do, and those dead officers are never far from our thoughts."

CHAPTER TWENTY

Hunter woke in the late afternoon, stretching and trying to mentally prepare for the night ahead. Everything was already in place and planned, but getting up earlier than necessary was crucial to reviewing every step with fresh eyes. It was a new beginning, and she couldn't derail the success of the game because of an early start.

Waking with a specific mission always filled Hunter with a nervous energy that would help only in the most complex of necessary sacrifices. The game was too fresh to kill the warrior, but it didn't mean the warrior's mate couldn't serve a purpose. That sacrifice would be like opening a wound that, while not immediately fatal, eventually would bleed the warrior dry emotionally and figuratively.

It was time to go, and Hunter picked up the kill bag, along with the directions to where the car was. The time to prove worthiness had come, and failure meant being trapped into watching the thrill of the kill from afar. If Hunter was relegated to being only a witness to the game, it would make death an easy option.

❖

"What are you wearing?" Sept asked softly into the phone while she had a minute of peace at her desk.

"My boring muumuu outfit, but I have a surprise for you underneath if you make it home in time to watch me take it off."

The quiet from Keegan's end meant she was in her office getting ready for the dinner rush. "Man, you know how to make the clock come to a crawl, babe." She watched Nathan on the phone, and he gave her a thumbs-up for some reason. "How about I come by later and take a peek?"

"Not while I'm working, honey. When you get me excited, I have a tendency to over-salt stuff."

"Then keep those pretty panties unknotted, and I'll come by for dinner, if you don't mind me bringing guests."

"Bring a crowd, if you want," Keegan said, sounding perkier. "As long as I get to stare at you for most of the night, I don't care who else is there."

"We're double-dating with Nathan and his new love connection, so no crowds. I'm trotting out my rusty social skills." She glanced at her screen, but still no report on the device they'd found.

"Your social skills are way above average, boo-boo," Keegan said and laughed. "At least I certainly think so. What time are you coming?"

"Hopefully later tonight when we're alone, since Jacqueline barged in on us and left me hard and ready for most of the day. But I'll be there for dinner around eight. Save me some bread-pudding soufflé."

"Thanks for putting that image in my head," Keegan said and sighed. "And we'll run out of wine before we run out of that, but dinner first, then dessert," Keegan said, making Sept think she'd be an excellent mother.

"If I'm lucky, you'll feed me dessert later in your new pretty panties." She lowered her voice again, not wanting to advertise her sexual fantasies to her coworkers. "I'm guessing white with plenty of lace and silk."

"Good-bye, Detective Savoie," Keegan said, laughing again. "No hints, so keep that sexy voice and all your guessing to yourself, but remember that I love you."

"Love you too, baby." Sept sighed when Keegan hung up, leaving her too restless to sit and wait any longer. The call Nathan had been involved in had ended as well, so she stood and put her jacket back on. "Let's go see Gavin and ask a bunch of annoying questions."

"That was Judy, and she's thrilled about tonight," Nathan said, following her out.

"Keegan's happy as well, since she loves to feed people, and I'm looking forward to talking to Judy. I don't think I've ever run across her on the job." The ride to the morgue wasn't that long, but Nathan managed to list all the things he really adored about Judy. He was like an eager beagle puppy sometimes, but it was part of his charm. That's what Keegan kept reminding her about anyway when she made too much fun of him.

"I thought you two broke up with me," Gavin said, leading them to where they kept the bodies.

"And miss Nathan throwing up every time he has to watch you work?" She handed Nathan a roll of mints, and she and Gavin laughed when he popped three into his mouth. "Not on your life. Our time's been blown to hell lately, and I mean that literally, so we had to keep postponing our visits."

"I heard about that." Gavin opened the drawer that held Bonnie first. "That's kind of nuts."

"We're waiting on the report on the bomb we found, but don't worry. I'll keep you updated. We'll also have the bomb guys check anyone we send you. I don't want you to cut into something that'll really ruin your day." She and Nathan stood on the other side of the gurney and waited for Gavin to put on gloves.

"You were right." Gavin pointed to a spot on Bonnie's shoulder. "We didn't miss it the first go-round, but since she had other track marks on her arms, we didn't highlight it." He pushed Bonnie back in, went a few drawers down, and pulled Lee Cenac out. "Lee Cenac, though, wasn't a known drug user, but she had the same puncture mark in almost the same exact spot. We took blood samples, and in both cases I expanded the screenings. With any luck we'll find out what this was, and it might lead somewhere."

"Thanks, Gavin. Anything else jump out at you with any of the bodies we've piled in here?" she asked, and he moved to another drawer that contained the charred remains of Nicholas Newton. His hands were frozen around his neck, and his arms were up as well.

"There's too much damage to what's left of him, but in my opinion he was stabbed before the bomb did its job. The shrapnel most likely finished him off, but that's a classic pose for an injury to the neck."

"What about Roger Breaux?" Nathan asked of Bonnie's boyfriend.

"No needle to the neck or shoulders," Gavin said, moving his arm to show the markings of a junkie. "These are self-inflicted, and the amount of heroin in his system means he never knew the bullet to the back of the head was coming. Even if he did, he probably didn't give a damn."

"Hopefully this is the last of them, and something you found will lead us to the asshole," Sept said as Gavin stripped off his gloves. "We'll be in touch."

"I'd rather have a lunch date than any more of this shit, and call

George tomorrow. I sent the bullets I took out of Breaux and the two teenagers for comparison. If it's the same gun, you know for sure the same guy pulled the trigger."

"Amen to lunch, my friend," she said, smiling when she glanced at her watch. "And I'll touch base with George in the morning. Come on, Nathan. We have time to relax over a drink before our meal."

"You're a lucky bastard, Sept," Gavin said, flicking the lights off.

"That's no lie, Doc, and I'm planning to keep it that way."

Hunter watched the woman hurry from her car and rush inside. This would be tricky, but the perfect time to strike was when the key went into the slot. No one ever did that one-handed, and taking them unawares was almost certain.

The blond head came up at the feel of the needle, and the expression of horror lasted only momentarily as the petite body went limp. The sacrifice was attractive, but this wasn't the moment to concentrate on superficial, unimportant things. Hunter stared only a second more before putting on the mask and dragging the woman inside. The altar was already made in the front room that appeared not to get much use, but it was the victim's fault. For such a beautiful home, the break-in had been easy.

The beginning part had to be fast, since the enjoyment came from the actual killing and not from watching the victim die as the drug suppressed their breathing to the point of death. But this one had to be quick. The warrior could interrupt, which was unacceptable.

"Are you ready?" Hunter asked when the blonde jerked awake, disoriented at first but then instantly afraid.

The woman opened her mouth, trying to speak around the gag, but it wasn't coming off. Nothing would stop this—nothing. The blonde kept struggling as Hunter took everything from the bag needed to complete the altar. This time would be different, since the weapon would have to be left behind as a gift for the god that would be invoked.

"So many bread crumbs, but none lead back to me. You, though," Hunter said as the sharp knife made work of the unattractive pants and top, "will be a real wake-up call for the warrior. Your protection should've been a priority, but it wasn't."

The salt circle looked about right, so Hunter centered the statue of Our Lady of Candlemas, or as the seller called her by her more popular name, *La Virgen de la Candelaria.* "It might seem silly to you, but I have to follow all the steps. Alex Perlis was calling the dead, and I'm here to answer the call."

Hunter glanced at the cheat sheet in the bag, ashamed, but there was so much to remember. The cut to the wrist did bleed plenty for the shepherd's crook on the bottom of the woman's foot and the number nine on the top. The blood really stood out on the creamy, pale skin.

The brown and burgundy candles were lit and illuminated the room enough for Hunter to see the blonde close her eyes as if in recognition of what came next. The fat tears that dropped despite the closed eyes meant the woman had resigned herself to her fate.

"I call on the fierce and powerful female warrior Oya to help me defeat the warrior and show the world what a false warrior she is." It took more force to drive the machete in, and Hunter had to really saw to get it to cut to the other side. Hunter used it to cut up into the chest as well before taking out the heart and dropping it into a sealable bag.

"What a waste, but it had to be done," Hunter said, placing a gloved hand on the woman's forehead before rising. "Oya, I can't finish your altar here, but I'll give you all you require where you live."

It was time to go, but Hunter had a few more things to do before ending the night and returning to the sanctuary of the condo. She left only what she wanted the police to find. Until the game was done, and beyond that, Hunter had to stay peacefully in the shadows. If not, she couldn't play the game anymore.

The bag was lighter now, containing only the last remaining necessities and the woman's heart. "Will finding it break yours, warrior?" Hunter asked, waiting to be outside before removing the mask. "If it does, you'll be that much easier to kill."

CHAPTER TWENTY-ONE

"Judy's set to meet us there," Nathan said, once they'd updated the team on what Gavin had found. For every new thing they uncovered, they had to hurry up and wait for the follow-up reports. "She wanted to change into something nicer."

"Great. Let's get going, and I'll buy you a drink. Call her and tell her to make sure to use the valet. It feels like rain, and she doesn't need to get soaked," Sept said, glad to turn her brain off from the job for the rest of the night. That wouldn't really ever happen, but flirting with Keegan did tend to derail the runaway train her mind could be.

"I'll lift a glass to a quiet night. Not that I don't love you, but I'd rather spend the night with Judy." Nathan wiggled his eyebrows at her.

"I'm crushed, but if you linger after dinner, I'm going to run you off with a few warning shots." She laughed and directed him to where the staff parked.

Keegan's missing cute little car made her worry for a millisecond, but she figured Jacqueline had most probably dropped her off. That would mean a nice walk home, and she looked forward to holding Keegan's hand and talking about her day. If she'd ever thought she'd find recipes and cooking techniques fascinating, she'd have had a good laugh at herself, but she could listen to things from Keegan's world for hours. Someone so passionate about their work tended to suck even the most reluctant kitchen enthusiast in.

"Let's head through the kitchen to the bar and wait for your date," she said, smiling at the staff who'd glanced up with welcoming expressions.

Keegan's number two, Louis Hibbs, was barking orders through, which made her glance at the office, but it was dark. Maybe Keegan had decided on a table in the dining room rather than the chef's table, she thought as her phone buzzed in her pocket. It was a blocked number, and the cop part of her brain knew it was no robocall or friendly reach-out from someone she loved.

"What?" Nathan asked as she answered.

"Savoie."

"Detective, thank you for taking my call." The voice was distorted by some kind of device, and the sound made her stand straighter. She couldn't know for sure, but this had to be the killer she was looking for.

"I'm sure you won't oblige me, but who is this?" She concentrated on any background noise and walked to the door for more quiet, but heard nothing but slight static.

"Nonsense. My name is Hunter," the person said, laughing. It sounded so strange in that mechanical tone. "I figured it was time for us to talk, and then I have a surprise for you."

"I'm not really one for surprises," she said, starting to take notes. She wanted to record the exact words this asshole used. "What do you want?"

"Please, Detective, don't you want to know anything about me?"

"I'm not asking, because assholes like you don't ever tell the whole truth." She stepped outside with Nathan right behind her, holding the phone a little from her ear so he could listen in.

"You aren't going to start with unintelligent vulgarities, are you? From what I've heard, you have more to you than that. After all, aren't you the great detective who caught Alex Perlis?" The deep breath meant that whoever this was didn't fear a trace on the line they were using. "That fact alone makes you a worthy adversary."

"I'm not interested in any games, Hunter, so drop the dramatics and tell me what this is about."

"Did you get my last note? Did you perhaps think I was kidding? I'm not ready to kill you, but you can't protect your own, and I took an important one tonight. Like the slice through the wrists that always starts the sacrifices, I've cut you tonight, and I'm going to bleed you slowly. In the end you'll pray for me to end the pain."

"What are you talking about?" Fear had never been a huge problem when it came to her job. It would be disingenuous to say she was never afraid, but paralyzing, all-encompassing fear would never allow her to wear a badge. Right now, though, that was exactly what washed through her like a rogue wave. It knocked her off the very axis of who she was and what she loved.

"She's waiting for you for one last good-bye," Hunter said, and like in a cheap thriller the caller hung up and left her thoroughly rooted in place.

"Who was that?" Nathan asked, raising his hands to her shoulders as if trying to get her to look at him. "What's wrong?"

"It was the killer," she said, the words coming out in a whoosh, and she suddenly hurt all over. The most acute pain was concentrated in her chest like her heart had been put in a vise, and perhaps when she figured out the meaning of the call, she'd indeed wish for a quick, painless death.

"How'd they know where you were?" Nathan asked, shaking her as if trying to snap her out of whatever was wrong and get her to focus.

She turned and ran back inside, grabbing Louis by the front of his chef's coat. "Where is she?"

"She had a little mishap and ran home to change. Usually she keeps another coat in the office, but they're all at the cleaners," he said, staring at her as if she'd lost her mind. "Is something wrong?"

She ignored him and called Keegan's cell. The kitchen had come to a silent halt, which made them all turn in unison when it rang from the office. She didn't have any more time to waste, and even with the possibility of what she'd find, she took off running toward the car.

"What's wrong?" Louis yelled after her, sounding upset.

"Call me if you hear from her," she said as Nathan unlocked the doors. "Gun this thing and take me home."

Nathan went lights and sirens the entire way, and she started choking up when she saw Keegan's car, but the house was dark. She fumbled with the key so much that Nathan finally unlocked the door for her, and she went inside with her hand on her gun. The place was quiet, so she pointed to the front of the house, and Nathan nodded and drew his weapon while she went up the back stairs.

A light was on in their bedroom, and she had to stop and blink away the emotions about to choke her and completely rob her of reason. The image of Roxie Stevens, Perlis's third victim whom he'd murdered in her bed, had wedged itself in her mind, and there was no dislodging it.

She slammed the door open, and Keegan jumped and screamed at the same time, her hands going from the top buttons of the chef's coat up over her head. "What the hell?" Keegan asked, stomping a foot in apparent frustration and anger. The outburst stopped when Sept fell to her knees and started crying.

The same type of sobs had come the day Joel had told her that Noel her sister and Sophie her niece had been lost in Katrina's floodwaters.

She fell forward and pressed her forehead to the floor, moaning from the relief of seeing Keegan standing there alive and unscathed.

"What's wrong, baby?" Keegan was on the floor with her, holding her and running her hands along her back soothingly. "Breathe, baby, breathe. Whatever it is, it'll be okay."

Nathan came in and dropped to her other side, placed his hands on her shoulders, and squeezed. "What did the bastard say?" he asked.

"What bastard?" Keegan asked, then seemed to understand when she sat up and held her. "I'm here, and I'm all right. Nathan, there's a glass on the nightstand. Can you get her some water, please?"

"I'm sorry," she said, pulling back and wiping her face. "I didn't mean to freak out and scare you."

"You're the steadiest person I know, so it must've been something important for you to come looking for me." Keegan brushed her hair back and kissed her. "Tell me."

She drank the water Nathan had gotten from the bathroom sink and told them about the phone call and what the person had said. "Once I realized you weren't there, I panicked."

"Was the call just to scare you? Like a practice run before they really try to hurt someone close to you?" Nathan asked, sitting on the bed.

"Perlis did the same thing, and it turned out to be bullshit, so this might be more of the same. The orishas might be different, but the crimes are basically the same. The way the caller threatened, though, made me believe someone had been hurt. It sounded like a done deal."

"The fucker is sick, so this was all to throw you off. Maybe those reports we're waiting on have something to them, and this diversion is to lead you away from some answer we're about to find," Nathan said. "Keegan not being at the restaurant was just a lucky break on their end."

"We'll find out eventually, but right now you need to get off my bed before I lose my shit again," she said to Nathan, and Keegan finally laughed.

"Go ahead and call your date and tell her we'll be there in a little while. After all this, we deserve a little downtime," Keegan said, and Nathan took the hint and left them alone. "Are you sure you're okay?"

She gladly welcomed Keegan on her lap after she sat on the bed. "If I hadn't gone completely insane, I would've scanned and searched the area. The only way this bastard figured out where I was is by watching."

"It makes me feel special, then, that you came looking for me instead of doing that." Keegan kissed her after she spoke. "I am sorry that happened."

"I really don't know how I'd handle it if something really did happen to you." She held Keegan for a while longer before they were ready to go. "Thanks for having my back, Nathan," she said when they got downstairs. "Park in the same spot, and we'll meet you there."

"Okay," Nathan said, tapping his phone in his hand.

"Problem?" she asked as Keegan leaned against her and she held her hand.

"Judy's not answering, so I guess she's already there," he said, but his tone held no conviction.

"Let me call," Keegan said, moving to the phone. Sept and Nathan stared at each other while Keegan spoke to the maître' d and the kitchen staff, and no one had met Judy Rollings. "She's not there."

"We'll drop you off and go check on her," she said, and Nathan walked out as if anxious to go. "Once I escort you inside, don't leave until I get back. I don't care what's going on," she said to Keegan. "I'll come back for you."

"Okay, but call me and let me know what's happening. I'm worried about you, and it's already been a strange night."

She walked Keegan into the kitchen at the restaurant and apologized to the staff. Before she went back outside, she called her father and explained the situation. Sebastian dispatched some units to Judy's house and said he'd wait for her follow up. Nathan turned the lights and siren back on once they were on St. Charles Avenue, and he drove like he'd made the trip often.

"What the fuck?" he said when they saw the blue lights flashing from the multiple police cars outside Judy's house.

"I called my dad to make sure Judy was okay. I'm sure she's inside pissed at both of us and only a great meal will get us out of trouble." She got out, and Joel came and held his hands up.

"You called this in?" Joel asked.

"It was only a check," she said, and the realization hit her. "What's going on?"

"Someone else called this in, and we were the closest unit," Joel said and scratched the back of his head. "I was getting ready to call you guys."

"Why?" Nathan asked, sounding as helpless as she had right after

Hunter's call. Joel held his hands up when Nathan started to walk past him.

"We've got another altar."

Nathan took three steps back until he hit a police car. "She's dead?" he asked in barely a whisper.

"Do you know her?" Joel asked, and Sept saw George walking up. "We haven't been able to find any kind of identification."

"She's one of us," Nathan said, grabbing Joel by the collar and shaking him, then just as quickly letting him go. Sept shook her head when Joel tried to hold him back, keeping him out of the house.

He moved into the house, pushing people out of the way. Sept was right behind him and went down to the floor with him when he reached the front room. If this was Judy, their killer had taken their time and done much more damage than at any scene before. Nathan glanced down at her naked and mutilated body and ran out.

"Don't let anyone near her, and get all these people out of here," she said to Joel and followed her partner out. She found him in the front retching into the grass. "Nathan, come on." He followed her compliantly, and she motioned for the EMS crew that had shown up to take him. They helped him rinse out his mouth and gave him a place to sit.

"We weren't like you and Keegan yet, but we could've been," he said, and the tears came as fiercely as hers had. "She didn't deserve that."

"You're right. She didn't. I need you to sit right here and let me take care of this."

"No. I'm not leaving her."

"Nathan, please." She placed her hand on the back of his neck and bent to get at eye level with him. "I'm not cutting you out, but you'd do the same for me. This is too important to let emotions overrule your head. We owe her more than that."

"You want me to go get Julio?" The way Nathan was shaking made her want the medics to sedate him, not send him off anywhere.

"Just sit and try to drink something. I'll have someone go get Julio." He nodded, and she called Julio, who promised to meet her there to save time. "Who called this in?" she asked Joel.

"I had the guys cue it up for you," Joel said, waving over one of the cops outside. "Go get the recorder."

Sept stepped back in the house and pressed Play. It was the same mechanical voice from her call and the same voice as in all the other 9-1-1 calls.

"The warrior's protégé wants so badly to earn a place by her side."

"Um." The operator hummed, and the voice stopped. *"What's that mean?"* the operator asked.

"Tonight he can join the game since he's paid the admission price. Go to this address, and he can collect his prize."

The call ended, and Sept punched her fist into her palm. Nathan was a good man, and while she'd never met Judy Rollings, she was sure she was a great match for him. That chance would never come, and she'd help Nathan get over the pain whatever way she could.

"Hey, baby," she said when Keegan answered the phone. "Don't leave alone, and I'll send one of the boys to get you if I'm not done. I know I promised to take you home, but this might take a while."

"What happened?"

"The phone call I got wasn't about you but about Nathan's date. All of these murders are horrific, but this one is a nightmare." She nodded to George and Jennifer as they moved to the body.

"How's Nathan?"

"He's me an hour ago. I don't want to leave him alone too long, but Rollings deserves my full attention." She took a deep breath, trying to prepare herself for the coming hours. "I love you, so please be careful."

"I love you too, and whoever comes to get me, have them bring Nathan with them. He'll feel better if he talks about it, and you're right. He shouldn't be alone."

"I love you for showing me every day why I'm so lucky to have you in my life. Try to have a good night. I've got to go."

George glanced up from his crouched position by the body. "What the hell?"

"Maybe it's the killer's love of the police, but this is way beyond overkill." She tried not to simply stare at the body, but it was hard not to. "This pretty much guarantees this son of a bitch doesn't make it to a trial."

CHAPTER TWENTY-TWO

Chloe Johnson stared out her twentieth-story window, ignoring the files on her desk and thinking of Jennifer and how she enjoyed this new job with George and major crimes. Most of the cases Jennifer was assigned to were tied to Sept Savoie, and that was the only reason she felt better about the whole thing.

The lights of the downtown area were beautiful, but Chloe knew that only ever seeing the worst of the city they both loved would change Jen, and she feared the distance it might cause because of it.

"Hey," she said when she saw Jennifer's name on the cell.

"Hi, honey. I don't have much time, but the last call out is going to take most of the night, so don't worry and wait up for me. You need your rest."

She smiled and placed her hand on her abdomen. They'd both been swamped at work, but they never missed the chance to try for what they both really wanted. She'd planned to share her trip to the doctor that morning with Jen tonight, but that would have to wait. "You too, so don't volunteer for anything else tonight. You're already doing enough."

"Are you still at the office?" The voices in the background of wherever Jennifer was were subdued, as if they were all being respectful of the scene.

"I was getting ready to leave, and I'll try to wait up for you if I can." She cleared her throat when Jen started to interrupt. "Ah, ah, ah," she said, and Jen laughed. "I said I'll try, but you know what the news does to me. It's like a sleeping pill in video form."

"Make sure you turn it on, and then I won't worry if you're sleeping. I love you, and I'll try my best to get there."

She disconnected the call and started packing her bag. "Hey, Chloe." Her assistant poked her head in, and she flinched in surprise, thinking she'd left already. "Sorry. I was getting ready to go, but you have a visitor."

"Visitor?" she asked, not really wanting to be stuck here any longer.

"Or pest." She saw Roger Smith's handsome face in her doorway. They'd graduated together and had been study partners from the beginning. "It's all in how you want to look at it."

"Get in here, pest," she said, smiling and holding her arms out. By luck they'd ended up in the same building, and they had lunch at least once a week. Roger had grown up pretty much like she had, and while they shared their success in work, Roger hadn't found the same in his personal life. "I missed you this week."

"Believe me, I'd much rather have been here, but Gretchen roped me into a case I don't want any part of, and it might piss Jen off."

"That's tough, buddy, but I can't see Jen getting pissed at you no matter what. I'll talk to her if she has the bad manners to prove me wrong. Believe me, I have ways of bending her to my will. Above all else, I think she finally understands that everyone deserves a defense thing." She went back to packing her bag and finished so they could get out of there together. "Are you free for dinner, or do you have a hot date lined up?"

"Come on. Let me feed you," he said and bowed deeply. "As far as the hot dates, I'm convinced that all the gay men in New Orleans are completely insane, especially the really good-looking ones."

"Way to generalize, drama queen," she said, taking his arm.

"Please. You thought that until you met Ms. Wonderful. Where the hell is Mr. Wonderful, I ask you?" he yelled in the darkened hallway and threw his other arm over his eyes.

"Shut up, you nut, and don't make me resort to setting you up again."

He gazed at her with a mortified expression. "Please, no. That last guy owned a snake, and I'm not talking about any kind of fabulous physical trait. I'm going to find the love of my life like every other person in this new age of modern technology."

"As compared to olden-times technology?" she asked and laughed when he stuck his tongue out at her. "All right. I won't tease you no matter what, but if you say eHarmony, you should know they won't find matches for spawns of the devil."

"If you're referring to my awesome gayness, there's no devil spawn about it, but I am talking about internet dating." He walked her to her car and took her bag and opened her door before getting in. "That way I figure, it'd be faster to click and delete instead of waste time and money on drinks. All the alcohol is murder on my pores."

"Poor, poor, pitiful you," she said, and he stuck his tongue out again. "And you never know. You could pointedly question a hot cop on the stand, then take her home. Oh, wait, that was me."

He snorted and smiled when she took a right on Poydras and headed to Ruth's Chris for steaks. "I'm still shocked you made it to the second date before chewing through her pants and that she hasn't figured out you're drugging her to like you."

"That was mean," she said, waiting for the valet to open her door. "But sadly true."

"Not the drugging part. Ms. Shultz is disgustedly and madly in love with you. Besides, she'd get fired if they ever popped a surprise screening on her." He held two fingers up, and the maître 'd sat them by the open windows that overlooked the nice alleyway outside that led to more bars and restaurants. "How's she holding up running with the big dogs?"

"She looks like a big kid heading to camp every day, so she's great. Because, I, like you, am an evil attorney, it limits our conversations at home. We don't talk about most cases, so there's no conflict, but she's definitely loving it." She opted for her usual petite filet and potato, with sparkling water.

"And you?" he asked after ordering. "How are you holding up?"

"I'm trying not to nag, and since Sept Savoie is leading most of what she's working on now, I'm not as concerned anymore."

He held his hand up, and she stopped talking. "Don't say anything else, since hot cop is causing a conflict between us. My new case, where more than anything I'm window dressing, is Alex Perlis. Gretchen and Fred are taking the lead, but they brought me in to fill the last chair at the table. If the jury sees we can sit next to him without cringing, they might not kill him."

"Wow, small world, huh?"

"Yeah," he said, taking a sip of his beer. "Considering Jen's new position, I tried to keep my distance, which is usually impossible since I love tough cases. Hell, I was a tough case for years, but this time Gretchen didn't give me a choice. Now I'm representing the creepiest human I've ever met, and Gretchen has loaded me down with research."

"Shut up before you get yourself into trouble. And I'll talk to Jen on your behalf. Had she heard it from anyone else, I'd fear for your life, but I was serious about her understanding what we do and why we do it." She took his hand and squeezed. Roger understood her and what she'd been through more than anyone.

"Thanks, and please know I realize how weird this is. It's bizarre that my client had a job that's now being done by my best friend's partner. It doesn't get any weirder than that."

"I feel for you, buddy. I've represented some real doozies in my time, but Perlis is truly evil." She smiled at the waiter.

"Everyone has at least one redeeming value or trait, but I'm still looking when it comes to this guy. Hopefully Jen won't have to deal with anything remotely close to what he did." He stopped talking and ate some of his salad, and she did the same to keep from commenting. "I did, though, get to meet someone famous."

"Don't tell me Brad Pitt is going to play him in the movie. That'll totally change my opinion of him. I don't care how many houses he builds to bring the Ninth Ward neighborhood back, that would be unforgivable." She followed his lead and stuck her tongue out at him, and he made a disgusted face when he saw her mouth was full of leafy green things.

"Brad Pitt will probably play Sept Savoie, that hunky thing. If anyone should've been born a man who then would fulfill my every fantasy, it should've been her." He pointed his fork at her when she started to open her mouth again. "But I digress. The writer Nicole Voles is all over Gretchen and this case. She's writing a book about it."

"From what perspective, I wonder?" She nodded when the busboy cleared her salad plate. "I read one of her books, and it was enough to see she was anti-police."

"I can't answer that, but Perlis fascinates her. No matter what, you know I'm firmly in the pro-cop camp."

"Thanks, buddy," she said, and they stayed clear of work for the rest of their meal. Now she prayed Jen made it home early enough for them to talk. He kissed her cheek and refused a ride home since he didn't live far. "Call me, and we'll do this again soon since Jen's been working so much."

"I will, and I love you," he said, hugging her tight. "And your little secret is safe with me until then."

"What?"

"Girl, you're glowing, and I'm already planning all my spoiling. I insist on being called Aunt Roger."

"I haven't talked to Jen yet, so I'm not confirming anything." She kissed his cheek again and stayed in his arms, enjoying the scent of him. "And I love you too, Aunt Roger."

❖

Hunter watched from the other side of the street as the two old friends said their good nights. Most of the other games were about random patterns. The victims might've fit a pattern the original killer found necessary, like all blond women or gay men. The psychology behind their choices indicated their hatred of their mothers or urges they wanted to suppress, but random was the rule.

New Orleans was different, though. All these people were like a large incestuous soup that connected them each to the new game. The one common denominator was the warrior, but each of these people had a part to play. They all also fit into Hunter's plan to keep bleeding Savoie until she was on her knees.

"Tonight you lost your partner. Little warrior Nathan will never forgive you for the loss of his woman. In a way she was one of yours, and you couldn't protect her." Chloe Johnson's car arrived, and she waved to Roger one more time before driving away. "I need to make a few more once-removed sacrifices before Chango is satisfied with your blood."

Chloe made a U-turn and stopped at the light close by. "Plenty of sacrifices that will chip away at what you count on."

❖

"Go drive Keegan home, and take Nathan with you," Sept said as the bomb squad ran everyone out while they checked. Her father had lectured all of them, but she figured this was one scene that wouldn't be rigged to blow.

"I don't need a babysitter for that, shrimp," Joel said, and she flicked his earlobe hard.

"He's staying with her because he's upset, Mr. Sensitive." The guys from the bomb squad came out and gave her the go-ahead. "The victim was his girlfriend, remember? Keegan doesn't want him to be alone."

"Will do, and I think that's your voodoo guy," Joel pointed to where Nathan was still sitting.

"Make sure you walk them both to the door before you hurry back." Before Joel got to them, Julio took a small pouch from his pocket and removed something that he then put around Nathan's neck. She wondered if the colored beads would help Nathan with his pain.

"Hello, Sept," Julio said when he joined her on the small porch. "I gave Nathan some tea to help him sleep. Keep him with you until tomorrow morning. His pain will need your strength."

"Thank you, and Keegan will take good care of him until I get home." She handed him some booties and a pair of gloves. "Excuse me a moment."

"Are you sure you don't want me to stay?" Nathan asked when she joined him at the back of the ambulance.

"I need you to go take care of Keegan for me until I'm done here. No matter what, know that you're not alone in this, my friend."

"Thank you," Nathan said and stood to hug her.

She watched him go, her heart aching for him. Julio placed his hand on her shoulder, and she smiled at him. "You've seen the worst Perlis could come up with, but you need to take a few deep breaths before you get in there."

"It's not an altar?" Julio asked as he put everything on. "When you called…I thought."

"Wait," she said, slowing him down. "It is an altar, but the body is way more mutilated than usual. Not that the usual isn't bad enough." She followed her own advice and took some deep breaths before leading Julio in.

Julio walked in and inhaled sharply when she moved to the side and allowed him to see the body. Judy Rollings had been stripped naked like everyone else, disemboweled like everyone else, but the killer hadn't stopped there.

"Do you see the differences?" she asked, worried she'd have to take Julio back out when he placed his hand over his mouth like he was trying not to throw up. "She was a police officer, and I'm still trying to decipher how this happened. There's no sign of forced entry, and she knows enough about these cases to not have gone willingly. I'd rather die on my feet than subject myself to this."

"Where are her breasts and her heart?" Julio asked, his eyes on the circle of salt. The only items in there, though, were the candles, a religious statue, and a child's snack-pack pudding cup.

"Tell me about this, and we'll try and figure it out together." She stood next to him, and George stopped what he was doing to listen. "What's this orisha?"

"The statue is *La Virgen de la Candelaria,* or Our Lady of Candlemas. Another not well known saint, but as orishas go, Oya is the owner of the marketplace and followed by plenty of business owners." Julio took a few steps toward the circle and pointed. "Her colors are brown and burgundy, and she loves chocolate pudding, but true followers would've made it from scratch. Her sacred number is nine, and she's also known for being a fierce warrior who wields a machete."

"That would explain this, then," George said, holding up the large evidence bag with a machete inside. "We found it driven through her mouth and stuck to the floor," he told Julio. "You can see the picture, but I couldn't look at her like that anymore."

"From what's here, what do you think the meaning is?" Sept asked, and she heard a few people coming in.

"Jesus H. Christ," Fritz yelled, placing his hands on knees. "What the fuck is this?"

"Sir, this is Dr. Julio Munez, the expert from Tulane helping us with the scenes," she said, thinking eventually someone new would contaminate the scene with puke. "If you could allow him to finish, I'll bring you up to speed."

"Oya is an odd choice, but I can only speculate as to why she was chosen."

"Speculation isn't a bad word, Dr. Munez," Fritz said.

"Alex Perlis stole the books from Estella Mendoza, then killed a woman in her store," Julio said, and something Keegan had mentioned made her guess where he was going with this.

"To duplicate Frieda Herns's murder would be tricky and almost impossible," she said, and Julio nodded. Keegan had questioned that if the murders had all completely duplicated Perlis's order, how would the killer copy that one. "Instead of choosing a place of business, the kill is dedicated to the goddess of the marketplace."

"Yes, but you're right about this being so different, since the heart and other pieces are missing," Julio said.

"What the hell?" Fritz asked, as if just noticing that Judy's breasts, ears, and heart weren't in the altar circle.

"The killer took souvenirs this time, sir. Did you think of something?" she asked Julio.

"Oya is also the keeper of the cemetery gates."

"I thought the cemetery was someone else's domain?" she asked, and Julio shook his head.

"The first day with the police officers, the killer marked them with the path of Afra, which linked them with the woman at Elegua's altar, but Afra is the gatherer of the dead. This orisha guards and keeps the gate where Afra's path leads them," Julio said.

"Excuse me." Sept stepped outside and told the closest couple of police officers, "Put a list together of all the cemeteries close to here, and I mean all of them. I don't care what religious denomination. I need it now."

"What are you thinking?" Fritz asked.

"I don't think the souvenirs were to keep." She cocked her head to Judy's body. "The altar's offerings had to go somewhere else."

"What does this asshole want?" Fritz asked Julio.

"Aside from the degradation of my religion?" Julio asked, breathing shallowly, as if not wanting to contaminate his lungs with the negative air in the room. "I don't know, sir. Hopefully people like Detective Savoie will eventually figure it out, but all I see here is someone who wants to kill for the simple sake of it. Nothing more than that jumps out at me."

"Why pick these crimes, of all things?" Fritz asked, but his question didn't seem directed at anyone in particular.

"We thought it might be a disciple of Teacher, or Teacher himself," she said, but neither of those choices seemed right.

"And now you don't?" Julio asked.

"I don't really know what to think just yet, but I do want to find the body parts and see if they lead us somewhere."

Jennifer had finished taking pictures from every angle, so George removed the black cloth from Judy's upper face and cursed. "Fuck me. The eyes are missing too."

"The eyes?" she asked, and something clicked in her mind. It had been something she'd read, but she had to do a few things first. She made a note to find the reference later, but something about eyes jogged her memory.

"I hope to hell for Judy's sake he did all this after she was dead," George said.

"I hope so too, but for now let's see if we can bury her with as much dignity as possible," she said, and Fritz turned around and stared at the door. "Julio, will you come with me?" Sept asked.

"Whatever you need, I'll try to help you."

"Then pray for answers, but for now we need to take a ride."

CHAPTER TWENTY-THREE

W hy so quiet tonight?" Brian Voles asked Nicole as he cut a piece of steak and waited for her answer before placing it in his mouth. "You're not thinking of giving up, are you?"

"I'll get what I need without police input," Nicole said, twirling pasta onto her fork. "The police are your take on the book and what's happening now, not mine." She gazed at him as she took a bite of her meal, licking her lips slowly when she was done. "What would you be doing if the current investigation was yours?"

"I'd concentrate on the explosives," he said, his nostrils flaring as she enjoyed another bite. "If they're the result of a serial bomber they'll have a certain signature. That's where they can find a lead to solving this case."

"The agents in Hicks's office won't share with you?"

"Anabel must be fucking someone in DC to keep this job." He chewed the meat like he was a vicious animal. "She's not taking my calls and has her people running interference for her. Her bomb experts are working with NOPD, which is unheard of, if you're true FBI. This should be her show, and the local idiots should be kept where they belong, on the sidelines. Either way, no one's talking."

"Maybe we should leak their lack of cooperation to the papers and news."

"If you did that to me, I'd shut you out permanently." He cut another piece of steak and dipped it into his mashed potatoes. "We need to start checking the police scanner and simply show up. Until we luck out, you need your NOPD contact to agree to a meet. I want to talk to him."

"You can do that alone?" She slid her hand across the table and touched the tips of his fingers. "I've got a few more meetings set up with Alex, and I don't want to miss them."

"Has he said anything interesting?" Brian didn't move his hand away from hers as he picked up his wineglass. "The fucker should do everyone a favor and hang himself before the city has to spend a fortune to try him."

"He's starting to trust me, and I think the thrill of being memorialized in a book is starting to thaw his frozen throat. A few more visits and I should have the whole story." She pushed her plate away, not hungry for any more food. "What do you think about the bombs?"

"In my opinion they're a diversion," he said, picking up his scotch. "It's the same with people. Usually loud showoffs are busy screaming at the world for attention, but it's when they're quiet that you should really be looking."

"And what are they usually doing?"

"The world is full of two kinds of people, sweet girl. Those who fuck, and those who get fucked over." He finished his drink, and she signaled the waiter for another.

"Where do we fall in the grand scheme of things?" She pulled on his index finger and smiled. "Maybe it'll give me a hint to get Alex to open up to me."

"Hopefully I taught you to always be in control and on top. You're too smart and too beautiful to be anyone's bitch." He smiled, and like in some instances, she found his expression more cruel than pleasing. "You have to grab him by the proverbial balls and squeeze. Then you simply have to demand he talk, and he will."

"I see." She leaned back and crossed her legs. "Back to the bombs. What are they a diversion from?"

"I can't say without the facts." He glanced from the new drink to her knee that her skirt riding up had exposed.

"You must have some idea."

"Maybe the killer should have skipped killing the two police officers since they drew attention somewhere unimportant." He swallowed half the new drink and began twirling the glass again.

"Why a mistake?"

"Doing anything that galvanizes every law-enforcement agency in town against them wasn't the smart play. That's my take, but my job is to find the bad guys, not plan the crimes. The FBI has taught me to think like a killer, but somehow I can't dumb myself down that much."

He finished his third drink and asked for the check. "Though I could be wrong."

"We'll see, I guess, but I'll always bet on you, Daddy."

"Shall we continue this at home?"

"I have another appointment, so maybe later." She lifted his hand and leaned over to kiss his knuckles. "Much later."

❖

"Sept," the radio dispatcher said after one of the uniforms handed his radio over and changed it to a secure line.

"Yes, ma'am. Go ahead."

"One of the units called in, and they found what you're looking for. That's all they reported since they said you'd understand."

"I know what they mean. Where are they?"

"Outside Lafayette Cemetery on Washington," the woman said. It was like a punch to the gut. "You know where that is?"

"Yeah, thanks." She waved to Julio to get into the car, and she sped off. Lafayette Cemetery was directly across from Blanchard's Restaurant. If it was what she was thinking, the bitch had made a point to leave a message. "I know exactly where it is."

The valets at the restaurant were all staring at the entrance to the cemetery and the police car with the blue flashing lights. "Turn those off," she said as she got out. "Where is it?"

"It's actually the entrance across from this one, on the other side," the officer said, pointing through the wrought-iron gates. "John sent us over here to cover the block."

"Do it without the pretty lights so we don't freak out the full and happy people coming out of there." She drove around the block and walked to the gate with Julio. A larger police presence was there, but they stayed outside as she and Julio headed right in and to the right of the gate, where the two candles flickered in the very slight breeze.

"Someone cut the lock," John said, stopping at a magnolia tree to the right of the gate against the wall, "and left this."

It was another altar, complete with candles and another statue like the one in Judy's home. She grabbed John's arm when he tried to move closer. "Call those bomb guys back."

"Why? You see something?" John asked but stayed next to her.

A heart, breasts, and ears lay in the circle, and she wanted to collect them, but she thought about her father's warning. "Something's hinky about this, so let's be sure."

They didn't have to wait long, and again the explosives experts cleared them out. Sept took a few minutes to call Keegan so she wouldn't be scared if she happened to look outside. "Can I stop by and see you?" Keegan asked. "Joel didn't mind waiting until we got through our busiest seating, since I didn't want to leave Louis in the lurch, but we're ready to go."

"Not this time, baby. Just go home, and I'll be there as soon as I can. Is Nathan still there?"

"I put him in the office with Joel, but I couldn't talk him into eating anything. This is the most bizarre thing. That poor woman."

"We'll talk about it later, but you're right about that." One of the bomb guys came out and held his hand up to her. "I'll call you later, but I have to go."

"Love you, and be careful."

"Love you too, and remember not to leave alone."

"Detective Savoie," the federal agent said. "We've got a situation, so good call."

"What'd you find?" The rest of the team came out to retrieve more equipment.

"The statue has enough C4 to take out everyone here. Whoever your perp is, the guy's got a seemingly endless supply of the stuff."

"Thanks, and be careful. We'll clear the area until you're done," she said, and the guy nodded.

"Might be a little while," the guy said, getting back into his protective gear. "We're trying to save it for the evidence value if it doesn't go off, but if it's too dangerous, we'll blow it in place."

"Take your time." She reported back to George and the others and apologized to Julio for keeping him so long. He stayed in the car with his eyes closed, softly mouthing prayers, but he wasn't leaving until he helped her. "Hey," she said to Gustave, "where are you?"

"Closing out the Rollings scene, trying to keep the chief and Dad from having matching strokes. You need something?"

"No. I was wondering if you found anything else."

"Gavin came out himself and said to pass along that he'd found the same needle mark on her shoulder area. They finished a few minutes ago and loaded Rollings for transport. As soon as we lock up I'll meet you there."

She told him what was happening and to inform their father. After the call, she joined George and Jennifer in their van, remembering the note she'd made to herself. "Did you ever get anything back from the toe someone sent me?"

"We handed it off for DNA testing," George said as Jennifer typed something into her laptop. "With everything going on, I haven't pushed them for results, considering where it came from."

"I need the results as fast as you can get them."

"Do you want me to have Gustave or one of the others follow up?" George asked.

"No. Tonight, all this made me think about it." The delivery on the happiest day of her life suddenly had her believing that the smallest clue that made no sense might be a key to unlocking something important.

The team came out of the cemetery with a metal box, which meant they'd retrieved the bomb without it going off. "It's clear, but we want to do one more sweep," the same guy told her.

They sat on their heels for another hour before she went in with Julio. The circle wasn't like any they'd come across, and it made her suck in a breath. "My God," she said.

Julio genuflected and lowered his head. "Yes, my God," he said, sounding like he was speaking around a lump in his throat.

The altar was missing the statue but was like a gruesome triangle of horror. Judy Rollings's heart, ears, and another cup of chocolate pudding made the triangle, and that was bad enough until you looked in the middle. The eyes that had been one of the things Nathan had on his list of things he adored about Judy Rollings sat there like macabre Halloween decorations.

"Can you figure out anything from this?" she asked Julio as she fought the fatigue that fell over her like a wet, hot blanket. She wasn't tired from her day, but from all this shit.

"This person is a sadistic bastard," Julio said and pointed to the eyes. "What's that?"

"George," she said, and they had to wait again while they took pictures and collected evidence. George and Jennifer collected all the body parts, leaving the eyes for last so they could investigate the square they were sitting on. "It's a laminated card," she said when George handed the last of the gore to one of his guys.

She waited until Jennifer placed it in an evidence bag. It was handwritten in block letters with a smiley face, of all things, at the bottom. "Was there a note in the other statue?" she asked Jennifer, getting her to glance up from reading the note.

"We found a folded piece of paper, but we always wait until we get to the office before opening these messages. Maybe that was a decoy, and this is the note."

Detective, do you see me yet?
Do you hear my voice in your waking dreams?
Do you get tired of carrying a title you don't deserve?
How long before the faithful desert you for your falseness?
Do you see what's right in front of you before it's too late?
Hunter

"If it was meant to be a decoy, Hunter would've left the first one empty. The second statue would've been the logical place to look, and if it had been on a motion trigger, it would've killed us all." She studied the altar again with only the candles burning. Why had Hunter gone so far astray from Perlis's methods?

"What?" Julio asked, as if trying to read her mind and failing.

"This isn't about the orishas or proving something to the warrior god Chango," she said, holding the taunting note up.

"I've told you that repeatedly from the day we met. Alex Perlis may not be crazy, but he's twisted my faith into this horror," Julio said, his head cocked slightly as if mesmerized by the candle flames.

"You're right about your faith, but Perlis was a believer. He might've twisted the rituals of your religion for something he desperately wanted, but he believed in what he was doing—that the altars and sacrifices he made would give him something he thought stolen from him."

George, Jennifer, and Julio stared at her as if expecting her to blurt out the end to the story and solve the case. "I understand what you're getting at, but where are you going with it?" Julio asked.

"This isn't some twisted religious fanatic following a path Teacher set out, and it isn't Teacher trying to get his disciple back." She said the words out loud, which helped order her thoughts as she glanced at the altar again. "Move," she yelled suddenly and startled them all into running for the gate.

"What the hell?" George said, out of breath, probably from the sudden sprint and the fright.

"Get back in there and throw something over those candles," she barked at the federal agent who was in the process of stripping his protective suit off. "Get back in there now. This sick fuck doesn't get to damage this place. Move."

The bomb squad ran back in, awkwardly carrying what appeared to be a heavy box. Her group all stood outside the wall and waited, and as if on cue, they heard a muffled explosion. That was it, though. She didn't see any kind of visible damage to the wall, but until the bomb squad came back out, she made everyone stay put. A minute later she heard another muffled explosion.

"How'd you know?" Jennifer asked, gazing at her like she'd set the damn things and, only through her kindness, saved them all at the last second.

"'Do you see what's right in front of you before it's too late?'" She quoted the note. "The statue was the decoy, the second one, I mean."

"Shit, you must be really good at the game Clue," Jennifer said, leaning forward and putting her hands on her knees. "Thank you. If I'd been blown up, Chloe would've been pissed."

"What were you going to say earlier?" Julio asked after laughing at Jennifer's attempt at humor.

"These copycat murders aren't about calling the dead or answering the call Perlis put out. They aren't about finishing Teacher's work. They're about showing all of us how much smarter Hunter is than any of us." The proof wasn't there yet, but it seemed closer than it had the day before, just a little beyond her reach. "She can kill with impunity even those of us trained to protect others."

"So the bombs aren't to throw us off any evidence left behind?" George asked.

"Yes, but it's more than that. This game is like any other one. It started at level one, and as we work our way up, the clues will get harder, and the penalty phases will carry more risk." She turned when the guys came back out, their box now a tangled mess. "Thank you," she told them. "This is hard enough without the preservation people on my ass."

"You sure you don't want to switch teams?" the federal guy asked. "You're damn handy to have around."

"Thanks, but I'm happy in my little pond. Usually it's not this exciting, but lately it's been a real blast."

CHAPTER TWENTY-FOUR

Sept let herself in and stood in the quiet, dark kitchen, needing the stillness around her. She didn't open her eyes when she felt Keegan press against her, sliding her hands to her ass. It was the first time in this very long night that she'd allowed herself to think about what Nathan had lost, and more importantly, what she still had.

Keegan went willingly when she bent over and lifted her, needing to kiss her to prove Keegan was fine, alive, and still the sexy woman who'd stolen her heart—her reason. She moaned when Keegan wrapped her legs around her and bit her bottom lip as if to get her out of her head and pay attention to the here and now. They weren't alone in the house, but right now she could give a damn. She needed to touch Keegan and forget everything but her.

She went up the stairs with Keegan wrapped around her, trying desperately to make it to the bed. It was difficult since she was as hard as the bullets in her gun, and Keegan was sucking on her neck like she was addicted to her skin. She closed the door as quietly as she could, flipping the lock before she walked to the bed to put Keegan down. They didn't exchange a word as Keegan pulled her T-shirt over her head before starting on the buttons of Sept's shirt.

"I've been waiting for you," Keegan said, tugging on her shoulder holster so she could get the shirt off. As Sept struggled out of her holster, Keegan made her intentions clear by unbuttoning her pants. "I know you need to talk, but first I need you to fuck me." Her words were like a hot shot of adrenaline to her groin.

The sleep pants Keegan was wearing almost ripped as she tried to take them off without moving her mouth away. It seemed like an eternity, but they were finally naked, and she knelt behind Keegan, the position giving her access to Keegan's upper body while she pressed back against her groin. She pinched and tugged on Keegan's nipples, loving the way Keegan's hips bucked upward like she was reminding her where she needed her most.

"Baby, I've been waiting all night," Keegan said, looping her right arm behind her head to make Sept lower her for a kiss. "I'm wet and so ready for you."

She flattened her hands over Keegan's abdomen and touched all the way down until she stroked through the wetness between her legs. "Fuck," she said as Keegan brought her free hand back up to her breast. "You're so wet."

"I've needed you since you left here," Keegan said, then moaned loud enough for Sept to feel the sound in her chest and groin. "Make me...damn." Keegan stopped as her strokes became firmer and faster. "I need to come, honey."

She moved her hand away, only to lay Keegan down and spread her legs so she could bend and put her mouth on her. The orgasm wasn't far off, and while she wanted to make it last, she wouldn't do that to Keegan. She slid her fingers in and sucked hard, her tongue moving over the hard clit in firm, fast swipes. Keegan seemed to be on fire, and she rocked her hips against her mouth and fingers.

"Jesus," Keegan said in a low, throaty tone. "I'm—" Sept took her fingers out and slammed them back in. "I'm coming—don't stop." Keegan moved her hips in time with her strokes and finally went rigid and tugged her head up by pulling on her hair. "Stop."

"Thanks, my love," she said, coming up and opening her arms so Keegan could press against her. "That's the best thing that's happened to me all day."

"Me too, and 'thank you' should be my line." Keegan kissed the side of her neck and moved on top of her. "I love the way you touch me." Keegan pressed her hand between them and rubbed her fingers over Sept's clit. The pace was excruciatingly slow, but no matter how much she squirmed, Keegan didn't speed up.

"Are you being overly cruel today?" she asked, since she needed to come, but Keegan's light, slow touch would keep her hovering forever.

"Tell me what you want?" Keegan asked, never stopping her fingers.

"I need you to make me come." She reached down and squeezed Keegan's ass.

"That's not helping my concentration," Keegan said, rocking her hips. "And I have a promise to keep." Keegan moved down and sucked her until she wanted to sob from coming so hard.

"Your mouth is a thing of beauty that should be worshipped," she said, so relaxed she was almost melting into the bed.

"You think my mouth should have followers?" Keegan asked, moving to cover her again. "I thought you were the jealous type."

"I am, and the cult following would consist of one member." She put her hands on Keegan's hips and smiled, not something she'd done all night. "Where'd you stash Nathan?"

"He's in the guest room next to Jacqueline, and Joel is downstairs on the couch. After we got home he didn't want us to be alone, so he stayed to protect us." Keegan rested her head on her chest and kissed the side of her mouth. "Nathan feels guilty for what happened. I think he wasn't in love with Judy, but having a good time really cost her." She kissed Sept again and rubbed the top of her shoulder. "I made that tea Julio sent with him, and he was out like I'd coldcocked him before I got the door closed. That's good, I guess."

"I'll make sure he's okay, but it'll be hard to forget the image we saw tonight." She blew out a long breath, frustrated they weren't further along in their investigation. "It was harsh, and I've seen some sick stuff in my time."

"Do you want to talk about it? It isn't fair that you carry this horrible stuff alone." Keegan moved her hand to the spot over her heart.

"Baby, I don't talk about it because I don't want you to have nightmares from just the mental image of it all. That's what wouldn't be fair." She rolled over and pressed herself to Keegan's body. "You help me by just being here and reminding me that we have love enough in both of us to overshadow anything."

"I'm tougher than I look, Seven, so my offer's good. More than anything, I hate seeing you suffer."

She nodded, then put her forehead down on Keegan's chest when her phone rang. "If this bitch killed someone else tonight, I quit."

"Answer it, and then you can explain the bitch part."

"Savoie," she said after getting the cell out of her pants on the floor.

"I didn't wake you, did I?" Jennifer asked. "Sorry for calling so late, but George put in a call about the DNA test for the toe you received in the mail. We have a profile, but the donor isn't in the system."

"Thanks. Not what I wanted to hear, but it'll give me something to think about."

"Bad news?" Keegan asked as she put her phone on the nightstand.

"Our gruesome gift remains a mystery." After Keegan piled the pillows against the headboard, she moved to a sitting position and sighed as Keegan straddled her. They could face each other while they talked, and she enjoyed the closeness.

"Tell me about the bitch comment."

"The day we were dispatched to the Cenac scene, there was an explosion in the Hilton parking garage. They didn't call us because they didn't think it was related." These discussions were so much nicer with a naked Keegan on her lap.

"I saw that on the news, but I didn't think it had anything to do with you," Keegan said, smiling, probably because her eyes had momentarily strayed from her face. "You're telling me it was related to your case?"

"A very relaxed person dressed like the Unabomber came out of the stairwell, walked calmly to the lot next door, and stole a car. That car then showed up at the Cenac scene with two dead teenagers next to it." She stopped when Keegan kissed her.

"Sorry, but I find your cop mode extremely sexy," Keegan said, kissing her again and pressing her hips down. "Go on."

"When we finally got a chance to watch the security tapes, something stuck out."

"What?" Keegan asked seriously.

"The hoodie and glasses obscured the face, but the walk was totally female. I think my suspect is a woman," she said, the thought more sobering now than ever. It'd take a totally cold-hearted bitch to do what was done to Judy Rollings.

"You're not kidding, are you?" Keegan pushed away a few inches as if to see her face better. "Do you think it's someone Alex Perlis knows?"

"In the morning I have to see the entire timeline and crime-scene photos again before I can answer that question. The missing piece hasn't hit me yet, but I'm positive it's there." She pulled Keegan closer and rubbed circles on her back. "Talking helps, so thank you."

"Are you sure you don't want to talk about tonight?" Keegan said softly against the side of her neck.

"Judy Rollings was mutilated, and unlike all the others, some of her body parts were left in the cemetery across from Blanchard's. It killed me that this happened to her only because she was dating Nathan and that her death came only because he's my partner. It really kills me that he walked in there and saw that."

Keegan held on to her tighter and kissed right under her jaw. "Nathan might not have a lot of family, but he has you, honey. It'll take time, but he'll get over it."

"I'd never met the woman, and I might not get over it," she said and couldn't help but yawn. "Sorry. It's been a long night."

"Lie back and let's go to sleep," Keegan said, moving off her, but not too far away. "All you need is some rest to clear your head."

"What I need is some luck," she said as Keegan rolled over and snuggled her butt into her crotch.

"What exactly do you call what happened in this room tonight, Seven?" Keegan said teasingly. "You're plenty lucky, and you better not forget it."

"You're right, and I've said that for months. I'm one lucky bastard."

❖

Nicole sat with the other five people in the visitors' waiting area at the jail and sighed. The night before had been frustrating, since she'd called her NOPD contact and the idiot had refused to pick up no matter what she threatened. She'd had to let that go right then and concentrate on getting Alex to open up to her.

"Grab him by the proverbial balls," she said softly, repeating what her father had said. He was right, but the way Brian expressed himself at times still made her smile.

"Ms. Voles." The deputy at the door yelled her name. "In there." He pointed to a room like the one where Gretchen had met with Alex. She'd have to call Gretchen later and thank her for the chance of privacy.

Alex shuffled in bent and slow, as usual. It would've been interesting to see him before his incarceration, because now he appeared like a ghost who could barely stand straight. "You can take those off," she said when the deputy started to leave Alex in his leg irons and cuffs.

"Are you sure?"

"I'm sure we'll be fine."

Alex stared at her while the deputy keyed open his feet first. The near haze in his eyes never seemed to leave him, and the madness appeared to be robbing him of any pride he had left. He no longer showered, and his hair hadn't been washed in the same amount of time. His hatred of Sept Savoie had also cooled, and the apathy of letting that go might give her father what he'd asked for. Alex wasn't too far from taking his own life.

"What do you want?" Alex asked, twirling a long strand of oily hair.

"You need to talk to me," she said gently. "I know you don't have any fear, having served Teacher and the orishas, but the gods will fall silent if you don't help me."

"You don't know anything. I killed plenty of bitches like you," Alex said, then laughed like a simpleton.

"You mean like your wife Sonya? Or maybe your little boy? They couldn't fight back, and I'd like to know if that made you feel like a man." She spoke in a low but firm voice.

"You don't—"

"Shut the fuck up and listen. You're nothing but a coward who loved beating on his family because he couldn't beat on someone like Sept Savoie." She pointed her index finger at him, and he caved sooner than she imagined. She'd have to thank her father later.

"What do you want from me?" Alex lowered his head and put his hands in his lap.

"Tell me why you did it." When he opened his mouth, she put her hand up. "And don't give me that crap about seeing your family again. That might've come later when you stole the books and understood what you were doing, but that wasn't the case in the beginning. Isn't that true?"

"That's all I wanted. I needed my family back, but that big bitch stopped me before I could finish." The tone he started with was low, but when he mentioned Sept his anger seemed to reignite.

"You can't lie to me." She leaned closer and stuck her finger into his face. "You know who sent me, and if you don't tell the truth, I won't tell you what you most want to hear."

"You don't know what I want, and you sure as fuck can't give it to me." His confidence was growing, and his whole demeanor as a hardened killer was emerging from hibernation.

"This is what I know about you, Alex," she said, trying to keep her outer façade neutral. "You're going to rot in here. Sept Savoie is going to convince them to put a needle in your arm and kill you. The last thought that will cross your pathetically feeble mind will be that she won. You'll be dumped in a hole, forgotten by everyone." She tapped her nails on the table and smiled. "The same will not be true of Sept Savoie."

The way Alex stared at her made her think that if he could get away with it, he'd kill her right then without regret. But when she didn't lower her eyes, his bravado seemed to falter. "That first guy was standing outside bitching about something, and I scared him when I entered that yard out back."

"Why were you there?" she asked, clicking on her recorder.

"I didn't want to be home after Sonya left, and I started walking where I could find people. The knife that belonged to my father just seemed like something to carry with me. I was all alone then, and I needed it." He recounted the story mechanically, and then something must've occurred to him when he balled his fists. "Does that bitch have it? I want my knife to go to my son."

"I'll take care of it," she said, playing along with his crazy. "Finish."

"The guy was scared at first, but I was wearing a police shirt, and it dropped his guard. We talked for a little while, and he told me what he did." The laugh he let out transformed his face, and she smiled, hoping he'd share the joke. "I could tell he was checking me out—he was that kind."

Good God, there were still Neanderthals in the world, but she didn't expect less from this guy. "You made a pass at him?"

"Better. I told him to close his eyes and I'd give him something he'd love." The way Alex was rubbing his thighs made her think he was reliving his kill, and it excited him. He then mimicked the motion as if he had a knife in his hand. "That guy died with this shocked look on his face, and he fell slowly. First to his knees, and then I pushed him to his back."

"You stayed, though. Why?" Above all else she wanted him to think she already knew all the answers.

"I thought someone would come kill me, but I couldn't walk away when I pulled my knife free and the blood came out like someone was squeezing it out of him. My pants were soaked with the shit, but I didn't care. I'd finally done it, and I proved all those fuckers who thought I was a loser wrong."

"Good, Novice," she said softly, and he stared at her as if he'd heard incorrectly. "Tell me about the second one. The one that brought me to you."

"Teacher?" He raised his hand and reached across to her. Their contact was brief, but he appeared happier when she touched his fingers. "It's really you."

"Tell me."

"The bitch in the park was to prove to you and to myself that I could do it. Once she was dead I was ready for you. I drew that stuff on her chest to call you."

"You did well, but another has started from where you failed."

"What do you mean?" His eyes were filled with tears that appeared to be about to spill but hadn't.

"My altars have come back, and the warrior is chasing a new novice. This time, though, they won't be caught." She turned the recorder off for this exchange, but it didn't matter. She'd remember the conversation verbatim.

"I did everything you asked," he said, and his tears finally started to fall. "You can't leave me."

"I'm not leaving you." She took his hand and smiled. "I still need you. I want to hear the rest of your story, and I'll tell you about the battles to come."

She stood and knocked on the door for the deputy. All she needed now was to fill in the blanks, and she could get the rest of what she was missing. "Remember to keep your mouth shut until I get back to you. Don't disobey me, or you'll pay."

"Yes, Teacher."

"You're not alone anymore."

CHAPTER TWENTY-FIVE

Sept sat outside sipping the coffee she'd made, content to watch Mike run around the yard sniffing things and marking his territory like it was his mission in life. She'd slept for a solid four hours and woke up so completely that she knew she couldn't sleep any longer unless someone anesthetized her. She had too much on her mind.

"I hate waking up alone when you're in the house," she heard Keegan say from the door. The sun was just coming up and the morning was cool, so she put her arms around Keegan when she sat on her lap.

"I was trying to be considerate and let you sleep." She kissed Keegan and handed over her mug. Keegan had changed plenty about her when it came to what she ate and drank, but she'd started small with her coffee. It was snobby, but now it was hard to take any cup that didn't come out of a Blanchard kitchen. "Did I wake you?"

"I think I sensed you were gone, and I had to come find you. What are you doing out here? Is the dog more alluring than me?"

"No one is more alluring than you. It's just that I haven't been back at work that long, and this woman has buried me in crap. It's overkill, but I think she's trying to fill my head with so much minutia I'll lose the big picture." She sighed but smiled when Keegan bit her earlobe. "I'm drowning and I'm worried. I need to see that big picture since it's where all the little stuff comes together."

"What are you worried about besides that?" Keegan asked, sounding so compassionate she wanted to carry her back inside.

"You," she said, closing her eyes because that's what had really woken her up. She could try to ignore that fear, but that's what it came down to. "I'm going to do what I can to try to help Nathan through this pain, but last night scared the hell out of me."

"What can I do to make you feel better?" Keegan didn't hesitate to offer to change her routine to take the pressure off her.

"You shouldn't have to change anything because of my job, sweetheart, and I'm not going to ask you to." She couldn't leave her such an open target either, and thinking about her getting hurt or worse made her tense.

"Honey, look at me." Keegan placed her hands on her cheeks. "If I can do anything to make you stop worrying so much, I'm willing to do it. I know how you tick, so I know that stopping altogether isn't in you. But something has to help you function better at work. The way I see it, if you're not obsessed about my safety you can concentrate on what will keep *you* in one piece."

"I'll think of something, but until then, you'll have to be happy with me watching over you."

"Don't try to fool me. You've already thought of something, but that last statement is just an excuse to look at my ass all day." Keegan pinched her cheeks. "Come on. You can chop stuff for me since we've got guests to feed."

They cooked together, and Joel joined them an hour later as Keegan placed a tray of biscuits in the oven. Sept's last single brother had spent plenty of time with them as he and Jacqueline flirted, but they hadn't moved much beyond that point.

"Thanks for staying last night," she told him as he poured himself a cup of coffee.

"I didn't mind, and it made me feel better to be here. Nathan was in bad shape."

"You can't blame him for that," she said as she started on the pile of fruit Keegan had put in front of her. "That scene was rough."

"Yeah, it was, and I had no idea he and Judy were dating. She was really sweet."

"You knew her?" Keegan asked.

"Not well, but we'd talked a few times when we crossed paths." Joel sat at the counter and smiled. "Who knew you'd become so domesticated, sis?"

"It's the private cooking lessons," Keegan said and winked. "They've warped my baby's mind."

"Does Jacqueline give those?" He winked back.

"If she does, bring some antacids with you," Sept said, jumping when Jacqueline pinched her hard on the ass. She'd come in from the front undetected and covered in sweat. "Did you go out alone?"

"Yes, and I go to the bathroom alone too." Jacqueline pinched her again, getting her to side-shuffle. "I'm all grown up."

"You are, but if you go running alone again or pinch my ass one more time, I'm going to put you over my knee," she said seriously. "You're either going to have to invest in a nice treadmill or come wake me up, and I'll go with you."

"Another bad night?" Jacqueline asked, as if understanding.

"Nathan's girlfriend was murdered," Keegan said.

"Man, poor Nathan," Jacqueline said and turned when she heard him come down.

"I'll be okay, I guess, but I don't know how I'm going to get there," Nathan said.

"When I lost my sister and niece, the same thing dominated my thoughts," she said, and Joel nodded. "The pain is still there, but time starts to dull it, and if you allow yourself the chance, letting someone in helps. Love is the best balm for any wound."

"Do I take the chance some other woman will end up in pieces, though?" Nathan asked, and Jacqueline shivered at the description.

"I know you won't believe me, but what happened to Judy isn't your fault. If anything, it's mine. I should've said something, since this perp is like Perlis and makes the game personal." She smiled when Keegan pressed against one side and Jacqueline against the other. "We all can't stop living our lives, but maybe we can get some advice from someone with plenty of experience on how to live it surrounded by heavily armed people."

"What's that supposed to mean?" Jacqueline asked.

"Royce or my father won't spare the manpower to watch over you when I can't, but I know someone who will. Trust me on this one."

"We trust you, Seven, but if this involves me or Jacqueline carrying a gun, forget it," Keegan said.

"No guns, but if you love me, you'll play along."

"We do love you, but keep in mind we inherited our revenge gene from Della," Jacqueline said, pinching her yet again and making her laugh. "Paybacks, stud. They are a bitch."

❖

Sept sat on the edge of the bed to put her boots on and stopped when Keegan walked out of the bathroom naked. They'd showered together after Joel left with Nathan with a promise to meet her at the precinct.

Joel had reluctantly agreed to the favor she'd asked of him when she'd gotten him alone, and part of her hoped she was wrong, especially after Perlis had eroded some of the public's trust in the police.

She leaned back slightly when Keegan straddled her legs and kissed her. "You're a cruel woman," she said as Keegan bit and tugged on her bottom lip. "Baby, I just got dressed," she said, but her resolve was weak.

"Take your pants off," Keegan said, standing up. "Hurry up, or I'm going to mess them up, and those just came back from the cleaners."

"Do fresh biscuits make you horny?" She stood, took her pants off, and handed them to Keegan. It was humorous to watch her fold them neatly over a chair, even though her nipples were hard as hell.

"You make me horny, and we ran out of hot water," Keegan said, sitting back down on her lap.

She spread her legs, which in turn spread Keegan's, and she could fit her hand between them. "Is this what you want, beautiful?"

"I want all of you," Keegan said, her eyes glassy. "Sorry. I think I'm ovulating or something." The comment stopped Sept's hand.

"Is there something you want to tell me?" She wet her fingertips and rubbed them over Keegan's hard clit. "You can, you know. I'll give you whatever you want, especially if it's something we both want."

"Even if that something is a baby?" Keegan asked, putting her arms around her neck. "I know it might be too soon, but I'm not getting any younger."

"If my answer is yes, can we talk about it later?" The way Keegan was rocking into her made her want to concentrate on the moment. She slid two fingers in and kissed Keegan as her hips pumped faster and harder against her hand. When Keegan stopped and went rigid, she cupped her ass with her other hand and held her. "If you use this method, feel free to ask me anything you want." Keegan laughed and squeezed her sex around her fingers one last time as she took them out.

"Actually, I was thinking this method." Keegan dropped to her knees and put her mouth on her until she dug her toes into the rug and came so hard she felt like she'd pulled a muscle in her butt.

"How about a cold shower?" she asked as Keegan kissed her sex before coming up to join her. "You can tell me more about our baby."

"I want you and me to have a family," Keegan said, shivering when she got in the shower after her as if to avoid as much of the cold spray as possible. "If you want to wait, I'll be okay with that but—"

"My love, I'd love nothing more than to share that with you." She kissed Keegan and held her before asking something important. "I've got one question, though."

"What?" Keegan's smile was beautiful.

"Della won't kill me if I get you pregnant before this big shindig, will she?"

"I'll protect you from Della as long as you make the appointment I scheduled in three days."

"Get out of here before we catch a cold."

They dressed and went down together, where Jacqueline was doing paperwork at the kitchen table. "I want one of those tankless water heaters for my birthday," Jacqueline said.

"Okay," Sept said, lengthening the word. "Is your birthday coming up?"

"No, but if you keep having sex in the shower, my health is going to suffer," Jacqueline said, pointing at her. "We're in the food industry, sexy. We can't afford to have the sniffles."

"I'll put that on my list." She kissed Keegan and grabbed her keys. "Be careful today, okay?"

Keegan and Jacqueline both nodded and walked her to the door. "You take that advice too, okay," Jacqueline said. "I love you, so don't mess that up."

She hugged Jacqueline and kissed her cheek before hugging Keegan and kissing her on the lips again. "I will, and I'll call you later. Don't take candy from strangers."

The sisters laughed, and it made her heart hurt to think of something happening to either of them.

"Can you spare five minutes?" she asked the person on the phone once she was in the car. "Great, where are you?" It was time to do something about keeping her family safe.

❖

"Hey, Sept, you can park inside. The boss said she'd make an exception for you," the big guy at the gate teased. This was the only spot on the property where you could see the house because of the large brick wall surrounding the place.

"Thanks." She drove in, and another guy pointed to the side of the house.

"If you're looking for a bribe, I gave at the office," Derby Cain Casey said as she clipped roses.

"I'm sure you have," she said and laughed. Cain was the "alleged" head of a large crime family in New Orleans, but they'd graduated from high school and Tulane together and become good friends. She'd never bend the law for Cain, and Cain would never ask her to, which was why they were still close. "I did come to ask a favor, though."

"Come on." Cain walked to the back of the house and entered through the kitchen. Sept knew it was to keep her away from the constant surveillance parked right outside. "You want some coffee?" Cain handed the roses to the woman in the kitchen, who left with them.

"If you've watched the news lately, you know I'm working another big case," she stated, trying to decide how to ask or if this was even a good idea.

"Sit down, you idiot, and tell me how you're doing first. It's not every day I've got a cop hero in my kitchen. I've stayed away because I didn't want to complicate things for you." Cain poured them each some orange juice and sat across from her. "Your mom fed me updates, but it's good to see you."

"Thanks for the bottle of Jameson for my health. It was all worth it to get Keegan in my life." She smiled when Cain punched her arm. The Casey family members were regulars at Blanchard's and some of Keegan's favorite customers, especially Cain's wife Emma.

"I heard the big news that you were off the market. You'd better behave, though, or Della Blanchard will mess you up."

"I do understand that about her." She laughed at Cain's words. Though the FBI didn't like her, Cain had friends in every corner of the city.

"Good. Tell me what you need so I can give it to you already," Cain said, lifting her glass and taking a sip. "Unless you want me to take Della out. Then you're on your own."

She smiled, then told Cain what she could about the night before and the call from Hunter. "That conversation left me cold. I'm so sorry for Judy, but had it been Keegan on that floor I would've eaten a bullet. I can't tell her that, but I'm sure you feel the same way about Emma."

"You must love her if you're talking like that," Cain said, tapping her fingers unevenly on her glass.

"I asked her to marry me, and she accepted. The thought of going on without her makes me crazy."

"Congratulations, and I'm guessing you need some help keeping your family safe while you chase this butcher," Cain said, and she nodded.

"I hate to bother you, but the department's already stretched thin, so the brass will never approve it. If you can't, tell me. I'll think of something else."

"Don't insult me. You know how much Emma loves Keegan. You go to work, and I give you my word your new family will be fine. I'll send my best guys, since we've been sticking around the house more lately."

She stood and embraced Cain for her generosity. It didn't surprise her, but the offer was more than she could've hoped for. "Thank you, and I'll do my best to pay you back."

"There you go insulting me again," Cain said, slapping her back. "You can send me a platter of that garlic bread from Blanchard's, and we'll be square."

"You got it, and I'll do my best to convince Anabel's people that you aren't that bad." Cain slapped her again and let her go but didn't move too far away. "I meant what I said—thank you. You don't know what this means to me."

"I do. You know what family means to me, and we're family, Sept. You don't have to ask, and that's what you should tell your bosses. Tell them I offered, and nothing else. I don't want any of this blowing back on you." Cain wasn't just giving, but she understood the politics and how to navigate it.

"Thank you isn't enough, but it's all I have for now."

"You cannot complain when we throw you an engagement party, and you know Emma will insist. Now get out of here and catch this guy."

She left smiling and wondered if there was some FBI file on her because of Cain. "Hey. Call Anabel Hicks at the FBI field office and ask if she'll see us," she said to Nathan. He probably should've stayed home, but she wasn't forcing the issue.

"Hold on," Nathan said and put his phone down. "She's in the office all day, so she said to come by whenever."

"Pick you up in about ten minutes."

He got in, appearing haggard. "What are we seeing Anabel about?" he asked and smiled when she placed her hand on his forearm.

"Are you sure you don't want to stay out of this today? You can hang out with Keegan and chop stuff," she said and smiled. "That's how she cured me."

"Really?"

"When we met, it hadn't been that long since Nicole and Sophie had died." She shook her head, remembering their first fight about using Grey Goose to drown the pain. "Keegan substituted pajama cooking lessons for vodka. I ended up falling in love and not concentrating on my sense of loss. She's a good listener. Remember that, and you can learn a few things about food."

"And the falling-in-love part?" Nathan asked, and she squeezed his arm.

"You try that with Keegan, and I'll use you for target practice."

He laughed at the threat, and some of his tiredness seemed to fall away.

"She's not likely to ever notice anyone else in this lifetime as long as you're around, and you're right about her listening. We talked last night—you're lucky, partner."

"You're not alone. I'll be happy to walk this road with you. I certainly have experience at it."

"Thanks, and thank you for not getting rid of me right off, even if I was probably an idiot."

She laughed and searched for a spot on the street to park. "You're welcome. Now let's go get some information that might lead us somewhere."

The receptionist walked them up to Anabel's office, and the bureau chief came from around her desk and joined them at the seating area by the windows. "Your father called me this morning and gave me the rundown about last night. I'm sorry, Nathan."

"Thank you, ma'am," Nathan said, and Sept respected him for keeping it together so far.

"Please, it's Anabel." She patted Nathan's knee. "What can I do for you two?"

She glanced at Nathan before speaking, but he waved her on. "Last night's scene was the same perp, but their signature changed when the victim's mutilation went a step farther than before."

"Sebastian said you investigated two scenes yesterday."

"Yes, and I could use your help on the second one," she said, handing Anabel the crime-scene photos. "We believe this perp is a woman, and she's copying Perlis's crimes for some reason but with her own style. The altar she left at the Lafayette Cemetery made me think of something, but I can't put my finger on what."

"What in particular?" Anabel asked as she flipped through the file.

"The eyes," she said, watching Nathan. He paled at her words.

"Can you run that MO through your system and see what pops up? We'll wait, if you don't mind."

"Stay here, and I'll have my team dig into that. While I do that, I'll get the head of our bomb squad to come up and give you a report on what we have so far."

"I'm sorry you had to find out like that," she said to Nathan, and he pressed his hands together.

"I can't look at those today, maybe never."

"I know, and it might help if, in Judy's honor, you—"

"What, quit or sit out?" he asked, angry now.

"Channel your anger instead of holding tight to the pain. You know what she did to Judy. Get pissed and dedicate yourself to hunting this bitch down."

"Detectives." The man from the night before came in and shook hands with them. He looked different in the gray suit and blue tie. "Thanks for coming in. Saved me a trip."

"I apologize. I didn't catch your name," she said.

"No problem. Last night we were worried about keeping all the stuff we were born with intact. I'm Will Butler, the explosives expert for the southern district." He sat and gave them each a copy of what he'd come up with. "Your suspect is an interesting killer."

"*That's* an interesting thing to say," she said, but hoped this led somewhere.

"A series of bombs happened in the mid-eighties that were classified at first as insurance fraud. You know, people destroying property they couldn't afford and couldn't ditch." Will tapped the first page of the file that contained a list of addresses.

"Did they get reclassified then?" Nathan asked.

"Turns out some of the places were successful businesses, so what had started in abandoned places morphed into something much more when the bomber picked places that had a few people in them, eventually killing fourteen." Will took her file and flipped quite a few pages into it. "The guy turned out to be a serial killer who escalated fast and had nothing whatsoever to do with the owners."

"I don't remember this case," Sept said, glancing at the file. "And what's it got to do with ours?"

"That's the design of John Moore's bombs, a unique signature when it came to the wiring and the detonation mechanism. He's now serving life in the Wyoming State Penitentiary. Most of his bombs went off in Cheyenne, but he was from a small town about a hundred miles away." Will flipped the page for her and motioned for Nathan to do the same. "This is the bomb you helped us find in the stolen car from your scene."

"You're saying they're identical?" she said, the implications making her head hurt.

"Down to the wire placement. Moore has an admirer of his work, who copied it," Will said with a little too much enthusiasm. "We've got another copycat that's most probably working with your perp."

"If that's true, this just turned into a cluster," she said, flipping between the two pages. The diagrams Will had put together were identical.

"I think we found what you're looking for, Sept," Anabel said, coming back in with Ivan and Catalina.

"If it's another copycat, my head might explode," she said, and Nathan nodded.

"There's a case in Newark that just wrapped," Anabel said, looking at her as if she didn't know if she was kidding. "Eugene Paul Masters ended up killing nine people with quite the unique signature. He called himself the butterfly killer," she said and explained why. "The lead detective was just found in his bedroom dead with the same MO."

"They got the wrong guy?" Sept asked.

Anabel shook her head and took a deep breath before answering. "The murder was almost perfect, except for the one thing Masters always finished with."

"It's the one clue the Newark department hasn't disclosed to the media," Catalina said.

"Somebody tell me," Sept said, raising her hands.

"Masters removed the eyes postmortem and placed them in the victim's shoes. When Detective Thomas Branson was found, his eyes were still in place, and that small detail marked his case a copycat," Anabel said.

"There's no way we've got three perps," Sept said.

"I don't think so either." Anabel pressed her hands together on her lap. "You've uncovered a pattern no one has seen before."

"We've got a copycat who didn't start with Alex Perlis," she said, and the realization was mind-boggling. "That's nuts."

"Nuts but true," Will said. "I didn't finish earlier. Moore's been incarcerated longer than he was a free man, but five years ago there was another string of bombs in Cheyenne. Same devices and same MO, and no known suspects."

"How many dead?" she asked.

"Fourteen."

"It's more than that, if you add in Detective Branson and all the bodies here," Sept said. "Can I speak to you alone, Anabel?"

Everyone cleared out, and Anabel moved to the seat next to her. "I'm going to have to report this, Sept," Anabel said to start.

"I know, but this asshole is in the city and is guilty of seven murders so far. Report it, but Chief Jernigan won't simply hand over the investigation to you—not without a fight."

"What do you suggest, then?"

"A joint task force, and I mean in every sense of the word. If this is a woman, she killed not only four innocent people, but three police officers on top of that. Fritz hands that over to you, and the mayor will have his balls, and you'll die in the flood when he pops an artery."

"You're so eloquent when you put your mind to it," Anabel said and held her hand out. "You're right, though, and to be fair, you're technically the one who put it together."

"Can you send Mora and Silva to our place, and they can start navigating the out-of-state stuff? Somewhere along the lines, something has to intersect."

"Probably a few more than Mora and Silva, including myself, so I hope you don't mind that. This isn't the type of case that comes along every day."

"That's great," she said and stood. "If you'll excuse me, though, let me go break the news to Fritz and my father."

"We'll be there as soon as we can put some stuff together. The most important thing, Sept, is to be careful. The butterfly cases worry me, because the copycat murderer targeted the man who captured Masters."

"If taking a shot at me brings this woman out of the shadows, I'm all for it."

CHAPTER TWENTY-SIX

Sept and Nathan drove to the precinct when Fritz said he and Sebastian would meet them there for a full report. What she had now felt like even less than what she'd started with in the morning. Certainly it was more information, but when she considered the scope, the killer had knocked them back a few pegs.

"Wow," Nathan said when they reached their workplace on Royal and it was packed. "It's like they're here for the second coming of the police god."

"You're hilarious." She parked on the street in the next block, and one of the uniforms waved her away from the car. "Thanks, man."

They made it to the conference room, where Fritz, Sebastian, and all the higher-ranking members of the NOPD were waiting. She took the pen for the whiteboard and wrote the names Masters, Moore, and Perlis at the top, then drew a line from every one of them to a circle at the bottom.

"This is what we know." She explained who Masters and Moore were and their commonality with Perlis. "Each is a serial killer who carved out a unique signature, but eventually all were caught." Each person listening seemed riveted. "Plus, the perp who identifies herself as Hunter copycatted all their crimes."

"What?" Fritz asked. "How can you be sure?"

"Right now, I can't, but after our team studied the CCT footage until their eyes bled, they found only one suspicious individual leaving the building to steal a car later found at a crime scene. It's highly improbable we have more than one killer duplicating crimes who were all involved in Lee Cenac's murder."

"But one guy responsible for all this isn't likely either," Fritz said.

"One woman, sir," Nathan said.

"That makes it even less likely." Fritz sounded exasperated. "If you're right, though, it'll certainly be an anomaly, since there aren't many female serial killers."

"It's an equal-opportunity world, sir," she said, and smiled to try to calm Fritz.

"Damn fine work, Sept, and even better since you kept the case where it belongs." Fritz literally patted her on the back. "What do you need from us?"

"Our team is working well, and having agents come from Hicks's office should streamline the process."

"We're all at your disposal, so get back to work," Fritz said, and the mob followed him out.

"What's first?" Nathan asked.

"Have Lourdes and the others find room for Anabel and her people. Then we have to make some calls."

She took the butterfly killer's case file back to her desk and thumbed through it. The police had kept the eyes part of the murders quiet, but she remembered where she'd heard about it. One of the victim's family members had given it up. The fallout hadn't been too bad, since Masters was already locked up.

"Can I speak to the detective working Detective Branson's case, please?" The call to New Jersey was more about curiosity than solving the case, but stranger things had happened. Mike had, she liked to joke, solved Perlis.

"This is Detective Lindsey Carter. How can I help you?"

"Thanks for taking my call," she said and introduced herself. "The bureau chief of our FBI field office explained that Detective Branson's murder was a copycat. Can you walk me through why you think so?"

Lindsey hesitated but finally started talking. "Everything was the same—the butterfly on the ceiling, the skin off the chest on his face, and his clothes cut off him and neatly folded at his feet. Only this time it wasn't his eyes in his shoes, but his testicles. The other weird thing was—"

"He was missing a toe," Sept said.

"How'd you know that?" Carter sounded defensive suddenly.

"It was sent to me by UPS while I was on vacation, out of town, away from my home."

"Why?"

"Good question, but I've got no answer. I'll inform the sheriff who still has possession of the toe and have it sent back to you. If Detective

Branson's been buried, maybe arrangements can be made to make him whole."

"Thank you, and if you don't mind, I'd like to stay in contact with you about your case. We're dead in the water when it comes to leads on our end. This might shake something loose."

"Let's hope. We could all use a break."

❖

Anabel and her crew had set up in the conference room, and the IT woman she'd brought with her had already found four other serial cases where someone had copied the original suspect's crimes after he'd been apprehended. If it was just one person and their time in New Orleans was almost done, their murders, along with all the others from different states, would possibly never be solved.

The hunt would have to resume only when or if Hunter resurfaced somewhere else and actually made such an egregious mistake that it'd lead to an arrest. If that happened, they'd have to wait their turn in the legal nightmare that would follow, and Hunter might never be tried and convicted in a New Orleans courtroom.

"You ready to go?" Nathan asked later that afternoon.

Sept's neck and back were stiff from watching a computer monitor for most of the afternoon as the agent researched cases. This rabbit hole couldn't suck up another one of her days, so she'd have to trust the agents to find the information. What had compelled her to stay was the number sixty-six. If one person had committed all the crimes, so far they'd found sixty-six murders.

"Come have dinner with me, and then we'll head back to the house and have a drink," she said to Nathan.

"I'm just going to head home," Nathan said, not getting up. "Go ahead, and I'll have someone drop me off."

"That wasn't a question, partner. It's a list of what you'll be doing tonight. You can wallow alone later, but you're coming with me."

The staff at Blanchard's were cleaning their stations as the first diners were set to arrive, which gave Keegan time to talk to them before she had to focus on her role in the kitchen. "Hopefully neither of you minds sharing the table with my family. It's inspection night, and you know that means Gran will be in rare form."

"Thanks for including me," Nathan said, and Keegan kissed his cheek.

"You might want to hold off on the thank you," Sept said as Keegan put her arms around her. "Especially if your phone rings during dinner. If that happens, pray Della hasn't ordered the steak and isn't holding a sharp knife."

"You might want to hold off on the sarcasm until you explain the big guy in the chair in the corner," Keegan said, pinching her, but she still had one of the waiters get them a drink. "Relax, and I'll join you once we get going. It'll give you time to come up with a good answer." An hour later, Della arrived with Melinda and two more burly guys. Jacqueline followed ten minutes after that but didn't appear at all perturbed by having a big shadow.

"Nathan, you have my sympathies, dear boy," Della said, taking his hands. "The mayor told me what happened when we had lunch today, and it's a horrible thing."

"Thank you, ma'am," Nathan said, bending so Della could kiss his cheek.

"Still won't save you from the phone if it rings," Sept said, and Della glared at her.

"Sit down, heathen, and try to act civilized. Any more comments out of you and I'll make you wear something with lace for the wedding." Della smiled when she pulled out her chair, unfurled her napkin, and placed it in her lap before the waiter could do it. "We'll make a restaurateur out of you yet."

"It can be my fallback if this cop thing doesn't work out," she teased.

"You might have more options than that if you can conjure up more good-looking men to show up at my door." Della pointed to Cain's man now standing right inside the open door of the office, as if to stay out of the way. "That young man appeared today and said he's not going anywhere. Any clue as to where he came from?"

"You mean there's something you don't know?" she asked, trying to convey shock.

"I spoke to Cain," Della said, rolling her eyes. "I know all, which you should keep in mind should you ever think about developing a roving eye."

"That'll never be a problem, so you cooperate and don't try to ditch your new heavily armed friend."

Della had opened her mouth to retort when the maître 'd came in walking backward, obviously trying to stop someone from following him. Nicole Voles didn't seem deterred as she pushed the guy out of the way. But everything did stop when the guy assigned to Keegan unholstered both his guns. It was impressive how quickly they were in his hands, leaving no doubt how fast he'd fire if Keegan was in danger.

"Whoa," Nicole said, her hands up.

Keegan stood behind Sept, who'd reacted as quickly minus the guns. "Ms. Voles," she said, not moving and feeling Keegan's hand on her back. "I believe Ms. Blanchard asked you not to come back. You have plenty of places to choose from to keep returning to a place you're not welcome. You seem intelligent enough to figure that one out."

The way Nicole smiled and glanced around her at Keegan made the urge to punch her in the throat hard to fight. "Zagat rated this place the best in the city for the heat in the kitchen, which I can certainly attest to, and the hospitality," Nicole said and chuckled. "I haven't gotten around to eating here, but so far I'm not feeling the second part of the equation."

"Lady," Cain's guy said, but Sept's ringing phone stopped him.

Sept glanced at it for a second, not wanting to take her attention off Nicole. It was a blocked caller, so she had no choice but to answer it. "Savoie."

"May I call you Sept?" The mechanical voice was getting old, but after the video footage, Sept understood the need for it. Someone's walk didn't confirm their gender, but their voice certainly did. "After all, we've experienced so much together."

"What can I do for you, Hunter?" She nodded at the guard, and Keegan and Nathan followed her into the office.

"I wanted to see if you enjoyed my eye-opening gift," Hunter said and laughed. "The little warrior's girlfriend was such a lovely prize."

"I'd think gloating and self-promotion were beneath a capable woman like you," she said as Nathan called this in since she'd agreed to a wiretap on her phone. The killer had engaged with her, not to gloat, but to get to know her last victim before moving on. There was no reason not to exploit that possibility.

"Are you so sure of yourself, Detective? Or can you only make deductions when you have a fifty percent chance of guessing correctly?" Hunter laughed again, then stopped abruptly as if it wasn't something she was used to doing. "You didn't enjoy my gifts at all? You should feel some comfort in figuring out my riddle with enough time to live."

"You killed a woman who'd dedicated herself to community policing," Sept said. Nathan sucked in a breath, and Keegan moved to him and held his hand. "Why would anyone get any pleasure from that?"

"We'll have to agree that you're wrong. The altars Judy completed were something to be admired. Once the word spreads, my religion will gain followers, and we'll entertain ourselves by watching you chase only what I deem necessary. None of it will lead to anything."

"Why call, then? Is that part of your game?" If wishes weren't child's play, someone would grant her the ability to reach through the phone and beat this bitch to death with her voice manipulator.

"The game is paramount, so don't forget it. It's my existence, and I'll never tire of it." Hunter paused, but Sept could still hear heavy breathing.

"Are you losing your grip?" She glanced out to the kitchen at the way Nicole was staring at her. Nicole's gaze was so intense she thought maybe she was trying to read her lips. "Is this the only way you think you'll earn respect? Teacher isn't real, and Alex Perlis will end up with a needle in his arm for the abominations he did in the name of your so-called religion."

"Careful, Detective, or you'll be blamed for those yet to come."

"You said there can only be one warrior. Stop hiding and trying to prove yourself with the innocent and face me. Then you can claim Chango as your own, but not until you defeat the true warrior. I'm his chosen, not you." Keegan covered her mouth and shook her head when she delivered the invitation. "Prove yourself, or accept that you're nothing but a butcher pretending to be something you'll never achieve."

The phone went dead, and she lowered it to stop the recording she'd started. She opened her arms to Keegan, who slapped her hands down on her chest. "Are you crazy?" Keegan yelled.

"There's a good reason, baby. You have to believe me."

"To taunt this maniac to kill you? Nothing you can say will make me believe you." Keegan slumped against her when Sept gave her the best reason she had—this nut's potential body count.

"We have to do everything we can to find her before she resets and starts a new game somewhere else," she said, kissing the top of Keegan's head.

"You'd better be okay. I've found my match, and I've got too much life ahead of me to spend it alone."

"I'll be around until all you can cook is soft foods I can gum in my old age," she said, which made Keegan laugh.

❖

Hunter had spent the day thinking about all the moves that hadn't been part of her meticulous plan. The conversation with Savoie an hour prior had been different, and it was extremely bothersome. Most calls of the same nature were all about stretching them with the hopes of tracing them to a location, but not Savoie.

"What do you know?" Hunter said out loud to the empty room. She was sitting in a meditative pose with her legs crossed. The worst mistake anyone involved in any game could make was to act as if they could change the outcome. "The game is mine, and you'll play by my rules."

That was true as the game came to a close, but something wasn't sitting right. Sept Savoie had something, and she wasn't going to share. It made sense that Sept would keep quiet while trying to push her to a certain action that would spring whatever trap Savoie was trying to set. If that was true, she wasn't taking the bait or the blame for the mistakes made.

To win, the most important thing was staying in a position of power. Invisibility until your prey was strapped to a table like Branson had been was the way of the hunter. Perlis had changed that strategy by taunting Savoie, and he'd been burned for it. The only way to play this particular game was to engage Savoie. If she didn't, the process would be incomplete.

"Perlis just had to call you to try to goad you into catching him." She closed her eyes and took deep breaths. "If I don't continue to do that, I don't deserve to play. Showing fear doesn't make me the best player, and you won't take that away from me."

Another deep breath brought no calmness, like it usually did, so she stood and headed for the kitchen and a bottle of water. The steps of the game that she had to complete were taped to the refrigerator, and this last play would end with Savoie's death. The game was incomplete, and adding another play made perfect sense. Mistakes beyond her control had occurred, but she could rectify them.

"You want to challenge me, then I'll give you your wish and punish the one person who should shoulder the blame for the hubris that skewered the plan." She very carefully laid the paper on the counter and neatly started writing.

"Once you prove yourself the fool I know you are, I'll enjoy building an altar for you on the graves of those you love."

She finished the plan, and after reviewing and considering everything that could go wrong, she knew it was time to put it into motion. She would have to go purchase what she needed for the altars necessary to teach Savoie a lesson about hubris.

"I thought you were a level above Branson, but you're like all the peacocks who wear the uniform. It's all for show."

❖

"You," Della said to Sept following their meal. "Come with me."

After the disturbing call, Keegan had decided to go back to work if Sept stayed, and they could go home together. Della had done an admirable job of keeping the conversation light tonight, but Sept could see the worry that bubbled just under the surface.

The bartender poured them both a cognac, and Della held her hand as they sat. "Do you remember the day I came and asked your permission to marry Keegan?"

"Are you sorry?" Della asked, and she shook her head.

"I'm asking because I distinctly remember telling you that I'd protect her, and her family, like you were my own. Today I asked an old friend for help, and it probably wasn't a wise career move, but no matter what it takes, I'll always put Keegan and my family first." She smiled and thought of her future with Keegan's family. "The essence of my life isn't my job. It's the people I love."

"Do I look like I needed convincing?" Della asked, making her laugh because Della never let her off easy.

"No, but I know you worry. Or maybe you needed reminding that I love you."

"This person sounds even more deranged than the bastard who killed Donovan and brought you to us," Della said, stopping to finish her drink. "I know that's true even if you won't tell me to save me from worrying."

"Can I do anything to alleviate your load?"

"I want my family where I can see them and keep an eye on them," Della said, and Sept wasn't sure what she was saying. That must've been apparent when Della went on. "My house is too small, but yours isn't."

"You want to move in with us?" The master bedroom downstairs was empty, since Keegan and Jacqueline hadn't wanted to take Della's room.

"Do you think that's a bad idea?" Della asked as the bartender refilled their glasses.

"You realize I don't sleep on the sofa, right?"

"Yes, but I don't have to like it," Della said, kissing the back of her hand before she winked.

Keegan joined them, standing in front of her stool and leaning back against her. "You okay?"

"Why do you think Nicole showed up again?" Keegan asked, and the question made her think about the bizarre encounter earlier.

The call from Hunter had taken precedence over some idiot whose agenda she hadn't figured out yet. "I'm not sure, but maybe she was trying to get a rise out of you and force you to say something."

"I'm not afraid of her or that, but I'm ready for her to forget all about me." Keegan sighed when she put her arms around Sept's waist. "What are you talking about?"

"We're getting housemates for a little while, but they promise to behave." The way Della laughed made her doubt that she would do anything close to that. "Have you cooked your quota for the night?"

"Another half an hour and we should be free to go. Nathan took the car, and he'll pick you up in the morning. Before you get mad, his parents were waiting for him." Keegan turned and kissed her. "And we rescheduled the big family Sunday lunch for this weekend."

"I'm glad I don't have anything else to think about or decide tonight," she teased, and Keegan bit her lip. "You need help with anything in there? I'm available and I'm cheap."

The Blanchards laughed, but she and Della followed Keegan back. She wanted to review her files and check if the agents had found anything else, but she could do that later. Right now she chose to provide those she loved some comfort by giving them her undivided attention.

It took less time than Keegan had said, and she gladly sat in the passenger seat and let Keegan drive her home. They showered together, and Keegan opted to go to bed, saying she didn't mind if she brought the laptop to bed so she could work. The agents had found another case where the convicted murderer had used drive-bys as his killing method.

The copycat was certainly multitalented when it came to killing people. Keegan was lying beside her, obviously sleeping, since her arm was thrown across her lap. If they could run down the gun used, the new case they'd uncovered might help them prove that the same person was active now.

"Hey. I'm sorry to bother you so late," she said to Jennifer softly.

"I'm at the office since Chloe's still at work. Do you need something?"

"We need to contact the Mississippi sheriff's office and get the ballistics reports from their case."

"What do you want to compare it to?" Jennifer asked, and Sept could hear typing. The dedication Jennifer had shown so far was admirable. For a second, a dark thought sped through her mind, and she tried to shut it down before she compared Jennifer to Perlis.

"The bullets that killed the two officers the day we found Bonnie Matherne. If we can match those two sets of bullets, we can prove the theory we're trying to put forth. If those are too mangled for a true comparison, try the bullets we took out of the teenagers."

"They're in evidence, so I'll get them in the morning," Jennifer said, and it sounded like she yawned then.

"Get some sleep and I'll see you then." The bullets might link another case, but some common factor had to tie them all together.

It had to be someone who could blend into their surroundings and had the freedom to move from place to place without raising any warning flags in their everyday life. The number of kills, and the gore of the most recent, probably were the work of a psychopath, and those kinds of people didn't blend in at all.

"Are you independently wealthy and don't need to keep a job that requires you to deal with people?" She continued to speak softly to herself, not wanting to wake Keegan.

The timeline showed the suspect wasn't following some kind of regular schedule that could indicate any type of pattern. All the copycat murders had started six years prior, and in that time, only one spree occurred some years in a certain location, but during some years up to three took place.

She answered her phone, rubbing Keegan's back to keep her asleep. "Hey, did your parents make it in?" she asked Nathan, knowing they'd moved to Shreveport after his father's retirement.

"Yeah. My dad gave me a pep talk, and my mom gave me a hug, the type only your mom can give you," Nathan said, and he sounded better. "Sorry I ran out on you earlier."

"You've met my mother, which means I totally understand."

Nathan laughed again. He did know her mother and had helped

with her parents' renovation on Sundays. They'd made progress on the house she'd grown up in, enough that her parents had been able to move in and live in the part they'd finished.

"What are you doing up?"

"The feds found another case of a copycat series of crimes. Drive-bys that killed four people right outside Biloxi. Sounds like the locals thought it was a drug war because of the neighborhood and the victims targeted—until they checked the bullets with the feds' records."

"Can I come over? I know it's late, but I can't sleep."

"Meet you in the kitchen, and bring your notebook. We've got plenty to cover, and I want this bitch to go down for every single crime I can pin on her."

CHAPTER TWENTY-SEVEN

The next morning at their precinct, Sebastian seemed engrossed with the ballistics report Jennifer had put together, and Sept allowed him to finish reading and lift his head before saying anything. She'd shared it with Anabel already, and they'd agreed that the gun used to kill the two NOPD rookies, the two teenage boys, and all the victims from the copycat drive-by shootings was the same one.

"What does this bring us, aside from being disturbingly interesting?" Sebastian asked, putting the report down.

"It's one step closer to proving Hunter is one of the most prolific serial killers of our time," Anabel said.

"And it should fill us with a sense of urgency to find the one clue that'll bring her down before she moves on. Once this game, as Hunter refers to it, is done, she'll be in the wind," Sept said.

"I agree with both of you, but like with Perlis, all of these crime scenes haven't yielded one clue we can use to narrow the field," Sebastian said. "If we can't do that, the mayor and the city council will demand a few people take the fall. Not that their threats should drive why we do this, but I'm only stating fact."

"We all realize that, Sebastian, and I agree with Sept on one crucial thing," Anabel said.

"What?" Sebastian glanced between the two of them before settling on Nathan.

"The answer is already here. We just haven't deciphered it yet," Sept said.

Nathan got up and turned the whiteboard around to where they'd written out the timeline they'd worked up the night before. From the information Anabel had provided, the map showed all the crimes they'd spotted and when they occurred. In their totality, only one discernable pattern was apparent.

"The crimes that someone copied all had one thing in common," Nathan said, pointing to the different states. "Hunter chose to duplicate all the crimes exactly in the same manner, on the same number of victims, as the original killer, and she took the same amount of time. It happened in every case," Nathan said, then placed his hand on Louisiana. "Except ours."

"That's where our questions come in," Anabel said.

"You lost me," Sebastian said.

"You were right about the near-perfect crime scenes," Sept said. "When they were planned, each location was clean." She made air quotes. "Hunter is a meticulous planner. She'd have to be to kill this many times without someone detecting her." The timeline was written in black, so Sept picked up the red pen as Gustave and Sharon walked in. At each location she wrote the method or weapon used to commit the crime. "In each spot the murders were copied, along with the same way the murders were done."

"Except for here," Sebastian said.

"We'd figured out the bomb part and the eyes, but the gun makes me think Hunter isn't very imaginative. When we say copycat, that's exactly what we mean. This time around, she couldn't adhere to the well-laid-out plan because she had to get some help. To take care of those loose ends, Hunter went back to the tried and true. She didn't think of anything new."

Anabel walked closer and simply stared at the board. "This is a killer who needs someone else's blueprint."

"Who knew Perlis would be the downfall of this plan," Sept said, and her father nodded. "It doesn't point to who, but we know her next play."

"Which is what?" Nathan asked.

"The same conclusion as all the other cases we've found." She pointed to the board. "The last victim in every case was the officer who arrested the killer. That might be the only original thing about all this."

"We've got an unoriginal killer who hates cops," Anabel said, and Sept nodded again. "If you're her next play, we need to drop a net over you, starting now."

"You can do that if you can do it without tipping her off. The bomb at the hotel, the call before Judy's murder, and a few other tips make me think Hunter might be watching." Sept stopped talking when someone she didn't recognize walked in. The blonde smiled and handed Anabel a sealed envelope.

"Relax. It's just my assistant," Anabel said as she ripped it open. Whatever it was, it was a quick read. "You have interesting friends who do you big favors."

"If you can provide the same care around the clock, I'll call them off," Sept said, not at all intimidated.

"You know we can't do that."

"Then get off Sept's ass and back to what's important," Gustave said, standing by Sept. "Keegan and her family aren't chips any of us are willing to gamble with."

"Okay, but it's part of the report now, and it puts you in a spotlight you might not want to make too bright." Anabel folded the paper and placed it back in the envelope.

"Trust me, Anabel, if I was interested in only the money that comes from being a dirty cop, I'd retire and serve drinks at Blanchard's. Keegan has more than enough to keep me, so to speak, but I'm a cop, and a damn good one." The bullshit that came from a simple friendship was unbelievable.

"Got it, and I was only giving you a heads-up. Enough about that and back to this case."

"We need a complete picture, so I'm not putting you off, but you and your team have to find the rest of the pieces, if they're there to find."

"We're working on it, and the profilers should have something for us soon. It might lead us in a direction we haven't thought of."

"Then let's find the missing piece and finish this," Sept said as Nathan grabbed his jacket. "Remember to stay in touch, everyone, and I'll buy whoever figures this out as many drinks as they want."

"Threats like that can move mountains, sister," Gustave said.

"Threats are for thugs, but alcohol is for closers."

❖

"You're a hard man to find," Nicole said to Sergeant Larry Nobles after she placed her hand on the back of his neck on the bandage he still had taped there. The crappy bar Larry had picked smelled of old booze and peanuts.

Larry's face was still bruised, and the small cuts had scabbed over, but he was due to return to work the next week. At least that's what the woman in his office had told her. "I've been recovering, so I've been at home with my girlfriend. The explosion put me on sick leave, which means if you're looking for some information, you're out of luck."

"Maybe I was worried about you and came looking for you." She took the barstool next to him and motioned for the bartender. "Maker's Mark neat."

"I thought you were strictly a wine person?" He took his eyes off his whiskey and glanced at her. "What do you want from me?"

"Tell me what happened to you."

"A few bombs went off somewhere I was working and did all this." He pointed to his face.

"Larry, I realize you made yourself clear about your reluctance to talk to me and don't care what I can do to you," she said, lifting her glass with her free hand.

"But if you have any sense at all, you'd realize your life as you know it is in the balance," Brian said, sitting on the other side of Larry. "Now, pay attention and cooperate, or you'll have more problems than with NOPD." Brian placed his FBI ID on the bar and smiled.

"What do you want?" Larry asked, his tone one of resignation.

"I want Savoie's notes from the Perlis case," Nicole said, not removing her hand from his neck and squeezing a little. "But right now, you're going to tell us all about these new cases."

"I don't know much about that. The only scene I worked was at that park where I got hurt, but only because we were short-staffed. My job doesn't get me out in the field very often." Larry grimaced, as if she was aggravating whatever was under the bandage.

"I know what you do, Larry. It's why I've paid you over ten thousand dollars already. I also know you can answer the questions we have even though you haven't worked the case." She squeezed one last time as hard as she could and let him go. "Let's start with the one you were actually at."

Larry started talking, and Brian took copious notes. The altar Larry and the others had found had only the fruit and pigeons the god was known to like, but no body parts. It had stood out as the only orderly thing in the trash mounds around it. "Whoever put it there had cleared the area like they wanted it to stand out. That shit was a trap, though."

"No one was killed, though, right?" Brian asked.

"The guys I was with all got hurt, but yeah, no one was killed."

"How'd you make it out so unscathed?" she asked, taking a sip of her drink.

"I was going back for the camera. The bombs went off when I was halfway back to the car."

"That was lucky," she said and smiled. "Are you usually that lucky, Larry? Or are you leaving something out?"

"Nothing," he said quickly, glancing around as if he'd spoken too loud and might attract attention. "Look, that's all I know. I'll get you the rest of what you need, and then we're done."

"We're done when my daughter says we're done," Brian said, placing a twenty on the counter for her drink. "When you send the notes for Perlis's case, send what's been catalogued so far in these new cases as well."

Nicole took Brian's arm and walked out with him, laughing at the fear in Larry's eyes. "Why do you suppose these new cases haven't benefitted Alex's status?" she asked as Brian opened her door for her.

"That's a good question, baby, but I need to read the case file before I can answer it accurately."

"This is exciting, isn't it?" she asked when he got behind the wheel.

"I'm sure Savoie doesn't share your sentiment, but it's a fascinating case that must have them scrambling. They should've taken me up on my offer." He pulled out, cutting off a small car, and the driver laid on the horn, but he didn't seem to care. Brian took what he wanted and did what he pleased. That's what she most admired about him.

"I'm sure it's only a matter of time, and they'll come begging for your expertise. That'll be the best part of this new book."

He looked at her and smiled. "I do my job, and that's it. You don't need to write about that, sweet girl."

"I want to," she said, reaching over and placing her hand on his thigh. He always felt so hot to the touch, as if the heat was a built-in mechanism to warn off those who couldn't handle it. "And you deserve the recognition."

"My time in the bureau is short."

"Then let's make the most of it."

❖

Joel Savoie sat in the unmarked car he and his partner Lamar Jones had checked out that morning and sighed. "I hate that she's always right," he said to Lamar as he tapped his thumbs on the steering wheel.

"You shouldn't have bet real money, bonehead," Lamar said

putting the high-powered listening device they'd borrowed from Anabel's people back in the case. He'd gotten close enough to hear their whole conversation.

They'd been parked across the street from the bar, and Joel was surprised that Super Special Agent Voles didn't pick up the tail. They'd spent two hours following these two around before the NOPD mole became apparent. Joel had bet Sept that morning at breakfast that one of their own wouldn't sell them out, considering what Perlis had done, but Sept's intuition and Larry Nobles's stupidity had proved him wrong.

"You want to wait for him to come out, or you want to go in and get him?" Lamar asked.

"Let's go." He climbed out and pulled his jeans up. Maybe something about this non-uniform part of the job did hold appeal. "God knows how long this fucker will be in there."

Larry resembled one of those dog ornaments people put in their cars as his head swiveled between them. "You're so popular, Larry," Joel said as Lamar placed his hand on Larry's shoulder in case he got happy feet. "All those visitors you're getting."

"Let's go for a ride," Lamar said, and Larry pulled away from him. "If this is your neighborhood hangout, don't make me handcuff you and drag you out, asshole."

"Problems, Larry?" the bartender asked.

"Just some guys from work. Put this on my tab, and I'll catch you later," Larry said, standing up once Joel moved.

"Yeah. If he owes you anything, he's got about ten grand and change," Joel said, and Larry appeared to be in pain. "No wonder Sept figured you out so quick. You're so expressive."

"Where you taking me?" Larry asked as Lamar sat in the back with him.

"You've got a date with Sept and Nathan, so start thinking of some really good answers to the questions you know she's going to ask," Joel said as he headed for the Quarter. "Then pray all you get is fired."

They each grabbed an arm when they arrived and led Larry upstairs to the empty office next to the conference room. He could hear his sister through the open door and left Lamar with Larry before she said anything Larry could sell later.

"I owe you twenty bucks," he said to Sept, and she smiled. "He just met with the Voles family, but it didn't sound like he was too anxious to continue their conversation."

Sept sat on the edge of the table and nodded. "This is one of those times when I'm not thrilled I was right." She combed her hair back and sighed. "Did you get it on tape?"

"Lamar got close enough to record it all, and with some enhancement, a jury will hear every word. Hell, you can make it out with the raw tape."

"Good and thanks. I know spying on your own isn't fun, but this one was important." Sept and her team listened to the tape, and it was enough for what she really wanted. A search warrant for Larry's phone records would hopefully prove her wrong, but that nagging suspicion from that night at the park had stayed with her. "Nathan, this should be enough to get us that warrant."

"On it," Nathan said.

"Anabel, want to join me for a chat?" Sept asked and rewound the tape. "Can you two put him in an interrogation room if he's not already in one?"

"What are you hoping to find out?" Lamar asked.

"One crucial thing, and if I'm right, it gets us that much closer to cracking this thing."

Twenty minutes later, all Larry was adamant about was that he had nothing to say. Eventually a good attorney might get him off, but for now she was arresting him.

"What now?" Anabel asked.

"Now we wait and let the very small room Larry will be sitting in do its magical wonders. Nothing like the threat of gang rape to loosen the tongue, if we threaten to take him out of solitary."

❖

"Why haven't they let Perlis out?" Nicole asked Gretchen Harrison as they shared dinner. It had taken some persuasion to get Gretchen out of her office, but she'd agreed to meet her at Le Coquille D'Huîte in the French Quarter. If she was barred from Blanchard's, another restaurant owned by the family was the next best thing. "They're the exact same crimes."

"I love your belief in my client, but it's not that simple," Gretchen said, picking up the small fork that came with the raw oysters she'd ordered. The restaurant was known for as well as named after the oyster shell, but Nicole wasn't a fan. "We're going to do our best to keep Alex off death row, but even I don't see us overcoming the mountain of evidence against him, and I'm good."

"I'm sorry. Did you not hear me?" Nicole asked, ignoring her salad for now. "The same murders are happening right now. Three of them, as a matter of fact. If Alex is in jail, then it's obviously not him."

"The team looked into the possibility, and the crimes are similar, but not at all the same." Gretchen mixed the horseradish and cocktail sauce together before putting a little on an oyster. "The police never share much, especially with me, but it's someone else."

"Shouldn't they have to disclose why they think so? Can't you take them to court and compel them?" Not knowing the facts was driving her crazy, and when she got her hands on Larry again, he'd need another month of sick leave. He had to have known this and kept quiet. "Alex Perlis doesn't strike me as the kind of man who kills five people."

"Don't forget one of those five was a cop, and three of the four attempted murders he's charged with are also cops. Since one of those three was Sept Savoie, she'd pin this on Alex if she could, but it's not the same person," Gretchen said softly, as if not wanting to be overheard. "He killed a policewoman in Sept's bed, for God's sake, which makes me think she went out of her way to try to prove it's someone working with him with the objective of clearing him."

"What do you know about the more recent murders?"

Gretchen shrugged. "Not much more than the news has reported. Sept isn't exactly an over-sharer."

"Can you find out? The addition of a like-minded killer would be great for the book." If she could cut this short, she would, but with more wine, Gretchen might be more forthcoming.

"Knowing Sept, you'll find out soon—"

"What are you talking about?" she demanded.

"Nothing." Gretchen stared at her like she was nuts. "Knowing Sept, you'll find out soon enough, along with the rest of us. Her brain doesn't work like everyone else's, and she's good at finding clues where none exist."

"Sorry. I'm just anxious about your case. I still believe Alex doesn't deserve the blow fate has dealt him."

"It's a good thing you're a writer," Gretchen said and smiled as she touched her hand. "Don't ever become a defense attorney."

"Why?" she asked, moving her hand so their fingers linked together.

"It'll break your heart, but since I'm always accused of not having one. I'm immune to the criticism."

"That's funny, but right now I'm not interested in your heart, Counselor," she said and winked. "But I can be patient."

"In the time it takes to finish dinner, maybe I can think of a way to repay you for all your help. Alex is actually talking again, and he swears he doesn't remember anything having to do with what he was arrested for. It might help in our diminished-capacity defense."

The table was cleared, and a few minutes later their meals were delivered. "I'm sure we can think of something," she said and released Gretchen's hand.

"I'm game as long as whatever we decide on doesn't go in the book."

She smiled and shook her head. "All my sex scenes are live performances."

CHAPTER TWENTY-EIGHT

Another week went by, and they were left with no more murders, no phone calls, and no hint Hunter was even still in town. Sept and Nathan had revisited every crime scene and re-interviewed everyone who might've been a witness. The only person on that list who had actually talked to Hunter was the operator who set appointments for Brandi Parrish.

"I thought you'd already talked to her," Brandi said as she sat by her pool in a bikini that left you wishing you had enough imagination to picture her dressed. Sept chuckled softly as she glanced at Nathan, who had his head back as if fascinated by the clear sky. For all his bravado, he seemed somewhat shy at times.

"I did, but I need to talk to her again." She smiled and tried her best to keep her eyes on Brandi's face. Her old friend made a habit of trying to make her sweat but wasn't overly obnoxious about it. "I promise I'm not secretly working with vice on some undercover sting operation to bring you down."

"As if," Brandi said, then rolled over to her stomach and held up a bottle of lotion. "Would you mind?"

"Nathan, you're up," she said, and his head dropped so fast she thought he'd fall forward.

"When you're done, she's waiting inside in my office. Try not to give her a hard time." Brandi glanced back at her and winked. "As a matter of fact, why don't you go in and talk to her? Nathan and I need a minute."

"You're a professional who charges a fortune—I'd hope it lasts more than a minute." The comment was totally inappropriate, but she couldn't resist. Brandi laughed, and Nathan blushed so scarlet his dark eyebrows really stood out.

"Get out of here, pervert. I want to talk to him, since I'm starting to like him more than you."

The woman Liza was sitting in one of the seats in front of Brandi's desk, sipping from a cup of coffee and not appearing too perturbed to be summoned again. She was older, Sept guessed late sixties, and had been in the business in her earlier years. Brandi valued her because she knew how to talk to clients, collect from them, and find out what they wanted so she could prepare the girls for their dates.

"Thanks, Liza," she said, sitting next to her. "I know I'm being a redundant pest, but we need to go over that call again. We've hit a wall, and I need something to get going again."

"Whatever you need, Detective. Brandi told me what was done to that poor baby I sent to that animal." Liza's hand shook as she placed her cup down, as if the memory upset her that much.

"Could it have been a woman who called?" The notes from the first meeting contained the entire conversation as Liza remembered it.

"It could've been, I said, but I can't be sure. The caller simply said what they wanted and promised to leave the money. I didn't think about it, since it was a deep voice asking for someone young who knew how to follow directions."

"Did you hear any type of accent? Anything in the background that would've clued you in as to where they were calling from?"

"They didn't sound Southern, but nothing like any other accent that would've stuck out. The background was quiet." Liza gripped the arms of her chair and took a few deep breaths. "Believe me, if I could help you, I would."

"I know, and I appreciate your time. Sometimes it takes a few days or weeks for something to click." The lack of anything to follow up was disheartening, but if it took doing it fifty times, that's what she'd do.

"You'll be my first call. The real shame was Lee's inexperience. She wasn't ready for this yet."

The statement made her nod. "Then why did you send Lee?" Maybe she'd been asking the wrong questions.

"You get a feel for people when they're talking about what they want," Liza said, sounding more relaxed with a subject she was familiar with. "They want it so bad they're willing to pay big money to get it."

"Why do you think that is?" Their talk made her think about the guy trying to pick up Erica the night Lee was killed. Some people allowed the side of their personality they kept hidden in their normal lives out when they were away from their families. Others might've thought about letting that part out to play but had better control.

"That's easy, Detective." Liza sounded as if the answer should be obvious. "They're churchgoing community leaders who marry and have children. Mostly they work and provide for their families and are rewarded once a week with the missionary position with a woman as interested in him as he is in her."

"Your business is built on a change of scenery, then?"

"Brandi's business is built on letting these guys ask for what they're afraid to at home. They want their cocks sucked, they want to eat pussy, and maybe they'd like to have a beautiful woman shove a big dildo up their ass while they fuck." The list Liza ticked off was in a way sad that you'd have to pay for it. "The repressed become the sexual gods they've always dreamed of being, and it takes only three grand to get there."

She smiled and nodded. "Thank God I'm not shy, then."

"Someone like you doesn't pay for sex, so thank God not everyone's wired the same."

"Do you make most of the dates?"

Liza stared at her for a long minute, and she smiled to ease any fear of reprisal for a wrong answer. "Most of the phone inquiries, but two more girls help me with that."

"Was Lee a popular date?"

"She was a beauty, but Brandi had her on a short leash. Not that she didn't trust her, but she wanted her to acclimate to the kind of customers we service."

"That means she has a short list of clients." It was probably nothing, but she had to ask.

"A handful since she's been here. Brandi picked some and trusted me to do the same."

"Anyone interesting? If you want, I can ask Brandi, if you're not comfortable answering."

"She said she trusts you, and that's good enough for me." Liza reached for her bag and took out a ledger. "You'd never guess how many John Smiths there are in the world until you do this, but every so often someone surprises us and uses their real name, or at least a real first name and a very real phone number."

Liza wrote down ten names and the hotel they'd sent Lee to. "That's a lot of John Smiths," Sept said when she looked at it.

"Some are repeat customers, except for this one." She tapped on number eight.

"Nicole," she read, followed by a phone number. "What's this area code?"

"Malibu, California," Liza said. "She wasn't into anything memorable, and she wasn't opposed to someone new. That's all I know, so if something was off about the date, Brandi might be able to help."

"Thank you, Liza." She folded the list and placed it in her notebook. "Where did Lee meet Nicole?"

"The Piquant, for most of the night. She's either got stamina or money to burn."

"Good question, but no worries. I won't ask. Ms. Nicole's secret is safe with me, but I can work around the information." She pocketed her notebook and pen, then stood to go. "I'm curious," she said when Liza took her hand. "What do you think I want?"

"That's easy. A woman who loves you and isn't afraid to give you even the things you're afraid to voice."

"Wow. You're good."

"Years of practice, and the fact you were able to walk away from Brandi in that swimsuit means you're really in love."

She nodded and laughed with Liza. "I'm definitely taken, but far from dead. Not even that suit could get me to cheat, though."

"Be happy, then, and call me if you need any more questions answered."

"Thank you, and call me if anything else comes to mind."

❖

Brandi's man Wilson nodded when she came out and accepted a glass of lemonade from him. "Get what you need?" he asked.

"Maybe something." She took a sip, humming because it was so good. "Did Brandi and Nathan come in?"

"You might want to let them finish. It was a long conversation. She's trying to be as compassionate with him as he was with her the night Lee was killed." Wilson went back to cutting up chickens and placing the pieces in a bowl. "He's a nice young man. Brandi really likes him. Real shame what happened to his girl."

"Hopefully whatever Brandi tells him will help ease his guilt."

"The boy's got nothing to be guilty about." Wilson made quick work of the last chicken and then washed his hands. "He just needs to be reminded that it don't do no good to crawl into the grave. He's alive and got plenty living to do."

"I hope that's true for all of us."

The back door opened, and Brandi came in wearing a large terry-cloth robe. Nathan's blush was so deep Sept clamped her jaws shut to keep from laughing.

"Ready?" Nathan asked.

"In a minute," she said and bent down when Brandi walked to her and kissed her cheek. "Thanks for getting Liza here, but I've a quick follow-up question."

"Shoot," Brandi said and rubbed Nathan's chest as if to calm him.

"The date she sent Lee out with, Nicole, did she mention anything about it?"

"It was one of her first women, and she said she didn't realize females could be so aggressive, but nothing made her overly uncomfortable."

"Thanks."

"No problem, and, Nathan, don't forget about Sunday afternoon," Brandi said. "We'll go for that ride and talk some more. I might also include a lesson on how not to blush. The rest you got down pat, darling."

Sept was proud of herself for not laughing, and it took ten minutes before his blush faded. "You okay?" she finally asked as she drove to the old Italian family restaurant on Canal Street.

"Please don't tell anyone what happened." Nathan started to get red in the face again.

"What. You had a conversation with Brandi about our case? That's what happened, right?"

"Thanks, and you should know I wasn't planning to *talk* to her," he said slowly. "She's just really good at making conversation."

"No problems, partner. Let's go accidentally run into the highly intelligent and talented Voles family." She'd called Joel and found out where they were, since he'd gone from following Larry to Nicole and her father. "It's probably nothing, but Nicole had a date with Lee Cenac before she died. Might not go anywhere, but excuse yourself after we get a table and call this number."

"And say what?"

"Nothing. Block your number and mute your phone." She got out and punched him in the arm. "Got that?"

"Sure."

The hostess hugged Sept and showed them to a table close to Nicole and Brian's. They were eating their starter salads and talking with their heads close together, and hadn't seemed to notice them come in. She cocked her head to Nathan, and he left as she raised her menu. Whatever Nicole was saying stopped as she reached down for her purse a minute later. She glanced at the screen and hesitated before taking the call. Hopefully Nathan had done as she'd asked. She put the menu down and stared out the window as Nicole's head came up and glanced around the restaurant.

The waitress came and took her drink order, but she made sure not to let her eyes stray to Nicole or Brian. She ordered two sweet teas and conveyed surprise when Nicole sat down. "What the hell do you want?" she asked, not having to pretend to be angry.

"Detective, are you following me because I kissed your girlfriend?" Nicole leaned in, and Sept found her perfume a bit overwhelming.

"I'm having lunch with my partner so we can review our case files. Why would I be following you?" Nicole was the owner of the phone, but it really only proved the bitch paid for sex. It was interesting, though, that she'd had sex with a call girl who'd been murdered not long afterward. "Paranoid much?"

"Did you just call me?"

"Did you need an excuse to come over here and hassle me?" Sept asked, leaning in as well and making Nicole back up. "And what was up with you barging into the kitchen at Blanchard's? I had to take a call, and you were gone when I was done."

"Keegan's an attractive woman, and I'm interested." Nicole shrugged and lifted her hands. "I didn't realize you and she were that close. I came to apologize."

"Your attitude didn't scream apology, Ms. Voles." She thanked the waitress for the drinks and returned her attention to Nicole. "If that's what it was, apology accepted, but don't make the mistake of showing up there again. If that's all, your father looks lonely."

"Shouldn't you be out solving crime?" Nicole asked as Nathan came back. "Are you ready to admit you need help?"

"From whom?" Nathan asked. "You or your father?"

"I'm just here to write a book, but my father's done nothing for you to treat him with such disrespect. He's willing to help you and offer his expertise."

"We'll let you know," Nathan said and pointed to the chair she was in. "Now if you don't mind, we're slammed for time and need to follow up on some new developments."

"Anything you can share?"

"It'll be in the paper soon enough," Sept said and waved the waitress back. "Two daily lunch specials." Nicole went back to her table, taking the hint, and the conversation with her father became much more animated.

"What's going through your head, aside from fantasies of punching that slimy asshole?" Nathan asked.

"The relationship she seems to have with her father is weird."

"Weird how?"

"He's got this fabulous career in California, but it's like she needs to prop him up. There's a story there, but I don't have time to figure it out." They had lunch, and after dropping Nathan off she went to see Gretchen Harrison again. Gretchen had asked her to come alone, but she figured it was an opportunity to ask her some questions on top of whatever Gretchen wanted.

Gretchen didn't stand when she came in and seemed cool. They had a history, but it was ancient and forgettable for its briefness. She was clueless as to why Gretchen wanted to see her if she was pissed about something, since they rarely spoke, much less saw each other.

"I'm not sure what you want, but you know what I want to talk about," she said to break the silence.

"You know we can't have any conversation about my client, Sept," Gretchen said, putting up her hand to shut her up. "I was hired to defend him, remember?"

"Gretchen, how long have we known each other? I'd never ask you to break privilege."

"Unless it got you something you wanted." Gretchen glared at her, and her voice rose a few octaves. "I was young and stupidly naive back then, and I thought we agreed to drop it and never let it happen again. Sort of how you dropped me when the case was done and you won."

"We agreed to forget it because you and I both knew your client raped five women, and you didn't exactly break privilege then, which makes this whole conversation moot," she said, getting irritated. "I'm only here because you called me, and I want to show you something."

"You've got nothing to say about the rest of it?" Gretchen didn't seem to be able to control herself over ancient history all of a sudden, which made Sept question her mental state.

"Don't try to rewrite our history together, Gretchen," she said, not raising her voice too much. "You fucked someone else while you were fucking me, and I didn't care enough to stay. That's the gist of it." The conversation was truly bizarre and not at all what she expected. "Why the hell are we even talking about this?"

"Maybe I've been thinking about it all this time," Gretchen said, walking to her sofa and dropping onto it. "Or maybe you did it again recently to someone I truly care about."

"You do realize I'm engaged and haven't thought of anyone else in a long time."

"Not what I heard," Gretchen said with her hand over her eyes.

"I'm not sure what the hell you're talking about, but let's start with what I want to show you." She handed over one of the pictures Jennifer had taken at the cemetery. "This is what I'm up against, and I'm trusting you not to let this go anywhere outside this room. If Perlis knows anything, tell me. I'm begging you to not let this happen to anyone else."

"Jesus, Sept, that's not something I can unsee." Gretchen pressed the picture against her chest. "I thought the pictures we already have were bad enough."

"That's what I think every time I show up at one of these scenes." She took the picture back and placed it in the file. "I don't want to pile on what you're already facing in court with Perlis, but if he knows who this is, or has said something, think about speaking up."

"Did you make a play for Nicole Voles?"

"What the hell did you just ask me?" She had to have heard wrong.

"It's a simple question."

Unbelievable, she thought. "I'm with Keegan, but that didn't stop Nicole from making a play for her. I walked in on her kissing Keegan by ambush."

"Is that what Keegan said?" Gretchen asked and grabbed her wrist when she went to move away.

"You're on thin ice, Gretchen. I thought we were friends, but if you say anything about Keegan, we're done."

"Please, Sept, just answer the question."

"Yes, that's what she said, and I believe her. She's never lied to me, and if you've met the Nicole I've become familiar with, you'd believe her too."

Gretchen nodded and let her go. "He hasn't said anything useful. He says he doesn't remember any of what he did, and nothing I ask will make him say otherwise. That's the truth, and if you think I'm lying, you can turn me over to the ethics board if you want to get back at me."

"Gretchen, I'm not here to mess with you. I'm seriously stuck, and I'm tired of having to walk in on these crimes scenes from hell. Believe me, if I knew some other way, I'd have tried it. My gut tells me Perlis might have some idea who's doing this, and he's enjoying every minute of it."

"Don't give up, and I can't promise anything, but I can always phone in an anonymous tip if he ever slips up."

"Thanks, and don't believe everything you hear about me." She tapped the file against her leg and sighed. "And I hope we can start over as friends."

"I'm sorry. I must be PMSing or something. I really haven't held anything against you at all over the years. This case is making me crazy."

"It'll be over soon, so hang in there." Her phone buzzed, and the text from Joel said Nicole was on her way up. She didn't want to run into her yet and chance something happening with no witnesses. "Thanks, Gretchen. And I'm here for you if you need anything."

She waited in the stairwell and hiked her eyebrows when Nicole exited the elevator with roses. "What's your game?" Why feed Gretchen some bogus story about her making a play for her? What did all that have to do with the book she was writing?

"You've made me curious," she whispered to herself and stepped back from the glass slot in the door when Nicole came back out and looked around. "I may not have time for you, but I'm going to make time."

CHAPTER TWENTY-NINE

Hunter opened her eyes two minutes before nine and closed them again briefly to enjoy the silence before the night she had planned began. The stillness was something special she didn't enjoy very often, but necessary before the world around her changed. The game was almost done, and the conclusion maybe should be something like what would happen tonight. It'd be fun to show the smug Savoie she'd never had a chance to win.

She walked naked to the kitchen and stared at the plan until she burned it into her memory. The last week she'd had ample time to walk through it more than once, so she was sure the timing was right. Only one thing would make this perfect, and that'd be standing next to Savoie when she found her gift. Perlis must have enjoyed doing just that.

The world was a simple place when you allowed your true self to flourish. Granted, sometimes you had to adhere to the public persona that helped people, but Hunter was always there scheming up ways to put all the miserable creatures she ran across out of their misery. Their deaths, like in this game, might not have been pleasant or easy, but the sweet relief of the nothingness she imagined that followed made up for not having to endure their pathetic existence any longer.

"I should've fucked before now to take the edge off." She'd been so busy she hadn't had time to indulge in what was so readily available to her, but the pieces of the game had to be perfect. "When I'm done and can take my time, it'll be that much sweeter. This will have to do until then."

She spread her legs, braced herself against the counter, and touched herself. Anticipation of the next few hours made her hard and wet, and it took only a few strokes to climax. The end made a tingle rush through her, and she stood a few minutes with her hand between her legs, knowing she'd have to do it again before she'd be calm enough to dress and get going.

"Fuck," she said, louder than she meant as she jerked against her hand hard enough to make her legs buckle. "Maybe I'll fuck you before I kill you, Sept. I want to see what all the fuss is about, since the world seems to love you enough to spread its legs if you ask."

She headed for the shower, not wanting to be late. "Believe me, once I strip away that façade you wear so effortlessly, they'll curse themselves for falling for your bullshit."

The uniform she'd need was laid out on the chair next to the bed, and she felt the same delicious tingle from before as she put it on. Everything was done, so she took her time slipping into it and lifting the kill bag, fighting the temptation to open it and check it one last time.

"You've got everything you need," she told herself. "All that's left is to complete the plan."

❖

"It sounded simple enough," Keegan said as she took the thermometer Sept had stopped for and placed it on the bedside table. They'd gone to their appointment and gotten the green light to start trying.

"It did." Sept lay on her side naked with a wide smile. "When you get hot, then we get hot."

"You're so poetic, baby." She laughed but stripped off her nightgown. "Now you just need to do your part."

"I'm always ready to do my part, beautiful." The way Sept wiggled her eyebrows made her laugh, but she'd left the task of talking to the Savoie brothers to their sister. "And I was going to surprise you with their answer tonight, so you wouldn't think I was slacking."

"Did they agree?" It was a lot to ask of someone, especially if they'd be acknowledged only as an uncle once the child was born.

"My love, you didn't think they'd say no to you, did you? Joel's the only one who hasn't made it, but only because I've got him hopping. The clinic's staying open later for him tonight. Then we'll be ready, and we've got plenty of material to work with."

"Material, serious?" she asked, laughing. "And way to work fast." She got on top of Sept and kissed her. "Our appointment was three days ago."

"We're all wired to protect and serve. They were glad to provide the serve part this time around. The best part is that Marjorie, Patrice, Claire, and Russ were more excited than we are, I think. I'm shocked one of them hasn't called and blabbed by now," Sept said of her sisters-in-law and her brother Jacques's partner Russ.

"Are you sure you're ready for this?" She smiled when Sept wiped her tears and knew her well enough not to have to ask why they were falling.

"It'll give me good practice to be alert for any late-night calls I get sent out on." The way they fit together made her heart full. Sept loved her for who she was and really strived to make her happy. This had never happened to her before, and it made her tears fall faster. "What's wrong? Are you not ready? It's okay to admit that."

"No, I'm happy—you make me happy, and I can't wait to be pregnant with you. Your job freaked me out at first, but your sisters-in-law and Russ helped me get over it. They learned how to deal from your mom, and I trust all their advice, especially Camille's. You and I are going to be a family."

Sept's phone rang, and she held up a finger since she had to take it. "Hold that lovely thought, sweetheart," Sept said, clearly in a good mood. Sept's smile disappeared instantly when she glanced at the phone, and she had to take a deep breath before she answered it. "Savoie."

"Hello, Detective." The mechanical voice was the same, but this time Sept heard a noise in the background that wasn't just the normal low static caused by the voice manipulator. "Lovely evening, isn't it?"

"It was," Sept said, and she leaned back some when Keegan pressed up behind her. "What do you want?"

"You're not pleased to hear from me?" The laugh that followed sounded as ridiculous as the first call. "I always come bearing gifts, which makes it unbelievable that you're not happy to be the fortunate one I called before."

"Before what?" The phone was a burner, of that she had no doubt, and it killed her that a trace to a specific person wasn't possible.

"Listen, Detective." The static stopped, and someone's moan took its place. It sounded muffled, like they were gagged, but the terror they were experiencing came through loud and clear. "I'm giving you something Alex never shared with you." The manipulator was back, as well as the laugh. "You're so close and yet too blind to see. Another one will be set free of you, and you're too ignorant to stop it."

"It's me you want. Come on, asshole. Let me trade places with whoever you've got," she said, and Keegan squeezed her shoulders as if in protest. "Or are you afraid?"

"Afraid is something you should feel constantly now. All these bodies you're responsible for. I'd love to talk to you about them, but I've got some cutting matters to attend to."

"Wait," Sept said, but it was too late. Hunter was gone with no clue as to who she had. "Fuck." She threw on a T-shirt and ran down the hall and opened Jacqueline's door. Jacqueline was standing by the bed in her underwear, glaring at her like she was contemplating a shoe to her head.

"Do you not know how to knock?" Jacqueline yelled as Keegan followed with Sept's briefs in her hand.

"Put these on before you freak out the rest of my family, please."

"What in the world is going on here?" Della said, coming out of the room Melinda and Carla were sharing. "Why is everyone half naked?"

"Keegan will explain. I've got to go," Sept said, sensing her face getting hot as Keegan helped pull her T-shirt over her ass.

"Thanks, honey," Keegan said, following her back to their bedroom. "Give us a couple of minutes, and I'm guessing someone with a gun will tackle anyone who tries to leave the house."

"Sorry about that," she said as she got her underwear back on and reached for her pants. "I need to scale my freak level back some."

"Where are you going exactly?"

"I have to pick Nathan up and head to work. Believe me, if I got a call, that means we'll be called out as soon as she's done." Keegan helped her button a fresh shirt and put on her shoulder holster. She held the badge until she'd tucked the shirt in. "Where's Carla? I doubt she's in danger, but I like being sure."

"Let me check with Mom, so don't leave yet."

All the Blanchard women were in the hall when she came out and joined them. "Please stay inside, and I'll call when I can," she told them all.

"Keep your ass in one piece," Della said, and she nodded. "It's cute enough, and for Keegan's sake I'd hate for it to get damaged."

Jacqueline laughed the loudest, and Keegan dragged her downstairs by the hand before she could come up with a retort. Cain's man Lou was sitting in the kitchen cleaning one of his guns, and he stood when she came down. "Hey, Lou, thanks for pulling a shift."

"You going out?"

"I have to go to work."

"Go with a clear head then," Lou said with a nod. "I got some guys outside, and no one will get through us. I give you my word."

"Thanks, and let me know if someone tries."

"Be careful, baby, and remember you've got a job to do in the morning here too," Keegan said before she kissed her.

"Get some sleep, and don't let Della make Lou nervous. I love you."

She waved to the other guards, not caring if someone was watching. If Hunter somehow did have an eye on her, she wanted her to see her family wasn't going to be messed with. "Get dressed. We got another call," she said to Nathan.

The recording she'd made of Hunter's message made her think of who the victim could be as she listened to it a third time. Quick calls to Brandi, Erica, and her family had relieved her mind of the most obvious choices, but whoever it was, her gut said she knew them.

Nathan got in and played the recording as they headed to the precinct, their team already going in, including Anabel and her people. "You can't think of anyone?" Nathan asked.

"I checked in with everyone important to us, and they're all okay. It's got to be someone we talked to, though."

"Why do you think so?"

"Hunter, like Perlis, has picked random victims, but in Hunter's case I believe only Bonnie was totally random. The rest have either been to send a message or clean up anyone who can identify her." She was about to cross Canal into the French Quarter when she made another quick mental review. "Gustave, you there yet?"

"Waiting on you, shrimp."

"Get Gretchen Harrison's number and call her. See if you can find her cell number."

"Wait up," Gustave said, and she heard him bark the order out for the number, which only took a minute. "Anything you want me to tell her? It's ringing."

"See if she's okay."

"Went to voice mail, and Jacques said the office number is being answered by a service."

She slapped the blue light on the roof and turned back toward Poydras and Gretchen's office. "I'll be there as soon as we check out her office."

"Not without backup."

"Meet you there, but Nathan and I are closer." She sped to the high-rise close to St. Charles Avenue and Poydras and parked on the sidewalk, leaving the flashing light on her car.

The lobby was lit, but no one was at the marble desk where the security guy usually sat, so she took her badge and banged on the door to try to get someone's attention. "I'll look around and see if I can find a number," Nathan said as she kept up her knocking.

"Wait," she yelled when Nathan was almost to the corner. An older, slightly overweight man in a security uniform walked as fast as it appeared he could to the door, screaming the entire way for her to stop before she broke the glass.

"What's the problem?" he asked, yanking the door open.

"Do you have a master key?" She pushed past him. He hesitated, and she wanted to hit him for the delay. "Do you?"

"Yeah." He held up a key ring. "There's one that goes to each floor."

"Did you let anyone else in through here? A woman maybe?"

"No. The only people here are the cleaning crew and the stragglers who work late."

"Give me the key to thirty-two, and stay here and let in our backup."

He hesitated again. "I'm not supposed to give anyone the keys."

"Do you really want the other cops coming to find you handcuffed to this door? I don't have time for this shit. Give me the key."

They got an elevator quickly because of the hour and rode it a floor past Gretchen's office, taking the stairs down. The floor appeared deserted, and the waiting area of her office was dark. If she'd guessed right, Gretchen was somewhere in there in big trouble.

"How do you want to do this?" Nathan asked.

"We go in and stick together until we clear the office."

She quietly unlocked the door once she had her weapon in hand and paused at the entrance and listened, but the place was quiet. The question of how long it took to disembowel someone and rip their heart out was on her mind, but she pointed toward Gretchen's office, then to her eyes. Nathan was right beside her as they headed to the solid wood door and swung it open, ready to fire.

The office was empty, and she exhaled in relief. She and Gretchen weren't close, but she was glad nonetheless she wasn't dead on the floor. "Thank God."

"Sept, are you upstairs already?" Alain asked when she answered her phone.

"It was a false alarm," she said, closing Gretchen's door.

"Someone just called in something from three floors down. The phone is still off the hook, according to the operator."

"What's three floors down?" They were back at the elevator punching the call button.

"It's another law firm, and when George was notified, he was really upset. The office the call came from is the firm Chloe Johnson works for. That's—"

"Jennifer's partner—shit." They forgot the elevator and took the stairs, willing to break in if that was what it took. The front door was open, but all the lights were off, so they entered the same way as before. She stopped breathing when she saw the flicker of candlelight from the center office, and she could've sworn she could smell the sulfur from the match used to light them.

They both stopped at the door when they saw three bodies on the floor, each with its own altar, but one was blessedly empty except for the burning candles. Thankfully, Chloe had been spared mutilation. Gretchen and the man next to her hadn't been as lucky.

"What the hell is this?"

CHAPTER THIRTY

Hunter took the service elevator to the basement, where the cleaning crews kept their carts. At this time of night, it should've been empty since the janitors were all working, but two women stood with a cart between them, gossiping in Spanish. They glanced at her and stopped talking, and that sealed their fate. She pulled her gun and emptied the clip, wanting to be sure.

"God damn it." She changed the clip and made sure the wig and hat were low on her head before she started to walk out. "The call was a mistake. Alex got caught, remember?" She spoke softly and took a deep breath to calm her movements. If she left like this she'd be caught for sure.

"Sept said to check the service entrance," a man said from right outside the door she needed to use. "Go in through here, and work your way up from there."

It wasn't time to panic, and she had every confidence in her training. She stepped back in and waited in the restroom. If she was right, most of the force would be concentrated upstairs, but there had to be another way out in case she was wrong. The sudden burst of noise from the next room meant she was wrong.

"Nine-one-one. What's your emergency?" It had taken way too many rings, but she still had a chance. "Is someone there?" the operator asked.

"Listen carefully," she said, lowering her voice and cupping her hand over the phone. She gave the address of the building, and the noise from the other end died away as if the woman knew who she was. "Tell Detective Savoie I left her enough explosives in the building to finish the job I started, and she didn't let me finish. But then again, two out of three isn't bad."

"Are you saying there are bombs in the building?"

"You figure it out, but I don't like to leave anything undone." She hung up and stood in the stall with her gun aimed and ready. Sept Savoie might figure it out for what it was, but she could take the chance. That do-gooder part of the detective said no, she'd evacuate the building until the bombs unit arrived.

"Radio call, sir," a man yelled.

"Get everyone out now," someone with a deep voice said, and the conversation was followed by running.

Hunter couldn't be sure, but the man who'd given the order to evacuate was Sebastian Savoie. If that was true, Savoie knew she was in the building and was tightening the noose. "What now, do you think?" she said out loud.

The five minutes she waited were enough to convince her the maintenance room was empty. "Way too close, so I hope this teaches *you* about hubris. The main thing that assures success is invisibility. Gloating before it's done will get you caught every single time."

She shook her head at the self-admonishment. "There's never been a single time, and I'm not going to get caught this time."

The service elevator stood open, which made her think about one thing. She took the keys off one of the dead women, realizing then that she'd left the set she'd stolen in the office upstairs. If this elevator stopped on every floor, she might find one spot the cops hadn't covered.

She punched the fifth-floor button and stood in a ready position again with her gun, but the door opened to an almost-abandoned floor in the parking garage. About six cars were there, which provided no cover, but she couldn't go back.

"Make sure y'all look under every vehicle," a woman said, but the searchers weren't on the floor yet. The empty concrete space made sound carry, so they were still one floor under her. She had only one logical option, so she left the elevator and headed for the stairs.

The majority of the cops searching seemed to be in the actual garage, so she made it down two floors, where most of the cleaning staff was obviously parked, and stood for a long while to make sure no one was out there. "Killing another cop won't help the plan. Only one is left, and the game is done."

She nodded and headed out to the row of cars. The keys she'd taken had Ford stamped on them, and luckily it was the second car she tried. Now she just had to sit and be patient.

"Eventually you'll realize how close you were."

❖

"Make sure you check every single one of them and cross-reference the list," Sept said, agitated that she'd been kicked out of the building. They'd announced over the seldom-used intercom that communicated to every room in the building for everyone to meet in the lobby. They'd spoken in three different languages to be sure, and it'd taken ten minutes for the group of over twenty to come down and instantly startle from the number of police waiting on them. The service they worked for had sent the supervisor to make sure there weren't any strangers in the group.

"They're all ours," the woman with the clipboard said. "We're only missing four, but one of those is home with the flu."

"Two are downstairs," Sebastian said, handing over the ID badges he'd recovered before they'd been tossed out. "Where's this woman?" He pointed to the last name with no check mark next to it.

"Rosario is one of my best," the woman said, waving one of the men over. "Have you heard from Rosario?" she asked him in Spanish.

"Her car's here, so she must still be in the building," he replied, and Sept understood enough to get what he'd said.

"Can you show me her car?" Sept asked in bad Spanish.

He nodded and seemed to understand the urgency as they ran to the parking structure. On the way he told her Rosario was his cousin, and not here legally. She might not have come out for fear of deportation, but Sept could give a crap about that. If she was right, Rosario didn't have a care in the world left.

"That one," he said, pointing, and she held him back and pulled her weapon.

"Get back, and see if Will's available to come down here," she said to Nathan as they backed away. "She's still either in the building or in there, but she's still here."

Will came via the elevator and checked the bottom of the car, making everyone stand back as he jimmied the door and trunk. "It's clear, but there's something for you," Will said, holding up a card with a gloved hand. The name embossed on the top was Gretchen's, which meant it had come off her desk.

Clever girl, Detective, but as always too late.
Thank you for the thrilling night, but you owe me one.

Whoever shall I pick to make up for your early arrival?
So many choices, and so little time left in the game.
Hunter

"I thought we had this place cleared?" she asked. It was maddening to have been so close and allow this bitch to thread the very small opening of escape.

"We did, but if she was in the trunk, we didn't open any vehicles," the woman who'd led the uniformed officers through responded.

"The rest of them are clear, Sept, if you want to open them and check," Will said.

"Open them up." The cops present started for the row of cars. They'd opened the first two when the first explosion rocked them into taking cover. That was followed by another one, and Sept saw debris falling from above. "Get everyone out."

"I'm staying put," Will said. "If those are the only two, then I'm heading up once the smoke clears and I can see what I'm doing."

"Why put the damn things out here?" Nathan asked as they made their way down the ramp to the street.

"It's a diversion. We can't take our eyes off anything out here and the other crime scene," she said, then doubled back and stopped Will. "Are you sure there's no devices in the office with the bodies?"

"We checked it, and cleared it, but if you're going back in, I'm coming with you. I'll leave someone here until we're ready."

"Okay," she said, pointing to all the possible exits out of the garage. "Nathan, have all the ways out covered, then stay here until every inch of every car that's in here is searched before it leaves."

"Got it."

"I'll be back as soon as George's done with the scene upstairs." She headed back, and the team was still outside waiting for the green light to reenter. "Where are Jennifer and George?" she asked Gustave.

"Jennifer wasn't leaving Chloe, and George wasn't leaving without the two of them, so they're still up there. It's a good thing too."

"What do you mean? If anything, Jennifer should be torn apart."

"Chloe came to—she's not dead," Gustave said, which relieved her.

"Let's head up. Try and get our Santeria whisperer over here. We were dodging exploding cars at the garage, so I haven't called him."

"Francois volunteered to pick him up," Gustave said, following her inside. The office was still dark, lit only by the candles, and the

EMTs were waiting in the hall since Chloe was wrapped in Jennifer's arms.

"Chloe," she said, sitting in a chair close to where the couple was on the floor. "I'm so happy you're okay, and I'm sorry this happened to you." Chloe smiled, and Sept saw the tears still falling. She'd never forget the fear she'd experienced when Perlis had her tied down.

That night as she'd watched Nathan and her brother-in-law Damien waiting to die with her, all she could think of was the people she'd leave behind. Her parents and siblings had already lost so much, and she had so much still left to do. They'd all survived, and even Damien had found himself a path back from the pain of losing Noel and Sophie. He was living with his parents and would be back at work in another month.

All that paled when she thought of leaving Keegan alone. The possibility still haunted her some nights.

"This can wait, Sept. She's been through enough already," Jennifer said.

"I know, but we need to respect the folks who didn't survive."

"It's okay, sweetie. She's right. I don't know how much I can help you, though. I was preparing for a case I've got tomorrow when Gretchen came in with a hooded creep with a gun."

"Was it a woman?"

"I never saw her face, but I'm pretty sure it was. She had us sit in my visitors' chairs and moved behind us. For like ten minutes she just stood behind us and said if we turned around she'd kill us." Chloe seemed not to want to glance at the bodies, and Sept placed her hand on her shoulder and nodded. "We both flinched when we felt a jab at the shoulder. I thought she'd stabbed me, but I woke up when Jennifer touched me."

"I don't have the words to express how happy I am you made it. Anything else you remember, Chloe?"

"Before I was out like a drunk on Bourbon, she kept repeating numbers and what sounded like instructions on what she was doing."

"Repeating the instructions?"

"It was strange. I mean, obviously she can kill, but she doesn't seem to have a stomach for it."

"God help us all if she gets any more comfortable."

❖

"Captain, we need a search warrant," Nathan said as the bomb guys walked back into the garage to get to the floor where the cars had exploded. "Do you want me to start the process?"

"The cleaning crew is all here, so call them over and have them give consent. That should get us started without having to wake a judge. If one person refuses, then we get a warrant for everything in here," Sebastian said.

"One more thing, sir." Nathan waved the uniformed supervisor over. "We need to run the plate of every car in there. We found stolen cars at a couple of locations, so it's probable one's here too. We might need more bodies out here to get through all this faster."

"Good call, and I have to say, I'm glad I partnered you with Sept. You two make a good team."

"Thank you, sir. Sept's been a great teacher and an even better friend." Nathan moved away and contacted an ADA to put them on standby, then took the time to text Sept and tell her what was going on. The radio on his belt came to life, and the NOPD bomb unit called to report.

"Two cars got blown to shit," the guy said. "Looks like the devices were attached to the gas tanks for extra pop. The team's checking the others, but nothing up here is drivable after the ones that were set off."

"Can I send people in to run all the plates?" Nathan asked.

"Stay put, and we'll walk the lot and radio them in. Once we do that we can send the wreckers in to start clearing this place."

"Thanks, and make sure you don't miss any floor."

"We'll start at the top and work our way down. A couple of my guys will check as we go, so make sure you don't send anyone up here. These calls are getting nuts."

"You aren't kidding," Nathan said and read the text he got. "And add opening the cars to your list. Our perp might still be on-scene."

"That'd be some shit."

"If it's true, though, you can go back to playing solitaire at work."

❖

"Jennifer, how about you take Chloe and have the EMTs check her out?" Sept said, placing her hand on Chloe's shoulder.

"If George can spare me, I'd rather take her to the hospital to get checked out," Jennifer said from behind Chloe, a spot she'd taken to better hold her, turning Chloe away from the bodies so close by.

"Go ahead, and I'll take care of this," George said.

"One more thing, Chloe," Sept said, and Jennifer's expression became even more concerned. "I identified Gretchen Harrison, but do you know who the man is?"

"Let me get her loaded up, and I can help with that," Jennifer said.

"Wait," Chloe tried to turn around, but Jennifer held her. "Who is it?"

"Please, baby," Jennifer said.

"Who is it?"

"It's Roger, and I'm so sorry," Jennifer said and held Chloe as she sobbed. "You know he would've done anything to keep you safe, and it looks like he did."

"Come on, Chloe. Let's get you out of here," Sept said, helping Chloe up and holding her until Jennifer took over. "Roger who?" she mouthed to Jennifer.

"I'll be right back," Jennifer said and walked Chloe out, stepping back in quickly and telling them who Roger was, what he did, and what he meant to Chloe. "He was her oldest and dearest friend."

"If Chloe was a target, I can understand Roger," Sept said as another team member took pictures for George. "What's Gretchen doing down here?"

"Sept, they radioed that Dr. Munez is coming up," someone yelled from the hall.

"I don't know, but this is a first," George said. "The two bodies, which should've been three, is a definite escalation. Thank all that's holy you figured this one out and got one out alive."

"That's what doesn't make sense to me, though. Why take a chance that I would figure it out before she was done? All this elaborate gory show takes time, and if I interrupted her with Chloe, there's no way she got out clean."

"How do you figure?" George asked as one of the techs started dusting for prints. The phone was full of blood, as was the door, but all of it was completely smeared.

"The two dead bodies downstairs that were found. Hunter must have been posing as the one woman who wasn't here tonight, and killing two people before you come up here to kill three more would've potentially gotten us called out sooner." She stepped behind Chloe's desk and covered the open files with paper from the copier on the credenza. The techs had taken all the necessary pictures of the scene, and she didn't want to take the chance anyone would see sensitive information.

"Hello, Sept," Julio said as he entered. The first sight of the slaughter made him reach for the beads around his neck. "Just when I think it can't get any worse than the last one," he said, tapping his chest rhythmically with the fist he held the beads in.

"I can't tell you how much I appreciate your continued help, Julio. These scenes can get overwhelming pretty fast, but you haven't given up on us." She waved him to a spot by the desk where he'd be safe from stepping on anything. "Not that the orishas have led us anywhere, but what's all this mean?"

"This doesn't make sense," Julio said, his eyes moving from one altar to the next.

"It's like the others with the circle and stuff in them."

"There are two altars, but the things on them represent Ibeji, one orisha. They are the divine twins but are seen as one entity. That's St. Cosme," he pointed to the altar by Roger, "and that's St. Damain." He pointed to Gretchen's.

"I think even my mother who's a good Catholic hasn't heard of some of these saints," she said as the techs finished around the bodies. "What else?"

"See how they both have the numbers two and four on their feet and the number eight on their foreheads? They're the same on both, but it's definitely Ibeji, and why he was picked makes no sense to me."

"Sounds like the twins are male and female, and that's what we've got."

"That's right, but why a third one?" Julio pointed to the altar that would've been Chloe's. "Please tell me this one lived."

"She did. This is her office, and I got here before she was killed. Unfortunately we found two more downstairs."

"That's good to hear, and the rest is right as well. The red and blue candles are their colors, and the dolls usually placed wear one of each color with white. The little bananas are their favorite, along with the candy."

"And what path do they walk, or what do they protect?" she asked.

"Nothing. They have no path but to be playful and curious. Their followers believe them to be universal in nature, the first twins ever born in the world, with Chango and Oshun as their parents."

"No warnings of death and war this time?"

"People who've had twins follow Ibeji, as do those who've lost one and the other child lived. The respect shown for the life of the child lost protects the other one from following them to the grave."

"You have no clue what this one would've been?" The empty circle suddenly became more interesting, since the other two were the same type of murders. "Some other of the orishas associated with them?"

"Their parents are highly regarded orishas, but one legend says Oshun shunned them, and Yemayá, the mother of all living things, raised them. Maybe this is what this altar is for, but I can't be certain since that's not the way of the followers." Julio bent to study the statues. "They must've searched for these because they're not common."

"They both look male."

"They are, and they were actual twins who died Christian martyrs. If I remember correctly, they were skilled doctors who were born in Arabia and died in the Roman province of Syria in the third century." Julio closed his eyes as he spoke, as if the answers were printed on his eyelids. "The orishas, though, are mostly seen as male and female, but I've heard of them as identical males or females."

"Thank you, and if you get any other ideas about the empty altar, please call me."

"Do you mind?" Julio asked, and opened his arms. When she shook her head, he embraced her and recited something she didn't understand. "It's nothing but a prayer of protection," he said when he finished. "You must remain strong and know we all pray for you."

"Thank you, and I need you to be careful. This killer has ways of finding people connected to this case or to me, and I don't want anything to happen to you."

"Matilda insisted I stay with her, so don't worry. And if I'm needed, you know where to find me. Maybe you should come talk to her."

"I will if I get the chance."

"Do you have a history of twins in your family?" Julio asked as what almost seemed like an afterthought.

"My brothers Jacques and Joel are twins, but not identical. Since they look and act nothing alike, no one ever believes they are."

He stared at her and took a few breaths, as if trying to decide about something. "Matilda said something about you that made no sense."

"Can you tell me? At this point I'm about to go sit with one of those psychics in the Quarter for answers."

"She said identical twins will come to you," he said, and smiled. "I'd hoped she meant Keegan and any children you might have, but you never mentioned anything like that. Perhaps she picked up on your brothers, or on this."

"If she says anything else, let me know, and if the name and address of the killer pop into her head, make me your first call."

CHAPTER THIRTY-ONE

O ne of the cars that blew up was reported stolen," Nathan told Sept after she finished upstairs and met him by the garage. "The bomb guys are still working through it, and the cleaning crew was allowed to drive away once everyone had agreed to have their vehicles searched. A unit checked on Rosario, the missing custodian, and she's really missing."

"Where and who was the car stolen from?" It was after three in the morning, and the thick clouds threatened rain, cooling the temps down.

"You won't believe it, but it was stolen from the same lot as before by the Hilton. Gustave went in search of security footage."

"All the other cars belong here?" The few drops that fell made her and Nathan seek shelter right inside the parking structure.

"I don't know about belong here, but they haven't been reported for any reason."

"Any jump out at you from this list?" she asked, and he handed it over. They both glanced up when a report of a shooting and possible homicide came through. "It's not like there's not enough going on."

"Hell. I'd love for us to be responsible for only one possible homicide instead of all this shit. Whoever got that call are some lucky bastards."

After two hours, they were called to the murder in the lower Garden District, and neither of them felt lucky. The guy who'd been shot in the head was one of the janitors at their earlier scene, and Hunter had obviously hidden under the back seat of the old Oldsmobile. But they couldn't figure out if he'd willingly allowed Hunter to escape or was surprised when he arrived home.

"Take a nap, and I'll swing by and pick you up after I finish mine," she said, dropping Nathan off. "I'll call you before I come back."

The drive home was quiet, and she went over the night again while she was alone. She had to be overlooking a clue because Hunter was simply a copycat and nothing more. By killing the defense team, or a majority of them, Hunter had screwed Perlis, so it wasn't about him and what he'd done.

"Lourdes." She'd called the precinct, knowing Lourdes had gone in on the off chance someone needed information.

"You're not dead on your feet yet?" Lourdes asked, then groaned. "Sorry. Poor choice of words."

"I am beat, but do me a favor and make a note to call Estella and ask her about religious statues, rare ones," she said of the woman who owned the books Perlis had stolen and used for his crimes. "Maybe we'll take a field trip to her place later."

"You got it. See you in a few hours."

"Let's hope we can go that long before something else happens."

❖

Their driveway was larger than most on the street, and it was still full because of the number of people in the house, but Sept wasn't about to complain. The crowd inside was easier to protect together than spread out over three different locations. She parked on the street and waved to the guys on patrol, impressed at how perky they looked.

She stopped at the BMW sedan Carla drove and noticed the sticker with the caduceus on it. The two snakes wrapped around a staff reminded her of Julio's history lesson on Saints Cosme and Damain. The two Christian martyrs were talented doctors who now also had followers in Santeria.

"Is there a problem?" the nearest guy asked.

"Were you here when the woman who drives this car arrived?" She found it hard to believe Carla was capable of these crimes, but could it be someone in the medical community who was using the murders as a way to blow off steam?

"She looked dead tired when she got here a couple of hours ago. Said it was a tough night."

That was an understatement. "Thanks, and it was. You guys need anything?"

"Go to bed, Sept. We got this."

She stopped and grabbed a juice and chatted with Lou. He told her Carla did in fact appear beat and was filthy from changing a tire. It was hard to find a doctor who did that, she guessed. Her own exhaustion made it easy to let her brain run off in a dark direction like she'd allowed it in the Perlis case.

The tone of Perlis's notes and why he was committing the crimes could fit Damien's life. Her greatest regret from that case was ever thinking her brother-in-law could be responsible for any of it. He'd come close to losing his life because of her assumptions.

"Hey, honey," Keegan said sleepily.

"Hey." She stripped her pants and shirt off and tossed them into the hamper. Her habit of leaving them on the floor had caused a long discussion two weeks after she'd moved in. "Open up for me before I take a shower and join you for a nap."

Keegan opened her mouth and closed it around the thermometer with a smile. The glance at her watch said she had enough time, and she took it out and read the digital window. "Thanks for being here for this. It's stupid, but I didn't want to do it alone," Keegan said.

"Wouldn't have missed it. You're running a little warm."

"You're sitting here naked, so of course I'm running a little warm," Keegan said and winked. "Do you want to sleep and skip the shower?"

"Shower first, trust me, and then I have time for like an hour." She kissed Keegan and got up to clean off.

"Let me sit and talk to you," Keegan said, following her in and holding her hand. "Anything you can tell me about tonight?"

"It started bad and went quickly to horrible," she said, adjusting the water. "When did your mom meet Carla?"

"Strange change of subject, hon. What's up?" Keegan raised her voice when she got under the spray.

"I'm only curious. How'd they meet?"

"Carla purchased a ticket for an event Gran hosts to raise money for culinary students. Part of me was excited for the instant spark since Mom had been alone so long." Keegan handed her a towel when the water shut off, her eyebrow was cocked in question. "Now spill, and you can, no matter what it is. You know I haven't always been the most supportive daughter, but I'm trying."

"I was only thinking of something, but I'm sure it's nothing."

"Like what kind of nothing? She really became a part of Mom's life, and if you're thinking there's some reason she shouldn't be, you have to tell me right now," Keegan said, holding her by the biceps.

She explained the orisha the killer had chosen and what Julio had said about it. "I'm just tired, baby, which means you shouldn't listen to me right now. The sticker on her car made me think of her profession and the difference between brilliant doctors of the two saints to their orisha's counterparts."

"What do you mean?"

"I don't think Carla is a vicious killer, but I do think the woman doing all this defines that difference. During her normal life she's most probably respected, but in the role of Hunter she can leave all that behind and indulge a part of herself not everyone has, much less understands." Sept quickly dried off and put her arms around Keegan. "Believe me, if I thought Carla was dangerous, I'd take her out. You know I love your mom, and her safety is important to me."

Keegan nodded against her chest and exhaled deeply. "Who was killed?"

"Two attorneys, Gretchen Harrison and Roger Smith," she said, and Keegan held on to her tighter. "Do you know them?"

"Gretchen was a lunch regular, so I know her from that. I don't know the guy."

"There should've been three victims, but we got there in time. We found Chloe Johnson alive, and that was a relief since she's the partner of our new team member, Jennifer."

Keegan had glanced up at her and opened her mouth when Sept's phone rang. "Do they think you can be awake twenty-four-seven?" The question held some heat, but she went and got it for her.

"Savoie."

"Sept," Gustave said, sounding as beat as she was. "I just left the precinct, and a message came in for you last night. I thought you'd want to know. The crap from Harrison's office happened, so it got lost in the shuffle."

"What is it?"

"Gretchen called you, and if Gavin's time of death is right, it was an hour to forty-five minutes before she died."

"What was the message?" Their last conversation might've sparked Gretchen to finally do the right thing.

"She wanted you to call her because it was important you two talk. Do you think there might be something in her office that'll clue you in?"

"If there is, the firm won't let us search. Gretchen and Roger might be gone, but their firm is still responsible for Perlis in court." She sat on the bed and smiled when Keegan sat pressed against her. "This might be a more finesse thing. Give me a couple of hours, and I'll make an appointment with the managing partners."

"Get some sleep, and let me know if you need anything from me."

"Thanks." She lay back and took Keegan with her and told her about the call.

"Close your eyes and go to sleep," Keegan said, cuddling up to her.

"Your temperature's up, and you don't want to practice?" she asked, squeezing Keegan's butt.

"I love the way you commit to practice, but you need to sleep."

"And the way you inspire my practicing trumps anything and everything." She squeezed harder. It didn't take long, and as she drifted off to sleep she thought about her love for Keegan and how Gretchen's chance of being this happy was gone.

What had Gretchen done to draw the attention of a killer?

❖

Hunter had walked to the nearest bus stop once the driver who'd allowed her escape was dead, but after thirty minutes of waiting, she started toward downtown on foot. It was the driver's own fault for lingering around the piece-of-crap vehicle after he'd parked it. She was too close to the finish line to leave a potentially devastating witness alive.

It would be a long walk back to her sanctuary, and she stayed vigilant for patrol vehicles that might stop a lone walker at this hour. This was the closest any opponent had come to catching her, and it solidified her decision.

The cool air was glorious after all her running around that damn building, so she didn't mind the distance she had left to go. "I have to think of what tipped Savoie off before I was done," she said, still baffled by how fast Savoie had arrived. "You're so good, I almost want to extend the game," she said of Sept, "but we can't take any more stupid chances."

The night hadn't followed the plan at all, but it had been thrilling.

Only her intellect had saved her, and her experience under pressure had kept her eerily calm throughout the whole thing. She'd been lucky, so she needed to quell the temptations that warred in her to keep playing with Savoie. It was time to end the game by taking the main player off the board.

"Only one more, and we move on. It's time to kill Sept Savoie and be done with it."

CHAPTER THIRTY-TWO

Y ou really need more sleep," Keegan said as they both got ready for work.

"I agree with you, but I have to go convince some lawyers to give me something they'd rather die than allow me." Sept buttoned her shirt and tucked it in, with Keegan's help, which made her smile. "I'll do my best to finish early and be waiting when you get home."

"Try to call me so you don't make me insane."

"I will, and you have a good day." She stopped and picked up Nathan to head back to Gretchen's office.

The parking garage was still closed, and a majority of the businesses had elected to keep their people at home until everyone with a badge gave them a 100 percent promise the building was completely safe. Gustave's call earlier had told her that the managing partners had come in to assess their office space and Gretchen's permanent absence from their firm.

"Detective Savoie." The silver-haired man who introduced himself as Walton Waters shook her hand, and she realized Waters was the first name in the string of them on the door. "Do you have any leads? This can't go unpunished."

"You might be able to help me with that," she said, and all the partners leaned in. "Gretchen was a friend, and catching her killer is important enough to me to ask for something I realize won't be well received."

"Whatever you need, we'll do it," another older man said.

"I need to search Gretchen's office."

All the partners shook their heads like they'd practiced uniformity. "Anything but that, Detective. You realize she was working on the Perlis case, and you going through those files would spell total malpractice on our part. We cared for Gretchen deeply, but our obligation to our client is paramount."

"Therein lies our conundrum, gentlemen. Gretchen called me right before her death, and I need to know why. It was urgent I call her back, and I think it was because she connected something from the Perlis case to the copycat murders we're investigating now." She flattened her hands on the conference table and gazed at each of them. "It's important to our case, and I came here first before getting a subpoena. All I need is access to her assistant, a member of Perlis's legal team, and an idea of what's on her desk."

"Could you give us a minute?" Walton asked.

Sept recognized Jennifer's father, David Shultz, coming in and extended her hand, but he ignored it and hugged her. "Whatever you need *ever*, it's yours. Thank you for saving Chloe and, in turn, my child from the pain it would've left her with."

"Thank you, sir, and you can help me right now." She explained what she needed and why. David didn't say anything else and entered the conference room. The door opened five minutes later after the screaming had subsided, and Walton invited her back in.

"Fred Peller and Gretchen's assistant will help you go through the contents of the office. Ask as many question as you want, but try to stay clear of anything having to do with privilege," Walton said. "We want to cooperate and thank you for not turning this into a legal battle."

"Are Mr. Peller and the assistant here?" The quicker they did this, the better.

"Fred's already in there, and we called the assistant."

The young man sitting at Gretchen's desk appeared distraught, but he wiped his face and stood when he noticed them. "Mr. Peller. Thank you for your help."

"Anything," Fred said, waving to Nathan to close the door. "I'll do anything to catch this animal. Gretchen was my mentor, and I was supposed to stay last night, but I had a date. Roger filled in for me."

"Do you have any clue why Gretchen called me last night? It was right before she was killed."

"She didn't mention anything, but let's see." He sat back down and flipped through all the files. "We're working exclusively on Perlis right now." He stacked all the ones he'd checked to the side.

"Anything new on that? I mean anything you can share?"

He shook his head but seemed to be thinking more than refusing to answer. "Alex just recently started talking to Gretchen but not saying anything that would help our case. It makes me wonder…"

She glanced at Nathan, and he shrugged. "Wonder what?"

"Gretchen recently got close to that writer Nicole Voles, and Nicole convinced her to let her visit Alex alone. Supposedly it was to do research for the book, but if Alex never said anything, why keep going back?" He kept searching as he spoke, which made Sept think back to Larry Nobles.

The cop who'd sold information to Nicole was in solitary for his own safety in central lockup, but he'd refused to talk to her. Maybe it was time for another visit. "Do you know if Ms. Voles ever told Gretchen about those visits?"

"Not that I know of," Fred said, and his voice trailed off again.

"Fred, whatever it is, it won't go any further than this room. You have our word," she said.

"Gretchen was always professional," he said hesitantly. "This case, though, started like that, but then Voles arrived. It was the first time I'd ever seen Gretchen not exactly do anything unethical, but bend her normal rules to please Voles."

"And it was like that until last night?"

"I got an email from her early last night telling me to review the case and implement what she and Roger were working on. She didn't say what, but the tone of her writing was different—it was like she was pissed about something."

"Is Voles still visiting Perlis?" Nathan asked before she could.

"As far as I know. She's hot to write this book and ever more anxious to help us however she could."

"Did Gretchen restrict his visitors?" she asked.

"Yes, since a bunch of reporters and sickos want to talk to him. Access is limited to us and Ms. Voles."

Nathan took his phone out and called the jail when she gazed at him. It was a short conversation. "Ms. Voles's name was removed yesterday afternoon."

Fred appeared as surprised as she was. "Shit," Fred said. "I have no idea why she'd do that."

"Can you access her email?" she asked, and Fred shook his head more firmly this time.

"I can, but I'm going to have to call our IT guy to unlock it. No one has Gretchen's password but her."

"Phone him, and then call me back when you're in." She took out her card and handed it over. "The answer we need might be in there, so please make it a priority."

"Don't worry. I'm on it."

"One more thing." She was picking up on something and wanted to be sure. "What's your impression of Nicole Voles?"

"She seems nice enough, but something's off there."

"Thanks for your honesty, Fred, and I totally agree."

❖

Nicole sat at her small desk and tapped her fingers on the keys but didn't actually strike any. The news had reported the murders from the night before, and it had left her restless. She stared at the phone when it rang and contemplated not answering it, but talking to someone might pull her out of the funk she was in.

"Have you fallen in a swamp?" Gwen asked. "I haven't heard from you, and you haven't sent any more sheets. The publisher called this morning and needs an update."

"I should've gone with my first instinct and not answered." The place was quiet since her father had gone out but hadn't told her where. "I've been busy with research, which means I don't have anything other than what I sent you to look at. That means stall the publisher."

"Are you okay?" Gwen sounded softer. "Do you want me to come down and help?"

"Not yet, and Daddy's still here. Anything new aside from the deadline warnings?" She stood and walked to the window. As excited as she was about the new book, she needed to get out of this city.

"I've got everything under control and look forward to seeing you. This place is dull without you."

"It's Malibu, darling. Go to the beach or something." Her attention went from the river to the street below. The guy walking on the opposite side of her building looked familiar.

She stepped back some but kept her eyes on him. He stopped at a dark SUV and got in the driver's side, but then the vehicle sat there. Had he been there that morning? "I'm sorry. What?"

"Do you want me to send you this month's numbers? Are you sure you're okay?"

"I'm fine, and yes. Send them, but I've got to go."

She stood there twenty minutes, but the car didn't move. The guy seemed like someone she should know, but nothing came to mind. "I'm either paranoid, or this writer's block is making me crazy," she said out loud. "Only one way to prove it."

She threw on a pair of jeans and a sweater, placing her wallet in her pocket. Her father hadn't taken the car, which gave her an excuse to drive to the market for supplies. When she got downstairs she followed her routine of using the side entrance, which led to the parking space, and noticed that the SUV was perfectly parked to see both the lot and the front door.

The traffic wasn't bad getting out, but she took her time, not wanting to lose the tail, if that's what it was. She clicked her blinker on and turned at the corner, and surprisingly the vehicles didn't move. For the rest of the trip she checked the rearview without trying to appear obvious, but no one was following her.

"I'm losing my shit," she berated herself, yet still glanced behind her.

It was time to call Larry and see if she was a target of something. What, she had no idea, but perhaps she'd pushed Sept Savoie too far.

"If this is your doing, you're going to pay."

❖

"What do you think?" Sept asked Estella Mendoza as the voodoo shop owner held the statue of Cosme with gloves on.

"I'm not an antiques dealer, but these look really old. If someone used them for an altar for Ibeji, they gave up something precious. Usually the orisha dolls are something like African primitives holding drums. That's true especially now that Cosme and Damain are hard to find."

"There was another altar next to these two," Sept said as the tech placed the statue back in the evidence bag. "Any idea what it was for?"

"What was in it?" Estella stripped her gloves off and followed her outside.

"It was empty, which is why Julio had no idea." The sun was bright, warming up the afternoon to the point she'd taken her jacket off.

"Do you mind if I ask Matilda? Maybe between the two of us we can think of something."

"Thanks, Estella." Sept walked Estella to her car and opened her door for her.

"I'll be in touch."

Sept went back inside to George's office and picked up the statues without taking them out of the bag. Both were solid wood and hand painted, so they didn't have a hollow for a note. It was the only scene without one, not counting the one they'd found in Rosario's car.

"What are you thinking?" Nathan asked.

"You heard her—they're old, so let's have them checked out." She found Della in her contacts and asked her for a good dealer that'd get them more information. The guy Della recommended and promised to call arrived twenty minutes later, ready to help.

"Della's a good woman to know," Nathan said and laughed.

"Bernard Rosemount, and I agree, as long as you don't piss her off," Bernard said. "I'm more versed in art pieces, but I'll take a look and recommend someone if necessary."

Sept handed him some gloves and showed him the pieces. He took a magnifying glass out of his pocket and studied both of them like he'd have to take a written test when he was done. "Anything you can tell me?" she asked after ten minutes of silence.

"Do you mind if I make a call? I'll do it on speaker. That way you can follow along, but I'll ask the questions."

"Go ahead."

Bernard called a religious-artifact dealer in New York, who immediately demanded pictures. After he promised not to share them, Nathan took some shots and texted them to the guy.

"Detective," the dealer said after a long stretch of silence, "I'm not sure where you got these, but they're exquisite. I'd say they're around six hundred years old, but I might be off since I haven't handled them. I'll check around, and if they were purchased at auction, I can get you the buyer's name."

"Thank you, and our contact info was attached to the pictures," she said, thanking Bernard as well. "That might actually lead somewhere, but why leave something like that at a crime scene? They're obviously valuable."

"I'd say it's a gift to the gods, but that's bullshit," Nathan said.

"Never heard of these saints, but the one orisha with no path might actually lead us somewhere."

Their next stop was central lockup, and she smiled when the guard led Larry in, holding his way-too-large pants while he shuffled in with leg irons. His bruises had turned deep purple, which clashed with his orange prison garb. "Hey, Larry, good news," she said, and he glared at her. "I got Chief Jernigan to start your termination papers, and as soon as they go through, you can get out of your cell."

"It's about damn time. I want my rep."

"I'm so glad you're ready to join the general population," Nathan said, playing along.

"What are you talking about?" Larry tried to raise his hands, but the cuffs kept them by his waist.

"You asked for a rep and clammed up, and that's going to cost you your job. If you're let go, there's no reason to keep you separated. You're going into a regular cell."

"Sept, come on. You can't do that," Larry said, scooting his chair closer to the table. "I'll be dead by morning."

"Sucks to be you," Nathan said.

"You sold information to someone who shouldn't have had it. From the beginning of these cases, someone's been trying to kill me." She spread her hands and cocked her head to the side. "How do I know you aren't helping someone try to kill me and my partner? Three cops are dead, so why should I give a crap about you?" She stood up, and Nathan followed her to the door.

"Wait," Larry shouted and tried to turn around. "Just wait."

"You know what I want to hear."

"I waive my right to counsel, so ask me whatever you want."

Sept turned around and stared at him. "You fuck with me more than you have already, and not only will I turn you over to the mob, but I'll introduce you." He nodded but appeared ready to cry. "What exactly did you turn over to Nicole Voles or her father?"

"She wanted the whole case file to get an idea of Perlis's MO. She said she needed it for the book, and she was willing to pay. The storm really screwed me, so I needed the money."

"But that's not all, is it?" she asked, and Larry started rocking.

"That's it—I swear."

Nathan placed a small recorder on the table and turned it on. The conversation with Brian and Nicole played, and when Larry started to say something, she pointed at him to keep him quiet. She made him listen to it all the way to the end. The button clicked off, and she held her hand up again.

"That doesn't sound like that was it."

"She wanted your notes. For some reason she thought something was buried in them that she could use."

"Okay," she said and smiled. "One more thing."

"What? I don't have anything else."

"But I do. Something about the night you were injured in that bombing that hasn't set right with me. To satisfy my curiosity I pulled your phone records. You didn't mention getting a call from a blocked number right before you said those bombs went off. What was that about?"

Larry started to cry, and she wasn't moved. "I don't know who it was, but they told me to run."

"Was it a woman?" she asked, exhaling. "That's an easy yes or no."

"It could have been either. They sounded like a machine." Larry pressed his arms against his side and kept crying. "I didn't say anything because you'd think I was in on it, and none of that shit was me."

"The fact that you wear a badge pisses me off, and now would be a good time to tell me whatever you've got." The show of emotion Larry displayed was sickening, but he had something she needed, so she'd keep his head above water for now. "I'll talk to Fritz to keep you in protective custody, but you might have to call Voles for me. Refuse, and I'm not going to be on your side."

The guards practically had to drag Larry out. What he'd said about her notes caught Sept's attention the most. What could be hidden in them? A book was one thing, but Nicole wanted something much more.

"What are you thinking?" Sept asked.

"I'm glad that piece of shit is getting fired."

"Eventually he will, but I bent the truth a little," she said and winked. "Larry doesn't get the truth just yet."

Sept spent the rest of the afternoon in the conference room putting the pieces together and finally thought she'd figured out the thing Nicole wanted most. "Delivery for you, Sept," Lourdes said, dropping an envelope on her desk.

The large yellow envelope had only her name on it. "How'd this get here?"

"One of the bicycle couriers in town," Lourdes said.

"Get George here, and tell him to hurry." This had to be the note she didn't receive at the last crime scene.

The envelope went into an evidence bag, and Sept sat in the conference room and stared at the board where all the information from each scene was written. She wanted to read the note, but an idea was starting to take root.

George arrived, and she was surprised to see Jennifer with him. "Believe me, I wanted to stay home, but Chloe and my mother made me come to work," Jennifer said.

"Is she okay?"

"She's alive, and that makes everything manageable. I have you to thank for that, and I'll never forget it."

"You don't owe me anything, but I'm here for both of you."

"Yes, I do. Chloe's pregnant, and losing her would've killed me."

"Congratulations. I'm so happy for you both."

George smiled at her and sliced the envelope open, taking the paper inside out with gloves and tweezers. "You were right. It's another note."

You have played a good game.
You were so close.
You were a good opponent.
The game is now done.
We will never meet.
You will be the one who lives.
But what kind of life will it be when you question if I'm really
    gone?
The day you know the truth will be your last.
My happiness will come when I see you most days, and you'll
    look right through me.

"Do you think they put a lot of thought into these?" George asked.

"It's supposed to strike fear in all of us, but really it's just irritating," she said, and she read it again. "She's leaving, but not really, since she'll see me most days."

"She's talking in circles," Nathan said.

"Not really, but it's a clue I've got to check out now."

"Are you sure?" Nathan asked.

"I'll be okay. Believe me. I'm not headed into a dark alley by myself."

She made a call on the way out and headed for the hospital. Carla was in an office she shared with two other doctors and smiled when she knocked. "Thanks for seeing me," she said, sitting after Carla did.

"Are you hurt?" Carla asked, leaning back in the office chair.

"No. I'm fine, but I've got some questions for you." She opened her notebook and glanced down at the list she'd made. "Did you leave the hospital last night for anything?"

"What's this about?" Carla lost her smile and dropped her feet to the ground. "Do I need an attorney?"

"That's your choice, but I'm not trying to trick you."

"I was here all night covering in the ER. You can check if you don't believe me."

"Do you have access to this?" She showed Carla the sedative used in the ritualistic murders.

"I have access to a lot of things, Sept, and I don't care for this line of questioning. Where are you going with this?" Carla's voice and volume never changed.

"The direction is a solution to what I'm working on, and it's important."

"I understand you're under a lot of pressure because of the stuff you're working on, but I doubt you'll find the answers here or with me." Carla tapped her fingers on the desk and kept eye contact with her. "I realize the girls don't care for me, but don't you think this is extreme?"

"Extreme describes the scenes I've been investigating, and trust me, this is me being straightforward. I can do asshole if you want."

"I'd prefer the Sept I usually meet at dinner."

"Maybe later, but right this minute we've got a problem." She closed the notebook, but she already knew the answers to what she had left. "Have you been in contact with anyone or any business in New York in the last two months?"

"New York? You've seen me almost every day for months. I think Melinda and the rest of you would've noticed me gone."

"Actually, I do remember the conference you attended to present some paper. Melinda was happy for you." She took her phone out and opened the text message Bernard had sent her. "The same two days you were there, you did a little shopping."

Carla stared at her like she was totally making no sense. "I bought Melinda a little something. Is that a crime?"

"You also bought these." She handed her phone over and showed Carla the invoice for the Cosme and Damain statues. "That's an impressive amount of money."

"Who the hell are Cosme and Damain?"

"Third-century talented doctors who died martyrs."

"I have no idea what this about." Carla resembled an oscillating fan looking between her and the phone. "There's no way I'd spend that much money on these...what you're saying are religious icons."

"This is your name, I assume your account information, and you were in New York when the purchase was made."

"I don't pay my own bills. My accountant does that. Since I was in the city, she probably thought I'd made the purchase. I'm telling you I didn't do it, but what's the big deal? Are these highly expensive religious statues stolen or something?"

"No, but when they're left at the scene of a double homicide, it piques our interest."

Carla's reaction seemed genuine, but the profilers had said their suspect was a psychopath. Such people were usually missing normal emotions, so the truly talented ones learned to be chameleons. At the moment, Carla appeared deflated as she sat back with her body totally slack. "You honestly think I killed two people?" Carla asked, finally showing some fear.

"I'm not accusing you of anything, and it's not two people but twelve. That puts my suspect in a category we don't usually encounter." She stared at Carla, and Carla broke first and dropped her head. "I'm investigating a crime, and the clues led me here. If you think who you are and who you're with means I'll ignore that, you don't know me."

"If you think I did any of this, then you don't know me. I've spent my life trying to preserve life, not take it."

"I need you to come in voluntarily and answer some more questions, and I hope you take me up on that offer. The fury over this case doesn't give me any choice but to take you in."

"Will you think less of me if I bring an attorney?"

"Not at all—I actually recommend it." Sept took her phone back and stood, not anticipating that Carla would give her any problems. "Just remember that the truth here really is the key to your freedom."

CHAPTER THIRTY-THREE

The team working in the conference room quieted when Sept and Carla entered. Sept escorted her into the empty office they'd been using and told her they'd wait for her attorney before they began. Nathan appeared as shocked by the development as Carla had been, but it had to be done.

"Come get me when her attorney shows up, but I have to make a call," she told Nathan and Gustave. She wasn't relishing this, but a warning to Keegan was in order.

"Sunday at your house should be interesting," Gustave said, shaking his head. "Are you sure about this?"

"Nathan, check and see if Bernard sent a copy of a receipt he texted me, and I'm not sure about anything," she said to her brother. "But I have to do my job."

She walked out to the courtyard some of the support staff used for cigarette and lunch breaks, glad it was empty. "Hey, love," she said when Keegan answered in that tone that sounded like pure happiness. "Do you have a minute?"

"For you I have all the minutes you need, and if you're free for lunch, come by and eat some duck."

"Any special reason I want to do that?" She smiled, enjoying the conversation before she dropped a bomb on Keegan's day.

"I'm swimming in duck, so you can have it three different ways. We had a mix-up in our order, so the suppliers gave me the surplus instead of wasting it. If you're not in the mood for duck, work your way up to it by Sunday. That's what we're having."

"Put your knife down and listen to me. And believe me, I'd much rather keep talking about duck."

Keegan's end grew much quieter, which probably meant she'd stepped into her office. "Hey, Jacqueline, could you give us a minute?"

"Actually, could you put me on speaker, since it really affects all of us?"

"Do you remember how you promised not to freak me out any more? It's not working."

"Sorry, sweetheart, but I finally got a clue that led me somewhere," she said as she cocked her head back and enjoyed the sun on her face. "Or should I say led me to someone."

"That's fantastic, no?" Keegan asked.

"That depends, I guess, because we all know who I have upstairs in an interrogation room."

"Are you trying to be dramatic or annoying?" Jacqueline asked.

"It's Carla." Like with a bandage, ripping it off fast was the way to go.

"Mom's Carla?" Jacqueline and Keegan asked together.

"That's her." She sighed, knowing the day would only go downhill from here.

"Honey, what the hell happened? She's not our favorite, but I doubt she's a serial killer." Keegan wasn't pissed yet, but she was working up to it, from the pitch of her voice.

"Okay, listen." She nodded to Nathan at the door and put two fingers up. "I've got to go, but I promise I'm not picking on Carla or your mother. I'm following a legitimate lead until I can clear her."

"Or not," Keegan said.

"Let's hope it doesn't come to that," she said, hating to hang up, but she had to. "I'll call when I can, but could you call your mother if Carla hasn't already and warn her just in case?"

"We promise, and don't forget to stay in touch," Keegan said and hung up.

"Sept, I can't believe it," Nathan said on the way back up.

"It's not up to us to believe it. It's up to us to prove it." She stopped before getting to the second floor and let Nathan go by her. "What can I do for you, Anabel?"

"Tell me you don't believe this? There's no way Carla St. John is some accomplished killer with dozens of kills to her name."

"I'm not accusing her of anything yet, but they pay me to run down leads and arrest bad guys. You don't excuse someone because they took out your gallbladder. Believe me, I hope it's not her."

"I still have my gallbladder, thank you, but St. John isn't our perp."

"Let me get in there, and we'll see." She made it up the stairs, and Anabel grabbed her arm.

"One last thing. Why question her up here? Why not an interrogation room?"

"We already have someone in lockup because they sold information. I want a room with no opportunists behind the glass or watching the video."

Anabel nodded and let her go. The conference room was still quiet, and she didn't want to waste any more time, so she let Nathan go in first and closed the door before anyone else got any cute ideas. She dropped her file onto the table, and Carla looked at her warily.

"I need to start by informing you of your rights," she said, and Carla's hands went up.

"I can't believe this is happening," Carla said, but Nathan Mirandized her.

"Your attorney will tell you the best thing is to keep quiet, but last night I got my first real clue, and it led right to your door. That's not like a parking ticket I can fix and it's forgotten." The pictures of the statues made both Carla and the woman in a great suit sitting next to her look down. "According to the store's records, you purchased these during the trip you took to New York."

"Carla told me about this, Sept, but let's be reasonable. She's going to buy these things in a way that can be traced to her, then turn around and leave them at a scene where she supposedly killed two people?" The attorney seemed to try and failed at not being sarcastic.

"I'm not after anything but an explanation," she said, holding up the picture.

"I didn't buy those. I was at a conference, and the only shopping I did was to pick up some earrings for Melinda. I ate at the hotel every night, and I was gone only three days." The way Carla spoke made Sept think the usually cool doctor was about to unravel.

"Listen to me, okay," Sept said, flipping the page over. "We've got your bank records, and they confirm what I'm saying. The amount to cover these was wired from your bank. You did buy these."

"I was hacked, then," Carla countered. "Come on. The shop had to have surveillance videos or something, if these things really cost that much."

Someone knocked, so Nathan got up to answer the door. Her father was waiting to get in to talk to her. "Nathan, could you give the captain an update?"

"Sure."

Once they walked out, Sept gazed at the attorney and paused before she spoke. "Carla, if you trust me at all, I need to talk to you alone."

"No way," the attorney predictably said.

"I don't want to question her about anything. I want to talk to her as someone who knows her. That's it, and it's up to you," she said, staring at Carla.

"I'll be okay," Carla said to her attorney.

The woman moved slowly but did go. Carla placed her elbows on the table and rested her chin on her upturned hands. "Want to finish me off?"

"Listen to me, and you'll get through this. I give you my word."

They allowed Carla to leave through the back to avoid being seen. Sept told the team she was taking off early to make up the sleep she'd lost from the night before. The only people she lingered with were Nathan and her brothers.

"So you don't have enough to hold her?" Jacques asked, sitting on the table where she'd interviewed Carla.

"More than enough, but if it's her, she didn't leave enough evidence except for the conveniently found receipt and choice of orisha." The private conversation she'd had with Carla had gone surprisingly well. "She's on her way back to her house, and Melinda will most likely join her."

Her cell phone rang, and she was surprised Julio was calling her. "Sept, I know you'll think we're crazy, but I've got to warn you."

"Hey, Julio," she said for the benefit of the people around her and because of her amusement over his telephone etiquette. "What's wrong?"

"I know you said not to discuss the case," he said, and she sighed, staring at the ceiling, "but I didn't think you'd mind if Matilda knew only the basics."

"That's perfectly fine," she said, even though it wasn't. "Did she think of something? Did she figure out who Chloe's altar would've been dedicated to?"

"Her best guess is Chango's wife Oshun, since the other two were for Ibeji, their children. That doesn't really lead us anywhere except that Oshun will turn bitter if crossed." Sept heard a woman she assumed was Matilda speaking in rapid Spanish, but the voice was too muffled to understand. "Today is the fourth of the month, and there's a full moon."

"You lost me," she said, hoping this was the last case of her career that involved religion. It entailed so much to remember, and rituals weren't her forte.

"Chango's feast day, or most important day, is December the fourth. That was months ago, but still months to come. Do you think the killer will wait that long? Especially if the fourth falls on the fourth day of the week." Julio was speaking so fast she had to concentrate to understand him. "If Hunter's game is to kill you—tonight will be the night."

"Thank you for the warning, because I do think Hunter plans to kill me as an end to all this."

"Matilda says to be vigilant and don't take the beads off."

"I haven't since she put them there." She hung up and told the guys what Julio had said. "For the night, I need you to put a car in front of Carla's place and one behind it."

"You think she'd try to kill you now?" Nathan asked.

"I didn't finish what I wanted to say before this call. Remember our case with Perlis. This time around, Carla is playing the role of my brother-in-law Damien. All the clues we could link to someone were too easy. She's not an amateur one second, then a proficient killer the next." She'd figured the night before, after the momentary insanity of suspecting Carla, that the choice of saints who in life had been doctors wasn't random. "The divine twins were doctors, and a doctor I know buys the statues at a crime scene, but the surveillance footage shows a flunky picking them up? I don't buy it, especially if one of the saints is named Damain. The spelling of the names is different, but it's pronounced the same."

"Then why watch Carla?" Gustave asked.

"Remember what happened to our Damien, or what almost happened to him and Nathan? I wasn't going to be Perlis's only victim that night. Hunter set Carla up for a reason, and whatever that is probably includes killing her. Whoever you send, make sure they're invisible."

"The owner of those types of vehicles is right outside," Jacques said. "I'll get Anabel to send the smallest, most nondescript thing in her fleet."

"Sounds like we need to drop a big circle of protection around you," Gustave said. "Hunter will go after you, if tonight is some special night."

"She had three on her slate the other night, so don't underestimate her."

"We need a plan, then," Nathan said.

"I have time to cover what it is only once before the sun goes down."

CHAPTER THIRTY-FOUR

Hunter was ready to tell the world about her brilliance, and this night would be the best of her career. Her next moves would prove that. "You've come as close as you're going to get, Sept," Hunter said, packing the trunk with what she needed. Once Savoie was dead, she had one thing left to do, and then she'd be ready to begin the next chapter.

She'd followed Savoie home, and the place was surrounded by goons. She was trying to think of a way to lure her out when Savoie slammed out with her slut screaming behind her. "You've finally shown your true stupidity, and the price of failure will cost you this life," she said, smiling as she pulled out before Sept made it to her car. Wherever Savoie went, she'd find her later because of the tracker she'd placed on her car. "Time to prepare."

That had been a couple of hours ago, and she couldn't have asked for a better outcome if she'd written a script and Savoie had agreed to follow it. The great warrior had gone back to work, then headed for St. John's place. Obviously getting her rich little bitch to talk to her again was more important than procedure.

The house had to be under surveillance, so she parked two blocks down and came in from the side instead of the front or back. Carla's house was perfect because it was raised and the trap door from the utility closet was now accessible after she'd undone the boards that had been placed to secure it.

It was a tight fit, but she came up next to the air-conditioner unit, where she'd placed the bag she'd put there two weeks before. She was here, and both her targets were waiting for her, which was a testament to how well her plan had worked.

"I ask you again," Carla said, sounding angry, "why are you even here?"

"I have a job like you do. You can't blame me for doing it," Savoie said just as defensively. "You know I had no choice, so you didn't have to turn Melinda and every one of them against me."

Hunter smiled, since her predication was correct. Eventually everyone in Savoie's life would turn their backs on her, and that was half of the equation of what she'd planned. Killing someone only to make them a martyr or hero wasn't as satisfying as completely stripping them of honor and dignity before their last breath.

The closet she was in was off the back door, which was perfect to peek out of since it was visible only from the back and the laundry room across from it. She doubted Savoie was arguing and pleading her case over a load of dirty clothes.

She loaded her weapon and carefully cracked the door, seeing the area was clear. They must've moved to the large den off the kitchen. "You challenged me to face you, and here I am," she said softly as she swung the door open and squeezed out.

The argument had stopped, so she shouldered her weapon and walked toward the den, not making a sound on the tile floor. "I didn't turn anyone against you—you did that yourself with the dumb move today," Carla said, and it seemed like she was headed toward her, so Hunter stopped.

Carla appeared from behind the half wall with a can in her hand and stopped at the sight of her. She had no chance to enjoy the fear in Carla's expression before she pulled the trigger, and the good doctor fell backward with her lips forming a perfect *O*. Savoie, like an idiot, came running with no weapon in hand, and Hunter pulled the trigger again.

"Wait," Savoie got out before she fell pretty much the same as Carla. The way she gasped for breath and grimaced made her move closer and place her crossbow on the granite counter. The double-tipped bolts, guaranteed to bring a big buck down, had worked beautifully. She removed Savoie's weapon and placed it next to the bow.

"Alex should have hobbled you before the kill. Right now, your lung is collapsed and probably filling with blood, but that's what the warrior craves, isn't it?" She bent and studied Savoie's face, which was a perfect mask of pain. "Believe me, you'll bleed plenty more before we're done."

"You...bitch," Savoie said, each word sounding like it took tremendous effort.

"No. I was nice and waited until you were healed before we played the game. I didn't want any excuses of how you were cheated of a chance to win because you weren't at your best." She went back for her kill bag, already anticipating escape down the trap door and out of this place as much as the kill. She wished she could witness all the law enforcement coming in and finding these two dead.

"Let her go," Sept said, taking a deep breath and wincing even more. "It's me you want."

"The truth is, I want both of you, so I can't let either of you go." She dragged Savoie to the den, admiring her for not yelling.

"Let me see your face, then," Savoie said, and Hunter cocked her head, considering the request. No one had ever asked her that, not thinking it was the most important thing at the moment of their imminent death.

"Did you guess anyone but Carla?" she asked, keeping the mask in place since it was always a rule to do so. "You really do owe her and the little women an apology. You got this so wrong."

"Nicole, I just needed you to tip your hand," Savoie said, looking pleased with herself. "You should've chosen, ah..." Sept said weakly, placing her hand against the shaft of the bolt when Hunter pressed down on it. "Chosen another god than Ibeji. Using the statues to try to blame Carla was a huge mistake," Sept said with great difficulty.

She took the mask off and combed her hair back, glad to be out of the confinement of the leather. "I'd waste time asking you why you think that, but the game is done. You're supposed to be the last piece, but it's your time."

The large coffee table at the center of the room was a perfect place to tie Savoie up and finish the altar Alex couldn't. She dragged Sept over and zip-tied one wrist to the iron leg before securing the other one. "Ripping your heart out will be one of the most satisfying accomplishments of my life." She poured the salt and lit the red and white candles. "Who knows? Maybe I'll make it a point to drop by the restaurant and console your little bitch."

"Fuck...ah," Sept said when she touched the bolt again.

She placed the hand-carved statue of St. Barbara above Sept's head. "Another beautiful thing you purchased Dr. St. John," she said, loud enough for Carla to hear her from the kitchen after she quieted

Sept. The last two things were cornmeal and bananas so Julio Munez would declare it a true altar to the king of the orishas. "Now it's only missing your heart, but that's easy to fix."

The moment had come, and it would make a great chapter in the book she'd write for herself. Those volumes would become public only after her death, but they contained the most accurate story of the chameleon killer. She'd mastered every possible way to kill, and she'd enjoyed the ride.

"Good-bye, warrior." She raised the knife over her head and took one last look at Sept's face for any type of expression. What she saw was defiance before the surprise that made her lift her head suddenly. The laser sight was pointed at her chest. It made her bring her arms down to finish, but then she saw only darkness.

Her game was done.

CHAPTER THIRTY-FIVE

"Took you long enough," Sept said as one of the SWAT guys cut her loose so the EMTs could get to her.

"Surveillance didn't pick her up, so thank Carla for not holding a grudge and calling me," Gustave said. "Good thing is, your plan of baiting the trap worked. Sounds like Voles wanted you both."

Sept groaned when they loaded her, and she put her hand up when they got close to Carla. "I'm so sorry this happened. I didn't think she'd already be in the house."

"Don't apologize," Carla said, taking her hand. "Maybe my injury will soften Della up."

"If it does, then put in a good word with Melinda for me."

Gustave directed the EMTs through the front door, and she smiled when Keegan's face appeared above her. "Why is an arrow sticking out of your chest?"

"I found the missing piece from Lee Cenac's altar. It's the arrow of the hunter," she said slowly, the pain overwhelming her.

"I'm so glad you at least kept the promise to come back to me," Keegan said. Earlier when they'd had their "fight," in case Nicole was watching, Sept had explained her plan to go to Carla's to lure their killer out. Melinda had thankfully agreed not to follow Carla home once they all knew backup was in place to prevent the worst. She and Carla were on their third version of the same fight when Nicole finally materialized.

"Always," she said with the last of her reserves. "I have that thermometer job to do." Keegan pushed her way into the back of the ambulance and prayed as they got a large police escort to the hospital. Sept had passed out, but the guy sitting beside Keegan assured her she was breathing on her own and her pulse was strong.

The hospital's emergency room was a zoo again because of the officer-down call and also because they were treating one of their own. Carla was a respected staff physician whom the hospital workers really liked.

"You should marry her, Mom," Keegan told Melinda when they took Sept and Carla into surgery. "Don't let her get away."

"I never thought…well, you know, seeing me with someone new…" Melinda shrugged as if she didn't know how to go on.

"Mom, we loved Mama, but you're too young and have too much to offer to be alone. Carla loves you, and if Sept plans to end every case getting impaled with something, it'll be good to have her around," Keegan said, hugging her mom. "You might want to convince her to sell the house so there won't be any bad memories, but Jacqueline and I will be happy for you."

"Listen to your daughter, Melinda," Della said, and they all sat to wait.

The bolts were removed and thankfully had only punctured a lung in each woman. Healing would take time, but no other organ was damaged. The Blanchards and Camille Savoie were moved to a private, more comfortable waiting room, but Nathan and the Savoie cop family waited outside, surrounded by what seemed like half the NOPD.

"Thank God we don't have to worry about Nicole Voles any longer," Jacqueline said.

Sebastian had told them what had happened and how one of the snipers had taken Nicole out before she stabbed Sept through the heart. "Maybe we'll have some more months of normalcy before Sept starts investigating major crimes again," Keegan said in agreement. "If it's a murder case, let's all pray for one-and-done next time."

"Amen to that," Camille said as Keegan put her arm around her.

"Hopefully it won't be too much longer before this investigation is wrapped up and it'll really feel like it's done," Keegan said and stared at the clock. "I have a happily-ever-after to get to."

❖

Sept heard people around her, but it was like swimming through ink to find a way to wake up. The pain in her chest was still there, though not as bad as it had been, and that at least was an improvement. She really wanted nothing but to find Keegan. She'd just seen her, but none of the voices around her was the one she most wanted to hear.

"I'm going on my break, but it's time to wake Detective Savoie," a woman said, and Sept agreed. It was time to regain consciousness. "You want to handle that, and I'll do Dr. St. John when I get back?"

"Sure. I'm new, but I can handle that." The second woman sounded so familiar, and Sept did her best to clear her head, but her body wasn't cooperating. "If you need anything, Diana is in the next room over. We got the easy load tonight with our two VIPs."

"They're in good hands."

The talking stopped, and Sept took a few breaths and tried to will her eyes open. She squinted because of the fluorescents, but it was progress. The shadow over her made her heart rate feel like it sped up, but maybe it was Keegan.

"Are you in there?" the woman asked and pried her eyes open with no gentleness.

The sight had to be a hallucination. Sept had watched Nicole get slammed back by a fatal shot to the forehead. That the idiot had tried to kill her and not take cover was amazing, but Nicole was dead. She was sure of it, even if she wasn't sure about anything else.

"Did you think you'd survive this?" Nicole asked as she reached into the lab coat she wore and took out a vial and syringe. "I wanted to rip your heart out, but this will do."

Nicole tipped the vial over and started to draw out whatever was in it, and Sept's panic started to kick her brain into gear. She needed to get out of here and away from this crazy bitch who'd obviously walked away from a bullet to the head. The way Nicole slowly pulled the plunger of the syringe out was torturous, and Sept pawed at the blankets covering her with one hand and the railing with the other.

"Forgot my wallet," the woman who'd been there before said as she reentered. "What the hell?" she asked loudly, which got Nicole away from Sept. "Hey, what are you doing?"

Sept made it to a sitting position and figured there was no way to make it over the railing, so she was dead once Nicole took care of the nurse. Her only option was to lean over and press the alarm on the wall that triggered a code. Nicole could maybe overpower one person, but not a whole team. Once the alarm went off, she pulled her IV out and crawled to the end of the bed and fell onto the floor.

Hitting the ground sent such a jolt through her chest she could sense herself slipping back into the black ink she'd just surfaced from. Maybe she'd find Keegan later and all this would have been a bad dream.

❖

"How the hell did this happen?" Sebastian yelled at no one in particular. The commotion from recovery had been so loud it caused more than one officer to run in and find five medical staff members practically sitting on Nicole Voles. "I thought this bitch was on ice at Gavin's."

"She is. I just called," Nathan said. "This isn't Nicole Voles, or the dead one isn't Nicole Voles. They had to be identical twins." They both stared at the woman sitting in the back of the cruiser cuffed and screaming obscenities. "At least one of them should match the fingerprints from the piece of note we found."

"Gustave," Sebastian yelled again. "Get warrants for every place she's been in the city and tell anyone who's interacted with her it'd be a bad idea to not answer questions. Start with her father, and work your way down from there."

"Yes, sir," Gustave said, but he and his partner Shawn didn't move. "We'll do it as soon as we lay eyes on Sept."

"Della's made enough noise that we can go into recovery four at a time, so Keegan and Melinda can stay in there. Who would've fucking guessed this?" He seldom used profanity, but this called for it.

"Matilda Rodriguez did," Nathan said, and they all stared at him like he'd lost his grip on reality. "She did, but we never would've thought she was right."

"She was, and since Brian Voles is one of ours, we'll have him picked up and delivered to wherever you want him," Anabel said. "I took the liberty of securing warrants in California for Nicole Voles's house and office. Her assistant's being questioned in the LA office."

"Thanks, Anabel. We'd like a shot at her too, so if it takes flying some of our people out there, we'll get it done."

"Do you mind if I go in and see Sept?" Anabel asked.

"We'll let you cut the line so you can start working this case," Gustave said.

"Sir." One of the uniformed officers jogged up and stopped by Sebastian. "The sheriff needs to speak to you."

NOPD was the force on the streets every day, but the sheriff's department ran the jail in New Orleans. Sebastian knew Sheriff Chip Hamlin but didn't speak to him often. "What can I do for you, Chip?"

"The kid who answered my message told me what's going on, so

I won't keep you, but I thought you'd want to know Alex Perlis hung himself in his cell today."

"This day gets more bizarre by the second. How'd that happen?" The news wasn't exactly unwelcome, but it was shocking, since Perlis had stayed defiant despite what he was facing.

"It was the damnedest thing. My people said he got a visit from an FBI agent that lasted twenty minutes. When they were done, Perlis went back to his cell, took a nap, then hung himself during shift change."

"Thanks for letting me know, Chip, but who was the agent?"

"Special Agent Brian Voles, but he doesn't work for Anabel. Told my guy he was a friend of the family."

Sebastian filled everyone in, and at the mention of Brian Voles, Anabel made a few calls. They were still discussing it when a nurse said they could start going in to see Sept. The police allowed the family the first rounds, and then Sebastian walked Anabel and her agents Mora and Silva in.

"Once you're stronger you can tell us how you figured out Nicole was the killer, but for now we came to thank you," Anabel said, taking Sept's free hand since Keegan held the other one. "You saw what no one had and took a dangerous animal out of circulation."

"I totally missed the sister, though. That was a shocker," Sept said, sounding sleepy. "Give that nurse at the station a kiss for me before you leave."

"Will do, and heal fast. We still have lots of work to do on this case. Hell, I might write a book about you after this. You did a damn fine job, Detective."

"Don't worry. She'll be ready as soon as her cape gets back from the cleaners," Keegan said, and Sept smiled and yawned.

"It's all about the team," Sept said and closed her eyes.

❖

When Sept woke up again she was in a different room, and Keegan was sitting on the bed holding her hand. It was still dark outside, but Keegan's smile when she noticed she was awake warmed her. "Have I ever told you how beautiful you are?" she asked, and Keegan blushed.

"Yes, you have, but I never tire of hearing you say it since I'm glad you think so." Keegan stood so she could lean over her. "You have a way of scaring the hell out of me, Seven, but I love that you always come through and back to me."

"That's because I belong to you." She closed her eyes when Keegan kissed her. "I asked you to marry me, right?"

"You did, and I said yes." Keegan kissed her again. "We celebrated by getting a toe in the mail."

She laughed at Keegan's bright outlook in every situation. "I made a plan to catch Nicole, and it taught me something important."

"What's that, my love?"

"I'm good at making plans—well, mostly. The only glitch was the double crossbow. Didn't see that coming."

"I'm just glad it wasn't something more lethal."

"Me too, but that's not why I mentioned it. I want to make a new plan."

Keegan nodded and smiled. "Do you want to tell me about it?"

"It's a long one—I'm talking sixty or seventy years, and that one might have some glitches in it too, but we're going to have fun making it work."

"I give thanks for you every day, baby. I wish for the same things and all that comes with a long and happy life. We're going to use your mom and mine for inspiration, aren't we?"

"If we do that, we'll end up with nine kids. We'll have to move if you want that."

"Nine might be too many, but we can compromise at maybe three," Keegan said, and the door opening broke their kiss. "Hey, Sebastian."

"Hey, sweetheart. I hate to bother you, but is this a good time?"

"Come in and sit," Sept said when her brothers and Nathan followed him in.

"We wanted to catch you up on what we know so far," Sebastian said, and Keegan sat back on the bed as if signaling she wasn't leaving. "Perlis is dead. He hung himself after having a talk with Brain Voles, so we have one less thing to worry about. That's a closed case."

"I thought about doing the same thing after some of my talks with Agent Wonderful. What did he meet with Perlis about?" Sept asked, enjoying the warmth of Keegan's body.

"That remains to be seen. Anabel dropped him in a dark hole, so we'll have to wait until she's done with him," Gustave said. "The dead woman we first thought was Nicole didn't match the prints we have, but Nicole two point one does."

"We sweated the guy at the building where Nicole leased a condo, and it turns out the sisters lived over each other," Nathan said. "We have the survivor in custody, but she and Perlis have something in common in that she's keeping her mouth closed. They're identical twins, so now we just have to figure out which of them is Nicole and which of them is Darla Voles."

Joel stood at the foot of the bed and put his hands on her feet. "How did you guess it was her?"

"The night she kissed Keegan made her stand out. Well, at first I wanted to use her for target practice, but you add Perlis, and Larry Nobles, and it made me concentrate on her."

"Something about her seemed off," Nathan said.

"I took a chance my hunch was right when she tried to frame Carla by talking Carla into posing as bait with me to see if Nicole would go after the target she wanted most. I'll never forgive myself for getting Carla hurt, though."

"I stopped by and saw her," Sebastian said, and smiled. "You have nothing to worry about. Melinda's in there making over her, and I can't be sure, but I think they're engaged."

"Get some sleep," Alain said, and they all kissed her and Keegan before they left.

"Maybe we'll have a double wedding," Keegan said, which made her laugh. "Or we'll let them go first so I get you all to myself at the altar."

"And if you're pregnant before that happens?" she asked, putting the arm of her uninjured side around Keegan when she lay back.

"Then it'll be me, you, our baby, and Gran with a shotgun."

She laughed until she had to stop because of the pain. "No matter who's up there with us, I'm looking forward to it."

EPILOGUE

Eight Months Later

"Do you have everything you need?" Keegan asked Sept as she stirred the grits she was making.

"I'm ready to go, babe. Stop worrying," Sept said, standing behind Keegan with her hands on her hips.

"She's fine, so finish telling me," Jacqueline said from her stool at the counter.

"The woman killed at Carla's was Nicole Voles, and the twin on death row is Darla Voles. They took turns writing the volumes of manuscripts found in their house in Malibu, and each book outlined every murder they committed," Sept said, reviewing the death penalty case they'd just finished, which landed Darla a date with the needle. "It sounds like super-agent Brian Voles was nothing more than a child abuser and molester."

"They took turns? Wasn't Nicole the writer?" Jacqueline asked.

"Do you really want to talk about this today?" Keegan asked as she leaned back against her.

"Yes. I didn't get to go to court much," Jacqueline said, throwing a napkin at Keegan. "What good is living with Elliot Ness if not to give me the details of a good story before she has a date with *60 Minutes*? She might get too famous and blow me off."

"The abuse and their mother's denial twisted them in a way that made them hate her, but—" The buzzer went off, and she put her finger up and moved to the oven.

"That's understandable," Keegan said, taking her hand after she put the tray of biscuits on the counter. "What kind of mother ignores that?"

"The kind who was Brian Voles's victim first. He beat her until their twins were old enough to replace her, and by then she didn't have enough fight for anyone else." She stopped to kiss Keegan until Jacqueline threw another napkin. "Darla and Nicole, though, reacted differently, in that they did everything possible to please him, but like their mother, one was more mentally strong than the other."

"This is sad in a way," Keegan said, and Sept kissed her again.

"It is." The trial had peeled back the complicated layers of the Voles family, and it was a perfect case study of how trauma, violence, and manipulation can change someone and make a person a killer. "Darla couldn't take it and had a breakdown in her senior year of college that led to a suicide attempt."

"And they wrote all this down?" Keegan asked.

"Pretty much. It took a long time to find them, but it was a slam dunk in the evidence department once we did and helped convict Darla Voles."

"Finish," Jacqueline said, making her smile.

"Nicole needed Darla to survive, and Darla didn't want to, so they erased her, and Hunter was born. As they worked on the books Nicole was known for, one met with the killers who were the subjects, and the other committed the crimes." Their writing style was slightly different, but not enough for their publisher or anyone else to notice. "In cities like New Orleans, where they killed in a spree, they took turns with the role of Nicole and Hunter."

"That's messed up," Jacqueline said.

"It truly was, but that's how their rebellion against their father manifested itself. Their mother withdrew, but they chose a half-life that would challenge how Brian Voles saw himself. They constructed puzzles for him to figure out and challenge his mind." She'd had to smile at the satisfied expression on Anabel's face when she recounted the experience of cuffing Voles and taking him in. "He figured out by their second copycat set of murders and coached them on the mistakes they made to keep the game going. The murders they committed turned him on, so he did nothing to stop them."

"Jesus Christ. That's disgusting." Jacqueline shivered for effect. "How'd you finally figure it out?"

"Actually, I was shocked when the mask came off after she shot me. After checking her travel records to verify she'd been in most of the cities where the copycat murders took place, I had my suspicions. That she led such a productive life made me doubt myself, and when

Darla ended up at the hospital to kill me, that really shocked me. At first I thought the drugs were making me hallucinate, and then I thought I was in a Lifetime movie."

"I wonder why no one else ever figured this out," Keegan said, taking the pot off the fire and turning in her arms.

"I'm not brilliant. In every city, the killer twins stuck to their meticulously crafted plan of one type of murder. Here there were too many variables, and they blamed each other for the mistakes they'd made that required the bombs to clean up."

"You are brilliant, so stop acting so humble. That's annoying as hell too," Jacqueline said as they heard Della and Melinda coming down the stairs. They'd spent the week preparing for the big day. "And what do you mean by too many variables?"

"It was Darla's turn to start as Hunter, which means the first time you two met Nicole, it really was Nicole. Their first target was Bonnie Matherne, and Darla copied the crime to a T, but she added the murders of the two rookies." She stopped to pour Della and Melinda some coffee and prepared it to their liking.

"Suck-up," Jacqueline teased her.

"You could learn from this one," Della said, kissing Sept's cheek. "Please continue. I was there for your whole testimony, but it's an interesting story."

"The gun Darla used was the one from another string of murders, and killing two police officers here made Fritz throw more people at the case. The more intense focus made the twins think they had to take drastic measures to wipe their tracks." They all moved to the table, and Keegan sat on her lap. "One working serial killer is something out of the ordinary, but three is kind of like a statistical improbability."

"I think the jury made the right choice when they put her on death row," Melinda said, and Della nodded. "Think of how many lives they took, and all the pain they caused. You and Carla were hurt, but it would've devastated us to have lost you two."

"I'm still so sorry she got hurt, especially after she agreed to be brought in and questioned, then act as bait. I planned to draw Nicole to me, but Nicole surprised us. I had to play it that way because I didn't know if Nicole had another Larry Nobles feeding her information, but I wish I'd figured it out sooner to at least save Gretchen and Roger."

"You did your best, baby, and because of you, there won't be any more victims," Keegan said.

"You're good for my ego, love," she said and kissed her. "The night she broke into Carla's for the second time, the sisters finally decided to show imagination with the crossbow. To follow Perlis's case, they needed another person to blame, and this time they picked Carla for some reason. It was the double reason for the choice of Ibeji as their last successful altar. It honored the divine twins and the doctors they were. That one of them was Damain was a bonus as an homage to Perlis picking Damien as his scapegoat."

"You got that she was trying to frame Carla from that?" Jaqueline asked.

"The receipt that Carla had purchased the statues at the scene made me realize they were trying to frame Carla. To me that's the most amazing thing about this whole situation."

"What? That she tried to frame Carla?" Melinda asked.

"No, ma'am. That they planned that far in advance. Carla's trip was a week after Perlis was caught. Nicole was still in California finishing her last book, and Darla was researching all of us but chose to start with Carla."

"Thank you for what you did to catch these monsters and for making today possible," Melinda said.

"Thank you for not shooting me all over again when you found out about Carla."

"You can make it up to her later," Della said, making a shooing motion. "Get out of here, and don't forget to turn off your phone. If it goes off today, *I'll* shoot you."

"Yes, Gran, and we've got some news for you later," she whispered in Della's ear as she kissed her cheek. Then Keegan kissed her on the lips to shut her up.

The courtyard behind the restaurant was decorated beautifully, and the guests were seated and waiting. Sept stood at the altar watching the garden gate, looking forward to seeing Keegan walk down the flower-lined aisle.

"Are you nervous?" she asked Carla as she stared in the same direction.

"Are you?" Carla asked, placing her hand on her shoulder. "This will be you in a couple of months."

"I can't wait, and I'm really happy for you."

Carla laughed and nodded. "Me too, but when Della Blanchard

tells you to propose to her daughter or face certain death, I dropped to one knee. Thank God I love Melinda more than anyone I've ever known."

"Don't worry. That means Della's come to love you. She doesn't bother to threaten if she doesn't care."

They stopped as the music started, and Sept couldn't believe that her eyes watered when she saw Keegan. While the trial was going on, they'd decided to wait until it was done so they could enjoy the ceremony and what came after. That gave Carla and Melinda the chance to go ahead with their wedding.

"Our family has enjoyed feeding people and being present for so many of their celebrations," Della said as she stood for the first toast after the ceremony was over. "Those moments are even more special when they're your own. Today we celebrate two of the most important things in life—love and family. They are the cornerstones on which our lives are built. Today I welcome Carla into our family and thank her for loving my child and committing herself to her happiness. A mother couldn't ask for more. Take care of each other, and I wish you years of happiness." Della raised her glass, and everyone did the same. "To Carla and Melinda."

That got the party started, and an hour later Della sat with her and Keegan. "Great party, Gran," she said, opening her mouth since Keegan held up a piece of cake.

"Stop trying to kiss my ass and tell me the news," Della said.

"You know how much I love your granddaughter," she said and smiled.

"Enough to repeat this party with even more people in a couple of months," Della said, accepting a piece of cake from Keegan.

"You know that, and how I'm going to love her forever," she said, and Della slapped her arm as if to get her to talk faster. "Go ahead and tell her, love."

"When we stand at the altar, we won't be alone, Gran."

"I know that, but what's the news?" Della asked, missing the point completely.

"We won't be alone because it'll be me," she pointed to herself, "Keegan," she kissed Keegan and smiled, "and our babies." She placed her hand on Keegan's abdomen, a new habit she'd developed from the moment the doctor verified and showed them the sonogram of their twins.

"Babies," Della said with a huge smile. "As in more than one?"

"Two," Keegan said, putting her hand over Sept's. "We're having twins, so she's got to make it up that aisle."

"Congratulations," Della said, kissing them both. "You certainly have been exciting to have around, Sept Savoie. I'm happy for you both."

"Thanks, Gran, but we're going to dance while I can still see my feet," Keegan said. "We'll fill everyone else in tomorrow at brunch before Mom leaves for her honeymoon, but Sept wanted you to be the first to know."

Sept put her arms around Keegan and swayed to the music away from the crowd. "You are the most gorgeous woman I've ever seen," she said, holding Keegan tighter. "And I can't wait to put that second ring on your finger and meet these guys."

"Could be girls, you know, or one of each," Keegan said kissing her neck. "But you're right. I can't wait."

"Dad offered me the desk job again," she said, willing to go along with whatever Keegan wanted.

"Seven," Keegan said, tugging her toward the corner of the yard. "Your job scares the shit out of me." Keegan placed her hand inside her shirt over the scar the arrow had left. "You're really good at it, though, and you need to keep doing it. Only tell Nathan it's his turn to get shot or whatever next time."

"Are you sure?"

"As sure as I am about the great future our babies and I are going to have with you. Our adventure is just beginning, but you finding and convicting people like the Voles family is part of that. The world needs you, Seven, but I've got first dibs." The kiss Keegan gave her was full of promise for later and for years to come. "Are you ready for all that?"

"I love you, so I'm more than ready for anything and everything as long as you're with me."

About the Author

Ali Vali is the author of the long-running Cain Casey "Devil" series and the Genesis Clan "Forces" series, as well as numerous standalone romances including two Lambda Literary Award finalists, *Calling the Dead* and *Love Match*, and her 2017 release, *Beauty and the Boss*. Ali also has a novella in the collection *Girls with Guns*.

Originally from Cuba, Ali has retained much of her family's traditions and language and uses them frequently in her stories. Having her father read her stories and poetry before bed every night as a child infused her with a love of reading, which she carries till today. Ali currently lives outside New Orleans, Louisiana, and she has discovered that living in Louisiana provides plenty of material to draw from in creating her novels and short stories.

Books Available From Bold Strokes Books

A Wish Upon a Star by Jeannie Levig. Erica Cooper has learned to depend on only herself, but when her new neighbor, Leslie Raymond, befriends Erica's special needs daughter, the walls protecting Erica's heart threaten to crumble. (978-1-163555-274-4)

Answering the Call by Ali Vali. Detective Sept Savoie returns to the streets of New Orleans, as do the dead bodies from ritualistic killings, and she does everything in her power to bring their killers to justice while trying to keep her partner, Keegan Blanchard, safe. (978-1-163555-050-4)

Friends Without Benefits by Dena Blake. When Dex Putman gets the woman she thought she always wanted, she soon wonders if it's really love after all. (978-1-163555-349-9)

Invalid Evidence by Stevie Mikayne. Private Investigator Jil Kidd is called away to investigate a possible killer whale, just when her partner Jess needs her most. (978-1-163555-307-9)

Pursuit of Happiness by Carsen Taite. When attorney Stevie Palmer's client reveals a scandal that could derail Senator Meredith Mitchell's presidential bid, their chance at love may be collateral damage. (978-1-163555-044-3)

Seascape by Karis Walsh. Marine biologist Tess Hansen returns to Washington's isolated northern coast, where she struggles to adjust to small-town living while courting an endowment from Brittany James for her orca research center. (978-1-163555-079-5)

Second In Command by VK Powell. Jazz Perry's life is disrupted and her career jeopardized when she becomes personally involved with the case of an abandoned child and the child's competent but strict social worker, Emory Blake. (978-1-163555-185-3)

Taking Chances by Erin McKenzie. When Valerie Cruz and Paige Wellington clash over what's in the best interest of the children in Valerie's care, the children may be the ones who teach them it's worth taking chances for love. (978-1-163555-209-6)

Breaking Down Her Walls by Erin Zak. Could a love worth staying for be the key to breaking down Julia Finch's walls? (978-1-63555-369-7)

All of Me by Emily Smith. When chief surgical resident Galen Burgess meets her new intern, Rowan Duncan, she may finally discover that doing what you've always done will only give you what you've always had. (978-1-163555-321-5)

As the Crow Flies by Karen F. Williams. Romance seems to be blooming all around, but problems arise when a restless ghost emerges from the ether to roam the dark corners of this haunting tale. (978-1-163555-285-0)

Both Ways by Ileandra Young. SPEAR agent Danika Karson races to protect the city from a supernatural threat and must rely on the woman she's trained to despise: Rayne, an achingly beautiful vampire. (978-1-163555-298-0)

Calendar Girl by Georgia Beers. Forced to work together, Addison Fairchild and Kate Cooper discover that opposites really do attract. (978-1-163555-333-8)

Cash and the Sorority Girl by Ashley Bartlett. Cash Braddock doesn't want to deal with morality, drugs, or people. Unfortunately, she's going to have to. (978-1-163555-310-9)

Lovebirds by Lisa Moreau. Two women from different worlds collide in a small California mountain town, each with a mission that doesn't include falling in love. (978-1-163555-213-3)

Media Darling by Fiona Riley. Can Hollywood bad girl Emerson and reluctant celebrity gossip reporter Hayley work together to make each other's dreams come true? Or will Emerson's secrets ruin not one career, but two? (978-1-163555-278-2)

Stroke of Fate by Renee Roman. Can Sean Moore live up to her reputation and save Jade Rivers from the stalker determined to end Jade's career and, ultimately, her life? (978-1-163555-162-4)

The Rise of the Resistance by Jackie D. The soul of America has been lost for almost a century. A few people may be the difference between a phoenix rising to save the masses or permanent destruction. (978-1-163555-259-1)

The Sex Therapist Next Door by Meghan O'Brien. At the intersection of sex and intimacy, anything is possible. Even love. (978-1-163555-296-6)

Unexpected Lightning by Cass Sellars. Lightning strikes once more when Sydney and Parker fight a dangerous stranger who threatens the peace they both desperately want. (978-1-163555-276-8)

Unforgettable by Elle Spencer. When one night changes a lifetime... Two romance novellas from best-selling author Elle Spencer. (978-1-63555-429-8)

Against All Odds by Kris Bryant, Maggie Cummings, and M. Ullrich. Peyton and Tory escaped death once, but will they survive when Bradley's determined to make his kill rate 100 percent? (978-1-163555-193-8)

Autumn's Light by Aurora Rey. Casual hookups aren't supposed to include romantic dinners and meeting the family. Can Mat Pero see beyond the heartbreak that led her to keep her worlds so separate, and will Graham Connor be waiting if she does? (978-1-163555-272-0)

Breaking the Rules by Larkin Rose. When Virginia and Carmen are thrown together by an embarrassing mistake, they find out their stubborn determination isn't so heroic after all. (978-1-163555-261-4)

Broad Awakening by Mickey Brent. In the sequel to *Underwater Vibes*, Hélène and Sylvie find ruts in their road to eternal bliss. (978-1-163555-270-6)

Broken Vows by MJ Williamz. Sister Mary Margaret must reconcile her divided heart or risk losing a love that just might be heaven sent. (978-1-163555-022-1)

Flesh and Gold by Ann Aptaker. Havana, 1952, where art thief and smuggler Cantor Gold dodges gangland bullets and mobsters' schemes while she searches Havana's steamy red light district for her kidnapped love. (978-1-163555-153-2)

Isle of Broken Years by Jane Fletcher. Spanish noblewoman Catalina de Valasco is in peril, even before the pirates holding her for ransom sail into seas destined to become known as the Bermuda Triangle. (978-1-163555-175-4)

Love Like This by Melissa Brayden. Hadley Cooper and Spencer Adair set out to take the fashion world by storm. If only they knew their hearts were about to be taken. (978-1-163555-018-4)

Secrets On the Clock by Nicole Disney. Jenna and Danielle love their jobs helping endangered children, but that might not be enough to stop them from breaking the rules by falling in love. (978-1-163555-292-8)

Unexpected Partners by Michelle Larkin. Dr. Chloe Maddox tries desperately to deny her attraction for Detective Dana Blake as they flee from a serial killer who's hunting them both. (978-1-163555-203-4)

A Fighting Chance by T. L. Hayes. Will Lou be able to come to terms with her past to give love a fighting chance? (978-1-163555-257-7)

Chosen by Brey Willows. When the choice is adapt or die, can love save us all? (978-1-163555-110-5)

Gnarled Hollow by Charlotte Greene. After they are invited to study a secluded nineteenth-century estate, a former English professor and a group of historians discover that they will have to fight against the unknown if they have any hope of staying alive. (978-1-163555-235-5)

Jacob's Grace by C.P. Rowlands. Captain Tag Becket wants to keep her head down and her past behind her, but her feelings for AJ's second-in-command, Grace Fields, makes keeping secrets next to impossible. (978-1-163555-187-7)

On the Fly by PJ Trebelhorn. Hockey player Courtney Abbott is content with her solitary life until visiting concert violinist Lana Caruso makes her second-guess everything she always thought she wanted. (978-1-163555-255-3)

Passionate Rivals by Radclyffe. Professional rivalry and long-simmering passions create a combustible combination when Emmet McCabe and Sydney Stevens are forced to work together, especially when past attractions won't stay buried. (978-1-63555-231-7)

Proxima Five by Missouri Vaun. When geologist Leah Warren crash-lands on a preindustrial planet and is claimed by its tyrant, Tiago, will clan warrior Keegan's love for Leah give her the strength to defeat him? (978-1-163555-122-8)

Shadowboxer by Jessica L. Webb. Jordan McAddie is prepared to keep her street kids safe from a dangerous underground protest group, but she isn't prepared for her first love to walk back into her life. (978-1-163555-267-6)

Racing Hearts by Dena Blake. When you cross a hot-tempered race car mechanic with a reckless cop, the result can only be spontaneous combustion. (978-1-163555-251-5)

The Tattered Lands by Barbara Ann Wright. As Vandra and Lilani strive to make peace, they slowly fall in love. With mistrust and murder surrounding them, only their faith in each other can keep their plan to save the world from falling apart. (978-1-163555-108-2)

Captive by Donna K. Ford. To escape a human trafficking ring, Greyson Cooper and Olivia Danner become players in a game of deceit and violence. Will their love stand a chance? (978-1-63555-215-7)

Crossing the Line by CF Frizzell. The Mob discovers a nemesis within its ranks, and in the ultimate retaliation, draws Stick McLaughlin from anonymity by threatening everything she holds dear. (978-1-63555-161-7)

Love's Verdict by Carsen Taite. Attorneys Landon Holt and Carly Pachett want the exact same thing: the only open partnership spot at their prestigious criminal defense firm. But will they compromise their careers for love? (978-1-63555-042-9)

Precipice of Doubt by Mardi Alexander & Laurie Eichler. Can Cole Jameson resist her attraction to her boss, veterinarian Jodi Bowman, or will she risk a workplace romance and her heart? (978-1-63555-128-0)

Savage Horizons by CJ Birch. Captain Jordan Kellow's feelings for Lt. Ali Ash have her past and future colliding, setting in motion a series of events that strands her crew in an unknown galaxy thousands of light years from home. (978-1-63555-250-8)

Secrets of the Last Castle by A. Rose Mathieu. When Elizabeth Campbell represents a young man accused of murdering an elderly woman, her investigation leads to an abandoned plantation that reveals many dark Southern secrets. (978-1-63555-240-9)

Take Your Time by VK Powell. A neurotic parrot brings police officer Grace Booker and temporary veterinarian Dr. Dani Wingate together in the tiny town of Pine Cone, but their unexpected attraction keeps the sparks flying. (978-1-63555-130-3)

The Last Seduction by Ronica Black. When you allow true love to elude you once and you desperately regret it, are you brave enough to grab it when it comes around again? (978-1-63555-211-9)

The Shape of You by Georgia Beers. Rebecca McCall doesn't play it safe, but when sexy Spencer Thompson joins her workout class, their nonstop sparring forces her to face her ultimate challenge—a chance at love. (978-1-63555-217-1)

Force of Fire: Toujours a Vous by Ali Vali. Immortals Kendal and Piper welcome their new child and celebrate the defeat of an old enemy, but another ancient evil is about to awaken deep in the jungles of Costa Rica. (978-1-63555-047-4)